Abou

Clive Hart lives in the ⸺⸺⸺⸺⸺ ⸺⸺ ⸺⸺ ıds as much time as he ca⸺ ⸺ ⸺ ⸺ ⸺ . He is a small part of an international community dedicated to recreating medieval mounted combat as close as it originally would have been.

The horse on the cover is Charlie, owned by Historic Equitation, and is the author's jousting and tournament horse.

For information on other books, please visit

www.clivehart.net

By Clive Hart:

The Rise and Fall of the Mounted Knight

The Legend of Richard Keynes series (six books):

Book One: Golden Spurs
Book Two: Brothers in Arms
Book Three: Dogs of War
Book Four: Knight Errant
Book Five: King Breaker
Book Six: Crusader

For Nik and Luke, who always help everyone else, even when it isn't deserved. And also for being the only people to buy this book in paperback.

Contents

REUNIONS

'Is this a good idea?' Bowman asked.

Richard had felt quite good about the idea on the voyage from Ireland, but now that they were in England and they stood outside the castle of Geoffrey Martel, he didn't find himself feeling quite so certain.

The wooden castle before them lacked stone and was not as impressive as many Richard had seen. A keep crowned a tall mound raised up on a long grassy hill that crept like a finger across the landscape. Ringing this mound was a simple wooden stockade that contained several wooden buildings, but as Richard approached the gateway, the sole and bored-looking guard sprang to life. He wore no armour to mark him out as a soldier and carried only a spear as a weapon.

'Are you sure they are going to let us in?' Richard asked Nicholas.

The Martel man with green eyes and blonde hair shrugged. 'I don't see why not. I used to stay here sometimes so they should know who I am. They won't know that my father ignored my ransom and abandoned me, so why would they give us trouble?'

'What if Eustace is here?' Richard asked.

'He only ever comes here when he's off with our father on one of his longer hunting trips. This is just the place where my father keeps my mother out of public view, so there is no reason for anyone else to be here. It's a quiet place.'

Richard really hoped he was right. They approached the guard and looked down from their horses at the young man who wore a surcoat with a red and yellow chequerboard pattern. The youth eyed the five men who rode up to his normally lonely gateway. 'Who are you and why are you here?' he asked, more weakly than he'd intended.

'Your voice crackles like a girl,' Nicholas said, 'don't you remember who I am? I've seen your face here before, you know mine.'

'There is a fee for entrance to the castle,' the youth said, 'I know who you are but your friends will still have to pay.'

Nicholas laughed and the black wolf-pelt that hung around his shoulders shook. The dead eyes of the beast upon his head looked down at the youth, who retreated a step.

Behind Nicholas, his half-brother laughed. 'Once a Martel, always a Martel,' Bowman chuckled.

Nicholas ignored him and pressed his legs onto his horse and walked straight up to the guard, who wisely stood aside.

Bowman looked back over his shoulder down to where the River Trent meandered through grassy plains. 'I'm not sure what I think of being back in these parts, or if I even want to speak to her if she's inside.'

'Speaking to her is why we've come here,' Richard said, 'that was the whole point of us riding east across England instead of just sailing back to Normandy.'

'But I haven't seen her for so long,' Bowman replied, 'how do we know she even wants to see me?'

'She will, she's your mother,' Richard pushed Solis through the gateway and into the bailey of the castle. Smoke stacks wafted into the grey sky from some of the scattered buildings. One was a decent sized two storey stable, which is where they headed. They quartered the horses there after letting them have a long drink from a trough. Soon Solis and the other stallions leaned out of their new stalls, sniffing down the stable block to inform Richard of the presence of mares at the far end. Leaving the horses to rest, Richard followed Nicholas towards the high grassy mound with its three storey keep.

'Fifteen years, I think,' Bowman mumbled as they crossed the yard with Gerold and Brian in tow.

Richard turned to his father's man, who he knew would have travelled here during his time with Uncle Luke. 'This makes me think about my parents and what it would be like to see my father again,' Richard said.

'Such thoughts lead only to pain,' Gerold said. The older man still wore the colours of Keynes, along with a thoughtful look on his face. 'For me, such thoughts burn deeply because I was not there in the Holy Land with your father when he died. Had I gone with him to the east, I feel sure that I could have prevented his death.'

'Did you ever hear what happened to him?' Richard asked. 'You must have spent much time with Luke in Eustace's company, did they ever speak of it?'

The older man nodded grimly. 'I regret every moment of it, you can be certain of that. Your uncle was an unpleasant man, a man who never got over his jealousy of his old brother, and he never found for himself a place in the world. When he found Eustace, he didn't find that place, he just found someone to tell him what to do. And they never spoke about your father and what happened to him, it was as if the matter was closed. Or undesirable. I regret I cannot help you understand the circumstances behind your father's death.'

That did not surprise Richard, if anything, it just made him more certain that either his uncle or Eustace were to blame. 'Did my uncle ever do anything good?' Richard asked.

Gerold shrugged. 'You should feel no guilt for killing him. I saw only atrocities and shameful things in the company of Luke and the Martels, they are the subject of my prayers so that the Lord may forgive me for my inaction.'

'Inaction?' Richard asked.

'I am old enough to know right from wrong, and old enough to know I should have acted to stop some of what they did. But I am weak, so I pray instead.'

Nicholas stopped at the foot of the mound which had steps cut into its turf-covered and very steep sides. 'You are blameless,' the Martel knight said to Gerold, 'I joined in with them because I thought what they did was right. I questioned none of it. I'm still not sure which of the things I went along with were actually barbaric and sinful. They twisted my whole being.'

Bowman lagged behind everyone, so Richard waited for him. 'I can't believe you're nervous,' he grinned to his tall friend.

'I'm not nervous,' Bowman said then softened, 'I just don't know what to say.'

'She's your mother,' Richard said, 'how hard can it be?'

'When you appeared before your grandfather and he realised you were alive, he died there and then,' Bowman said, 'so there's that.'

'He didn't want me to be alive,' Richard said, 'your mother will be glad to see you aren't dead.'

Nicholas sniffed and climbed the steps up the mound. 'I told everyone that I saw you in the woods back when you poached our deer,' he said, 'maybe they'll all believe me when you stand before them in the flesh.'

'Hopefully Geoffrey and Eustace aren't here to find out,' Bowman said.

Richard shook his head. 'There were no expensive horses in the stables and I didn't see any stallions, so I don't think they're here.'

Bowman grunted. 'You always know everything, don't you?'

Richard ignored him and climbed up behind Nicholas. The mound was as steep as the staircase in his own keep back at Yvetot, just five times longer, and the climb made him lose his breath. Birds flew overhead and the wind ruffled his hair. Richard knew this venture into the heart of English Martel territory was a gamble, but if they could be gone before nightfall, no one ever needed to know they'd been there.

Green countryside stretched out to the horizon in all directions once they reached the summit. Richard's cheeks were red and Brian puffed heavily at the top, his breath rasped sharply and he sounded uncomfortable.

'You could have stayed down below,' Richard said to him.

'I don't want anyone to talk to me,' the monk replied, 'everyone who has heard me speak so far has sworn at me or called me names.'

Richard wanted to reassure him, but he couldn't think of anything to say, for the English so far had scoffed at meeting an Irishman. Instead, he followed Nicholas into the keep, which was small enough that each floor contained only a single room. They bypassed the ground floor kitchen by climbing yet more stairs, up to the first floor entrance to an empty hall. Above it, at the highest level, they found a door made from a heavy hanging fabric.

Nicholas pushed it aside and stepped in. Curtains of solid colours draped the wooden walls of the chamber, creating a blaze of light that looked a world away from Richard's own drab bed chamber. A solitary single window had a curtain rolled up and tied above it so that the breeze and daylight both bathed the room. The wooden beams running across the ceiling drew his gaze, for they were all painted bright red. The ceiling between them was a pale yellow. He wondered how anyone could afford all that paint.

'Nicholas?' a woman asked. She sat on a finely carved chair which was painted in more reds and yellows, and with four women sitting on stools around her. Two children chased a black and grey dog around the room and ignored the newcomers.

'Mother,' Nicholas approached her.

The woman had long blonde hair in two long plaits on either side of her head, wore a red dress, and was instantly recognisable as Bowman and Nicholas's common relation. Her face set into a frown. 'Geoffrey told me you'd died in France,' she said. 'But I still felt you, so I thought it untrue.'

'Did he?' Nicholas sighed. 'I'd been hoping that my father had never received the ransom note, but actually it turns out that he just doesn't care about me.'

'Notes, not note,' Richard said, 'I sent more than one.'

The mother considered Richard. 'Son, have you brought the knight who captured you into my home?'

'It's not like that,' the Martel knight replied, 'we aren't enemies. Although I'm not sure what we are if I'm honest.'

'Your father will not be happy.'

'When is he ever happy?' Nicholas asked. 'He was never happy with anything I did.'

'He's a hard man to please, everyone knows that, but that is only because he has high standards.'

Bowman snorted, but before his mother could look too closely at him, Nicholas walked nearer to her and blocked her view. 'You were not pregnant when I left,' he said.

His mother smiled and rested a hand on her belly. 'I think you're going to have a sister.'

'Great, another one,' Bowman groaned.

Richard kicked him and nearly knocked over a stack of wooden panels piled up against the wall. One had a scene from Greek mythology painted onto it and their installation would lift the bed chamber into an even more colourful state.

'Why are you wearing that?' Nicholas's mother asked him, a finger pointing to the wolf-pelt. 'You look like you are acting out a story for a singer.'

The fur from Ireland he wore over his mail had smelled in recent days, and the mail itself had rips and an orange dusting. They'd all suffered from rust recently, the party had remained armoured as they rode through England, especially once they'd reached Martel land.

The Martel knight stroked one of the paws tied under his chin. 'It was a trophy from some Irishmen who nearly killed me and my brother.'

'Eustace?'

'No,' Nicholas said, 'we have just come from Ireland.'

'We aren't telling people that,' Richard said.

'But Eustace hasn't been in Ireland,' the noblewoman replied, unsure of what her son was telling her.

'No,' Nicholas turned away from his mother to reveal Bowman.

The blonde man stood next to Richard and scratched the back of his neck.

'Nicholas, what do you mean?' their mother's eyes looked Bowman up and down.

They had the same eyes.

Bowman stood still as the children caught hold of one of the dogs, and it barked back at them with happy excitement.

His mother beckoned towards one of her ladies. 'Would one of you fetch the water bowl? Our guests would like to wash off the road.'

'Go on,' Richard said to Bowman, 'say something.'

The blonde man swallowed and stepped back towards the doorway. He bumped into the unremarkable figure of Brian, which stalled his retreat.

Richard grabbed Bowman by his mailed sleeve and halted him. 'We've come a long way through lands I'd rather not be going through to do this,' Richard said, 'this could be your only chance.'

Bowman looked like a puppy himself as the dog slipped free from the children and bounded towards Richard. The dog was a crossbreed, the greater part was clearly sheepdog, but it had dark markings and angry eyes even though it played happily. It slammed to a stop underneath Nicholas and tilted its head up to look at his wolf-pelt. It sniffed the air.

'Robert?' the woman narrowed her eyes.

'Mother,' Bowman whispered.

'Robert?' Brian tried to suppress a laugh. 'His name is just Robert?'

'I thought you were dead,' Bowman's mother got up from her chair.

Nicholas folded his arms. 'A common problem in these parts, it seems.'

Bowman's eyes reddened. 'I'm so pleased you are well,' he said.

His mother swept across the chamber and embraced him. She was much shorter than Bowman, but the power of her approach nearly knocked him over. She gripped him tightly, and he slowly found the right place to put his hands to hug her.

The younger of the ladies brought over a pewter bowl of clear water and held it for Nicholas to wash his hands, face, and neck. The dog ran off and rolled around on the rushes from the river that covered the floorboards, sending them flying in all directions in a cloud of dust.

Bowman's mother cried tears of joy. 'I tried to forget you, but you should know that I have thought about you every day.'

'Mother, how can you be happy with that man?' Bowman asked.

'He is always kind to me,' she pulled her head back and looked up at her son, 'and he has provided me with a better life than most women could pray for.'

Richard took the offered pewter bowl, but the water swirled with a mixture of dust and orange rust from Nicholas's mail. He splashed it over his face anyway, but leant forward so the drops would avoid his mail shirt, even though rust already heavily stained it.

'Does he hurt you?' Bowman asked.

His mother stepped back and laughed. 'His wife is the woman he is required to have, I am the woman he wants to have. Geoffrey has never hurt me, Robert, I am quite safe here. I am happy.'

8

The dog sat next to Richard. He squatted down and scratched under its chin as its tail wagged, sending more rushes flying in all directions. The children giggled as one hid inside a large chest in a corner of the room while the other held its hands over its eyes.

Bowman watched the other pretend to search for it and looked at Nicholas. 'You had a childhood like that, didn't you?'

Nicholas nodded. 'Of course, until I was eight and was sent away to my uncle,' he said.

'And you still turned out like this,' Bowman replied.

'Now, Robert,' his mother said, 'there's no need to be jealous of your brother.'

'Half-brother,' Bowman replied.

'Not this again,' the Martel knight said, 'are you done now? Can we just go?'

'You've only just arrived,' their mother said, 'you should stay a few nights at least, there must be so much to tell me.'

Nicholas frowned because she had spoken to Bowman. 'At least your father didn't pretend you were dead,' he said.

'Your father is the problem here,' Bowman said, 'it's his blood that has you howling at the moon.'

'I've never howled at the moon,' Nicholas replied, 'and I tried to tell everyone you were alive.'

'Your father banned all mention of Robert's name when I questioned him,' their mother said, 'and everyone learns very quickly to never repeat a question. But to see you alive makes me the happiest woman in the world.'

Bowman teared up.

She looked up into his eyes. 'My heart springs with joy because your life means that something of your father will live on after him. Until today, sadness had always cast a shadow over me, but now I am freed.'

Nicholas walked over to the open window and looked outside.

'I am Isabel,' she said to Richard, 'who are you?'

Richard hesitated. 'It's probably better you don't know,' he said.

Her eyes passed to her other son. 'Jealousy doesn't suit you, Nicholas,' she said firmly, 'you had everything Robert did not. You had a sheltered life, while he was cast aside, though not by my choice. My taking was against my will, I arrived with your father by force, did you know that?'

Nicholas turned back from the window, a pained expression on his face. He shook his head.

'Your father threatened me with death if I told you, but now I no longer need to fear that.'

'Death?' Nicholas gasped. 'Why would he threaten death?'

'So that you continued to follow him and be useful to him,' Isabel said, 'but now I sense you have left us. Left me.'

'I don't want to leave you,' he said, 'but my father has decided for me. He clearly doesn't want me anymore.' Nicholas checked himself. 'Wait, what did you mean when you said you were taken by force?'

His mother left Bowman and moved to her younger son. 'That truth should make little difference between us, you are still my child.'

The young Martel blinked. 'So I am the product of a violent union,' he said, 'I am the result of my father's sin, and that sin flowed through into me. That must be why evil has been following my thoughts. My half-brother is the lucky one, you have never looked at me the same way you just looked at him.'

Brian slid up to Richard. 'Is this was what was supposed to happen?' he whispered.

'Be quiet,' Richard replied.

'What evil has followed you?' Isabel asked her son.

'In Ireland, ever since a house fell on me, I have lost time. And I wake up with blood all over me whenever something hits me on the head.'

'You're getting carried away,' Richard said, 'the blood is always from a fight, a fight you're supposed to be in. You don't turn into a demon at night.'

'Well, I never remember it,' Nicholas shrugged.

'Both of you are my children and I cherish the two of you equally. I have lost three before they reached the speaking age, there is no need for jealousy. And I do care for Geoffrey, you will have to learn to accept it.'

Bowman groaned. 'How can you care for him after what he did to me? After what he did to your apparently beloved husband? My sister? He destroyed our family.'

Isabel frowned at Bowman. 'The Lord works in mysterious ways.'

'Not that again,' Richard mumbled.

Bowman half rolled his eyes.

'If you care for us equally, why did you not press for my ransom to be sent? It isn't as if father couldn't afford it,' Nicholas said.

His mother sighed. 'I told you, Geoffrey told me you were dead. You will have to ask him about it.'

Nicholas shooed the dog away as it tried to rub its head on his leg. 'I don't need to ask him, I'm leaving with Richard.'

'You weren't supposed to say my name,' Richard groaned.

'It's settled,' the Martel knight continued, 'I'm leaving with him, he actually cares whether I live or die. Even my half-brother tried to save my life at least once.'

'Tried?' Bowman blinked and half laughed. 'You're standing here still breathing, aren't you?'

'I still owe this man my ransom,' Nicholas said to his mother, 'as my father won't pay it, I'm bound by honour to earn it.'

Bowman snorted loudly enough that one child looked over.

'Now you have returned, your father may pay for you,' Isabel said.

'I doubt that,' Nicholas said, 'I need to pay this man myself.'

'You mean Richard,' his mother said.

'Fine,' Richard said, 'that is my name.'

'He does need the money,' Bowman nodded to Richard, 'he is extremely poor.'

'You don't have to mention that, either,' Richard said.

Bowman pulled a face. 'Who cares? She doesn't know who you are.'

Their mother waved away the lady with the pewter bowl. 'Very well, but I would like it very much if you could return to visit me, if you won't stay tonight.'

No one replied.

Isabel looked at Gerold, narrowed her eyes, and then Brian. 'At least you have a man of God with you,' she said.

'Him?' Nicholas said. 'He's just an Irishman with nowhere else to go.'

'I'm not sure he's even a man of God,' Bowman added.

'An Irishman?' Isabel squinted at Brian. 'I'm so sorry.'

Brian looked to Richard for help, but he could only shrug back.

'Perhaps you could find an English priest,' Isabel said hopefully.

'Why are you sorry?' Brian asked.

'Oh, my dear boy,' she said, 'I can barely understand your uncultured tongue.'

Brian said something in Latin that sounded sarcastic.

'His very words torture my ears,' Isabel frowned.

The monk shook his head and stomped off back down the stairs.

Bowman and Nicholas exchanged a glance, but neither corrected her.

'I should go after him,' Richard said.

'Perhaps we should all go,' Bowman said.

'Must you?' his mother asked. 'Would there be any harm in staying one night?'

Bowman looked at Richard, uncertainty etched across his face. Richard tapped his foot on the floor. He didn't want to be caught by surprise inside his enemy's castle, but Bowman looked like he needed a second chance to leave his mother on happier terms.

'Maybe one night, if we leave early in the morning,' he eventually suggested.

Isabel beamed.

Brian ran back into the room, his breathing sharp. Everyone looked at him.

'What now?' Bowman asked.

'Men,' the monk panted, 'some men have arrived.'

Nicholas yawned. 'Nothing to worry about, I'm sure. It's probably just some clerks or someone delivering something.'

'What did they look like?' his mother asked. 'If your feeble mind is capable of remembering such things.'

Brian glowered at her, then looked at Richard. 'Two finely dressed men on horses. With hounds and a huntsman.'

Nicholas's eyes widened.

'You said your father and Eustace use this castle as a hunting lodge,' Richard said, 'could it be anyone else?'

Nicholas bit his lip.

'Idiot,' Bowman said.

'Don't call him an idiot,' Isabel replied.

'What do we do?' Richard asked. 'There's only one way down the mound.'

Nicholas put a hand to his sword. 'There are three of them and four of us,' he said.

His words hung in the colourful chamber and the ladies who had been pretending not to listen gasped.

'He is your father,' Isabel said, 'there will be no bloodshed here.'

'We need to get out, then,' Richard made his way out of the chamber, where he ran straight into the imposing bulk of Geoffrey Martel.

'Your horses are in my stalls,' Geoffrey said dryly, 'who has such impudence?'

Richard backed into the chamber and Bowman whirled round as all their hands dropped to their swords.

The elder Martel sneered at their surprise and walked in. He was large, with broad shoulders and his family's piercing green eyes. His dark hair was shoulder length, and it was immediately obvious that he belonged to the highest ranks of the nobility.

And that he didn't fear them.

'Nicholas,' Geoffrey said flatly, 'this is unexpected.'

'Is it?' he replied. 'Or do you mean displeasing?'

Geoffrey cleared his throat. 'Your absence has weakened your manners.'

Richard wanted to lick his lips, but he focused on Geoffrey's sword-hand in case it acted.

The head of the Martel family looked around the group. 'I saw Luke's white and blue saddle in the stables, but he is not here. Gerold, where is he?'

The man from Keynes coughed. He wanted to look at Richard but held his nerve and looked the Martel lord in the eyes. 'We have returned from Ireland.'

'I can see that, do not waste my time.'

'Luke died there, along with many others,' Gerold said.

Geoffrey didn't react. 'I told him it was a foolish venture, what is there in Ireland worth taking?'

Brian didn't dare take offence.

'But I don't know you,' Geoffrey said to Richard. His eyes lingered on Bowman for a moment, a longer moment than was safe.

'We are friends of Nicholas,' Richard said to break his gaze.

'In that case, we should speak in the hall, not in a woman's chamber,' Geoffrey turned his back on the men whose hands had remained on their swords. He descended the staircase.

Bowman looked at Nicholas.

'I don't know,' the Martel knight hissed, 'we have to go down with him.'

'We'll talk until he's done, then we'll go,' Richard said.

'Or until we have to kill him,' Bowman said.

'Robert,' Isabel said, 'there will be no killing.'

Richard swallowed and led everyone down the stairs and into the hall. He stopped two paces into it when a man bending over the hearth stood up. His hulking body could only be one man.

'Eustace,' Richard said under his breath.

The big Martel turned to him and laughed. 'Of all the things today could have brought, this is the last I expected,' his green eyes glinted as the new fire caught.

'You know him?' Geoffrey asked.

Eustace grinned. He looked so like his father that it was only wrinkles that told them apart.

'I am Richard of Yvetot,' Richard decided indecision would show weakness.

Geoffrey Martel sat down in his chair, a chair painted red and with carved legs that ended in the paws of wolves. Those paws were black.

Nicholas walked in, his face frosty.

'Take that ridiculous thing off your shoulders,' Geoffrey said, 'you look like a savage yet to see the light of Christ.'

A third man already sat at the table, the green cloak around his shoulders covered in so many twigs that he picked some out and placed them in a growing pile on the table.

Gerold walked in and tried to stand in front of Bowman. Brian's face quivered and he stayed in the doorway. He looked down the final flight of stairs with longing.

'Gerold,' Eustace said, 'where is Luke? I saw his saddle.'

'In Ireland,' Gerold answered.

'They just told me he's dead,' the Martel lord answered for him.

Eustace laughed. 'He never was quite as capable as he thought he was. He never managed anything without me being there for him. Frankly, he was starting to irritate me.'

For a strange moment, Richard felt offended by the insult to his family member, but then he recovered himself. A trio of dogs bounded up the stairs and ran around the table chasing each other. One came too close to Eustace and he kicked it away. It let out a whine and ran behind Richard, where it sat and looked up at him. It was male, black as night, with silky hair.

'Simply for my curiosity, what happened to Luke?' Geoffrey looked at Gerold.

Luke's former man tensed the hand on his hilt.

Eustace prodded the growing fire with an iron rod that in his hands was probably as deadly as a sword.

'Well?' Geoffrey looked over to Richard. 'Are none among you man enough to answer a simple question? Or are you all struck dumb by some Irish curse?'

Eustace twirled the iron poker in his hand, which nearly hit another dog. 'Tell me, Richard of Yvetot, how is your marriage?'

Richard steeled his eyes. 'Never better.'

'Have you moved the rock that fell down from your church on your wedding day?' Eustace smirked.

'You still owe me a ransom for back then,' Richard replied.

Eustace laughed. 'I escaped so I owe you nothing. You, however, owe me, don't you?'

The knight responsible for hunting stopped picking twigs from his cloak.

'Actually,' Nicholas said, 'we could balance that for my ransom, then everyone could be happy.'

Eustace rammed the poker down into the table so hard the huntsman winced and the dogs all ran away. Except for the black one, which sat behind Richard and barked at Eustace.

'You are not worth the Pinnacle, do not flatter yourself, half-brother,' the Martel man sneered.

'The Pinnacle?' Geoffrey said as his memories fell into place. 'You are the man who sent me the note for Nicholas.'

Richard frowned. 'Notes, actually, I sent more than one.'

'So you trespassed in my French castle, and now dare to come to one of my English homes?'

'They didn't take the Pinnacle for themselves and they don't occupy it now,' Eustace said, 'but they helped the new occupant to steal it from us. The ransom we looked after for a while was under the care of this Richard.'

'Then this Richard here is not a very careful man. Or boy. It is either very brave or very foolish for you to be here, which is it?'

Their group had travelled with their mail on, and Richard wore both of his mail shirts, whereas the hunting party were equipped only for the chase. Maybe this was the best chance he'd ever get to inflict revenge on Eustace for what he'd done to his sister.

Geoffrey chuckled. 'You have a look about you, boy. You have the audacity to be eyeing us up, as if the three of you have even the smallest chance of besting us.'

Nicholas stepped forward and looked his father in the eyes. He had to look up. 'It is the four of us against the three of you,' he said. The eyes of the wolf were level with his father.

'Take that thing off, it is absurd,' Geoffrey said, 'but I am more interested in why you are here.'

Nicholas fumed. 'You ignored my ransom note.'

'Notes,' Richard added.

'And left me to rot,' Nicholas continued, 'a father takes care of his sons, that is how it is supposed to work.' He prodded the Martel lord in the chest.

Geoffrey looked down at the finger. 'I'll forgive that this once, because I did ignore you, but prod me again and you will lose the finger.'

'Father,' Eustace said, 'forget him, he's only a half-blood, it is Richard that will interest you.'

Geoffrey brushed past Nicholas to look at Richard. He peered down with disdainful eyes and Richard felt himself sweating.

'You owe me a castle,' Geoffrey said slowly, 'and that is what I am setting your ransom at.'

'My ransom?' Richard asked. Then he understood and the sweat on his back turned icy cold.

'You can fight here, but the result will still be your capture,' the Martel lord said, 'you and your little friends have walked yourselves right into my power.'

'They aren't worth much,' Eustace pulled the poker out of the table, which left a crack running along its length, 'it wasn't long ago that Richard was still a weanling at Castle Tancarville, hanging under the Chamberlain's teats for milk.'

'Tancarville?' Geoffrey studied Richard. 'I suppose you will tell me that this is the same Richard who was involved in the death of my son?'

Brian furrowed his brow. 'Are we talking about a third son? Or a fourth son?'

Eustace twirled the poker around and pointed it at Richard. 'The conclusion of that matter was that a boar did for Simon, and if you look at Richard's hands, you'll see they tested him over it. But this is the very same Richard.'

'I liked Simon,' the Martel lord said with a stern expression, 'he was a dutiful son.'

'Yes, and I wager you would have ransomed him,' Nicholas said.

'I would sell my soul for him to live,' Geoffrey shouted, a shout that hurt Richard's ears.

It hurt Nicholas more, and he looked tearful.

'I wrote a letter about you and Simon to Lord Tancarville,' Geoffrey said to Richard, 'he was to send you to me, but he never did. It would seem that God saw fit to undertake that task for me himself.'

'God had very little to do with our arrival,' Bowman stepped out to face his step-father. His hands bunched into white-knuckled fists and fire erupted in his eyes. 'Do you know who I am?'

'They call you Bowman,' Eustace said from behind his father, 'a rude squire.'

Richard really hoped Bowman would keep his mouth shut.

'You also know me by another name,' the blonde man told Eustace.

'Did you have to?' Richard sighed. 'This is complicated enough as it is.'

Eustace took a step closer. He raised the poker back up and pointed it right between Bowman's eyes. 'You,' the Martel knight's eyes flickered in recognition.

'Me,' Bowman replied and his hand went to his sword.

'Enough,' Geoffrey shouted and his lone word echoed off the wooden walls and stilled everyone.

'Not yet,' Richard said and Bowman snarled.

'Who is he?' the elder Martel asked.

'It all makes sense now,' Eustace kept the poker a hand's width from Bowman's eyes, 'he is the half-blood's own half-brother.'

Geoffrey fought to make sense of it. 'Isabel's son? He's dead.'

'I tried to tell you,' Nicholas said, 'but no one listened.'

Eustace laughed and half lowered the pointed iron rod. 'I actually think he's come back to kill me, nearly twenty years after the first time. What do you think will happen now, Robert? It was Robert, wasn't it? Do you think you're better off than back when you were a snivelling child?'

Bowman's veins pulsed.

'We didn't come back to kill anyone,' Richard said, 'we just wanted them both to see their mother. For her sake as much as theirs. Allow us to leave in peace.'

Geoffrey held his hand out and pushed the poker down. 'I care not for Robert, and you cannot spill his blood below his mother. You can do that once we are outside this keep. Nicholas however, you are my concern and you belong to this family. To me.'

'You don't own me,' Nicholas said, 'slavery is almost gone in England, you can't make me stay. If you wanted me to remain, you should have paid my ransom.'

The Martel lord shook his head. 'You should have escaped like your brother did.'

Eustace grinned. Richard remembered Eustace riding away from him at Yvetot, on his wedding day to Sophie, and the thought angered him. That debt would need paying.

'I might care for your mother more than anyone else alive,' Geoffrey said, 'but when the day of judgement comes, you are a bastard son and not worth a ransom. I can make more of you. You may have served a useful purpose as an agent within our lands, but you never had enough ambition to make you of real value to me. You are a follower and not a leader.'

Eustace laughed so hard he had to fight to control his breathing.

'I think we should be going,' Gerold said.

'Did I ask your opinion?' Geoffrey asked. 'Beyond your name, I barely remember a thing about you.'

'I served with Luke for years,' Gerold replied, 'you saw me every day for half a year.'

Geoffrey shrugged. 'Then you cannot matter much.'

'I am still standing here,' Bowman said, his chest heaving up and down under his mail shirt.

'And what do you want me to tell you?' the Martel lord asked. 'That I am sorry your mother is happy here? That I'm sorry Eustace cut off your father's hand and cut out an eye with an eating knife? Will that pacify your soul? Will that give your life meaning? Will that stop you wasting my time?'

'Calm down,' Richard said softly to Bowman.

'Listen to the boy,' Geoffrey said, 'if we spill blood all over the floor today, there will be no room for my huntsman to sleep here tonight.'

Gerold put a hand on Bowman's shoulder. 'Back away,' he said.

'Listen to the old man,' Eustace cut the poker through the air at one of the dogs which ran around the table again.

Gerold grew almost as red as Bowman.

'I am tired of this,' the elder Martel said, 'whatever you ragtag band of layabouts are, I have no interest beyond the fact that you are trespassing on my land. What are you but an angry giant, an old man, a half-blood failure, a boy, and a monk? Why would men like you even have a monk?'

'Why shouldn't they? What do you know of God?' Brian said without thinking.

Geoffrey laughed at him. 'That is an Irish accent, rough and painful to the ear. I heard that good Norman men are killing thousands of them as we speak. And you dare to ask me what I know of God?'

'Spare us the piety,' Eustace put his hands on his hips, the poker hanging down like a sword, 'no one cares about your crusade.'

'Silence, I shall answer the barbarian monk to educate him,' the Martel lord said, 'I have journeyed to the Holy Land, I have fought the heathen and bled for my God. I have ridden knee-to-knee with men like Raymond of Tripoli, Bohemund of Antioch, and Hugh of Lusignan.'

'Lusignan?' Richard interrupted, 'the father of Guy? He told us that his father was lost in the Holy Land.'

'Lost, yes,' Geoffrey said, 'he was captured with many other great men. He died there in captivity.'

'His son thinks he lives,' Richard said.

'Why should I care?' Geoffrey asked. 'But I have made my point to the heathen monk.'

'I'm not heathen,' Brian shouted.

'Quiet,' Eustace said, 'I want either a ransom worth a castle or Richard's head.'

'Well, boy, do you have a ransom worth a castle?' Geoffrey asked wryly.

'He has his honour,' Gerold said, 'which is more than can be said for you.'

'Honour?' Geoffrey laughed. 'Honour neither protects my family nor my king. Be silent. It is time to draw this matter to a close. Nicholas will return to my service, and Eustace can do whatever he likes with Robert and Richard down in the bailey.'

'We shouldn't take him back, father,' Eustace said, 'not after he betrayed us.'

Their father sniffed. 'He is not really part of this family, so I barely even view his pathetic attempt at rebellion as a betrayal. He is just a spoiled child and shall be treated as one.'

Nicholas looked unable to speak, as if the weight of his father's disdain might crush him.

'What about me?' Gerold asked. 'You speak of the others, but what do you want to do with me?'

Geoffrey laughed, and Eustace readied himself to walk towards Richard with the poker.

Richard's fingers slid closer to his sword.

'You, old man,' the elder Martel said, 'are so insignificant I would hardly notice if you vanished.'

Gerold lunged. 'Notice this,' he shouted as his fist connected with the lord's nose and it cracked under the blow. Geoffrey fell backwards and Eustace tried to push around him to get to Gerold.

'Go,' Richard shouted, 'run.'

Brian was already gone.

Gerold pulled Bowman around and fled down the stairs with him.

'Come on,' Richard shouted at Nicholas as the wolf-covered Martel knight drew his sword and faced his half-brother.

'I'll give you time,' Nicholas said.

Richard remembered when Sir Wobble had pulled the same self-sacrificing move, and he would not let that happen again. He drew his own sword.

Eustace howled, pushed his father aside and swung the poker at his half-brother. Nicholas batted it aside but the bigger man slammed into him and threw him back onto the wall.

Richard cut at Eustace but the large man swatted the attack away without having to look at it.

The black dog, hackles raised, barked at Eustace.

Nicholas blocked a thrust of the poker but Eustace was quicker. He thrust the poker towards Nicholas and the point thudded into the mail around his ribs. The black dog leapt and sunk its teeth onto Eustace's poker-arm. He fell back trying to shake the snarling beast off.

Geoffrey drew his sword clumsily and held his bleeding nose with his left hand. The knight of the hunt threw aside his cloak and drew a long knife.

'We should go,' Richard said.

'Probably,' Nicholas collected himself and followed the others out of the hall.

Richard ran down the stairs behind him, which creaked and moaned under their mailed feet. The sounds of barking and shouting echoed from the hall as Richard flew down the wooden stairs and then down the steps cut into the grassy mound. The air was cool and the openness of the landscape calmed his frantic mind. Half way down the mound he had a flashback to his escape from Keynes, where he'd run away from Eustace the first time. But this time was different, he thought with an unexpected sense of elation, this time he wasn't leaving anyone behind.

Gerold and Bowman overtook Brian and rushed into the stable building.

The young guard on the gate wandered over with his spear held low, trying to work out what was happening.

Richard reached the bailey floor and ran. Nicholas made a howling sound and laughed as they went. Richard wanted to call him mad, but he had no breath to spare for that.

They readied their horses as fast as they could, and when Richard dragged a sleepy-looking Solis outside to mount, he saw the Martels descend the steps at a leisurely pace.

Geoffrey still held a hand over his nose, and blood stained his dark blue tunic.

Eustace rubbed the bite wound on his arm. 'You won't leave the country before we find you,' he shouted across the bailey, 'we own everything as far as you can see, how far do you think you'll get?'

The Martel's horses would be tired from the hunt, so Richard was happy to try his luck.

The black dog bounded down the grassy mound, shot past Eustace, and ran over to Richard with his tail wagging.

'I think you've made a friend, young lord,' Bowman landed in his saddle.

'I did want a dog,' Richard looked over to Brian, who had already managed to mount. The monk had forgotten to hook the curb chain under the horse's chin, so it flapped about, but there wasn't time to correct that.

The young guard grabbed his spear with two hands and pointed it at them.

Nicholas laughed and howled at an imaginary moon. The youth backed away.

Richard walked his yellow-coated stallion out of the castle. 'I'm not running from them, not this time,' he said when Gerold wanted to go quicker.

'They aren't really chasing,' Bowman looked back.

The Martels reached the bottom of the mound as Richard rode out of the open gate with no idea of what had just happened to them.

The black dog, panting, walked comfortably behind Solis, who kept swinging his neck round to look at the animals at his heels.

'Which way are we going?' Richard asked.

'Away from here,' Nicholas said.

'They know we'll ride to a port,' Bowman said, 'and they will be able to track us.'

'So we need to be quicker than them,' Nicholas said.

'Or just smarter,' Richard said.

Bowman laughed. 'That's probably easier than outrunning them.'

'What do we do?'

'We have to go south because that's where the ports are,' Bowman said, 'so ride south while we're in view of the castle. Then we go east until we reach the Great North Road, then ride down that. Once we're on that road they can't track us because it's so busy. If we go east today, we'll reach Grantham on the road around dusk.'

'Grantham?' Richard asked. 'Lord Tancarville was going to send me and Sir Wobble there after Simon died. He owns it.'

'Ha,' Bowman cried, 'there we are then, we can get ourselves a decent night's sleep through association.'

'What are you talking about?' Nicholas asked.

'Don't worry,' Richard said, 'we'll find somewhere to sleep and then we can work out what happened here.'

'I have no idea,' Bowman said, 'I think I've more anger than when the day started. We should never have come here.'

'I know,' Richard looked over his shoulder but no one had yet left the castle in pursuit.

'I know you tried though, young lord,' the blonde man grinned, 'as usual.'

Nicholas let out a deep breath. 'Honestly, I think I feel better after that,' he said, 'thank you for punching my father in the face.'

Gerold grunted an acknowledgement and Richard hoped the older man felt better for finally standing up to the Martels.

They rode at a strong pace south, then turned east along a road that tracked around shallow hills and through increasingly dense woodland. They crossed other roads as the skies blackened, and sometimes there were riders behind them in the distance. From other hilltops they saw no one, and a gentle breeze took over and cooled them. They reached the manor at Grantham in the evening's chill as an owl hooted, but Richard was too tired to notice. Some clerks let them in when Richard spoke about Lord Tancarville with just enough detail to seem convincingly on his business.

Exhausted, they sat around a great hearth in a cavernous hall as embers floated up into the dark ceiling and their hosts engaged them in friendly but idle talk.

A clerk whose features resembled a mouse told them that Lord Tancarville was ignoring the King's summonses, and that his son was the talk of Normandy for the rumoured murder of some women.

'If you've been in Ireland,' a clerk with an impressive double-chin said, 'you probably don't even know about Becket.'

'The archbishop?' Richard asked.

'Exactly, King Henry had him killed,' the clerk said.

'Well,' the mouse-like clerk said, 'he is saying the knights did it on their own account, which knowing those knights, I can believe.'

'The archbishop is dead?' Richard remembered the book Becket had given him and hoped it remained safely tucked up in his castle in Normandy.

The clerks both nodded. 'King Henry is in Canterbury now, or at least so they're saying, doing penance for the whole thing.'

Richard stared into the oranges and yellows of the flames and remembered the Breton villages that had burned at King Henry's command. Although, Henry had been good to him after that, especially once he had done the King some favours.

'We'll go to Canterbury,' Richard said, 'Geoffrey and Eustace can't touch us if we're with the King.'

'The King?' Nicholas asked. 'Do you not remember his message to Strongbow in Ireland? That all knights who stayed there and didn't return home will forfeit their land.'

Richard ginned and the fire reflected off his teeth. 'But we have returned, have we not? Besides, we don't need to tell him we were there.'

'We did agree that Ireland never happened,' Nicholas said even as he stroked his wolf-pelt.

Bowman ignored them and looked into the fire himself, his mind drifting back to Eva who he surely would never see again.

Richard left him to it. 'We're going to the King,' he said, this time with certainty.

'Why?' Nicholas asked. 'What's he going to do for us?'

Richard smiled. 'We're going because the King holds Keynes now, and I want it back.'

THE YOUNG KING

Canterbury was far busier than during Richard's previous visit. On that occasion, Thomas Becket had helped Richard on his way and gifted him an expensive and precious book. This time around, Becket was dead and pilgrims flocked from across the land to venerate him.

'I have waited my whole life to come here,' Brian said as they stopped their horses in the square facing the monumentally vast stone building that was the cathedral.

'I think you'll be the only one who isn't here for Becket,' Richard said.

The monk grinned and almost jumped down from his horse. Richard nodded to himself, for the monk had steadily become accustomed to their horses and saddles.

'We aren't going in there, are we?' Nicholas asked.

'I'm not,' Bowman said.

'They wouldn't let either of you in,' Richard smiled, 'but fear not, we just need to hide Brian and his Irish accent somewhere while I find the King. So this works for everyone.'

The monk handed his reins up to Richard. 'I don't mind when you come back for me, I could pray here for days.'

Bowman groaned.

'When we're ready I'll come in and get you,' Richard said.

Groups of pilgrims walked around the square, but most were in a tightly packed throng around the huge double doors into the cathedral. Excited chattering intermingled with the shouts of street vendors, and the fouler smells of human cities mixed with the sweeter smells of human cooking. Brian disappeared into the throng and was gone as quickly as his short legs could take him.

'You're not going to buy a pilgrim badge, then?' Bowman asked with a grin.

Richard considered the street sellers with pewter badges who loitered around trying to make sales. He thought he'd get one for Sarjeant as a joke, but before he could, the entrance crowd was parted by unarmoured knights who held them back to create a path out of the cathedral. The crowd grew louder and more enthusiastic as others flocked to see who was leaving.

'Someone important must be coming out,' Richard said.

'Obviously,' Bowman replied, 'I don't think they're doing that for Brian.'

The knights wore tunics and cloaks as fine as Geoffrey Martel's, but none had entered the church with any weapons, for not one wore a sword belt. A stream of churchmen marched out of the long channel they'd created. They wore white with purple trims, and everywhere was gold, tall hats, and staffs with jewel encrusted crosses at their heads. A stocky man with bowed legs and red hair on his head followed them apart from everyone else as if in a bubble.

'I thought finding the King would be harder than this,' Richard said.

'Don't get too excited, I don't think he'll want to talk to you right now,' Bowman said as the King, dressed only in white linen undergarments, left the cathedral with bare feet.

Some in the crowd booed.

'They're brave,' Bowman said.

King Henry ignored them, his head fixed forwards as dozens more churchmen followed him out of the cathedral. The procession passed a pile of wood meant for scaffolding, and a crane which unloaded a large stone block from a cart. At the rear of the procession, as it left the square heading south, was a vermin-faced monk.

Richard sighed. 'I'd just about forgotten about him.'

'God's toes,' Bowman sank in his saddle, 'every time that monk is here we end up dancing with death.'

Brother Geoffrey, his eyes sweeping back and forth through the crowd, couldn't miss them. He looked up at Nicholas. 'I see you are openly in league with the devil now, Richard. That at least is finally honest of you,' he said.

'It's just a pelt,' Nicholas said.

The monk frowned. 'Why are you here, Richard? Are you here to mock the faithful?'

'No,' Richard said, 'one of my friends has gone to pray inside.'

Brother Geoffrey looked around the group, who had remained mounted. 'You seem to gain more and more friends, I don't understand it. The lure of the devil, perhaps. What do you promise them?'

A family walked by, saw Nicholas's pelt, and rushed on their way.

'Is it wealth that attracts these new men to you?' the monk asked. 'A hidden wealth perhaps? Drawn from a hoard of gold?'

Bowman laughed. 'He's the poorest knight I've ever met.'

'I have no gold,' Richard said, 'do I have to carry another red-hot iron bar to prove it to you?'

'I can arrange that if you like?' Brother Geoffrey said hopefully.

'He really is dirt-poor,' Bowman said, 'he cannot afford to even buy a dog.'

Richard looked down at the black dog which had refused to leave them. It drank from a puddle that Richard thought looked less than clean.

'We're going to find the tournament circuit over the sea and make our money there,' Richard said, 'that's what we're on the way to do. Once I've got my family village back, anyway.'

Brother Geoffrey spent a moment deep in thought. He scratched his cheek and sniffed. 'If you are contemplating something as preposterously stupid as seeking money on tournament fields, then you cannot have a pile of gold.'

'Why is everyone talking about gold?' Gerold asked.

'Don't ask,' Bowman said, 'and there isn't any gold, I swear that on my mother's life.'

'That doesn't reassure me,' Brother Geoffrey said, 'but if you wish to play at being errant knights, then perhaps I can help you.'

'You? Help us?' Richard laughed. 'All you've ever done is make my head ache or blister my hands.'

'Ah,' the monk said, 'but do you know anything of tournaments? Do you have a company to join? Everyone knows new knights are preyed upon and picked off by sinfully dishonest older knights. How will you avoid that?'

Richard didn't know, because he'd never thought about it. He'd never even heard about any of that.

'You haven't, have you?' Brother Geoffrey looked smug.

Richard watched a group of men missing limbs instead.

'I can get you into a company,' the monk said, victory in his voice.

'Fine,' Richard replied, 'but what do you want from us?'

The monk smiled a rodent-like smile that made Richard think twice about continuing their conversation.

'It is not what I want,' Brother Geoffrey said, 'it is what the King will want.'

'The King?' Richard raised his eyebrows.

'Indeed,' the monk walked south, 'you can help him. Follow me.'

Richard looked at Bowman.

The blonde man shrugged. 'We can see what he has to say,' he said.

'Just the devil's boy,' Brother Geoffrey said, 'the rest of you are certainly not welcome in the court. How would that wolf-skin look at the time Henry is trying to look sorry for the murder of an archbishop?'

'I'll go,' Richard said to Bowman, 'you just keep Nicholas away from anyone who might want to burn him.'

Bowman grinned. 'I'll do my best,' he said, 'maybe.'

Richard ignored him and rode after the monk who walked in the same direction the King had gone. The dog followed at his horse's heels, who by now ignored its presence.

The monk led Richard through the teeming streets of Canterbury, which was slow going, until they left the main urban area and Canterbury Castle loomed into view.

The castle occupied a square piece of land surrounded by a ditch and water-filled moat, lined by a modest stone wall. Two gatehouses guarded the only entrances, but they were barely taller than the surrounding wall. Some houses were built up to the inside of the wall of the square bailey, and a keep took up one quarter of the space to tower over the far corner. The keep, unlike the walls, was impressive. Many storeys tall, and with towers at each corner, the giant cube of flint and sandstone was a full-scale Norman fortification complete with arched windows and arrow slits.

Whereas Canterbury was full of people, the castle bailey was full of horses. The horses were tied to wooden frames that criss-crossed the earthen ground, and the animals were eating piles of hay or cut grass. The mounds of fodder were so freshly cut that the sweet smell crept into Richard's nose and reminded him of his childhood. Several carts loaded high with horsebread sat in the middle of the yard, and servants and grooms distributed the food to the animals, as well as cleared up after them.

Solis entered the yard and his head shot up, his ears flipped forwards and he sniffed the air. He shouted a stallion cry, but the other horses ignored him entirely.

Richard patted him on the neck and he snorted back.

'Tie him somewhere and we'll go in,' Brother Geoffrey said.

Richard dismounted and looked for a space on a wooden rail that wasn't too near any other horses. A servant walked past with a bucket of water so Richard gave his horse to him and asked him to deal with Solis.

Brother Geoffrey regarded Richard. 'You act like a knight now, you have grown since Castle Tancarville,' he said.

Richard had to laugh. 'Is that a compliment?'

'Don't get cocky, boy, you simply have mail and a sword, if I wore that the servant would have obeyed me, too.'

Richard didn't believe that. The black dog started to follow Richard, but he told it to stay and to his surprise it sat down. Richard then let the monk show him towards the imposing keep. Well-dressed men were everywhere, some in mail, and the scene reminded Richard of the army camps of the Breton campaign.

The guard at the entrance to the keep's own small gatehouse nodded at Brother Geoffrey and the monk wafted passed him with his head held high. Richard followed him inside, out of the daylight and into a chamber crammed full with people. Torches flickered away in sconces lining the walls, and rafters with red painted beams supported the lofty ceiling. Tapestries hung on every side depicting biblical scenes or tales from Rome. Incense floated through the air and Richard pushed past men with cloaks worth more than his own village.

Brother Geoffrey stopped where the crowd stopped. A short open space separated everyone from a raised dais, on top of which King Henry pulled a blue tunic down over his head. He already wore a rough spun hair-shirt directly against his body, which the blue tunic obscured. The hair-shirt was supposed to be a private penance no one else was aware of, but by dressing in front of everyone, the King was making it public knowledge that he endured it.

Heny sat down on his throne, a gold and red chair with orbs topping the backrest, and scratched at his chest. 'This is damn uncomfortable,' he said.

'That is the point,' Brother Geoffrey stepped forwards.

'What do you want? Others were here first,' Henry said.

'Do you know who this is?' the monk pointed a bony finger at Richard.

The knights and squires craned their necks to see and jostled to get a look at him.

Richard suddenly wanted to draw his cloak around himself, but instead stood very consciously still.

King Henry squinted down at him. 'Ah yes, the English lad with that ramshackle village in Normandy. The one with the yellow horse that kept trying to bite mine,' he said.

A few people spoke amongst themselves in the vast crowd.

'Why have you brought him to me then, monk? There's always a reason with you.'

Brother Geoffrey approached the King and bowed. 'I have brought him to help you with your problem.'

'Spit it out, monk, I haven't got all day. Which problem?' the King asked.

'The big problem,' Brother Geoffrey whispered.

'The Becket thing?' Henry replied.

'No, the other big problem.'

'The rebels in Poitou?'

'No, Your Majesty,' the monk sighed, 'the serious big thing.'

King Henry scratched under his armpit and swore. 'The serious big thing? King Louis of France?'

The monk lowered his voice. 'No, the serious thing we spoke about in your chambers in private. The thing we can't talk about with all these people here.'

The King's eyes flashed red for the briefest moment before he regained his composure. 'Well, why didn't you say so? What is it with you churchmen?'

'Can we speak somewhere in private?' Brother Geoffrey asked.

Henry let out a deep breath. 'I've just walked further on my own two feet than I have before in my entire life. I am not leaving this hall until those two feet stop throbbing.'

The monk fidgeted with his fingers.

Henry bellowed a deep laugh. 'Calm down, I'm not sending you away.' The King made to stand up, thought twice, then remained seated as he raised his voice. 'Clear the hall. Everyone out, go on. Now.'

There was some argument as the more high-ranking men in the hall glared back with tight lips, but one by one, the well-dressed occupants left.

As soon as they were gone, the hall became cavernous and sounds echoed from the tall, ice-cold walls.

'There you are, monk,' Henry said, 'some of them are so petty they will run home and plot rebellions against me for this. Whatever you are about to say had better be worth it.'

Brother Geoffrey nodded. 'I think it will be. You see, Richard here wants to join the tournament circuit.'

The King slapped his thigh and laughed. 'Why ever would you want to do that? You'll lose your horse within moments of the melee breaking out, if you even survive the grand charge.'

'I need the money,' Richard replied.

'Then you'd be better off being a knight for hire, real knights fight in real wars.'

Richard wasn't going to tell him how that had gone in Ireland.

'Yes, Richard,' Brother Geoffrey said slyly, 'why don't you try that?'

'If the King plans any more campaigns, I'd be happy to serve with him again,' Richard answered.

'A good response,' Henry's eyes shone, 'we certainly had some moments in Brittany, didn't we?'

Richard nodded.

'However, I'm too busy with this ridiculous Becket thing,' the King said, 'I need to play the humble penitent for as long as possible, so I will wear hair rather than mail for some time.'

'If I may,' the monk interrupted.

'You may not,' Henry said, 'I would rather talk to this man about our war stories than talk to you.'

'You sent away everyone for a reason,' Brother Geoffrey said, 'I would like to propose something to you.'

The King sighed. 'Very well.'

'Richard wants to play the tournament knight, but he has no company to ride with. On his own, he is all but certain to end up horseless and armour-less. It is therefore believable that he would approach a company to join. He has a history of violence that will endear him to the sort of knights who frequent tournaments. And you, Your Majesty, have a son with his own company who you suspect of plotting rebellion.'

Henry put two and two together in an instant. 'You want to plant a spy in my son's household?'

'Precisely. You already assigned loyal men to some of the important posts in his household, but the Young King knows exactly who they are. When he last tried to rebel, those men refused to join him and returned to you, leaving us with no one to inform us of his intentions. Anyone you appoint, he knows their history, so they cannot spy because he simply doesn't confide in them. He never even speaks to them.'

The King stared at Richard. 'I think he's loyal, do you think he'll turn rogue like the last one?'

Brother Geoffrey clasped his hands together in front of him. 'That was most regrettable, but your decision to use him was still the correct one. The rogue has taught your son the use of arms better than anyone else could have.'

'Damn that rogue,' Henry raged, the words spitting from his lips with sudden anger.

'We simply misjudged his childlike view of loyalty,' the monk said, 'by giving him a new lord, our spy took it rather more literally than any other knight would have done.'

'Will you?' Henry asked Richard. 'Will you betray me like the Marshal did?'

'Marshal?' Richard blurted out. 'William Marshal?'

'How many Marshals are there?' the King shouted. 'There is only one, a fact that the Marshal himself can't seem to stop spouting from his treacherous mouth. And after I paid for his ransom. The ingrate.'

'If I may,' the monk said quickly, 'the Marshal still is loyal to you, he just sees the whole matter differently. You assigned him to the Young King, so he is now loyal to his new lord. Albeit above and over you.'

'I am the King of England, I rule from the frozen wastes of the north to the mountains that separate us from the Spanish Kingdoms. I rule twice as much land as the King of France, and yet this one knight takes my son as his lord above me.'

Brother Geoffrey ignored him so calmly that this couldn't have been his first tirade. 'That is all very true,' he said, 'but it also is the reason Richard here might be accepted.'

Henry's face cooled and his arching eyebrows asked the monk to explain.

'Richard was at Castle Tancarville with the Marshal. They were quite close, something I saw with my own eyes. The Marshal will advocate for him, I am sure of that. The Young King will therefore accept him, first at a distance, but over time I'm sure he will trust Richard. This boy seems to have a knack of drawing in people who should know better. He can warn us if another rebellion is being planned, and tell us who is involved.'

The King nodded. 'It pains me I cannot trust my own son, but ever since we placed that crown on his head and made him a king in the eyes of God, he has been insufferable. Having turned on me with force of arms once already, I feel in no way bad for spying on him. Richard, you will do this for me.'

Richard didn't like the sound of that, but the King hadn't asked his opinion.

'Why did you crown him?' Richard asked instead.

'Why indeed?' Henry shot Brother Geoffrey a biting glance. 'Because it makes the succession clear. It stops barons speculating on who should be the next king and causing a civil war. We cannot have another time of anarchy such as we have only recently emerged from. My son, young Henry, is now a crowned king, and will follow me onto this throne. You will serve him, Richard, and tell me when he gets impatient and wants to take my throne before the proper time.'

'Again,' Brother Geoffrey added.

'Stay your tongue, monk, do not get above yourself,' Henry said, 'but I am sick of squabbles amongst my children. My son's younger brothers follow his lead, but I may give them land just to spite him. That will show him who really wears the crown. It might peel some of his followers away from his side, too.'

'That is a wonderful idea,' Brother Geoffrey said.

'I know that, monk, and trying to flatter me so crudely doesn't make me like you any more.'

'Your Majesty,' Richard bowed.

Henry cocked his head slightly. 'What do you want? Is your task not clear enough?'

'It is painfully clear,' Richard replied, 'but I had actually journeyed here to Canterbury to speak to you about another matter.'

'Had you now?'

Richard nodded. 'A while ago, my grandfather gave over my family lands to you in order that my uncle could run them. But this was a trick of my uncle, who convinced my grandfather I was dead. The land should be mine.'

Henry yawned. 'Do you know how many such family disputes I hear every day?'

Richard shook his head.

'Well nor do I,' the King said, 'because they all send me to sleep.'

Richard held the King's gaze but said nothing.

'Fine, don't look at me like that,' Henry said, 'that's how my wife looks at me when she will not let something go.'

Richard opened his mouth to ask how the Queen was, but closed it when he imagined Henry's response.

'Who is your uncle? Do I need to care about him if I dispossess him?'

Richard scoffed under his breath. 'He recently died.'

'That makes this easier, then,' Henry said.

Richard's heart skipped a beat. Would the King grant his wish here and now?

Two knights walked into the hall but the King bellowed at them and they turned and fled.

'I would not award it just yet,' the monk said, 'let the boy prove his loyalty with your son first.'

Richard's eyes shone fury, and he turned on the monk.

'You've hit a sore point, monk,' Henry laughed, which stopped Richard from pummelling the smug monk's rat-like face.

'Consider Keynes as the hostage for your good behaviour,' the King said, 'if you stay loyal to me, unlike the Marshal, then I will give it to you.'

Richard fumed, he had been but a word away from reclaiming his rightful lands.

'Oh calm down,' Henry waved a hand at him, 'this is how business is usually done. Almost everyone seems to betray me, so what choice do we have? You will join the Young King's household, earn his trust, and report to Brother Geoffrey every time you move on, or any word regarding rebellion or disloyalty comes to your ears. Needless to say, if you turn your cloak on me like the Marshal has, Keynes is forfeit, along with whatever your village in Normandy is called.'

Richard didn't answer.

'Do not tell your old friend we have had this conversation,' Brother Geoffrey added, 'he is still loyal to King Henry, but now he is loyal to the Young King first. You cannot trust the Marshal.'

The name sounded strange in Richard's ears. Sir Wobble sounded right. He knew Sir Wobble, but did he know the Marshal?

'Shall we go?' Brother Geoffrey asked. 'You have much to do.'

Richard accompanied the monk back to the bailey, which was now full of the dozens of men the King had evicted from his hall. They watched Richard go with scornful and jealous glances. The black dog had gone to lie down behind Solis, and both animals turned their heads when he appeared to retrieve them. A black horse next to his palomino had a new hoof print on its flank, so Richard removed Solis quietly and left the castle with Brother Geoffrey.

The monk looked smug as they wound their way back to the cathedral, probably because he finally had something real to hold over Richard.

Bowman slept in his saddle as one cart carrying stones snapped an axle and square stones slid off and thumped into the square. The noise woke Bowman up with a start and he noticed Richard's return.

'Took you long enough,' Bowman said, 'are we going to Keynes or Normandy?'

'The King will give me Keynes if I do something for him. It's probably best if you don't know what.'

'You're holding back from us, are you?' Bowman asked.

'It's safer for you if you don't know.'

'He's right,' Brother Geoffrey said, 'if you don't know, you can't blurt it out when you're drunk.'

'You think I can't hold my drink?' Bowman said, too loudly.

Richard couldn't help laughing. 'Do you remember when you got drunk in Waterford? That didn't go so well, did it?'

Bowman narrowed his eyes, then pretended to look up at the cathedral.

'So Keynes will have to wait?' Gerold asked. He'd been almost silent since they'd left the Martel castle.

'For now,' Richard said, 'we just need to do something before I can get it back. Before *we* can get it back.'

The old Keynes man nodded. 'I serve your family, not your lands, but it would mean something to me if we can recover them. I would wish

Keynes to be in your name, to honour your father's memory. Our law, and God's too, dictate that Keynes should be yours.'

Richard couldn't agree more. 'We'll do this one last thing for the King, then justice will be done.'

Gerold nodded, the grey streaks amongst his black hair shimmered in the light as the sun started its evening descent. 'I will follow you wherever the King needs you to go,' he said.

Nicholas swept back his wolf-pelt so he could itch his scalp. 'It's a bit too warm when the sun's on it,' he said.

Bowman turned to him. 'I don't suppose you're having second thoughts about staying with us, mother's boy?'

Nicholas grunted. 'Me the mother's boy? Our mother preferred you. If anything, you're the mother's boy.'

'Enough,' Richard said, 'I know you're both coming with me, and I'll need all three of you on the tournament field.'

'So, we're still doing that?' Bowman asked.

Richard nodded. 'The burden of the King's task is mine alone, but we are still going to earn some ransoms across the sea.'

'Will the monk want to come and watch that?' Bowman asked.

'I'm right here,' Brother Geoffrey said, 'and I am certainly coming with you.'

'Not you,' Bowman said, 'our monk.'

'Your monk?'

'Him,' Richard nodded over to the cathedral, from which a glum-looking Brian emerged.

Brother Geoffrey frowned and Richard wondered if he was somehow jealous of Brian.

'I thought you could spend days in there?' Richard asked.

Brian pushed his way around a pilgrim with a growth on his neck. The monk reached Richard and shook his head. 'There is no peace inside. People kept pushing me, one fat man knocked me into a wall trying to get past. Everyone talks loudly and there are men in there selling water blessed by the old archbishop. You are not supposed to sell things in churches, Richard.'

'Who is this?' Brother Geoffrey asked bitterly.

'This is Brian, he's one of us,' Richard answered.

The Irish monk's face flushed with pride before he swallowed it down. 'Who are you?' he asked the older monk.

'Brother Geoffrey of Cluny. Why do you accompany Richard? I hardly believe it can be because of his piety.'

'We don't have time to go into that,' Richard said.

'Is he a real monk?' Brother Geoffrey asked harshly, 'tell me, if you are really a monk, who was Bernard of Clairvaux?'

Brian snorted. 'He founded a Benedictine abbey in a clear valley, which is what Clairvaux means. He helped to forge the Rule of the Knights Templar, telling them what they should and should not do. That is why their Rule looks a lot like the Benedictine rule, and Templars act so much like Benedictine monks.'

Brother Geoffrey stood motionless.

Richard looked at him. 'Is he right?'

'Perhaps,' Brother Geoffrey replied.

Brian grinned at Richard. He stared Brother Geoffrey straight in the eyes and asked him. 'Is this bitter old man really a monk?'

'How dare you,' Brother Geoffrey said.

Richard's black dog growled at him and the older monk looked at it out of the corner of his eye.

'Very well,' Brian said, 'name the three sites in England that adhere to the way of Cluny, your supposed home.'

All eyes turned to Brother Geoffrey. He hesitated. 'I have not been to Cluny in a long time.'

'He's not asking you about Cluny,' Bowman said, 'he's asking you about England, which isn't so far away, is it?'

'Yes,' Richard said, 'tell us the three houses.'

Brother Geoffrey rolled his tongue around his mouth. 'The youth of today have no respect,' he said, 'which can only be expected when they come from somewhere as dark and pagan as Ireland.'

'How pagan can he be if he knows more about your holy order than you do?' Richard asked.

Bowman laughed.

'You would do well to respect me,' Brother Geoffrey said, 'you will need me in the court of the Young King.'

'The Young King?' Bowman asked. 'What's he got to do with us?'

'We need to join his company,' Richard said, 'then we'll be safer during the tournaments.'

'And where will we find him?' Bowman asked. 'There are tournaments from Brittany to Flanders and right across to the Empire. He could be in Paris for all we know.'

Brother Geoffrey sighed. 'This is why you need me, you are all foolish and ignorant.'

'I think Brian proved that you're ignorant, too,' Richard smiled.

Brother Geoffrey pretended he hadn't heard. 'Make no mistake, you are foolish, Richard. How many men were in the King's hall?'

'I didn't count. Fifty?'

'And how many horses were outside?'

'Two hundred.'

'So you counted those,' Bowman scoffed.

Richard shrugged back. 'So?'

'My boy,' Brother Geoffrey said, 'who is ignorant now? Where do you think the other hundred and fifty men were?'

'Oh,' Richard nodded, 'the Young King is here?'

'Indeed. And without me, you would have boarded a ship and sailed away from him tomorrow. So do not mock me. Go to him now and ingratiate yourself. Reach his inner circle. I will seek you out daily, but will not go with you to him now so he does not see us together.'

Bowman narrowed his eyes. 'Why do you need to be in his inner circle?'

'That's the thing it's better that you don't know about,' Richard said.

Bowman groaned.

Brother Geoffrey took his leave and melted into the bustling crowd around the cathedral.

'Can we go now?' Bowman asked. 'Just standing here has made me feel unwell.'

Nicholas nodded, and the wolf on his head nodded with him. 'I think it would be good to be amongst our own kind,' he said.

'No one is your kind,' Bowman grumbled.

'Come on, we'll go to the castle and find the Young King,' Richard said.

'Another strutting peacock, I'd wager,' Bowman said.

'It's funny you should say that,' Richard said, unsure whether he was happy about it, 'because our favourite peacock is with him, and I think he's going to be more insufferable now than ever.'

Bowman sighed.

They left Brian to mind the horses in the castle bailey, a task he volunteered for because he was worried the knights would not be sparing in mockery of his accent.

This time Richard led the others up a staircase to the first floor of the keep and into a wide hall. Unlike the one below, this one did not house King Henry. This hall had three huge arched windows on one wall that let in three great pillars of light. Wooden wall panels painted in reds and blues obscured the stone behind, so bright that they almost offended Richard's eyes.

It was noisy, too, for at least a hundred men, many of whom were mailed, spoke, shouted, and laughed at each other across the vast space. Some wore surcoats of bright colours, and others of red which looked like those worn by King Henry's household in Brittany. A few knights walked about with a hawk or falcon on their fist, a very unsubtle display of status. Bowman complained about them and Richard had to tell him to mind his courtesy.

As his father had been arranged in the floor below, the Young King sat on a throne on a raised platform at the far end of the hall, but unlike his father, his household officials surrounded him. A thin crown of gold hung at an angle from one of the golden orbs on his throne behind his head.

Richard slowly pushed his way through the ranks of men until he reached the front and Sir Wobble caught his eye.

He remembered the last time they'd met, when his friend sulked about Richard delivering his ransom even as he set him free. Then refusing to help him with the Little Lord because Richard had taken too long to deliver that ransom. Richard's anger rose with the memory of it, and the memory of the long campaign in Brittany he'd had to endure in order just to earn that ransom. And the finger he'd lost in the process. Then he remembered Keynes was at stake, so he took a moment to calm himself.

Sir Wobble stood tall on the Young King's right-hand side, wearing his mail and his tattered green knighting cloak that had been shredded during the Battle of Neufchatel. His dark face more resembled that of a man now, and his stature was proud and confident. He wore a sword with a red jewel embedded in the hilt, too gaudy for Richard's taste.

The Young King was also tall and broad-shouldered. He had a long neck, but unlike Sir Wobble had pale skin covered in freckles. His bright, wide eyes laughed at something someone was telling him, and he ruffled his reddish hair occasionally as if it was a habit.

Although he looked like he might be a year or two younger than Richard, he looked a much more agreeable man to follow than the elder King Henry.

To the Young King's left stood a man in his twenties with curly brown hair and a surcoat over his tunic with the same yellow and red chequerboard pattern the Martels had. He looked nothing like a Martel though, and when Richard prodded Nicholas and asked him if he knew the man, the Martel knight said he didn't.

Behind these three stood an array of older men in civilian clothing who yawned and scratched their beards. These must be the men the King had installed to guide his son, their age and manner marked them out as different to almost everyone else in the hall.

Sir Wobble's eyes lit up as he recognised Richard. 'You,' he shouted loudly enough that the Young King looked up at him with a frown.

'Richard,' Sir Wobble said, 'where have you been? It's been far too long since we saw each other.'

Bowman choked down a cough of disbelief behind Richard, for they had both expected a far frostier welcome.

'Well?' Sir Wobble asked. 'Are you here to see me, or join our company?'

'Both?' Richard replied.

The Young King studied Richard's face and his eyes flickered down momentarily to his missing finger. 'Marshal, is this a friend of yours?' he asked in a high, warm voice.

Sir Wobble nodded. 'He is, introduce yourself Richard.'

'I am Richard of Yvetot, a small village in Normandy. I have three knights with me and I wish to fight on the tournament circuit.'

'A knight with a small village who yet travels with three other knights,' the Young King mused to himself, 'if your village is small it can only be worth a single knight's fee, so your knights cannot hold land from you.'

Richard shook his head in agreement.

'Are they family?'

'No,' Richard replied.

'Then why do they stay with you?'

Richard shrugged. 'You'd have to ask them.'

The Young King broke into a smile. 'I think they follow you because of you yourself. Most unusual.'

Pride welled up and Richard felt a slight urge to admit to the Young King about his father's spying scheme.

'What are you best at?' the Young King asked, his eyes soft and friendly.

'Best at?'

'Every knight who wishes to enter my service stands before me and exclaims that they are the best rock thrower, the fastest runner, or can ride for the longest out of all the knights in our realm. What is your claim?'

Richard contemplated saying something about riding. A worry surfaced that he might be asked to prove it, and Solis was just as likely to embarrass him as vindicate him. 'I can't really think of anything,' he said instead.

Nicholas, who was mindlessly standing in another direction looking up at a tapestry on the wall depicting the death of Caesar, opened his mouth. 'He's actually quite good at killing kings.'

The knights, barons, and counts in the hall, not to mention the crowned Young King himself, fell to silence. Ice crept across the chamber and up Richard's spine. He gulped down hard.

'I told you,' Bowman nudged Richard, 'he's a liability.'

As a hundred eyes drilled into him, Richard was inclined to agree.

'I think you need to explain that,' Sir Wobble's hand dropped to his sword.

Richard had an idea. 'We have just returned from the campaign in Ireland,' he said.

'I thought we weren't mentioning that,' Bowman said.

The onlookers spoke amongst themselves in hushed tones.

'Ireland?' the Young King said. 'My father forbade that venture.'

Richard nodded. 'And yet we went.'

Bowman grunted and then whispered in his ear. 'Very clever, young lord.'

The knights nearest made approving noises.

Sir Wobble removed his hand from his weapon. 'Ah, so you killed an Irish king?'

Richard nodded and the Young King visibly relaxed in his chair.

'How did you kill him?' the curly haired man with the red and yellow surcoat asked.

Nicholas opened his mouth again but Bowman stomped his heel down on his toes, then pretended to apologise.

Nicholas shot him an angry look and kept quiet.

'With the blessing of God,' Richard said.

The Young King laughed. 'I like you, you are amusing. I can see why the Marshal has a fondness for you.'

'I wouldn't go that far,' Sir Wobble said.

'But your knights seem ill-disciplined and rude,' the Young King said.

'I can't argue with that,' Richard said, 'but when you're standing in a blood-soaked ditch with only them and Raymond the Large by your side, and two thousand screaming Irishmen are charging you, I wouldn't ask for anyone else.'

More hushed conversations sprung up in the crowd behind Richard.

'You were at Baginbun Head?' the Young King asked, his voice more quiet than before.

Sir Wobble's face turned red. 'When did Bowman get his golden spurs? He's even less nobly born than you are, and you can't afford the gold to knight him.'

'Raymond the Large knighted him as the Irish crested a hill and poured down on us,' Richard lied.

Bowman stood tall beside him and puffed out his chest.

'Who's the peacock now?' his half-brother said.

Sir Wobble didn't look as happy anymore. 'But I was knighted before you,' he turned to his lord, 'Richard was knighted after me when we fought at Neufchatel.'

'Marshal, you're doing it again,' the Young King said, 'you don't need to prove anything to me.'

'I heard stories about you, you're famous across the world,' Richard said to Sir Wobble. The peacock might envy his recent adventures, but Richard still needed his friend to vouch for him.

Sir Wobble half smiled.

'I heard about a tournament where you won a pike and defeated all before you,' Richard said.

'The pike was at Pleurs,' Sir Wobble smiled fully, 'I fought so many foes, and withstood so many blows, that my helmet was beaten onto my head so closely I couldn't take it off. I had my head on a smith's anvil so he could hammer it free. It was still stuck on when they delivered the verdict of my victory. My left ear still rings from that,' he rubbed it without thought.

Many knights in the hall laughed, but some groaned and rolled their eyes.

'He's not changed, then,' Bowman mumbled.

'I remember him being extremely sulky,' Nicholas said, 'but then that was at Castle Lusignan.'

Sir Wobble peered down at the knight and his wolf-pelt. 'You? What are you doing here? I remember you from the forest when you tried to arrest us for...'

Bowman coughed loudly, and everyone looked at him.

Richard decided it would be best if they didn't admit to poaching in front of a crowned king. 'This is the same man, but he serves me now,' he said.

Sir Wobble licked his lips. 'You have always kept strange company, Richard,' he said.

'Most entertaining company,' the Young King said. 'I must confess I am quite jealous of your stories. There is, for my part, the story of myself and the Marshal at the Anet tournament,' most of the knights chuckled, 'but these are mere shadows of deeds done in war. I have seen war, but it did not go well. Unfortunately, I never had the chance to lower my lance at an enemy. Perhaps that is why I lost.'

'You were badly advised,' a man behind the Young King said. He had a head that was wider at the top than the bottom, and big round eyes that seemed kind. Those eyes narrowed at Sir Wobble. The surcoat over the man's mail was yellow, blue, and green.

'Thank you, Adam,' the Young King said, 'but I know what happened. I was there. Next time will be different.'

Richard held his breath. The King's worries about rebellion were justified.

The Young King pointed at Richard and laughed. 'Look at him, he is shaking like a baby in the cold.'

Sir Wobble put his hand over his mouth and stifled a snigger.

Richard half laughed and half shook his head.

'I'm just having fun with you,' the Young King said, 'if you can't take a joke, then you'd be no good to have around.'

'You shouldn't tease the fresh knights,' Adam said, 'tease the ones who've earned it. Tell the joke about the Marshal at Anet, don't pick on the young ones.'

'This young one has fought at least one full campaign,' the Young King said, 'how many have you fought, Adam?'

Adam looked away with annoyance.

Richard couldn't take his eyes from Adam's surcoat.

The knight looked back and caught Richard's gaze. 'Yes?' he asked.

'My apologies, I thought I've seen those colours before. Where are you from?' Richard asked.

'Yquebeuf.'

Bowman coughed. 'I'm sorry, is that a place or an illness?'

Adam ignored him. 'It is my family's manor in Normandy.'

Richard remembered that combination of colours. 'Do you know Sir Roger de Cailly?'

Adam looked at Richard a little deeper. 'He is my lord. His manor is the next one over from mine.'

Richard smiled. 'He was my lord too.'

Adam nodded. 'I know who you are, and where Yvetot is.'

'You can marry each other later,' the Young King said to a ripple of laughter from the watching knights.

Sir Wobble crossed his arms and scowled in Adam's direction.

'I can feel your eyes, Marshal,' the Young King said without looking at him, 'you should save your envy for your old friend, he'll be the talk of my court for weeks.'

A man with a chest like a wine barrel pushed through the front of the crowd and inspected Richard. 'This man?' the newcomer said. 'He's but a boy.'

His accent was English, but rough and even further from French in sound than Richard knew his own was.

'Calm down, Henry,' the Young King said, 'your precious Marshal is still the greatest knight in this hall.'

'And none should fast forget it,' Henry replied.

'This is Henry the Northerner,' Sir Wobble said, 'do not mind him or his ill-ordered words.'

Richard thought little of Henry the Northerner, he was nearly as old as Gerold but his face was too smooth and soft to be a man of war. His deep voice boomed across the hall and echoed from the rafters high above.

'The baby looks at me like I'm devilled,' Henry the Northerner said, 'he cannot compare to the great Marshal.'

'Call off your dog,' the Young King said, 'before I have to kick him. You know his voice grates me.'

'Henry,' Sir Wobble said, 'I've known Richard for longer than anyone else here, do not attack him. Besides, he will surely be the talk of the court only for a day or two.'

'This is childish, can I go?' Bowman asked Richard.

'No, learn to put up with him.'

'Put up with him?' Henry the Northerner said. 'He is the greatest knight in the kingdom. You should bow with him.'

'To him,' Richard corrected, 'you should bow *to* him.'

The Young King chuckled and looked at Sir Wobble. 'Are all the knights from Lord Tancarville's little school so self assured?'

'Not all in the same way,' Sir Wobble replied.

Henry the Northerner pointed a chubby finger at Richard. 'You might have known him first, but I've been here beside the greatest knight.'

'Nobody cares,' the Young King waved at him to leave.

Henry looked between the Marshal and the Young King, and the Marshal nodded. Henry stalked back into the crowd.

'You should chain him to a post outside,' Adam said to the Young King, 'he brings us all down with his lack of courtesy.'

'He is the Marshal's man,' the Young King replied, 'and I will never command my beloved Marshal to do anything he doesn't wish to.'

'He's harmless,' Sir Wobble said, 'he's just enthusiastic.'

The knight with the blue, yellow, and green surcoat sighed. 'Well, if Richard here ruffled Henry the Northerner's grubby feathers so much, I'm for admitting him into your retinue.'

'What do you think, Marshal?' the Young King asked.

Sir Wobble nodded. 'He'll be useful on the field.'

'Thank you, Sir Wobble,' Richard said.

Sir Wobble recoiled at the name. 'I am the Marshal now,' he said haughtily.

'The peacock has grown too big for his own feathers,' Bowman said quietly.

'Sir Wobble?' the Young King peered at the young man out of the corner of his eye.

'An old name,' the Marshal replied, 'a child's one. We don't use it anymore.'

'Very well,' the Young King said, 'and Richard, you will stay with me and we shall see how you fare in your first tournament. If you show valour, I will retain you and your ill-mannered knights.'

'Thank you,' Richard bowed and allowed himself to relax a little.

'Adam,' the Young King said, 'the Marshal's place is by my side, so take Richard away and tell him how things work.'

Adam nodded and stepped off the platform.

'I will now return to the business of lawyers, clerks, and ruling my lands,' the Young King said loudly, then cocked his head, 'of course though, I won't, because my father won't grant me any lands.'

The hall erupted in laughter, but a tinge of something else invaded the young man's voice.

Adam motioned at Richard, who followed him out of the crowd.

'Is the Marshal really your friend?' Adam asked. 'He is insufferable.'

'That's the word I used for him,' Bowman said once they were out of earshot of anyone else.

'He's not so bad,' Richard said.

Adam chuckled. 'Maybe not when you had child-names for each other. But the Young King told me to speak of things here, and I don't want to, so this will be brief. The Marshal has taught the Young King the way of war, and for some reason has his full trust. The Old King's officials try to keep a check on his spending and extravagance, but they fail. Many noble and rich men try to become the Young King's friend, but the only one who is near equal to the Marshal, is Count Robert of Meulan, who is here somewhere. The other knights are many and of every sort. The Young King maintains twelve only himself.'

'Then what are the rest doing here?' Richard asked.

Adam smiled. 'When the Young King plays the knight errant and roams the tournament fields, he employs several score more.'

'He's off to tourney now?'

Adam nodded. 'Of course, he has been confined in England for too long.'

Richard remembered his task from Brother Geoffrey. 'Where is the first tournament? Where are we going?'

'Lagny,' Adam said.

'Where's that?' Richard asked.

Adam shook his head. 'You fight in Ireland but don't even know of Lagny? Lagny is but a single day's ride from Paris. Richard, we're going to France.'

THE CIRCUIT

Richard forewarned Brother Geoffrey of the destination of the Young King's household the first chance he'd got, which had been as the old Roman lighthouse inside Dover Castle faded away behind them, and waves lapped the sides of their ship as they crossed the narrow sea. The monk had almost danced in celebration, for he hadn't yet been able to uncover that news for himself.

Richard was glad the sea crossing was short, and it was Nicholas, clinging to the wood high on the prow of their ship, that spotted the lighthouse of Boulogne first. Despite the daylight, a bright light shone from its tower atop a hill overlooking the port. The crew, efficient and accustomed to their task, slid out oars and slowly navigated their way to shore and to France.

As they waited to disembark, Richard leant on the side of the ship with Bowman, the black dog sitting between them.

'Are tournaments different from how they are in the stories?' Richard asked.

The blonde man shrugged. 'I've never seen one, young lord. I've spent most of my time back in England, where they've mostly been forbidden.'

'Why?'

'The King thinks they are a hotbed of rebellion and lawlessness,' Bowman explained.

A knight and two clerks from their ship argued with some officials from Boulogne over the customs fee for their entrance. That fee was waived the moment the officials realised the Young King was onboard.

Unloading the three ships took half the day, and Richard noted that more knights disembarked here than had done so as part of Strongbow's Irish invasion fleet.

Boulogne was under the control of Count Philip of Flanders, and traded under his banner. That yellow banner flew from a pole above the port, a proud black lion in its centre, a recent addition according to Adam, one that put Philip at the forefront of fashion. Richard remembered it had been the Flemings they'd fought against at the Battle of Neufchatel and wondered if Count Philip had led them into that battle himself. Richard was therefore pleased when they rode south and out of Flemish territory, and two days later reached the bustling town of Amiens.

Amiens straddled the River Somme, and the town turned out in great numbers to welcome the Young King and his retinue. Even before the houses of the town appeared, families and local knights lined the road to glimpse Angevin royalty, throw flowers at him, or even try to walk up and touch him. Richard rode at the very front with the Marshal, within a vanguard with the duty of ensuring the road ahead was clear of danger. Danger seemed a long way off as they entered the town, where cheering people hung out of upper storey windows to get the best view of the procession. Richard's dog loped behind them with its pink tongue hanging out happily wherever they went.

'I've never felt so loved,' Bowman contemplated the crowd as he rode next to Richard.

'It's not for you though, is it,' Richard replied.

A group of young women ran up to them with wreaths of flowers. The Marshal took one with a wide grin and hung it over the front of his saddle. Solis intercepted one with his teeth and ripped it away from a woman who yelped in surprise. The stallion shook it around in his mouth before it flew out and hit Henry the Northerner's horse on its rear. That brown horse kicked out and clipped a young girl with a wreath on the arm, causing her to drop it and cry out in pain.

'Control your horse, Henry,' the Marshal shouted at him, 'we're trying to look good.'

Bowman laughed and Richard ignored the icy stare Henry shot towards him once he'd regained control of his horse.

A trio of brown dancing bears greeted the procession as they entered a bridge over the Somme. A pair of horses backed away from the bears and bumped into each other as their uncertain hooves drummed the road. The Marshal pushed his horse ahead of them, insulted their riders, and the more wary animals followed his lead. Beyond the bridge lay most of Amiens, and it was in the centre of the town that the column paused.

The rich and powerful of the town turned out with their brightly coloured tunics and cloaks, their best hunting dogs beside them and their falcons never far away. One leading merchant had two dancing monkeys that the Marshal found hilarious as they jumped and spun, white teeth showing in either a grin or a snarl. Richard didn't trust their tiny eyes and their needle-sharp teeth.

Richard waited on his horse as the crowd jostled to get a view of the Young King when he stopped at the dignitaries. The Young King remained mounted while there was a fight over who could hold his right stirrup to aid his dismount. The merchant with the monkeys won thanks to a well aimed punch, and once the Young King was on his own two feet, the merchant beamed as if he'd won some grand prize.

'This is very different to what we're used to,' Richard said.

Bowman nodded. 'I could get used to it, though.'

'If we do well in the tournament, we might be able to. But I need to find out how to do that.'

'Go and ask the peacock,' Bowman said as the Marshal found a knight he knew in the crowd and went to talk to him. Everywhere the air hummed with cheers and shouts. Music came from at least four different places, and the various sounds merged together into an incoherent cacophony that made Richard feel crowded in.

Nicholas rode his horse with Richard, but when the townspeople saw his wolf-pelt their cheers dimmed and they shuffled away. The Marshal told Richard to go away and leave him alone if Nicholas was going to scare the locals.

In one corner of the square the beat of a drum started up and soon a collection of flutes joined it and people danced around the musicians.

'He's not even their king,' Bowman mused as the Young King, golden crown on his head, spoke to the local notables. The red-haired man crouched down by a dancing monkey and tickled it under its chin, which sent the onlookers into raptures of excitement.

'He's just tickling a monkey,' Bowman said, 'if I did that, they'd probably lock me up.'

Henry the Northerner rode his horse, which had the slightest limp, behind the Marshal and announced his name to the masses. The words boomed over the heads of those nearby and some rushed to see the famous knight.

'He's loving this,' Richard said.

'Too much,' Bowman added, 'and that loud dog he has following him around shouting his name is getting on my nerves.'

Richard laughed, but Henry the Northerner was close enough to hear and ceased his proclamation of the Marshal's name. 'It's nothing to do with you,' he snapped in their direction.

'Just do it a little quieter if you can,' Richard couldn't wipe the smile from his face.

'No one asked for your opinion,' Henry shouted, 'who do you think you are?'

'Whatever we are,' Bowman said, 'it's better than being a peacock's dog.'

Henry kicked his horse on and charged towards them as the residents of Amiens cheered their new and unplanned entertainment.

Henry flashed his sword out and waved it at Richard. The black dog raised its hackles and barked at Henry, but the sound was lost in background.

Richard pushed Solis out of the way and towards the Young King. His assailant followed, then slammed to a stop when he saw the Young King turn and look up at him.

'What are you doing?' the Young King asked. 'Put that sword away, this is a celebration, not a battle.'

Henry the Northerner turned bright red and replaced his weapon. 'Richard caused it,' he said.

'I don't care who caused it,' the Young King said, 'end it.'

Henry backed his horse up, then rode back towards his master with a foul look on his face.

'You should probably stop antagonising him,' Bowman said once he was gone.

'I think you did the antagonising,' Richard replied.

The Young King handed some gifts to the dignitaries and remounted his horse. It was not a warhorse, but his parade horse he'd ridden specifically for the town. Its coat shone white under the sun and its legs stepped high and with great energy. The stallion arched his thick neck as the Young King pointed him out of the square. As it went, it sometimes moved sideways and sometimes performed small jumps in the air to delight those who lined the streets leading out of Amiens. Richard had heard of parade horses, they were immensely valuable and never to be risked in war. Instead, they reflected glory onto their riders by proudly displaying movements a warhorse couldn't, or at least shouldn't, perform.

The Marshal joined his lord, not to be outdone, on his own black parade horse which bounced along the street mostly on its hind legs, as if constantly jumping over a log, the Marshal unmoving in the saddle and waving as he leapt by.

Once they passed through Amiens' southern walls, both men swapped to travelling horses, their parade mounts dripping with sweat and panting with exertion.

'How far have we still got to go?' Richard asked the Marshal when they took their place again at the head of the procession.

'Two days to Lagny from here,' the knight replied, 'but my lord has asked me to go ahead and secure lodgings for him. The town will overflow with knights soon, and we must find him the very best of the houses. If a lowly knight, or even a count has already taken the best house, we are to throw him out.'

'Will you tell me what I need to know of tournaments?' Richard asked. 'I don't want to make a fool of myself.'

The Marshal frowned at Richard with confusion in his eyes. 'But you have fought across Brittany and Ireland, and apparently killed a king. Shouldn't you be the one teaching me?'

'I doubt it,' Richard replied, 'you never taught me how to wield a sword properly and I've lost count of how many times I've dropped it in battle.'

'I'm sure you can figure it out,' the Marshal said, 'but we need to get ahead of the Young King, are you ready to ride quickly?'

Richard nodded and his friend looked down at his palomino stallion.

'I see you still can't ride another horse, or can you simply not afford one?'

Richard frowned. 'Don't worry about me, I'll keep up,' he said. It was Brian he was worried about if they were to travel faster than an amble.

In the end Brian kept up, and he even stayed on his horse. The Marshal led them at pace until it was too dark to travel, but as soon as morning broke they were in the saddle again and pressing towards Paris and Lagny.

Forest flanked the road, in some places so thick the land felt wild. Despite the remote feel, traffic was at first heavy with carts pulled by oxen or horses. The Marshal was keen for progress however, and only as the sun peaked on that second day did he slow the pace.

The road became quiet, a straight line that cut through green sycamore trees and blackthorn bushes.

The Marshal jumped from his horse and waited for a servant to take it from him. 'I'm tired so I'm going to have a sleep,' he said.

Richard looked at Bowman. 'I expect Brian wouldn't mind a rest either.'

Bowman slid off his horse and stretched his lower back. 'Nor I.'

'Mind the ground though,' Richard said, 'horses shouldn't eat those sycamore seeds.'

Bowman shrugged and sat down on the ground with his back to a tree, his reins looped around his foot. The Marshal found his own tree by the roadside and was snoring softly within moments of finishing an apple.

Richard dismounted, but having no servant to mind him, he had to make do with letting Solis attack a blackthorn bush. The stallion kept at it, despite having to spit thorns out after every mouthful. The black dog at least could lie down and close its eyes in peace under a thorny bush.

Other riders dismounted and rested in whatever way they could, but at least the woods provided shade and calm. Birds chirped overhead, and the air was pleasantly cool.

Henry the Northerner handed his horse to one of the Marshal's servants and sneered at Richard. 'Where are your servants?' he asked.

'Don't rise to it,' Nicholas said from the other side of the road.

Richard decided to make a peace offering. 'I don't mean for there to be any trouble between us, could you tell me about tournaments?'

Henry's eyes narrowed as he searched Richard's face for signs of bad faith.

'I'm just trying to get along with you, no one else is helping me. Can you?' Richard asked.

The sturdy man softened his expression.

The sound of hooves rang out from the south. Solis shot his head up and his ears pricked toward the clattering of iron shoes on the Roman road. Richard glanced in the same direction, and after a moment two horses appeared from the trees travelling in the ambling gait. The first horse, almost floating along the road such was the smoothness of its movement, carried a tall man, thin in limb and body, dressed in fine silken clothing. His cloak fluttered out behind him like a banner and was lined in fox fur, which meant that although he was a rich man, he was not a noble.

The lady who rode behind him on a smaller chestnut palfrey was more glamorous. Her black-speckled white ermine fur caught Richard's eye as the pair of them rushed by. A shower of loose stones and grit flew from their hooves, which coated the sleeping Marshal.

The resting knight sprung up, wiped dust from his eyes on his way, and shouted after the riders. 'Stop or we'll chase you down,' he roared.

Bowman stayed still but opened one eye to watch, as did the black dog under its bush.

The rich merchant turned around, saw the fire in the Marshal, and pulled his horse up. His companion rode on until she realised the merchant had stopped.

'Ignore them,' she told him, 'come with me as you promised.'

The merchant thought about it, but he had not yet cleared the knights alongside the road and he knew he would not outrun them.

'Come back here, now,' the Marshal shouted. Richard wondered if his old friend had grown too used to giving orders.

The merchant turned his horse and walked it slowly towards the head of the Young King's vanguard, his face nervous.

The Marshal strode forwards and pointed at himself. 'Can't you see what you've done with your carelessness?'

'I am afraid I cannot,' the merchant said in an accent that rolled smoothly off his tongue.

'You've got dirt in my eye,' the Marshal poked it with his finger, 'where is your courtesy?'

The merchant struggled to find words. 'I am very sorry.'

'Wait,' Marshal said, 'you're not even a knight, are you?'

'I trade,' he replied.

The Marshal snorted. 'That explains the rudeness. Why do you travel with such a noble lady? It is highly inappropriate.'

The merchant's ermine-wearing companion rode up alongside him. Thinly built and with long brown hair under a silver circlet, Richard stared at her. Her dress was long and a dazzling blue, but most strikingly she looked furious with her companion. 'You don't have to stop for them,' she said harshly.

'My dear,' the merchant replied, 'one must stop for a knight, we can hardly run away, can we?'

She shot him a look but her lips stayed sealed.

'Why are you in such a hurry?' the Marshal asked. 'And why is a noblewoman not travelling with someone appropriate?'

'I am sorry for covering you in dust, please accept my humblest apologies,' the merchant half bowed.

'Grow a backbone,' the noblewoman hissed at him, 'let's ride away.'

'You will do no such thing,' the Marshal stepped closer to them. 'I am a knight and will investigate this matter. I shall dispense justice if wrongdoing has taken place.'

'Wrongdoing?' the merchant cried. 'We are but riding.'

'So let us continue,' the woman turned her horse away.

'Stay where you are,' the Marshal ordered, his voice echoing off the leafy trees around them.

The merchant noticed Brian rubbing his legs. 'You, monk. Can you aid us with this unreasonable knight?'

Brian looked up with wide, startled eyes.

Richard walked over. 'Leave him out of this, he's not involved.'

'Do I know you?' the Marshal asked the woman. 'Your face seems familiar. Have I seen you before?'

The noblewoman shook her head. 'Your accent is like dysentery in my ears, your words enter the air like stones in a soup.'

'I suppose that's a no,' Bowman opened his second eye and propped himself up.

Richard ignored him as the Marshal stepped right up to the riders and examined their horses. 'Maybe I know a relative of yours who shares your features?' the Marshal asked.

'That is more likely,' the woman replied, 'I am a niece of Count Philip of Flanders.'

'What are you, such a highborn lady, doing with the likes of him? A base merchant with no regard for honour or duty.'

'When did the peacock have a regard for honour or duty?' Bowman asked.

'Shut up,' Richard replied, 'come on Sir Wobble, leave these people to go away on their business.'

The Marshal neither paused nor looked away from the couple. 'Explain yourself, merchant.'

'We are fleeing to start a new life.'

'You weak man,' the woman said, 'how did you ever make your fortune with the nerves of a scolded child?'

'Runaways,' the Marshal scratched his chin, 'and you intend to live off your fortune?'

'Well, of course,' the merchant answered, 'I will buy and sell in Rouen and we shall be able to live off the profits.'

'How disgusting,' the Marchal grimaced. He stepped towards the merchant and prodded a finger up into the man's waist. Then he grabbed something which made a sound like grinding metal. 'You carry your fortune in coins?'

The merchant nodded. 'It is all we have.'

'How much do you have?'

The merchant remained silent.

'Let go of that,' the woman screamed, 'and let us go, my uncle will have your head for this.'

'I rather think he won't,' the Marshal smiled the way he had back at Castle Tancarville regardless of his situation, 'because your uncle would be devastated if you escaped. Think of the scandal, such a well-born lady living off trade? It will not do, I owe it to Count Philip to save you from this terrible fate.'

'I want to leave,' she said, 'this has nothing to do with you.'

'I am acting for your uncle, and also in your own interest,' the Marshal let go of the purse and tunic that covered it, and held his palm out.

'No, my God, no,' the merchant shrank back from it.

'Don't give it to him, ride off,' his companion ordered.

Richard sighed. 'This woman is distressed by you, let them be.'

The Marshal beckoned with his outstretched hand. 'This is for her honour as well as her uncle's.'

The merchant sobbed as he dropped the fat purse in the knight's palm. The Marshal opened the leather thong that drew it shut and looked inside. 'To save me the trouble of counting, how much is here?'

'Fifty pounds,' the merchant wiped his nose.

Every knight, squire, and servant along the road stopped what they were doing and stared dumbfounded at the merchant.

'How much?' Bowman's eyes bulged.

'Fifty pounds,' Richard blinked to himself, 'imagine what I could do with even five pounds.'

'I told you in La Rochelle, young lord, we should be merchants,' Bowman groaned.

'I can buy ten horses with that,' the Marshal's eyes lit up, and he pulled the drawstring tightly shut.

'It's not yours,' the woman said curtly, 'give it back.'

'His punishment for kidnapping you is to lose his ill-gotten money,' the Marshal said.

'He didn't kidnap me, I'm with him because I wish to be.'

'Just let us go,' tears ran down the merchant's cheeks.

The woman sighed at him and shook her head.

'Your punishment,' the knight told her, 'will be to either starve with this merchant, or return to Count Philip and leave this man behind. You may choose which.'

The noblewoman walked her horse away from the merchant and next to the Marshal. Her eyes looked down at his red surcoat and his swarthy face.

'What are you doing, my darling?' the merchant sniffed.

Richard wondered if his old friend even knew what a woman was.

The Marshal frowned at the noblewoman. 'Are you looking for an escort back to Count Philip's lands? Because we're going the wrong way, so I'm afraid we can't help you,' he said.

The woman's eyes lingered on the pouch longer than anywhere else.

Bowman pushed himself away from the tree and onto his feet. 'She's after the coins, peacock, get rid of her.'

'What are you saying?' the merchant asked.

Richard groaned. 'Can't you see? She doesn't care about you. She's already moved on. Get away from here and go back to whatever life you had.'

Nicholas approached the merchant and held a hand of berries out for his horse. The merchant on his horse however, could only see the head of the black wolf. He paled, spun his horse around, and flew along the road as fast as his horse could take him.

No one was much interested in his leaving.

'Are you married?' the noblewoman asked the Marshal.

'He's waiting for a rich heiress,' Richard said, which made Bowman laugh.

The Marshal shrugged. 'He's right, I'm waiting for a very rich heiress with vast lands. Unless you are that heiress, you best go back to Count Philip.'

'I am an heiress,' her face shone and her eyes were bright.

'Really?' the Marshal said. 'I'm a good friend of the Count, I've said that already haven't I? Maybe you should come with us, for he'll be at the tournament.'

'Will he?' the woman's face dropped.

The Marshal nodded. 'We will meet him tomorrow.'

'Nevermind,' the woman stepped her horse sideways away from him.

'Give Count Philip my regards,' the Marshal told her.

The woman rammed her legs onto her horse. It bounded away and took her back along the road until she disappeared into the leaves and was gone.

'Count Philip will be pleased when she returns,' the Marshal smiled and tucked the pouch away.

Bowman laughed. 'You're an idiot.'

'That was theft,' Brian looked up at the newly enriched knight, 'you just took it from them.'

'Their fleeing together was repulsive,' the Marshal said, 'they are lucky I didn't take their horses, they would have deserved it.'

The monk looked at Richard. 'Is this normal here?'

Richard wasn't entirely sure. 'Knights exist to dispense justice,' he said, 'and that woman was clearly up to no good.'

'Don't think too much about it,' Bowman said, 'either of you.'

'I'm not very tired anymore,' the Marshal looked around for his horse, 'it's time to get to Lagny, I've got some coin to spend.'

It wasn't long before the Marshal led them through Saint-Denis and past its famous chapel, which because Brian wasn't allowed to enter, caused him to fall into a sulk. They never saw Paris itself and arrived at Lagny as dusk had taken hold and braziers sent flickering light up the sides of the buildings. No two buildings looked the same, some were covered in pebbles, others plastered, and yet more plastered and painted in bright colours.

Freshly erected gallows stood at the entrance to the town, and Richard remembered what Bowman had told him about lawlessness and rebellion. Ignoring any such misgivings of disorder, inquisitive townspeople braved the dark to glimpse the new arrivals.

The Marshal's mail shimmered in the brazier light as watchmen pushed them aside to speak.

Richard pulled his cloak around himself to ward off the evening chill. Fortunately, they didn't have to wait in the cold for long, because as soon as the Marshal mentioned who their lord was, the watchmen led them to the grandest house in Lagny. The two-storey building had an overhanging top floor with red painted beams gleaming in the glow of the lanterns carried by the watchmen. They waved with their wood and horn lanterns at the building and the Marshal dismounted and knocked on the door.

A portly man with a magnificent grey beard appeared. 'I am the magistrate, what do you want?' he asked.

'The Young King requires your house for lodgings,' the knight replied.

The magistrate gasped and bowed. 'It would be my honour, I will have my family and dogs out of the house before you've stabled your horses.'

'You can leave the dogs,' the Marshal replied as the man rushed back inside.

'Aren't we going to tell him the Young King isn't here yet?' Richard asked.

Bowman swung his leg over the back of his saddle and dismounted. 'Of course not, we want to stay here tonight, don't we?' he grinned.

The magistrate was true to his word, and when Richard walked into the building after lodging his horse and the black dog in the same stable, there was nothing alive in the house except for three huge wolfhounds. Candles burned on shelves and the table in the hall, and a hearth already smouldered gently to send the sweet smell of well-seasoned wood across the chamber.

Bowman sniffed the air. 'We have slept nowhere this nice since before Ireland.'

Richard slumped into a chair by one of the two long tables and yawned. 'I've never been this far east, either,' he said.

'This is indeed a long way from Keynes,' Gerold inspected some pottery on the table in search of drink.

The Marshal sat at the centre of the largest table and relaxed into his chair. 'Now for the quiet before the storm,' he said to himself.

'Why? What happens next?' Richard asked.

'When word gets around we're here,' his friend replied, 'the local knights and rich townspeople will flock to see the Young King. They aspire to be of use to him, sometimes they just want to look upon him. It's a bit odd, really.'

Gerold drank something from a cup and nodded with surprise at its taste. 'Richard, this is the night before the tournament, all the knights are excited and will roam around drinking at each other's lodgings. There will be some fights, some things will be stolen, and in the morning heads will be sore.'

'That sounds about right,' the Marshal grinned, 'and everyone always clusters around us because we have the most famous and skilled knights.'

'You mean because we have the Young King,' Richard said, 'they don't care about you.'

Henry the Northerner slammed a cup down on the table but the Marshal held his hand up. 'Calm down, he's my friend.'

'He can't talk to you like that,' Henry said.

'I can say what I want,' Richard replied, his patience worn down by the four days they'd been on the road in his company.

'This is how it starts,' Gerold said, 'the stupid arguments and then the pointless fights. Your father didn't like tournaments, Richard.'

'My father never once mentioned tournaments to me, did he know them?'

Gerold chuckled then coughed. 'Your father fought in one at Northampton, even though the king at the time forbade it.'

'How did he fare?'

The older man shook his head. 'Well enough, but he thought them an extravagance, war is real.'

'War is dangerous,' Richard said, 'and in my experience, not very profitable.'

'Tournaments are dangerous too,' the Marshal said, 'but they are more enjoyable and glamorous than war.'

Adam walked into the hall, his green, yellow, and blue surcoat flowing behind him. 'There's already a crowd outside,' he said, 'every country knight within a day's ride is waiting to see the Young King. I think this is going to be one of the biggest tournaments we've ever seen.'

Richard felt a heady mix of excitement and nerves. His throat dried up, so he reached for a jug to see what was inside.

Nicholas added a couple of logs to the hearth, and the light from it dimmed until they caught.

Richard sank into his chair and closed his eyes. It was time to relax.

People came and went, but Richard's moment of calm was shattered when the Flemings arrived.

'Count Philip,' the Marshal jumped from his chair and held his arms out towards the tall, gangly man who strode towards him. The count had long legs, long arms, and even longer blonde hair. He wore no armour, indeed nothing other than a mustard yellow tunic and a black cloak. His household was mailed and wore yellow surcoats with a black lion, just as Richard had seen on the banners above the port of Boulogne.

The Marshal grabbed him, and they embraced tightly. Richard wondered what they had been through for that welcome to be normal, the Marshal had certainly not tried to embrace Richard when he first entered the court of the Young King.

'Where is he?' the Count asked.

'He is behind us, I don't know how you didn't meet him on the road,' the Marshal replied.

'I came not from my land,' Count Philip said.

'Then you will not know about your niece,' the Marshal replied.

'My niece?' the tall man frowned.

'We met her yesterday,' the English knight told him, 'she was riding with a merchant, escaping to live sinfully from the profits of selling.'

Count Philip's mouth dropped.

'Worry not, I rescued her and sent her back home.'

'On her own?' the Count asked.

'Of course,' the Marshal replied, 'she seemed quite capable of looking after herself.'

Count Philip pushed the knight away. 'You sent her off all on her own? Are you having some joke at my expense?'

The Marshal looked hurt. 'You know I would never do such a thing.'

'I know,' the Count said, 'but my niece is but ten years old.'

Bowman didn't bother trying to hide his laugh. 'I told you, but you didn't listen, did you?'

The Marshal's face changed to confusion. 'Your niece was only a year or two younger than me,' he said, 'she had a sharp tongue on her, too.'

Count Philip sighed. 'My dear William, my only niece is ten years old, and presumably safely at home with her guardians. Whoever you met, she was nothing to do with me.'

'Not so clever, are you,' Adam held a cup up, 'to the naïve peacock.'

'I'll drink to that,' Bowman stood up to thud his wooden cup onto Adams.

The Marshal returned to his chair to sulk.

Richard was ignored by almost everyone as the Flemish knights noisily crowded the table and Bowman drank with Adam.

At least Nicholas and Brian sat with him. 'We're the outcasts here, aren't we?' Brian pushed an empty cup around the table.

Nicholas shrugged. 'They all know each other, except for my half-brother who seems to be one of them already, but that's no loss.'

The realisation dawned on Richard that his first tournament would be the next day. 'I'm not so sure this was a good idea,' he said.

'Fear not,' the Martel knight said, 'everyone keeps telling us how good our company is, we can surely watch what everyone else does and stay out of trouble tomorrow.'

'I'm sure someone will get killed,' Brian said, 'someone always does.'

'Would you like an excuse to leave this hall?' Richard asked the monk.

He nodded back. 'There will be fights, and when they're all drunk, they'll just mock me.'

'I would like you to write a letter to my wife for me. I need to tell her I'm alive and where I am.'

'She's going to be angry at you,' Nicholas grinned.

'I'm quite aware of that,' Richard said, 'but I need to tell her I'll go home between tournaments, it can't be too far to Yvetot from here.'

Brian's eyes lit up. 'I'll find ink and parchment, we rode by an abbey on the way into town,' he said.

'Thank you,' Richard said as the monk scurried off.

'What about me?' the Martel knight asked. 'Have you got anything for me to do?'

'Not really,' Richard replied, 'just stay here so I'm not sitting on my own.'

Richard took his cloak off and threw it onto his bedding piled up against a wall. A dozen Flemish knights in the hall drank together with the Marshal's vanguard, and combined with the roaring hearth, the chamber heated up.

Cheers and excited yells floated through the air from outside and ears pricked up at a rush of footsteps on the earth.

'I'm guessing the Young King has arrived,' Nicholas said.

'I don't know how all his knights are going to fit in here,' Richard said, 'I bet we get thrown out first.'

Before they could complain any more, the Young King entered the hall to a great cheer from everyone already inside. His smile was wide and his freckles glowed in the candlelight.

Count Philip greeted him with a bow and another embrace, but the Young King's face straightened when he looked at the table. 'Marshal, why is my table so bare?' he asked.

The Marshal glanced over the table himself. 'I'm sorry, my lord, we haven't been here long enough to arrange for food.'

'You mean you got carried away?'

'He does,' Adam said, which drew a snigger from Bowman.

'Someone find some women to cook for us, and someone else bring me all the wine in Lagny,' the Young King ordered loudly.

More cheers erupted as some of the newly arrived knights left the hall to round up all the food and drink they could lay their hands on.

The Young King took his place at the centre of the larger table, around which knights sat on benches so close together that some could barely breathe.

Count Philip and the Marshal flanked the young Angevin king, and Richard almost felt weak when the Young King stood up and pointed at him.

'Richard,' he said, 'come and join us, I want to hear of your war deeds. Your scarred face puts these baby-faced knights to shame.'

Richard blushed, which made the jagged white of his scar more visible, and stood up.

'Don't mind me,' Nicholas said, 'I'll just sit here quietly.'

'Sorry,' Richard made his way gingerly up to the big table.

The Young King looked around the huddled knights and grinned at Henry the Northerner, pressed up to his master's side. 'You,' the Young King said, 'make way for Richard.'

Henry turned red and clawed at the Marshal. 'Expelling me will bring shame to you,' he said.

The Marshal shrugged. 'Just get up.'

Henry looked around for allies, but found none and vacated his place on the bench for Richard.

'You'll pay for this,' he whispered as Richard approached.

'Have you ever sat at a high table before?' the Young King asked him.

'No,' Richard replied.

'It is a great honour,' the Young King twirled an unlit candle in his fingers, 'honour is a funny thing, don't you think?'

'I suppose so,' Richard replied as he squeezed into the small gap between the Marshal and another knight.

'Honour and status, you can't touch them, so how do they exist?' the Young King considered the faces around the table who hung on his every word. 'But they are such powerful things.'

'Everyone looks at you,' Richard said, 'with more love than they do your father.'

The Young King's eyes twinkled. 'There, there is the flattery every other knight usually begins with. You see Richard, these men love me more because while my father was only the son of a count, I am the son of a king.'

Count Philip banged the table with his fist and laughed, followed by howls of approval from the other knights.

The Young King smiled at Richard. 'Ask me a question.'

Richard swallowed. 'Can you tell me about tomorrow, what will happen?'

'A little boring, but easy enough to answer,' the Young King nodded. 'Our team is based here at Lagny, but to our south another team is based at the hamlet of Torcy. The River Marne is the northern border of our happy battlefield, which lies across a thousand paces of meadows and streams. To our south, at the same distance, lies Bussy, some shabby little place that serves as our southern border. Between here and there the land lies blanketed in woods and groves. The tournament area is within these far-reaching boundaries, you see. Knights may not leave that area, but may take refuge in the lists at Lagny and Torcy.'

'Lists?' Richard asked.

'A wooden palisade guarded by infantry, a haven to adjust armour, treat wounds, and store captive men and mounts. Next to our list here at Lagny there should be a timber stand for the crowds to watch. It is in view of this list that the tournament begins with the grand charge.'

'Thank you,' Richard said, 'I've been trying to find someone to explain that for four days.'

The Young King laughed. 'There is no shame in your ignorance, Richard, not when you've killed kings in Ireland.'

'It was only one king,' Richard replied.

The table laughed. 'Tell us a story,' one knight shouted.

'I think I've spoken enough,' the Young King swept back his red hair, hair unhindered by his crown.

'Tell us the story about Anet,' another knight cried.

The Marshal groaned so slightly that only Richard heard.

'You must all be sick of me telling that one,' the Young King laughed lightly, 'and our new war hero Richard doesn't want to hear stories of how the Marshal lost a captive, however funny it is.'

Richard did quite like to hear it.

'That's one of my favourites,' Adam shouted from the lower table.

The Marshal smiled with his teeth showing, but his eyes narrowed.

The Young King began to re-tell the tale of Anet, but a band of young ladies sailed into the packed chamber in bright dresses, and aroused a chorus of shouts from the knights.

Richard couldn't understand who they were or what they were

doing in the hall, but they surrounded the high table and knights left it to break away and speak to them.

The Marshal expelled a deep breath and stood up. 'Anyone who wants to joust in the morning had better keep a clear head,' he bellowed.

A few knights looked twice at their cups, but the Flemings jeered back.

'Why do you care?' Richard asked him.

'It's my job,' the Marshal said, 'I'm responsible for military matters.'

'I thought the tournament was just a game?'

His friend pulled a sour face. 'Maybe to you.'

'I didn't mean to offend you,' Richard said, 'what jousts are you talking about?'

'Before the main tournament begins, certain knights face off in individual contests with the lance. These duels are fought below the stands where all can see. The leaders of companies often watch to look for rising talent, for it is usually newer knights who joust.'

'It's just for show then?' Richard asked.

'And winnings,' the Marshal smiled, 'in my first few tournaments I won many coats of mail and horses from my jousting victories.'

Richard rubbed his chin. A battle with swords wasn't his best discipline, but with the lance and only one opponent to face, he felt more confident. He'd defeated Sir John in such a contest, he remembered as his fingers ran around the top of the dagger he'd taken from the Norman knight.

'You're getting the idea,' the Marshal smiled at him.

A hand tapped Richard on the shoulder and he looked up into the dead eyes of Nicholas's wolf.

'How long have you been standing there?' Richard asked.

'You and your family stole my ransom,' the Marshal snarled at the Martel knight.

'It wasn't really me,' he replied, 'I was just following my brother.'

'I was in that cell at Castle Lusignan for a few days longer than I needed to because of you.'

'Leave him alone,' Richard said.

The Marshal turned to Richard, which nearly knocked him off the bench. 'And it's your fault I was there for *months* longer than I needed to be.'

'We've been over this,' Richard held up his hand, 'I lost this finger to earn your ransom.'

'I overheard about the jousts,' Nicholas said, which snapped the Marshal out of his mood.

'So?' Richard asked.

'If I can capture a knight for you, then I've paid my ransom,' Nicholas said, 'a knight for a knight.'

Richard shrugged. 'That sounds fair.'

'Ask our lord,' the Marshal said, 'he decides who will joust.'

The Young King turned his head to them as if he'd been listening. 'I would quite like to hear more about this stolen ransom, my Marshal has always been very vague about his captivity. But you, knight of the wolf, may joust tomorrow. If that is, you wear that pelt upon your helm.'

Nicholas grinned.

'I should like to joust, too,' Richard said.

'Find an animal to wear and you may,' the Young King chuckled to himself.

Bowman appeared next to his half-brother and nudged Richard. 'Look who's here,' he said.

Standing by the lower table, with a woman on each side of him, and with a smile that showed his missing front tooth, was Guy of Lusignan.

The Marshal saw him and jumped to his feet. Or at least he tried, because he was so tightly pressed between his lord and Richard, that he wedged himself in and couldn't stand up.

'What is the matter with you?' the Young King asked.

'That's Guy who killed Uncle Patrick, it was he who imprisoned me.'

'I remember taking that castle for him,' Bowman said, 'and how well Eva shot her arrows at the Martel garrison.'

Nicholas frowned, having been one of the garrison, but it was Bowman who looked the more forlorn at the memory.

'I'll kill him here and now,' the Marshal pushed Richard away to make himself room to squeeze out.

'You will do no such thing, I forbid it,' the Young King told him sternly.

The Marshal paused.

Richard had half a mind to join him as the memory of Long Tom falling from the siege ladder in Brittany flashed before his eyes. But Guy was also unpredictable, and Richard preferred to have nothing to do with him. 'I don't think I want him on my side during the tournament,' he said, 'I'd fear a knife in my back.'

The Young King grabbed the Marshal's arm and gripped tightly. 'No fear, Richard, Guy is staying at Torcy tonight, he'll be riding against you rather than with you.'

The Marshal returned to the bench with a thud. 'Good,' he said, 'I'll settle this matter with iron.'

'Mind yourself,' the Young King released his grip, 'your duty it to my protection, we've spoken before about you riding off for your own reasons.'

One woman at Guy's side turned and revealed her face.

'Isn't that?' Richard started.

Bowman laughed.

'Count Philip's daughter?' the Marshal said questioningly. 'What's she doing here?'

'She's probably never even been to Flanders, let alone a relation of Count Philip,' Richard said.

'I don't know how this is confusing you so much,' the Young King said.

'Because peacocks have very small brains,' Bowman said solemnly.

The woman's eyes widened as she realised the trouble she was in. She whispered something into Guy's ear and then fled with a slow casual walk that fooled no one. Richard couldn't help admiring the walk.

Guy looked over and smiled.

'If he comes over,' the Marshal said, 'I doubt I can stop myself from knocking some more of his teeth out.'

Richard couldn't help a snigger. 'I thought you were the most gracious, humble knight there ever was, Sir Wobble?'

'Don't call him that,' Henry the Northerner reached down to Richard from behind and tried to drag him clean off the bench. Nicholas grabbed the unwelcome arm with both hands and swung Henry away. The stocky knight lost his footing and fell headfirst into a cup-board on the wall. The plank of the board snapped, and three ornate silver cups hit the floor with a clatter. One landed on a wolfhound who was asleep, and it jumped up and sunk its teeth into Henry's leg.

While half of the knights in the room laughed at him, the burly Englishman kicked the dog off and whirled at Nicholas.

'You don't touch him,' the Martel knight said.

Henry looked into Nicholas's unreadable eyes, and his resolve for a fight melted.

'Enough,' the Young King said, 'that dog could have bitten me. You need to swallow whatever jealousies you have for each other.'

'I'm not jealous,' Henry the Northerner folded his arms.

Nicholas smirked at him, because while he was half Henry's weight, Nicholas felt no fear for him whatsoever.

'They disrespect your greatest knight,' Henry said to the Young King, 'you must do something.'

'You want to fight to settle this, do you?' the Young King asked.

Nicholas grinned. 'Can I joust him tomorrow?'

The Young King shook his head. 'No, I want you and your wolf to unhorse a Fleming tomorrow, to put the fear of God into their ranks before the main charge.'

The Martel knight grinned at Richard. 'See, someone appreciates my wolf.'

'Who is the peacock's dog fighting then?' Bowman asked.

The Young King gave the blonde man a sideways glance. 'The Northerner has a point, Richard, your men are undoubtedly disrespectful.'

'I said before,' Richard replied, 'it's a price worth paying when your life is at stake.'

'Well,' the Young King said, 'I think maybe you shall joust tomorrow, you shall take on the Northerner and we shall close this matter. You do need to find an animal to put on your helmet though, and I want the Northerner to wear peacock feathers on his.'

The knights all found that hilarious and started to drink and joke.

The Marshal looked up at his man. 'Don't embarrass me tomorrow,' he said, 'leave this hall and get some sleep.'

Richard looked at his friend. 'Do you want him to beat me?'

The Marshal shrugged. 'I'd rather you win, truth be told, but I don't want him to lose badly for that would reflect poorly on me. Can you just knock him out cold rather than toy with him like you did with Sir John?'

'How do you know about that?' Richard asked.

'We all know about that,' the Young King said, 'you knocked his teeth out.'

'Only one or two,' Richard replied.

'He is the Chamberlain of Normandy's first knight,' the Young King said, 'and you defeated him in a duel. Every knight has heard the story.'

The Marshal made a grunting sound.

'Never you mind, Marshal,' the Young King smiled at him, 'you've had your time in the joust, it is Richard's turn to show us how a war veteran rides.'

Richard swallowed, tomorrow was going to be an even bigger day than he'd expected.

The Young King cast his eyes around the hall. More knights had entered, and they crammed together so closely that a fight broke out over a spilled drink. Sweat, stale drink, and leather all mixed together in the close atmosphere. The Young King stood up and cleared his throat. 'The air in this chamber is thicker than the Marshal's ransom list.'

Everyone laughed.

'Everyone in this hall whose name is not William is to leave.'

Richard looked at Bowman, who could only shrug back. 'At least it isn't just us being evicted,' the blonde man said.

'Now,' the Young King shouted, 'all of you, out.'

Richard squeezed himself off the bench as everyone not called William left the merchant's house and had to find other entertainment for the evening. Richard wasn't worried about that though, because the next day he was going to joust in front of thousands of people. But if it went well, he might just claim his first winnings.

RISING STAR

Richard checked Solis's shoes, but their iron nails still held them securely onto his hooves. Richard placed his battered white saddle with his family's painted blue line onto the horse's back and did up the girth strap. Chunks of the wooden saddle were missing, eaten away by the endless rubbing of mail links, and patches of once white paint had been rubbed down to bare wood. This saddle had originally been carved out of a single tree trunk, and that strength had held it together despite all it had been through. Richard held the stallion's bridle in his hands, the leather worn and cut in places, but Solis lowered his head to take it all the same. The leather breastplate that he tied around the horse's chest had needed cleaning for months, but was still sturdy enough to bother attaching.

'You can't put it off all day, young lord,' Bowman held a linen bag in each hand, the bags that contained Richard's mail.

Richard sighed. 'There will be so many people watching, what if I humiliate myself?'

Bowman dropped the linen bags at his feet. 'If you're the last to arrive at the lists,' he said, 'then you certainly will be humiliated.'

Richard had already laced his leg armour onto each leg, so he slipped the tighter-fitting of the two mail shirts over his body.

Nicholas slung his shield over his mailed body on the other side of the yard. Servants ran back and forth with fodder for various horses. Gerold tied the leather lace at the back of the Martel knight's neck tightly, and the mail coif took its proper close-fitting shape around his chin and neck.

Nicholas jumped up and down to test the fit. His mail did not fall down over his eyes, eyes which blazed with enthusiasm. 'This is going to be the moment my life changes,' he said.

Bowman sniffed harshly at his half-brother as he brought Richard his helmet. Tied on top of it was an owl. A dead, stuffed, owl.

Richard had known finding a dead animal had been Bowman's plan, but seeing it for the first time was another matter. The lifeless eyes looked nowhere in particular and unnerved Richard. The last time he had been this close to an owl it had been nailed to a victim of the Fallencourt massacre. On that day the heat from the burning village had been intense, and although in the past, Richard could almost feel the heat on his cheeks once again.

'Ah,' Bowman said, 'I hadn't thought of that. Sorry.'

'It's fine,' Richard said sharply, 'once it's on my head, I won't see it.'

'Just bury your lance in that idiot's face,' Bowman said.

Richard took the helm and laced it under his chin. Oil from his mail coif came off on the back of his hand as it scraped over the rings.

Gerold held Nicholas's shield up to him.

'And you shouldn't be so cocky,' Bowman said to his half-brother.

The Martel knight frowned. 'Why not, I won't fear whoever I face.'

'If you do lose, though,' Bowman said, 'you'll have no horse or armour. Richard can't replace them, so what if the Young King decides not to help you?'

Nicholas's shoulders slumped. 'Why did you have to say that? I'll just find a corner to curl up and die in if it comes to it. Like a cat under a hedge.'

'Seems appropriate,' the blonde man said under his breath.

'Enough of that,' Richard said, 'he's proven himself more times than it should take for you to at least be polite to him.'

Bowman gave Richard his shield, a red one from the Young King, who had two carts stacked high with spares.

'Now I'm worried about losing,' Richard said, 'maybe I should leave my second mail shirt off so I've got a spare?'

Bowman took the shield back from him and passed him the linen bag that contained the baggier shirt. 'No, young lord, better to be alive and poor than dead with a mail shirt sitting here unused.'

Richard sighed and donned the larger shirt over the tighter one and then took his shield. He still wasn't sure it was the right decision, but if he lost, he'd lose his horse, too. Richard glanced over to the stallion and felt wetness in his eye. He couldn't wipe it away either, because he knew he'd just leave a greasy mark on his cheek.

Bowman wiped his fingers clean on his green tunic. 'You've got dirt under your eye,' he said and wiped Richard's face for him.

Richard had to move his eyes away. 'Thank you,' he mumbled, 'but if I lose Solie.'

'I know,' Bowman said, 'I remember the first time. Concentrate on that northern lout, young lord. End him.'

'I'm not aiming at his face, this is a tournament,' Richard said.

'Just say you aimed at his shield and the lance skimmed off,'

Bowman grinned, 'no one will be able to say differently.'

'I'm pretty sure that's murder,' Richard said.

Bowman laughed. 'At this point in our lives, would that even matter?'

Richard managed a gentle laugh, but for him it did matter.

Gerold draped the wolf-pelt over Nicholas, the head resting on top of his iron helmet and making him seem the size of his other half-brother, Eustace.

'You certainly scare me,' Gerold said.

Richard belted the Little Lord's old sword around his waist and took a deep breath. The mail on his shoulders added no noticeable weight for him anymore, so perhaps he was ready for what lay ahead.

They led their two horses out of the courtyard behind the merchant's house and went to the wooden platform used for mounting horses. Their breath misted in the air and long streams shot out from their horse's nostrils as they stamped their feet in the fresh air of the morning.

Bowman clapped his hands together for heat, but Richard was heated from within. In the distance a cockerel crowed and a dog barked. Richard's black dog drank from a puddle and sniffed the air every time he heard another dog.

Richard and Nicholas mounted so that the iron mail on their legs would stay free from mud. Bowman and Gerold glumly picked their way through the modest layer of mud that was the local street, following their riders at a slower pace. Richard hadn't seen Brian yet, hopefully he was getting a letter to Sophie sent and staying out of trouble.

A handful of knights rode their parade or travelling horses along the road towards the list outside Lagny. They were unarmoured because the main event was still many hours away and they were not taking part in the morning jousting. Indeed, many knights were still in bed, or simply not bothered enough by the jousts to actually attend them. Some hungover knights dragged themselves out of the town to wake themselves up, but it wasn't just knights who were on the move.

The townspeople trampled through the mud to see the most exciting thing to visit their town all year. Richard had to wait while groups of them unstuck themselves in the mud, or blocked the street having conversations with each other.

In smaller numbers, there were also the traders and merchants who exploited the event. Just outside the town, the horse dealers had set up paddocks full of horses for sale, and next to them saddlers carved saddles, and farriers re-shod horses to prepare for later in the day.

Some traders set up stalls on their carts displaying leather goods and even maces and daggers. A blacksmith pounded a helmet into shape and an extended family were busy repairing mail shirts for knights who stood waiting in abject boredom. The richer knights sent their squires to wait for them.

Past the hammering, clinking, and neighs, Richard and Nicholas rode to the south of Lagny, past the abbey that had scorch marks from a fire along one wall, and out to the lists.

The other team's village, Torcy, was somewhere to the southwest, but it was far out of view. In view however, were the lists and stands in the open pasture. The lists were huge, larger than the promontory fort at Baginbun Head, large enough for a thousand or more knights to ride their horses within. A sizable ditch ringed it, and a short wooden palisade stood on the ditch's spoil heap. The lists were a genuine fortress.

'They built all this for a game?' Richard asked.

'There'll be another one at Torcy,' Bowman replied despite being out of breath from the walking.

A group of knights walked past, one with a leopard on a leash that Richard's dog barked at but wisely stayed away from.

'Can you put a rope around his neck and keep him out of trouble?' Richard asked.

'It's not your dog,' Bowman said, 'and if you die here, I'm not looking after it.'

Richard frowned. 'I'm not planning on dying here.'

'No one ever does,' the blonde man sighed. 'Do you need anything or can I find the food sellers?'

'What are you going to pay them with?' Richard asked.

Bowman laughed. 'Promises,' he walked away even though Richard hadn't answered if he needed anything else or not.

Behind the stand, and stretching out to the fields beyond, stood a forest of tents. Hundreds of tents, many painted in blues and reds, clustered around fires and groups of horses. The knights not famous enough to evict the townspeople had to make do with the open air, but even they had canvas between them and the elements. Richard remembered the single tent of the Irish campaign and shook his head in disbelief.

'Are you ready?' Richard asked Nicholas. Mud streaked up the legs of their horses, but at least the animals had warmed up their cold muscles.

The Martel knight grinned. 'Whichever Fleming rides against me will never forget this day,' he said.

Richard was quite sure he was right.

'What about you?' Gerold asked from the ground beside him.

'I've been waiting for this for over a year,' Richard said, 'maybe longer. If I'm accepted into the Young King's tournament team, then my money troubles are over. My village can be repaired and defended. Sir Wobble might have mocked that merchant he stole from, but money is everything when you haven't got any.'

'Well said,' Gerold nodded, 'for a moment there I was looking up at your father.'

Richard gripped the lance he'd taken from another of the Young King's carts tightly. He gazed up at the sharp point to think about something else.

'If this is a game,' Richard said, 'why do we use sharp lances?'

Nicholas laughed. 'Why would we make this safer? Then what use would it be for training for war, that's what this all is. Even under the gold, silver, and drink.'

They reached the tall timbered tiered stand upon which some local knights were seating people according to their status.

A master carpenter shouted up to them to make the lighter people sit at the top.

Gerold laughed. 'Did you know the carpenters are paid with the timber once the event is over?'

Richard shook his head. 'I suppose it's no wonder then that they don't want the whole thing to collapse,' he said.

At least two hundred people occupied the stands. The most richly dressed spectators stood at the front, and merchants and poorer knights had to content themselves further back. Those who had nothing stood on the grass behind a rope fence that marked the boundary of the tournament field. A contingent of spearmen with colours from Paris stood here and there along the boundary to keep people off the field.

They let Richard on without questions because he looked the part, and he suddenly felt alone with just Nicholas for company when Gerold stayed by the rope. The two of them rode over the dewy grass with their breath clouding the air until they reached the twenty other armoured knights who waited for the jousting to begin.

The Young King and Count Philip rode their parade horses amongst the group and paired knights off together.

'The Breton should joust one of yours,' the Young King said.

The Count nodded. 'And the big German should face an Englishman. Both think they are better than the other.'

'I agree,' the Young King said, 'and I would like my knight of the wolf to face one of yours, to gauge him against a man we know.'

Count Philip considered the knights still available. He pointed to one. 'Arnulf, you will joust the Young King's wolf-knight.'

Arnulf wore the yellow colours of Flanders and had a black lion painted on his shield. His eyes rested on the wolf on Nicholas's helmet and for a moment they looked unsure.

'You've got him,' Richard managed a small smile.

'He's only a bit bigger than me,' Nicholas said, 'and wolves always chase lions off in the mountains.'

Richard wondered where the young man got his confidence from. He searched the knights around them for Henry the Northerner, and spied him at the back with another knight from their company.

The first two knights to joust rode on their own towards the stand, long lances reaching high into the sky as they rested the butt ends on their thighs. One knight had a light blue surcoat, the other a top half of black and a bottom half of mustard-yellow. They split apart and rode to opposite ends of the stand, a sensible distance away from the dividing rope, so that their jousting course would occur right in front of the spectators.

As the blue knight turned to face his opponent, his horse pawed at the turf and clods were dug up and thrown into the air. The blue knight held the excited horse firm as the German knight in his black and yellow held his lance up high into the air to signal his readiness.

Both knights did not charge from far away, slowing gathering speed. Instead, as in war, they held their energy until they were nearly upon each other. Only when they were a javelin throw apart did they launch their horses. The horses reached full speed in an instant. Both knights thrust their lances up into armpits and lowered their points at the same time. The blue knight's exuberant horse ducked a step to the side at the last moment, the crowd groaned, and both lances missed their mark.

'He needed more outside leg,' Richard mumbled, an instruction that some in the stands also shouted at the knight. Some booed him for his failure to control his horse as both knights turned again for another course.

This time they signalled while turning and flew towards each other without pause. The blue knight's horse only moved a little away from its opponent this time, and crashed his lance into his foe's shield. The German knight's lance skated off the blue knight's helmet, but he reeled backwards as the blow threatened to unseat him. The crowd burst out into a cheer as the blue knight turned to them and held his lance aloft in what he felt was a victory.

The black and yellow knight remained in his saddle and righted himself, but the Young King and Count Philip halted the match.

'You can have the German,' the Young King said, 'my side is larger so you can have the knight who can take a blow. I'll take the one with the difficult horse.'

Count Philip didn't seem too bothered either way, and Richard felt nerves in his stomach as the next pair were called forward.

A knight with the white and black colours of Brittany rode out. Richard was sure he'd seen those colours in the battle at the castle he'd forgotten the name of, back when King Henry almost fell into the hands of the enemy.

A Flemish knight in red took his place underneath the stands, and the more noble of the spectators cheered him. Bowman stood next to the stand, feeding the black dog what looked like cooked chicken. From somewhere he'd even found a rope for it.

The Flemish knight rode well and struck the Breton with a mighty blow on his shield. The sharp lance tore through it and the Breton fell backwards as the back of his wooden saddle snapped. His left foot stayed in the stirrup though, and as his horse cantered away his head bounced along the pasture. The crowd gasped and cried out as the rear hooves of the bolting horse got tangled up with the flailing knight. His horse tripped, came down, rolled, and pushed itself up again. The knight lay motionless on the floor as the horse snorted and shook itself. All the mounted noblemen who loitered about rushed over to the stricken knight, and the Young King himself jumped down from his saddle to tend to him.

When the young Angevin stood up and shook his head, Richard suddenly felt his palms sweating. 'I thought this was just a game,' he said.

'It's still riding horses,' Nicholas yawned, 'and the lances are still sharp.'

'How are you so relaxed?' Richard asked.

The Martel knight looked very much at ease. 'I used to worry about things, but ever since Waterford, it seems to be only my half-brother who can bother me.'

'You mean since a house fell on your head?'

'I don't remember that,' Nicholas replied.

While some servants dealt with the loose horse and the dead knight, Nicholas and his Flemish opponent were called for.

'Good luck,' Richard said.

'I don't need it,' Nicholas rode away. That left Richard to watch the black hair of his wolf atop his horse, which from the back looked like the wolf was riding it.

Richard could see Guy of Lusignan in the stand, and the woman that was not Count Philip's niece. She cheered at Nicholas as he turned his horse and waited motionless for his adversary to signal.

The Fleming's surcoat comprised many horizontal red and white stripes, and a good number of the richer spectators cheered him. A slight breeze ruffled the hair of the wolf-pelt, but otherwise Nicholas could have been a statue.

The Fleming raised his lance but Nicholas still didn't move. The red and white knight pumped the lance up into the air in frustration and his horse bounced on the spot, knowing very well that the course was imminent. Richard had a moment to marvel at the game his captive knight was playing, then just when it looked like Nicholas would never signal, his lance thrust up as if to pierce the morning sky.

His horse surged forward, a horse seasoned in Ireland, a horse that its rider knew would run straight. With that confidence, Nicholas couched his lance and leant into the weapon. His foe's spear flashed past his face, and ripped a gash in the flesh of the wolf-pelt, but Nicholas was undaunted. His own lance hit the Fleming's shield in the exact spot where the lance couldn't be deflected, and pushed him right out of the saddle. The poor knight's horse was stunned by the force of the blow, and as his master hit the earth behind him, the horse could only catch its stride and then stop to look back at the Fleming sprawled on the grass.

Nicholas gently eased his horse to a stop, and without looking back at his fallen opponent, rode over towards the Young King.

'The wolf defeats the lion of Flanders,' the young Angevin shouted loudly. Everyone in the stand erupted in a cheer, especially the poorer spectators. The knights raised their own ovation as the fallen Fleming got to his feet and brushed himself down. His helmet lay several paces away, his head newly covered in brown mud.

Nicholas had neither broken a sweat nor lost his breath. 'I would like to pledge my captive to Richard in return for my own ransom owed to him,' he said.

The Young King smiled. 'I see no reason why not, your victory is beyond doubt. A knight for a knight is perfectly reasonable. I must confess, wolf-knight, that you frighten even me. I have rarely seen such a professional performance in the joust, most young knights are nervous of fighting in front of a crowd of thousands.'

Nicholas shrugged. 'Usually when I fight in front of thousands, half are in an army trying to kill me. This is child's play,' he said.

Count Philip laughed. 'If you had an army of wolf-knights, I'd pay homage to you for Flanders right now.'

The Young King's face turned hard. 'Maybe you should.'

Both men paused for a moment. Then they laughed at each other.

'Who is next?' the Count asked.

'The peacock against,' the Young King looked at Richard, 'against the owl, apparently.'

Richard could feel the weight of the animal on his head and he worried it would tip his helmet off.

'I think all knights should wear animals on their heads,' the Young King mused.

Richard realised that the horse and mail belonging to Nicholas's fallen adversary were now his, which made him feel slightly better about the prospect of losing.

Nicholas rode past him.

'Congratulations,' Richard said, 'you're free, how do you feel?'

'The same as before,' Nicholas said, 'and I don't think I want to go anywhere. If it's all the same to you, I'd rather remain in your service.'

Richard blinked as their horses crossed paths. 'If you're sure,' Richard tried to turn his head to continue talking, but his mail coif restricted him, so he turned his eyes towards the way he was going instead. There, in front of him, and with a cluster of bright peacock feathers tied to the back of this helmet, was Henry.

His opponent waited for him, and clad in mail, a substantial opponent he was. Henry's mail coat was covered with a leather breastplate that made him look even wider, and his red shield, bright with fresh paint, seemed somehow intimidating just because of its colour.

'When I knock you from your horse,' Heny shouted at him, 'you'll be back down where you belong.'

'You won't bait me,' Richard rode Solis past his adversary and towards the stand. He rode right up to the rope and townspeople reached out and tried to touch him. Others laughed and joked about the owl on his head. One merchant pointed his scar out, which drew a cheer from those leaning on the rope.

The alluring woman who was not the Count's niece threw a piece of white linen at Richard. With no hands free he couldn't catch it, and it floated down to the grass and started to soak up dew. 'Joust for me,' she shouted.

Richard smiled despite his best efforts, but pulled himself away and turned to wait for Henry to get into place. The English knight raised his lance and Richard saluted in return.

Henry's horse walked a step and then broke into a canter.

Solis realised what was happening and his hind legs lowered and coiled underneath him before he sprung towards his opponent.

Henry the Northerner lowered his lance straight away, a tactic that sent horror through Richard. Only the most uncouth knights lowered at anything earlier than the last possible moment, because it meant the lance point would come perilously close to the oncoming horse's head. Richard turned his shoulders to his right so that his horse's head would turn the same way, away from the wickedly sharp point that came towards him at his eye level. Richard had to ride his horse at an angle, and he lowered his lance as anger replaced his initial horror.

Henry swept his lance sideways at Richard as if he were nothing more than a fresh squire, and because of his clumsy technique, he was far too early and the wooden shaft of the lance hit Richard across the nasal guard of his helmet.

Richard's vision exploded as the metal pressed into his nose, and the next moment it went black as the owl tipped forwards and flapped down into his face. The cold feathers pressed into his cheeks and eyes, and the beak pecked at his chin. Richard's mind flashed images of Fallencourt and his breathing sharpened out of control.

Solis kept going and Richard almost lost his balance, and the owl, all dead eyes and feathers, bounced up and down on his face. Richard regained his breathing and tensed his core to stop his horse once he took control of his breathing and fought the panic.

The stallion obeyed with a snort and turned around all by himself, ready to charge a second time.

'Not yet,' Richard shouted, and the horse stopped and stood still as if embarrassed.

Richard lifted his lance-hand up to his helmet and tried to undo the lacing.

'What's the matter?' Henry shouted from where he'd turned and stood ready to go again. 'Have you already lost your nerve?'

Richard only had one finger to undo the lacing, and he couldn't reach it with the long lance in his grip. He gave up and punched the helmet with the lance, even as the dead owl kept getting in front of his mouth and blocking his breathing. All he could smell was wet feathers. Richard punched the lance into the helmet again and the lacing snapped. The helmet, owl and all, fell to the ground.

Solis spooked sideways as the ball of feathers landed by his foot, and Richard nearly fell out of the saddle. He shouted at his horse again and the stallion lowered his head to sniff the owl. Solis licked it and a bunch of feathers came away in his mouth.

Richard turned him roughly to face his foe, anger raging in his heart for the embarrassment he felt for his panicked reaction to the owl.

'You can't joust without a helmet,' Henry said, 'I will accept your yield here and now, I do not need to slice your head open.'

Richard adjusted his grip on the lance and clenched his jaw. He would not lose Solis without a fight.

He raised his lance. The crowd cheered wildly, and Henry's face flashed with uncertainty. Solis surged forwards without being asked, and despite never saluting, Henry cantered to meet them.

Richard's eyes focused on his foe, and the rest of the world disappeared. It might as well have been a battle, and Richard aimed Solis at the head of Henry's horse; this was no longer a game.

The English knight's horse realised the yellow stallion was heading resolutely for him, and he veered away to avoid a collision. Henry had again lowered his lance far too early, and as his horse veered to the right, he could no longer bring his lance to bear on Richard.

Which had been the point.

Richard lowered his lance as the cool morning air rushed by his bare head and put all of his weight into the tip of the pointed iron head.

Richard's lance clipped the top of Henry's shield, ran up it, and went under the rim of his helmet. But it didn't pierce his face, instead it caught the top side of the mail coif and ran up between it and the inside of the helmet. The blow pulled the helmet clean from Henry's head, and would have taken the head with it had the lacing under his chin not snapped first. The peacock feathers detached and exploded into the air. Solis slid over the grass as he dug his feet in to stop and turn, the stallion acting on instinct alone.

Henry stopped his horse and hauled its head around.

Solis cantered at him, and Richard prepared to lower his lance again.

'I didn't signal,' Henry shouted, 'you can't charge yet.'

Richard charged.

Henry's horse wavered, and as his rider did nothing to reassure him, the animal sprung to the side and rode away from the oncoming juggernaut that was Solis and Richard's rage.

The laughter of the crowd broke Richard's fixation, and he pulled his horse up. The spectators jeered at the fleeing knight and Richard realised that the Young King was shouting at him.

Henry reached the young Angevin and argued something.

Richard walked his panting horse over.

'He broke all the rules, his horse and mail are mine,' the English knight cried, spit flying from his mouth.

'Quiet,' the Young King said, 'do not raise your voice in my presence.'

'You saw how early he lowers his lance,' Richard said, 'I expected better from a knight who serves the Marshal.'

He'd nearly said a knight who serves the Young King, but had just caught himself before it slipped out.

Count Philip nodded. 'That was unacceptable, I do not deny it, but you charged twice without signalling.'

'No one waits for a signal in a battle,' Richard said, 'how many horses has he hit in the head before?'

Henry gasped. 'How dare you accuse me?'

'Silence,' the Young King said, 'we all saw you gouge a chunk out of a horse's neck at Stamford, and don't think I've forgotten what you did to the horse of that Savoyard knight last year.'

Henry's indigence faded.

'Richard,' the Young King said, 'this is not a battle. You wait for a signal. You can also order one of your men to fetch your helmet for you, it is foolish to joust without one, we are not here to kill each other.'

Richard stayed stony-faced in silence.

The young Angevin sighed. 'But I can't punish you, they are cheering you in the stands. Your star is rising, you gave them excitement. You will both put your helmets back on and complete a fair course. You both signal and you both lower at the correct time. If either of you do not obey me, you forfeit your horses to me without appeal. Do you understand?'

Richard nodded, but his breathing was fast and his lips pressed shut.

'Go on, then,' the Count said, 'before he changes his mind.'

Richard briskly turned his horse away as Gerold picked his helmet up from the mud. Mercifully, the older knight removed the owl before he handed the mud-splattered helmet up to Richard.

'Thank you,' he said as he placed it on his head, the broken lacing preventing him from retying it, and took his lance back from Gerold.

'You must conquer your breathing, Richard,' Gerold told him, 'anger gives strength for sure, but it also creates recklessness. Your father was always calm as battles raged around him. He captured King Stephen because he fought his urges and controlled his thinking.'

Richard snatched the lance quicker than he should have and felt sorry for Gerold who frowned up at him. The knight's face turned to a smile as he ducked back under the rope.

A gaggle of brightly coloured musicians started up with drums and pipes next to the stand.

This time Richard raised his lance to signal his readiness. Henry waited with his down. Maybe he had seen what Nicholas had done and was copying. Richard remembered Gerold's words and remained where he was with his lance up and ready.

The assembled onlookers jeered at Henry for delaying, and Richard concentrated on his breathing. Solis snorted and tried to advance, but Richard tensed his whole body and the horse restrained himself.

'Get on with it,' the Young King shouted at the English knight, who relented and raised his lance.

Richard relaxed his clenched muscles and Solis sprung forwards with a squeal. He cantered towards Henry whose horse charged too, but with less eagerness than Richard's.

Richard focused his eyes on his target, the top of Henry's shield, and put the thought of his enemy's lance out of his mind. Richard brought his lance down and it struck the red shield. He turned his shoulders to his left, into his opponent, and the lance tipped Henry around. The English knight twisted violently and hung off the side of his saddle. His horse jumped at the sudden shift of weight on his back, but instead of trying to catch his rider, he jumped away from the weight and ejected Henry from the saddle. When Richard turned, Henry lay on the ground face first, trying to push himself up.

'A fair course,' Count Philip cried as the musicians played and the observers in the stand jumped up and down in jubilation. The timber creaked beneath them, the carpenters shouted, and some of them abandoned their seating and rushed to the safety of the grass.

Richard felt exhilaration course through his veins. In triumph, he had a mind to trample the vile knight into the ground, and as if understanding, Solis lowered his head and ran at him. Richard had to haul him back and decided it would be better if he rode over to the Young King instead.

'That horse of yours is a true warhorse,' he said, 'you entered the jousts with high stakes by riding him.'

'I don't have another horse,' Richard replied.

The Count laughed. 'You have three now.'

'It has been a profitable morning for you,' the Young King said.

Henry dragged his horse over by the reins, slogging across the short grass and puffing. His mail coat was caked in mud and blades of grass, and he had left his shield behind. 'He broke all the rules,' Henry pointed at Richard.

'You broke some too,' Richard replied.

'I dispute his claim of victory,' Henry looked up at the Young King, 'it should not stand. He failed to signal even though he was ready.'

'Were you ready?' the Young King asked.

'No,' Richard said flatly, having to swallow the urge to smile.

'Judge it a draw,' the English knight said, 'didn't you see him aim his horse at me?'

'I don't care,' the Young King replied, 'if we have to employ judges to watch every aspect of these matches, it will suck all the enjoyment out of it. You are supposed to be a knight, accept your defeat and cease complaining.'

'He does have a point,' Count Philip said, 'your owl-knight did charge twice without signalling or waiting to see one, and I saw him aim his horse at his foe rather than aim to ride past him. Neither act displays good courtesy.'

'Where is the Marshal?' the Young King scanned the knights on the field.

'I have not seen him,' the Count answered, 'he prefers sleep to jousting, he is likely still in the hall.'

The crowned Angevin shook his head. 'Philip, will you see to matters here? I need to resolve this matter with the Marshal.'

The Count of Flanders nodded and rode away to find the next two matched knights.

'Both of you,' the Young King looked Richard in the eyes, 'come with me.'

Richard felt sheepish as he fell in behind his new lord and ignored the icy stares of Henry who pushed his way in front of him.

Gerold and Bowman appeared behind him but kept their distance, the black dog covered now in brown mud.

The horses were stabled, and both men disarmed before they traipsed into the merchant's house.

The hall was mostly empty now, and the Marshal stood with the Young King at the far end of the chamber.

Adam patted Richard's shoulder on the way in. 'Well done pegging the peacock down a notch,' he grinned.

Bowman stayed with Adam and Richard wondered where Nicholas had got to. Instead, he found a bowl of water and splashed the cold liquid up onto his face. Freshened, Richard looked for something to drink.

A man in a black robe handed up a cup of water. Richard stood in surprise when he saw it was Brother Geoffrey.

'Thank you,' Richard said after a moment and took the cup.

'What a surprise it is seeing you here,' the monk said, 'we should find somewhere to speak later.'

'Not here,' Richard said as quietly as he could, drank from the cup, and walked to the Young King.

Henry stood next to him already, imploring the Marshal. 'He cheated, you must back me,' he said.

The Marshal batted his hand away.

'I have no spare horses with me,' the Young King said, 'and the next shipment of coin from my father isn't due for weeks. The horse dealers here all refuse to give me any more horses until I settle my debts with them, so you'll just have to give Richard the horse and follow your master around on foot.'

'A knight must have a horse,' Henry cried.

'Ride your palfrey in the tournament,' the Young King said, 'and you do owe Richard your mail.'

Henry the Northerner shot Richard a stubborn look. 'He cheated three times, we cannot let dishonour lead to a reward.'

'You can keep your leather breastplate,' Richard said, half because he thought it might make him look merciful, and half because it was too big to fit him anyway.

'These matters always bore me,' the Marshal said to his lord, 'can you rule so I can go back to doing something more interesting?'

'You will never make a landed knight if you cannot bring yourself to hear disputes,' the Young King said.

The Marshal yawned. 'I can employ clerks and lawyers for that.'

The Young King looked annoyed at him, but then turned to Richard. 'I will make a ruling, a fair ruling, and then we can begin our preparations for the tournament proper,' he said, 'do you both swear to abide by my judgement?'

Richard nodded, and Henry crossed his arms and said nothing.

'Good,' the Young King said, 'both of you acted with a lack of courtesy during your match. This will not do, Henry, you will train with your lord until you learn to lower your lance like a knight and not some Spanish rogue.'

Henry nodded, and his face dared to show hope for the outcome.

'Richard,' the Young King turned to him, 'I understand you have come from the battlefields of our empire into our little world here, and I can forgive you forgetting where you were. This once. Never let me see you ride in a joust without signalling again.'

'You won't,' Richard swallowed.

'But you did still win the match,' the Young King said, 'the final course was fair and shall stand. My judgement is that Henry can keep his arms and armour, partly because we need him on the field later today, and partly so he will stop his whining.'

Henry grinned at Richard with so much smugness he considered punching him.

'But his horse must still go to Richard.'

Henry's face dropped. 'But my palfrey is lame, he cannot carry me through the tournament.'

The Marshal nodded. 'That horse has never faced an enemy, either, it would be more of a liability than not having Henry there at all.'

'Very well,' the Young King said, 'he is your man, Marshal, you can replace his warhorse out of your own pouch.'

'What?' the Marshal's face recoiled in disgust. 'Why should I give out money for anyone else? I hardly have a shilling to my name.'

Richard laughed. 'What about that fifty pounds you stole?'

'Stole?' the Young King turned to his Marshal.

'It was my judgement for the criminal matter of the Count's niece.'

Richard heard Bowman laugh at him from the back of the hall. 'I'll take coin over Henry's horse,' Richard added, 'if that helps everyone?'

'Fifty pounds?' the Young King smiled. 'Do you know how much I spend on knights every day?'

Richard shook his head.

'Two hundred pounds,' the Young King laughed, 'can you imagine what that costs me over the year?'

The Marshal groaned. 'Fine, my lord, I can see where you're going with that, I'll give Richard a pound or two.'

'That horse is worth at least five,' Richard said.

'What are you, a merchant?' the Marshal replied, genuine annoyance in his voice.

'Come on, Richard,' the Young King said, 'we are above bartering, accept the offer with grace and courtesy and we can leave this matter behind.'

'Fine,' Richard folded his arms.

The Marshal looked at his barrel-chested man. 'You'll pay me back for this,' he said.

'Good grace applies to you, too,' the Young King scolded him, 'all three of you are behaving poorly. I must say I'm quite disappointed.'

'I just think I shouldn't have to lose out because Henry lost,' the Marshal said.

'And why not?' the Young King rounded on him. 'Are you not ready for the responsibility of leading men?'

'It's just he isn't really my man.'

'Really?' the Young King tilted his head. 'You pay him, though, don't you?'

The Marshal almost bit his lip and threw his hands up in frustration. 'I'll pay Richard a pound, but I'm going to tend to my horse now,' he walked away and towards the door.

'I thought it was two pounds,' Richard said.

A withering look from his new lord silenced his hopes.

'Get out of my sight,' the Young King said to Henry, who scampered out after his master.

Adam made barking noises after him as he left, which Bowman found greatly amusing. The mud-caked black dog joined in the barking, which made the joke even funnier.

The Young King found his chair and slumped down into it. 'What am I going to do with you, Richard?'

Brother Geoffrey tried to make eye contact with the Angevin lord. The monk sat next to a Parisian knight who Richard had seen with Count Philip the night before.

The Young King groaned. 'Speaking to my enemies in my own hall is an unwise policy, even for you, monk.'

'This knight is hardly an enemy,' Brother Geoffrey replied, 'he is loyal to the Count.'

'Count Philip is friends with both the King of England and the King of France,' the Young King said, 'his loyalty to one is always balanced by the other. Get out of my hall.'

Brother Geoffrey pushed his chair back slowly and stood up. The French knight he'd been speaking to fled the hall as quickly as he could while trying not to look bothered or suspicious.

'Out,' the Young King said, 'everyone except Richard, get out.'

Adam pushed himself from the wall, and Bowman looked down at the dog. 'Shall we find you something to eat?' he asked it. The dog wagged its tail and soon Richard was alone with his new lord.

'I know who that monk is,' the Young King picked up a jug and swirled the contents around.

'I don't like him,' Richard replied.

'I know, the Marshal told me who he was when he appeared for the first time last year. I know who he answers to.'

Richard swallowed. He needed to feed the monk information, or he'd lose Yvetot and his chance to regain Keynes all at once.

'I heard about the trial by fire, show me your hands.'

Richard held them out, the old scars faint but unmistakable.

The Young King grasped his hands and ran his finger along a scar. 'It is true, then. You can never quite tell with the Marshal,' he said.

Richard wanted to run away.

'My problem,' the Young King let go of Richard's hands, 'is that you are a very capable knight. Your wolf-knight is effective, too, and I would like both of you to serve in my company.'

'Thank you,' Richard said, partly holding his breath.

'And I do want you to serve me.'

Richard let the breath out. He would have to be careful when he met with Brother Geoffrey.

'That is not my problem, though,' the Young King continued, 'my problem is your loyalty.'

'My what?'

'Your loyalty, Richard. Who did you serve in Brittany?'

'Your father,' Richard replied.

'Exactly, and who did you see before you came to me?'

'Your father.'

'Quite,' the Young King slammed the jug down so hard it made Richard jump, 'and who told Brother Geoffrey I was riding to Lagny?'

The question hung in the air like a sword. Richard worried his eyes gave him away, and he swallowed and struggled against an urge to cough.

'It's a simple question.'

It wasn't a simple answer, though. Richard had a choice, hope the Young King was bluffing or toying with him, or switch sides and go against the overlord of England, Normandy, Brittany, Aquitaine, and probably by now, Ireland. He kicked at a pile of yellowed reeds on the floorboards, then licked his lips.

'I did.'

His words lingered in the air for some time.

The Young King nodded. 'That was the right answer. I know you are spying on me. You are not the first, either. But if you tell the monk anything ever again, I will destroy you and everyone you care about. One bad step and you're finished, your reputation, lands, family, all will be taken from you. If you serve me with loyalty and love you will be rewarded, but if you cross me for my father's sake, Hell itself will come as a relief.'

Richard nodded. 'I will be loyal,' he said.

'Good,' the Young King filled a cup and pushed it across the table towards Richard, 'because make no mistake, I will be watching you.'

OF KINGS

Saddles, bridles, and shields lay everywhere. The courtyard behind the merchant's hall brimmed with knights shouting at squires and servants running back and forth with equipment. Younger servants brushed horses until they were clean, and those horses kicked their stable door because they knew something was about to happen.

The black dog lay in front of Solis's stable with a large bone in its paws, the only calm animal in the yard. He gnawed at the flesh-covered bone, and when a servant got too close, the dog growled at the boy with snarling teeth.

'Where did he get that bone?' Richard asked.

'There's a whole pile of them in the town,' Bowman replied, 'no one will miss one.'

'So you didn't ask for it?'

Bowman shrugged. 'I'm a knight, I don't need to ask for things.'

Richard snorted, aware that no one had ever knighted Bowman.

'But don't change the subject,' the blonde man said, 'what are you planning on doing about the Young King?'

Richard did not know. 'Avoiding him for now,' he said.

The Marshal shouted from across the courtyard. 'What are you avoiding?'

An armourer handed him a helmet while he waited for Richard's reply. The iron helmet had a flat plate of metal attached to the front of it instead of a simple nasal guard. It had two short rectangular vision slits.

'King Henry asked me to spy on his son, and the Young King knows,' Richard said, 'which means it must be obvious to everyone, so I won't bother hiding it.'

'Oh, that,' the Marshal held the helmet up and inspected it.

Richard crossed his arms because he'd hoped his friend wouldn't have discovered so soon. 'Maybe I should just go home,' Richard said.

A servant rushed up to the Marshal and slipped on the treacherous mud of the courtyard. 'There is a question from the Young King's mews. Should they avoid feeding some of his birds in the morning?'

'How should I know?' the Marshal lowered the helmet over his face, which muffled his voice. 'Go and ask our lord if he plans on hunting, he hasn't told me.'

The servant left delicately, but the Marshal's burden continued as a new one replaced him. 'One of the Young King's bratchets escaped and killed a bird of some sort in the town. Can you arrange for compensation for the bird?' the new servant asked.

The Marshal groaned in frustration. 'What was a bratchet again, a female scent hound? Never mind, it doesn't matter, was the bratchet one of the good dogs?'

'She is one of the older hounds, but is on the decline,' the servant answered.

'Then offer her to the owner of the birds as compensation,' the Marshal waved him away, 'a dog for a bird is a good trade for the owner, and as a bonus we'll be rid of an ageing animal.'

The servant bowed and left the Marshal to slide the helmet off his head. The knight considered the iron helmet and slid it back on.

'Do you like your position at the Young King's court?' Richard asked. 'I remember the days when all you wanted to do was eat and sleep.'

The Marshal turned his covered head to Richard. 'How do I look?'

'I don't know, I can't really see you.'

The Marshal took it off again. 'I am tired of the insignificant questions they bombard me with. Do I care if a hound has eaten some godforsaken pigeon? I don't care about hunting at the best of times.'

Richard chuckled. 'You got what you always wanted and you hate it,' he grinned.

'I don't hate it,' the Marshal said. 'My family name of Marshal made my appointment to be the Young King's Marshal inevitable. Which means I'm now the most important man in the entire court.'

'Apart from the Young King, you mean,' Richard said.

'Of course, but everything has a price, Richard, and that applies to your choice, too.'

'I can't really see how,' Richard said, 'both of my choices probably lead to me losing everything.'

'Your problem is just another pigeon to me,' the Marshal said, 'along with hiring carts for every journey we take and making sure none of the servants starve to death.'

'You know the Young King well,' Richard said, 'what can he actually do to me if I refuse him?'

The Marshal laughed. 'The worst punishment a knight can face at court is to be ignored. Our lord could simply forget you exist. You may continue to live, eat, and even earn ransoms in the company, but if you are ignored, you are no one. Do you see?'

'I can think of worse things,' Richard replied, 'it would at least be a quieter life.'

'You will tire of a quiet life quicker than you think.'

Richard sighed because his friend was right. He had grown bored with family and village life before they'd set out to Ireland.

'You need one of these,' the Marshal held the new helmet out, 'I'm going to see if our lord will pay for everyone in the company to have one.'

'Why?' Richard asked. 'Surely you can see nothing behind all that metal?'

'Sight isn't everything,' the Marshal pointed the helmet at Richard's face, 'you wouldn't have that scar if you'd been wearing one of these.'

Richard felt the scar. 'Or maybe I wouldn't have seen a blow that I blocked because my eyes were unobscured.'

'Suit yourself,' the Marshal said, 'but I can't afford to ruin my face like you until I've got myself that rich heiress.'

'Ruined?' Richard asked. 'I think it makes me look tougher.'

The Marshal nodded in pretend agreement. 'Heiresses don't want ruined men, Richard.'

'You're still holding out for that, are you?'

The Marshal nodded and grinned. 'I'm a man of note now. I met many fine women at the Queen's court, and the Young King's wife knows many more. Maybe I should introduce you to some of them. I'd wager she shall introduce me to my future wife, I'm sure of it.'

Most of the horses now stood in their stalls with saddles and bridles on. The courtyard rang with the clinking of their metal bits, or the clunk of those bits being rubbed against stable doors.

'Besides,' the Marshal said, 'we lose too many knights to eye and jaw injuries, and each time that happens, I have to sit with the clerks and do parchment-work. Did you know we have to record almost everything?'

'I wondered why you cared that the rest of the company had those helmets,' Richard said.

'I suppose it's a bit late for you,' the Marshal looked sad.

'My scar isn't that bad,' Richard went to turn away but stopped himself, 'I don't need your pity. I wanted your advice, but I suppose I'll have to do without it.'

'Calm down, Richard. You need to learn to be more calm,' the Marshal said, 'although, if I'm honest, I am disappointed that you agreed to spy on our lord.'

'Disappointed? King Henry made you do the same thing.'

'But I never told him a thing, Richard,' the Marshal said, 'I know you did. I saw Brother Geoffrey here. He only appears when the King has sent a new spy, the entire company knows it. Do you remember back in Castle Tancarville how we all knew what that monk was about?'

Richard did, but he'd forgotten and felt foolish for it. 'Well, what do I do now? Why did you change your allegiance?'

'I changed nothing,' the Marshal replied, 'I still serve the elder King and I am loyal to him. But now I am in the Young King's household, and he is my true lord. I must say, I really don't wish to be anywhere else.'

'The King will be angry with you.'

'Which one?'

'You know which one,' Richard said, 'he will treat your actions as a betrayal.'

The Marshal shrugged. 'My conscience is clear, so why should I care about anyone else's?'

'Just tell me what I should do. How did you do it?' Richard asked.

'Me?' the Marshal laughed. 'I did what I knew was proper. And this is your problem, not mine. I've got enough problems, as you've seen. They come and nibble at me ten times a day. How many of this? What to do with that? Solve your own problems.'

'Can't you speak to the Young King for me?' Richard asked. 'Tell him what a terrible position I'm in.'

'Terrible position?' the Marshal stamped a foot onto the mud. 'You left me in a cell with that oaf Guy of Lusignan for months. *That* is a terrible position, being locked up and never fed, forced to watch the man who killed my uncle lord it over me.'

'He only locked you up at night because you annoyed him, and he fed you as much as everyone else in that castle,' Richard said.

'I don't think you know what terrible means, Richard. You can live here, within the best company in Christendom, with the best King under God, and earn enough wealth to grow old happily. And yet you're complaining about it.'

'I don't think you understand what the King is going to do to me,' Richard said, 'he's going to take away my village.'

'Oh, no, how will you cope without your precious little village,' the Marshal sneered.

'Don't envy that,' Richard said, 'you have more men in your company than I have villagers. And I'd wager you've never had to execute one of your company before.'

The English knight narrowed his eyes. He took a breath and sighed.

'Maybe you're right. I shouldn't envy you, considering how famous I'm going to be. My advice would be to weather the storm, join the Young King, and ignore his father. Loyalty is everything.'

'That's the problem. I can't be loyal to two kings if they are at each other's throats,' Richard said.

'Worry about it later,' the Marshal said, 'just ignore the Old King.'

'What if I can't? I have to send him something, some scrap of news, to keep Yvetot?'

'The Young King can inflict a worse punishment than death on you,' the Marshal replied, 'he could ignore you.'

'I know, but that didn't sound so bad,' Richard said.

The Marshal gasped. 'But what could be worse? If the Young King turns his eyes from you, then you disappear into the blackness of history. I should kill myself if it ever happens to me, I could not bear the shame. The whispers behind your back, the jeers in your face, the petty jokes. Do not cross the Young King, Richard.'

A boy with wisps of hair on his chin jogged into the yard. 'Marshal, there is an argument with a farrier, you must come and help.'

'Why does it need my help?' the Marshal asked.

'The farrier is threatening to brand a squire in the face if he doesn't pay him,' the boy said.

The Marshal groaned and slammed the helmet down on a table the armourer had set up. He stormed off with balled fists and left the armourer to watch him go.

Bowman left his stable. 'I thought he'd never leave,' he picked up the new helmet and tested the strength of the face-plate by trying to snap it off.

'Don't do that,' the armourer said, 'it'll stop a sword, but not a clumsy fool like you.'

Bowman put the helmet on and turned his head back and forth. 'If I'm in a fight, I'll never breathe through all this metal,' he said, 'I'll pass out.'

'I had no trouble when I tried it,' the armourer looked offended.

Bowman dropped it on the table. 'It'll never catch on,' he said.

'Should we go home?' Richard asked him.

'Where's home?'

'Not this again,' Richard said, 'or do you want to go back to your mother? Because we might find it hard to get back into that Martel castle again.'

Bowman went to pick up his own mail shirt. 'I don't know, young lord,' he looked the iron rings over for rust.

'I will go back with you if you need to,' Richard said.

Bowman looked up. 'Her path has changed now, it has split from mine. I might even forget about her if it wasn't for my half-brother swanning around like a drunk in a wine cellar.'

'He has done nothing to you,' Richard said, 'except save your life once or twice.'

Bowman threw the bag of mail down onto the table, where it slid off and landed with a squelch in the mud. The blonde man went to kick it.

'Don't do that,' Richard said, 'and you need to come to terms with Nicholas, he's going to be around for a while.'

Bowman retrieved his bag and shook his head at the brown smear on the linen. He knew the moisture would soon soak through to the rings inside if it hadn't already. 'This is his fault.'

'It's not his fault,' Richard said, 'and you threw the bag. Why can't you get along with him? Or at least tolerate him?'

'He had the upbringing I never had, and look what he did with it. He went along with Eustace like a puppy, but a crazed puppy who savaged whoever his master told him to.'

'I think he's changed,' Richard said.

'I don't,' Bowman poured the mail shirt onto the armourer's table and found somewhere to hang the bag up to dry. 'He's the same man who was with his brother when they were planting flags in piles of corpses in Brittany.'

Richard had purposefully never asked Nicholas about that. 'Do you think we should stay here?' Richard asked.

Bowman shrugged. 'My advice would be for you to hold on to what I never had. Give your children a life, young lord, don't abandon them.'

'I'm here to provide for them,' Richard said.

'Are you?' the blonde man cocked an eyebrow. 'Or are you here because you enjoy it?'

'I'm not enjoying having two kings looming over me looking to pick me apart,' Richard replied, 'but the pay is twenty shillings a day, Ireland was two.'

'In Ireland, we left with nothing but scars and secrets,' Bowman said.

'Exactly, but the coins here are real,' Richard said, 'and after a few years earning this much, we'll be able to build up Yvetot and make it safe for my children. Until the walls can keep the Little Lord or the Martels out, I need to work.'

'I think you've answered your own question, young lord,' Bowman picked the mail shirt up and heaved it up over his head.

'Which king, though?'

'That's what I mean, you already know,' Bowman let the shirt fall and wriggled his torso until the metal fell down and settled in the right place. 'Geoffrey Martel thinks he is loyal to King Henry, so I'm going to side with his son.'

Richard frowned. 'I'm not sure that's a good reason for a decision,' he said.

Bowman belted his sword around the mail. 'Reasons don't matter, young lord, only actions do. Pick a king and stick with him.'

Nicholas walked into the yard leading his horse, in his other hand he held the owl that had been on Richard's helmet.

Bowman turned away and went back into his stable without looking at his half-brother.

Nicholas held the owl up, its ruffled feathers out in every direction, lathered in mud and grass. 'I thought you might want this back,' he offered it to Richard.

'Not really, I'd rather you got rid of it. I'm not that fond of owls.'

'Who is?' Nicholas tossed it over towards the black dog, who caught it midair and shook it vigorously. Feathers soared into the air and floated down in a cloud of white, black, and brown. The dog jumped about with the dead bird in its jaws and shook it so hard the head fell off.

'Well done in the joust,' Richard said.

Nicholas let go of his horse, which was happy to stand still and fall asleep on the spot. 'The other knight's horse wasn't as good as mine, that's all.'

'I think you impressed the Young King,' Richard said.

The Martel knight yawned. 'It made me hungry.'

The owl flew from the black dog's mouth and it thudded into the door of a stable, which caused the horse inside to jump and snort.

'You should give him a name,' Nicholas said.

'The right one hasn't come to me yet, and I think he might end up being Bowman's dog.'

The Martel knight rolled his eyes. 'He does need a dog, anything to stop him from moping around like one himself.'

'Don't be hard on him,' Richard said, 'he's jealous of what you had and he hasn't gotten over it yet.'

'He is the child my mother holds dearest,' Nicholas said, 'he's not the one who has a reason to feel sorry for himself.'

'You'll both have to deal with it,' Richard picked up the new helmet and tried it on.

'I think hiding your face makes you more intimidating,' the Martel knight said, 'under my wolf it would really terrify anyone I attacked.'

Richard took it off. 'I can't see anything through the metal, I wouldn't be able to see the top of my own lance when I lower it.'

'I'd have one,' Nicholas replied, 'the jousting is over though, so you need to prepare for the main event.'

'I'm preoccupied,' Richard said, 'I've got more important things to worry about.'

'Don't be so dramatic, everything will work out,' Nicholas ran a hand down the coarse and damp wolf-pelt, 'although I'm going to go inside to dry this out while we've still got time.'

'Which king would you choose?' Richard asked.

The Martel knight walked towards the merchant's hall. 'I wish I had a family to agonise over, and if I did, I would side with the Old King to save them. But I don't, so I'll side with the young one, because all men must die, and fathers tend to die first.'

'That's one way to look at it,' Richard said, 'and not really very helpful advice, either.'

Nicholas shrugged, but from where Richard stood it looked like it was the wolf that was doing the shrugging. 'If I were you,' the Martel knight said, 'I'd ready yourself for death first, then the choice will seem more trivial. It might make it easier.'

Richard opened his mouth as the knight went inside, then let out a long breath. No one was really being much help at all.

Richard checked Solis and made sure he was ready to ride, before leaning on the stable door waiting for time to pass. He thought about the tournament ahead, but thoughts about kings and villages pushed those out of his mind. Siding with the Young King felt like the easy option for now, but he had promised himself to be a good knight, a responsible father, and a considerate husband, and the latter two of those didn't sit well with being an errant knight.

Gerold returned fully armed a short while later with mud up to his mailed ankles.

'Where have you been?' Richard asked him.

'I saw the young Irish monk, my lord,' Gerold replied.

'I'd forgotten about him, where is he?'

'Apparently, Lagny has a famous abbey, and he is rushing around it like an eager child. There are monks from Amiens there now, and they are reading and arguing.'

'We saw the abbey,' Richard said, 'it had a fire, its walls were all burned and black.'

The old knight shrugged. 'That's not my concern, the monk wanted me to tell you he is happy to stay here as long as needed.'

'Did he send my letter?' Richard asked.

Gerold nodded. 'The monks were happy to pay for the messenger, apparently they are fascinated by his tales of his country.'

'Good,' Richard knew Sophie would be angry at him, but not sending her a letter would be far worse.'

'I am looking forward to seeing your village,' Gerold said, 'to see how you are as a lord.'

Richard swallowed. 'We have had a lot of bad luck in Yvetot. Storms, fires, and one sacking, so don't expect too much.'

'If you rule like your father, then your villagers will be content and productive.'

Richard grunted a reply, he dreaded to think how the old villagers were getting on with the new ones de Cailly had sent him.

'Tell me,' Richard said instead, 'everyone seems to have heard about the King's task for me, what would you do?'

Gerold grimaced. 'You are in a sore spot, my lord,' he said, 'and I will follow you down whichever path you take.'

'That's not really advice, is it?' Richard shook his head.

'Now, there's no need to be bitter,' Gerold said, 'making tough choices is why you do not have to break your back in the fields, or dull your knees praying all day. The more responsibility you have, the harder each choice becomes. Your father battled himself with his choice to go to the Holy Land, did you know he spent two years arguing with himself if he should go?'

Richard shook his head, he thought his father had made the wrong choice. 'Maybe I should leave and go back to Yvetot,' he said.

'Quite possibly,' Gerold used the corner of a building to wipe mud from the leather sole of his leg-mail. 'And my advice would be to see to your family and lands. They matter above all else, so bow to the old king, for he is still the one who wields power. Find a way to keep the Young King cordial, but maintain communication with that slippery looking monk. If King Henry takes your land, you will become nothing once more.'

'You seem happy with no lands.'

Gerold smiled. 'Not all men can own land, it is the way of things. I am content with my lot, I have no greed.'

'So you'd have me stay here but spy for the Old King?'

'Whatever you choose, my lord,' Gerold nodded to the gap in the courtyard that led to the street.

Richard turned around and as Brother Geoffrey picked his way through the light mud with exaggerated steps.

'What are you doing here?' Richard asked.

'Making sure you do nothing stupid,' the monk replied.

Bowman snorted from in his stable and Richard realised he'd been listening to everyone else while he'd been in there.

Brother Geoffrey looked towards Bowman's snort. 'That horse sounds unwell.'

'It's very unwell,' Richard replied, unable to hide his smirk.

'I heard that the Young King discovered our scheme,' the monk said.

'And everyone else in the company, apparently,' Richard said.

'I do not understand how they sniff my spies out.'

'I'm sure we'll never know,' Richard said, 'but you should go.'

'Do you have any news for me?'

'Why would I have anything for you now? Ask me again once the tournament is over,' Richard said.

'Be careful with your tone, boy,' Brother Geoffrey said, 'you need me. Without me the King will strip your lands from you. Don't forget that.'

'I can hardly forget it, it is entirely your doing,' Richard said, 'but please go before you're noticed.'

The monk narrowed his rodent-like eyes at Richard. 'One false step.'

'Yes, I know,' Richard turned his back on the monk and went to examine the new helmet again.

'We must leash the Young King to save the father,' Brother Geoffrey said, 'King Henry cheers when messengers bring word of his son's tournament victories, but at two hundred pounds a day, the kingdom cannot withstand his frivolities forever.'

'Have you tested these against a mounted rider?' Richard asked the armourer who stood behind the table pretending he wasn't there. The man shook his head.

Brother Geoffrey dragged himself through the mud so he could hiss in Richard's ear. 'The Young King leaves a trail of debt in every town he passes through. Do you know how much two hundred pounds is, boy?'

'Why should I care?' Richard put the helmet back down and rested his palms on the table. He spread his fingers out across the rough wood, his fingers running over knots and dents caused by dropped armour.

'Two hundred pounds is the income of a moderately wealthy baron. For an entire year. It is obscene and half the world disapproves of it. What we are doing is to help the realm.'

'It isn't really helping me much, is it?' Richard replied.

'Think of the kingdom rather than yourself, and come to me as soon as you have anything worthwhile to tell,' Brother Geoffrey said.

'Leave us,' Richard told the armourer. The man was eager for an excuse to leave and rushed into the Merchant's hall.

Richard lowered his voice. 'Look, I'll spy for you, but you have to help me not get caught. So I don't want to be seen near you, ever. I'll come to you,' Richard said.

'That is not how I operate.'

'It's how I operate,' Richard hissed, 'and the Young King can't know about it. Now go away.'

The monk stepped back and rubbed his chin. 'We'll try it your way,' he turned and slogged back through the mud which crept up the hem of his dark robe.

Bowman's head appeared above his stable door. 'I thought he'd never leave. But it's time for us to go, we want to make a good first impression.'

'Nicholas is still drying his wolf out,' Richard replied.

Bowman shrugged. 'Not my problem.'

Adam left the hall and waited at the edge of the mud for a servant to bring his horse over. 'What are you all standing around for?' he asked. 'We should be the first onto the field to show how well we can endure our arms.'

'You sound like the Marshal,' Richard said.

'I hope not,' Adam grimaced, 'he's not like us, he's a parasite.'

'What do you mean, us?'

'Men of Sir Roger. I know some of de Cailly's qualities must have rubbed off on you,' Adam said. The servant held his horse for him and Adam swung himself up into the saddle as if it were merely another step in a flight of stairs.

Richard watched him go, but his horse stopped and tried to bite another that rode into the courtyard. Adam ignored the newcomer and went on his way, but Richard looked up at Guy of Lusignan and wondered if he'd ever be able to leave the courtyard himself.

'I should have known you'd be here,' Guy sat tall in his saddle dressed in mail, but had left his blue and white shield behind.

'What are you doing here?' Richard asked. 'The tournament is soon to begin, and you have to start over at Torcy.'

Guy laughed. 'All the pruning idiots on both sides will take so long to smooth their feathers and fall into line, that I could ride to Amiens and back before being late,' he said.

'Why don't you do that, then,' Richard put his hands on his hips, 'I don't want to talk to you.'

'That's convenient, because I'm not here to talk to you,' Guy replied, 'I have come to see William, because I'd like to see how he's fared since his release. I have heard famous things.'

Richard's dog growled at Guy and his horse spun around to get a look at the black hound.

Bowman opened the stable door and pulled the dog into it by the scruff of its neck.

'You're here too,' the Lusignan muttered, 'if I remember correctly you still owe me your death.'

'Try and take it on the field if you want it,' Bowman said.

'Tell me,' Guy leaned forward and rested his arms on his high saddle, 'why can I not see your Irish princess here?'

Bowman clenched his jaw and disappeared into the back of the stable. He shut the door behind him and it rattled on its hinges.

The Lusignan turned his horse back to Richard. 'He's still prickly, then. Such a shame he didn't accept my offer.'

Richard thought about throwing the new helmet at Guy's face.

The knight looked down at Richard. 'I have heard about your ransomed friend, but I have heard nothing of you. Where have you been since you fled from my castle with your band of friends?'

'We didn't flee,' Richard said, 'and my doings are none of your concern.'

'That is amusing,' Guy said, 'because your very recent doings are very well known. Everyone at Torcy knows you're spying for the old tyrant on his demonic offspring.'

How did everyone find out so quickly? Richard wondered if it was Bowman's mouth or Brother Geoffrey's blatant approach that was to blame.

'That's a sore spot, then,' Guy chuckled at him, 'if you want my advice.'

'I don't.'

'Well, you can have it anyway,' the Lusignan walked his horse closer and the black stallion sniffed at Richard. Guy grinned. 'Suffer for the old despot. It would do me a favour, at least. The Old King's evil eye is fixed on me and my family, and it would be of a great help if you could distract him for a while.'

'I don't serve you,' Richard said.

'A shame,' Guy said, 'but I've got more advice for you.'

'I still don't want it.'

'Stay away from the Young King in the tournament,' the Lusignan said, 'I'm going after him, and I've come here to tell him that.'

'Why would you tell him?' Richard asked.

'Why not? I want to see what his reaction is,' Guy replied.

'You're mad,' Richard said, 'our company is the largest here, no one will get to the Young King.'

Guy smiled his incomplete smile. 'We will find out. You see, I want to find out what a king's ransom actually looks like. But if capturing him proves difficult, his head will do me just as well.'

Richard laughed. 'You're just trying to be intimidating now,' he said, 'you will not kill the Young King, even if you were stupid enough to want to.'

Guy smiled with his mouth but not his eyes. 'Did you know that pagans to the east sacrifice horses to their gods?'

Richard remembered enough of Guy not to be drawn in.

'No? Well, I think you still owe me for all the trouble you caused me, so remember that.'

'If you're threatening my horse,' Richard said.

Nicholas left the hall and threw the wolf-pelt around his shoulders. He stopped dead. 'You?'

'Me?' Guy replied. 'Don't tell me the great Martel family never paid your ransom?'

Nicholas frowned and Guy laughed so hard he had to wipe a tear from his face.

'And you're still with this boy and his angry friend,' Guy took a deep breath to settle himself. 'I'm so glad I came, this was worth the journey. Tell me, wolf-knight, how are your relations with your father?'

Nicholas tied the black paws below his chin. 'You destroyed my life,' he said.

'That's a bold claim from a Martel, and you must be an extremely useless one for that brood to have rejected you.'

Nicholas stormed forwards.

'Wait,' Richard shouted.

The Martel knight stopped as his feet hit the mud.

'Interesting,' Guy said, 'my congratulations, Richard, you have done the impossible and tamed a Martel.'

'He's not really tame,' Richard said.

'If we meet on the field,' Nicholas said, 'I will not be taking prisoners.'

Guy shrugged. 'If we meet on the field, young wolf, you'll never have the chance to.'

'Enough,' Richard said, 'we're leaving.'

Nicholas took a wide berth around Guy and went to fetch his horse.

Guy abandoned his horse in the middle of the courtyard, which was a brave move, and entered the hall.

'Richard,' Nicholas shouted once the Lusignan was gone.

Richard opened the stable door and led Solis out. The palomino strained to sniff the abandoned horse, but Richard held him back. 'Yes?' he replied.

'The Young King had a message for you.'

Richard's heart sank. 'Is he sending us home?'

Nicholas emerged from the dark stable with a grin. 'No, he's adding us to his personal guard for the tournament.'

'Is that good or bad?' Richard asked.

'I don't know,' Bowman led his horse out, 'but Adam told me that everyone always tries to capture the Young King, and there are two thousand knights on the enemy side here. Not to mention what that Lusignan weasel just said.'

'Great,' Richard replied, 'another chance for Sir Wobble to be heroic.'

THE IRON WORK

The hooves of a thousand horses churned the path to the list into a quagmire. Despite Richard's effort to arrive early to the field, most of his team already warmed their horses up within the fortified list by the time he reached it. Knights sporting all manner of colours turned circles and practised charges against each other, while others stood in groups and bragged about their upcoming heroics.

Richard led his knights through the single gap in the ditch and stakes and into the list. Their red shields were new and undented. Richard looked back at Bowman and Gerold, who both looked identical to him. Nicholas wore his wolf-pelt and received haughty looks from many noblemen as they made their way through the practising knights to the growing company of red-shielded riders.

Servants on foot ran back and forth with shields, lances, forgotten weapons, and jugs of water all across the list.

'There are more knights here than the King had in Brittany,' Bowman said.

Gerold halted his horse beside Richard. 'This is an unusual tournament,' he said, 'and the lists aren't normally this big, either.'

Richard adjusted the grip on his ash lance. The Marshal's new helmet bounced against his leg as he rode. He'd tied it to the back of his saddle because the Marshal's words about broken faces and eyes had lingered in his mind. That mind had flashed back to the crippled veterans who had so terrified him at Lillebonne, and Richard couldn't help but think that if he ignored the helmet, he was tempting a facial injury.

'We just need to survive the grand charge,' Gerold said, 'then the size of our company should protect us.'

A detachment of spear-armed infantry made its way through the slick mud and took up positions inside the entrance to the list. The Marshal led an ox-drawn cart into the fortification that was stacked into the air with new lances and a few replacement shields. The top so bristled with lances it resembled a hedgehog. Some servants unhitched and took the ox away, leaving the stash of weapons behind.

Richard shook his head. 'I can't afford to even buy myself a single new shield,' he said.

'Remember that you're owed the ransom for Henry the Northerner's horse,' Bowman said, 'you want to keep that in mind, because Sir Wobble will choose to forget it if you let him.'

Richard chose to count knights instead of potential ransoms. There were four hundred just in the red livery of the Young King. That was four times the number of knights that had conquered Leinster.

'I think I've picked my side,' Richard said.

Bowman grunted. 'I hope you know what you're doing.'

'If the Young King can draw this many knights to his banner,' Richard said, 'he is the future.'

'His purse draws them,' Bowman said, 'and don't forget who refills it.'

Richard didn't care, because when the old King died, the means to refill the purse would fall to the Young King.

'Look,' Nicholas pointed to the south-west, where a company of knights emerged in a narrow column from the woods beyond the list. Their colours were black and white, and they rode up to the stands and gained a modest cheer from the people already in it. Food sellers were doing a roaring trade nearby, and horse dealers were buzzing around waiting for the action to begin.

Two knights warming their horses up in the list collided and both their horses tangled up in a clash of legs and snapping wood.

'There's more coming now,' Bowman nodded towards the woods that lay a few bow-shots away from the list. A company of fifty gold and green knights arrived, their banner held proudly aloft before them. Behind them, and in dribs and drabs, more of the opposition team arrived from Torcy. The companies congregated at the far end of the stand until their numbers swelled to over a thousand. Mounted squires followed them with spare lances and set themselves up behind their knights.

'Those squires are fair game,' Gerold said, 'unless they hide behind the rope barrier.'

Nicholas grinned.

'We're not here to scare servants,' Richard said, 'we're here to guard the Young King and avoid getting captured.'

'Or killed,' Bowman said.

'Obviously,' Richard replied, 'but we need to protect the Young King to prove our loyalty to him.'

'So he's our new master now, is he?' Gerold asked. 'Are you sure?'

Richard nodded. 'We can serve both kings,' he said more confidently than he felt.

Bowman coughed. 'Fine. Why not.'

Count Philip of Flanders arrived underneath his yellow and black lion banner. He had a second identical banner behind him, and over two hundred knights in his company.

'That's who we need to watch,' Bowman said, 'I expect he has their team's largest company.'

Count Philip led his men past the rest of his side and over to the rope barrier that separated the field from the spectators.

The smell of cooking meat drifted over the field, and Richard's stomach rumbled. 'I never ate any breakfast this morning,' he said.

Bowman grinned. 'I did, and I gave the dog your share.'

'Thanks,' Richard replied.

Two bands of musicians played lively tunes from different sides of the stand, but in the list the sounds mixed and were painful in Richard's ears.

More and more companies arrived from Torcy until the groups were only small or sometimes only pairs of knights in non matching colours.

'I hate to say it,' Richard said, 'but Guy was right about the need to turn up early. I'm not sure who we are impressing by standing here.'

'At least it isn't summer,' Nicholas said, 'the sun isn't cooking us alive today.'

Townspeople flocked to the rope barrier until a sea of people waited eagerly for the action to begin.

'Some of the Flemings are dismounting,' Bowman said, 'surely they aren't giving up the idea of fighting?'

Some of the Count's knights removed their helmets and passed them down to servants, while others walked their horses behind the rope and seemed to leave the tournament permanently.

Two Norman knights in pale blue colours rode in front of Richard and he could tell one of their horses was lame on a hind leg. He thought about shouting a warning but concluded it was not his concern. Solis pulled his head down to eat the damp grass, which wrenched the reins from Richard's hands. Richard let him eat because action didn't seem imminent.

The Young King rode across the list area with the Marshal, Adam, and two dozen of his closest knights. Four men paraded behind him with red royal banners. Along with the Young King's, their horses shone resplendent in full red. Expensive red cloth caparisons with hoods stretched down to their hooves and covered them from nostril to tail.

'Count Philip is up to something,' the Marshal said. He had two swords and two maces belted around his waist, as well as a dagger.

The Young King halted his horse. 'It seems more than likely.'

'We should keep half our company in reserve to counter them if they spring an attack,' the Marshal said.

The Young King exhaled a long breath that hung in the air. 'That would show that I am capable of comprehending such behaviour,' he said, 'which I am unwilling to do.'

'You want to ignore two hundred knights who are clearly planning an ambush?' the Marshal pointed at them with a mail-covered finger.

'I do,' the Young King replied. 'I would rather suffer from the deception of others than indulge them by countering it.'

'He doesn't sound much like his father,' Bowman said.

The Young King viewed the blonde man with a wry smile. 'I can learn from his mistakes. I can be everything he is not.'

'No wonder the King is paranoid,' Nicholas scratched his ear under his mail coif.

Henry the Northerner scowled at him from on top of a fresh horse. 'There is only one king here,' he said, 'and it isn't old Henry.'

'Quiet,' the Young King said, 'Marshal, rein your creature in.'

Henry shrank back from the Young King, saving the Marshal from the bother of shouting at him.

Richard searched for more knights coming out of the forest but saw only green trees tinged with the first yellows of the year.

'I think it's time to leave the list,' the Young King said, 'Marshal, see to your work.'

Richard turned to his men. 'Whatever happens, we stick together.'

Everyone nodded back.

'I'm mostly talking to you, Nicholas,' Richard said, 'I don't want you running off on a killing spree, remember this is not a real battle.'

'You don't need to tell me that,' the Martel knight said.

'I think he does,' his half-brother said, 'but if you run off, don't expect me to come back for you again.'

'Again?' Nicholas asked.

'Have you forgotten that, too?' Bowman raised his voice.

'Enough,' Richard banged the shaft of his lance loudly onto his wooden saddle. 'We'll soon have enough men to fight without doing it between ourselves.'

'Well said,' the Young King smiled and Richard realised the young Angevin had been listening. He blushed.

The Marshal rode out closer to the middle of the huge list and barked orders at the top of his voice. Richard shook his head in wonder that the young man who in Normandy had devoured his meals and slept so soundly had transformed himself into a leader. 'I think I might stop using his old name,' Richard said to himself.

The Young King pressed his calves into his horse and the fine Italian beast moved off into a walk. Its coat was a grey-ish blue, but under its caparison, Richard could only see its pitch-black eyes. The bannermen walked along behind him and out through the stakes and the ditch. The infantry stood well clear and whispered to each other as the Young King swept by.

'I don't get what all the fuss is about,' Bowman said.

Richard pulled his horse's head up from the grass. 'He's famous,' he said, 'I think the locals would be happy if we invaded and installed him as their king.'

'That is probably his goal,' Gerold said, 'for the whole of France is his father's dream, even if he knows it's too much for one man to rule.'

Richard joined the exodus from the list, and horses jostled and bumped into each other, eager to get proceedings underway. Within their ranks the smell of leather, horses, and the beeswax mixture used to treat mail all mixed in his nose. It was the scent of war.

As knights left the list and spread out across the pasture, they engaged in excited conversations. Confidence overflowed and Richard started to believe that everything might go well.

The stand lay to his left, and opposite him the Torcy team formed a single, long line. Companies of knights moved along the line until it ran out, then made it longer. It soon reached from the rope by the stand out into the distance to Richard's right, where the knights were so far away all he could see were multicoloured blobs moving about.

'Form line,' the Marshal bellowed in a voice that didn't sound like it belonged to him, and the royal company pushed to the front and spread out. Richard found himself between Bowman and Gerold, a few horses down from the Young King.

'It will be an honour to fight alongside you,' the old Keynes knight said.

'I think the honour is mine,' Richard replied, 'and hopefully once the charge is over we can spend the rest of the day on guard duty. How long do these things normally last?'

Gerold chuckled. 'Until dark,' he said.

Richard groaned, Solis would be angry by then. He looked down at the grey scar down his horse's yellow shoulder where the hair had never regrown, and said a silent prayer for his safety.

'Things are going to happen quickly, aren't they,' Richard said.

'Four strides from them, four strides from us,' Bowman left his words to hang in the cool air.

'Remember,' Gerold said, 'once we are through them, gather up together and make for the Young King. Your father knew the knights who scatter are the ones who get picked off first.'

'I thought my father didn't approve of tournaments,' Richard said.

Gerold half turned his head, and a smile crept across his weathered face. 'That doesn't mean he didn't know how to deal with them.'

Richard wished his father had mentioned them just once to him back at Keynes.

'So when does it start?' he asked.

The Marshal stopped his horse behind them. The grey stallion sniffed at Solis, who swished his blonde tail back in his face. 'It begins when it begins,' the English knight said, 'when the first man charges, the game is on.'

'Seems a bit disorganised to me,' Bowman said.

Richard felt the Marshal sneer behind him without turning his head.

A small group of knights followed the Marshal. 'We will push in here next to you,' he said to Richard.

'Do whatever you like, you seem to be in charge,' Richard replied.

The Marshal narrowed his eyes for a moment, then laughed. A laugh which Richard had last heard at Castle Tancarville.

'This is just the start,' the Marshal said, 'when I have amassed more ransoms than any knight in history, potential brides will queue up for me.'

'He's full of,' Bowman began, but Richard pushed his shield with a crack into the blonde man's lance to silence him.

Nicholas stood furthest to the right, and he gestured with his lance further down the line. 'Someone's charging,' he said.

'Really?' Richard squinted to make out the coloured blobs of the opposite team in the distance.

'He's right,' Bowman shortened his reins and set himself into his saddle.

Adrenaline surged through Richard, his lungs pounded.

'To work, boys,' the Marshal shouted, 'to the iron work.'

The knights on either side shouted back at him. 'The iron work,' and cheered.

Horses up and down the line pawed the turf and snorted clouds into the air. Some reared up when they were held back by clenched reins, and some younger ones backed out of the line as their riders screamed at them. Solis snaked his neck, flattened his ears, and launched his jaws at Gerold's horse. Gerold's horse was black and twice the palomino's age. It stood firm and threw his head back at him, white teeth forcing Solis to retreat and think twice about doing it again.

'Go,' a knight to their right shouted.

'Should we?' Richard asked.

'They've already begun,' Bowman said, 'so we might as well.'

'Wait for the signal,' the Marshal said, 'our company is not some rabble, we charge as one.'

Richard was confused. Shouts to go, shouts to hold, horses snorted and bellowed, and orders of every kind all at once drowned out the noise of the crowd behind the rope.

A company in the enemy line to their right surged on, but they charged out from the centre and in a V rather than a line.

'Amateurs,' the Marshal muttered.

The black and white company directly in front of Richard lifted their lances up and down as a salute, and their horses fidgeted.

'Shout your war cries and charge,' the Marshal cried.

'Dex Aie,' the Young King's knights shouted.

'What does that mean?' Richard asked.

'God for us, or something like that,' Gerold said.

'Dex Aie the Marshal,' Henry the Northerner screamed at the top of his voice. The Marshal's other knights joined him.

Solis jumped forwards a step, and as Richard hauled him back, he glanced over and saw the Young King seething. His face, looking at the Marshal, was red and his eyes shone with anger.

The black and white knights shouted their own war-cries. Their horses coiled back on their rear ends, then exploded forwards.

The Young King's company responded in kind, but Richard was still backing Solis up, and Bowman and Gerold squeezed together in front of him and he lost his space.

'Dex Aie the Marshal,' Henry shouted as his horse flew by.

From behind the line, Richard could see that most of the Young King's red company were in a decent formation. To his right, the Marshal's sub-company were not. They charged after their leader, who raced ahead of everyone else.

'That's the Sir Wobble I remember,' Richard muttered as he spurred Solis in an effort not to be left behind.

Mud from the hooves ahead spun past Richard's face.

Lances in front lowered and disappeared from Richard's view. He lowered his own and pressed on to see what black and white knight might appear through the royal charge.

The two lines crashed together in the loudest sound Richard had ever heard. Horses collided, men spilled from saddles, and lances splintered and snapped with deafening bangs.

Bowman and Gerold's horses hit the same knight at once, the impact threw the hapless knight's horse back and down to the ground. Solis jumped the sprawled horse and the motionless knight, a jump which jolted Richard's back.

The two teams passed through each other in a frenzy. Black and white knights, who were Bretons, squeezed through between the red knights of the Young King's company. One lowered his lance at Richard.

Richard just managed to aim his own, but he missed as the Breton's lance dug into the corner of his shield and jarred Richard's left arm that braced it.

As the two sides all executed the tightest turns they could, the ground between them became strewn with men, horses, and broken lances.

Bowman's black horse sharply turned around in his path, and suddenly Richard had nowhere to go. Solis half jumped and half pushed his way through his friends as they charged back the way they'd come. A host of black and white knights turned too, and the second charge began.

Except that the two sides had already broken up. Companies from both teams surged back and forth chasing each other, and Richard saw the Marshal's men hurtle off in pursuit of five Bretons, one of which held their banner. The five had been separated from the rest of their compatriots and looked like easy targets.

Richard turned Solis away from them, tensing his core and pulling his horse around with his body rather than his arms. The stallion twisted and leapt off to chase his friends.

He bounded past Adam, who pointed at the Marshal. 'Come back, you fool, you selfish, small-minded, arrogant fool. Where is your famous loyalty now?'

Richard left him and his eyes fell on the royal banner. The whole Breton company ploughed towards it, funnelling themselves into a cluster of knights eager to be the one to take the Young King captive.

Such was the mass of men and beasts that both sides ground to halt and worked on each other with swords and maces.

Bowman and Gerold crashed into their own line and pushed into the melee around their new lord.

A horse mounted another one from behind, its flailing hooves knocked the knight from it without him ever knowing what had happened.

Another enemy contingent slammed into the royal company as Adam raced by Richard with his lance on its way down. 'To me, Dex Aie,' he cried.

The knights who, like Richard, had ended up out of place all flocked to answer Adam's call. They charged together into the fray.

Richard lowered his lance at a knight who wasn't looking at him. The knight was stationary and fighting someone else. At the last second, Richard realised this wasn't a real war, and he dropped the point of his lance. It missed the oblivious knight's face by a whisker and barreled into his shield instead.

The knight flew out the other side of his saddle, and Solis cantered on and crunched into the flank of black and white knight's horse. Richard swung his lance sideways, but the dense crowd made it useless. He dropped it as Solis bit the opposing horse on its rear and it kicked out at him in return.

Adam's horse pushed past Richard and his mace rang on helmets to his left and right. The Bretons in the area panicked at the attack that drove through them, and peeled away from the fight. A Breton streamed by Richard so he thrashed out with his sword and it dug into the man's hand, knocked his sword from it, and a freshly severed finger spiralled through the air.

Richard wondered how anyone was supposed to take captives in this mess.

Adam appeared in front of him, a toothy smile across his face. 'I noticed you followed me, well ridden,' he said.

'I can't believe that attack worked,' Richard said as the second company to attack the Young King fled the area in a flurry of hooves.

'This isn't my first dance,' Adam rested his sword on his thigh and caught his breath.

The fleeing enemy revealed the Young King unharmed beneath his four banners, three hundred of his red-shielded knights around him. Some took the surrender of any dismounted opposition who were on foot and therefore unable to escape. They rounded up these captives and led them back towards the list, their defeated heads low.

Loose horses bolted here and there, but many went straight back to their comrades, where servants rushed to reclaim them. Yet more servants already ran out of the list with bundles of fresh lances.

'I can't believe how efficient this is,' Richard said when he found Bowman.

'As soon as money is involved, everyone takes things more seriously,' the blonde man rubbed his forearm with the pommel of his sword.

'Are you alright?' Richard asked.

'Fine,' Bowman replied, 'truth be told, I expected more violence, young lord.'

Nicholas joined them with his broken lance still in his hands. 'Your friend has run off over there,' he pointed to the rolling fields that ran east and away from Lagny. Richard could see a bundle of red mixing with black and white, but couldn't tell who was winning.

A servant held out a fresh lance to Nicholas, who eagerly took it. Richard tried in vain to make eye contact with the servant to get one himself.

'Regroup the line,' Adam cried.

'Is he in charge now?' Nicholas asked.

'Why not?' Bowman asked. 'At least he's here.'

Cries of alarm rang out from the company.

'The Flemings,' Adam bellowed. 'Form, now.'

Richard spun Solis back towards the stands. His eyes caught men and women jumping up and down on the tiered seating, and their shrieks sounded like warnings. Because below them, and hurtling across the pasture at full speed, was Count Philip and his full company.

The yellow tide swept across the green grass, over some of the fallen horses from the first charge, and towards the rapidly reforming royal line. A squire ran at a royal knight with a fresh lance, but his horse baulked away from the running man and sent the rider crashing into those next to him.

Richard felt a flicker of pity for the squire for the punishment he'd receive for that, because Count Philip veered his formation straight into that gap.

'The peacock returns,' Bowman said as his horse spun around on the spot, the excitement getting the better of it.

Richard noticed a group of red shields in the distance cantering towards the list, several captured horses and knights in tow.

'Charge,' Adam cried, and others echoed it down the red line.

The Flemings accelerated from their centre and formed a wedge that crashed through the gap in the Young King's line and split his forces in half.

Richard charged.

Bowman managed to kick his horse on as it spun around to the right direction and leapt after Solis.

Richard's muscle memory went to lower his lance, but that still lay on the ground, so he had to hold his sword out in front of him instead. The Flemings, fresh and bristling with sharp lances, lowered them.

The sun glinted off the iron tips and Richard grimaced.

A Fleming homed his lance in on Richard's shield and hit it with a crunch. It pinned the shield back into his body, slid up it and flew away. Richard lashed out with his sword to his right and thumped it onto the upper arm of the knight whose lance hit Bowman on his helmet.

Richard held Solis and turned him. The scene he arrived at was one of utter chaos.

Red-shielded knights lay everywhere on the ground, and some horses pulled themselves back to their feet. The wave of yellow and black crashed through and started to turn back to finish the job.

Richard felt concern wash over him because the two sides were now evenly matched in numbers, but one side was far fresher. He spotted the red banners amongst a cluster of surviving royal knights, and made for them.

Count Philip made for them too. The tip of his wedge was still intact, and fifty knights arced around in a shallow turn, irresistibly drawn towards the stationary Young King.

Richard raced past Nicholas, who was remounting his horse.

Richard didn't reach the Young King in time, but had a clear view of the Flemings rolling over the King's guard and enveloping them. Swords flashed above helmets, shields cracked, men shouted and fell. Knights with red shields began to be taken away from the melee as captives.

Richard couldn't allow the Young King to experience that fate at the first tournament where he had joined his guard.

He aimed Solis at the Flemish knight leading one of the royal company away by the bridle. The pair moved at a canter, the royal knight unable to save himself with his reins in the hands of his captor.

Richard spurred his stallion. Solis responded with a burst of speed he normally reserved only for boar, and rammed into the side of the Flemish knight. His horse buckled in as Solis raised his front legs and pushed the knight out of his saddle. The horse fell to its knees and Richard caught the flailing reins in his sword-hand just before the royal knight's horse bolted away. Richard only had one finger on the reins and still clutched his sword as the horse yanked him around and realised it had to stop.

Richard tensed his core, Solis stopped, and he handed the reins back to the now free royal knight. Richard shook his hand, that finger was going to hurt later.

The rescued man gathered his reins up and took a breath. He had curly brown hair, and Richard recognised him from the Young King's court as Count Robert of Meulan. 'I cannot thank you enough,' Count Robert said, 'but we must see to the King.'

Richard nodded and together they charged back into the contest, the Count drawing an iron-topped mace from his belt as they cantered.

A handful of unhorsed royal knights remounted and attacked the Flemings that ground down the Young King's guard. They circled the Angevin like hungry wolves, his capture only a matter of time.

Richard and Count Robert rammed into the yellow mass and battered them with sword and mace. Solis pushed his way into the press and Richard clouted a knight in the nose with his pommel. While stunned, Count Robert knocked him to the ground with a great blow to the head from his mace. A sword dug into the rim of Richard's shield, the iron blade too close to his eyes for comfort, and Richard had a fleeting thought about the new helmet that was still tied to his saddle.

Count Robert took a sword blow to his arm, but never flinched.

A horse rode across Richard's path and Solis bit it on its rump. The animal jumped away and Richard went through the gap it left and back outside of the dense combat.

Out from the list, their prisoners safely stowed, galloped the Marshal and his knights. Richard rode towards them hoping to add himself to their impact when they charged.

The Marshal looked cheerful.

'Where have you been?' Richard shouted as he spun his horse around to join them.

'Gathering a few ransoms,' the Marshal said, 'it has been a fine start to the day.'

'The Marshal scattered all before him,' Henry the Northerner panted and could only just get the words out.

'Count Philip is about to capture the Young King,' Richard said.

The Marshal's face blackened. 'No, no,' he muttered, then he mustered a great cry, 'charge.'

'Dex Aie the Marshal,' Henry and the group shouted.

They rushed towards the Flemings, who were concentrating on their prize, and caused instant mayhem.

The Marshal rode at the head of his formation, his sword arced left and right as his horse surged into the enemy ranks. Fury powered his strokes and his sword broke arms and dented helmets. He rarely hit a shield. His knights behind him unhorsed and finished off the knights the Marshal had stunned or wounded, and within moments he had cut his way right through to the Young King.

Richard found himself with no one to face as the Flemings

regrouped away from the Marshal's fury.

The Young King sat emotionless with his banners around him, but his face was whiter than usual.

'Marshal,' the Young King whispered, but it was a whisper of anger rather than fear.

'My lord,' the Marshal said, 'there is good hunting to be had today, do I have your permission to leave and seek ransoms?'

The Young King blinked, and Richard thought he was about to lose his temper.

'Marshal,' the Young King said through gritted teeth, 'it would be more becoming of your station to defend your lord while he is under heavy attack. We have spoken about this. At length.'

'Very well,' the Marshal said cheerfully, 'we shall remain here and drive these Flemings off for you.'

Colour returned to the Young King's face in the form of rage.

The Marshal spurred his horse and led an assault on the Flemings, who had regrouped a distance away and readied their next charge. Henry the Northerner, Adam, and Count Robert all poured after him, so Richard joined in. The Marshal struck the foe before they could get moving, allowing the royal attack to penetrate their ranks and deal revenge onto the Flemings.

Richard aimed for Count Philip's banner but couldn't find a way through the red shields ahead of him.

The yellow banner retreated away from the melee and the Marshal's war cry rang out again as his knights gave chase.

'Hold,' Adam shouted after the Marshal and his joyous knights, 'stay with the Young King.'

Richard hauled Solis back next to Adam, even though the stallion strained to take part in the pursuit.

Count Robert of Meulan also had to roughly restrain his horse. 'Come back,' he shouted after the Marshal.

Richard gulped down some air, his body was hot and he felt his sword-arm ache around his shoulder.

'That young fool,' Adam said, 'he thinks he's so much better than the rest of us.'

Count Robert shook his head and returned to the Young King.

Bowman and Gerold turned back too, but thirty knights roved the pasture with the Marshal as the Flemish banner grew smaller and smaller as it disappeared over the rolling hills.

Richard went back with Adam, to where barely thirty knights still stood with the Young King. The bulk of the company roamed around the tournament field chasing prisoners, although they had lost a good few captured and plenty lay wounded on the ground.

'This time I won't forgive him,' the Young King said, his voice simmering.

'You give him too many chances,' Adam said, 'we should retreat to the list until he returns.'

'I will not retreat,' the Young King said.

'Do not be stubborn,' Count Robert removed his helmet to scratch his head through his matted hair, 'if we are hard pressed there is no shame in retreat.'

'But we aren't hard pressed, are we?' the Young King replied. 'The opposition are all gone.'

Bowman pointed over towards the yellowing woods beyond the fortified list. 'I'm afraid not,' he said.

Richard followed the blonde knight's gesture to where a party of knights burst out of the treeline. They wore shields with blue and white lines.

'Lusignans,' Bowman spat onto the churned up ground.

Horses and men still fought to catch their breath. The air around stank with sweat and wet leather.

'Prepare to meet their charge,' Adam shouted.

'We're outnumbered,' Count Robert sighed.

'We're always outnumbered,' Richard grinned back at him.

The Young King frowned. 'Your confidence may be misplaced,' he said, 'Guy's knights are seasoned, and they are fresh. See their tall lances? They have only now ridden from Torcy so they can attack us when we have fought a hard contest and need to recover.'

Richard rotated his tired shoulder and his brief burst of optimism evaporated.

Royal knights pushed into line, their horses snorted and sweat matted their coats. Richard closed his eyes and inhaled the sweet smell of exercised horses that saturated the air. As the horses chomped on their bits and shook their heads, the steam rose from them like fine rain falling in reverse.

Richard had a sudden idea, threw his helmet to the ground, and retrieved the new helmet from his saddle. He slipped it over his head and laced it up. The world became a darker place.

Shouting from the stands behind matched the Lusignan war-cry in volume, but Richard only had time to grip with his legs and accelerate as the Young King's line advanced to meet their white and blue attackers. No longer able to see his own horse or his own weapon, Richard focused on the only thing he could see through the eye slits of the face-plate, and that was the enemy.

A blue and white caparisoned horse headed straight for him. Richard resolved to ignore that knight's lance, who might have been Guy himself, and cut at him. The two sides rushed at each other and collided in another splintering crash. The sound of snapping lances boomed through the air and made Richard's ears hurt. Guy's lance bounced off the top of his shield and struck the face-plate. The iron dented and screeched under the blow, but as Guy disappeared behind him, Richard knew his face was unharmed, even if his neck shot with pain. The plate bent back towards his left cheek, and he could already feel the cold condensation from his breath on the inside of the helmet.

Richard swung Solis around and chased after the Lusignans, who made for the Young King.

Knights from both companies scattered as the fighting broke up and white and blue knights chased ransoms. Bowman clobbered a knight around the back of the head who slumped forwards before his horse raced away across the grass.

Guy clattered into the Young King, and they battered each other with their swords.

Richard aimed for Guy, an urge to avenge his dented helmet growing within. Four blue and white knights peeled off after a lone red one, who fled from them with his legs flapping on his horse to make it go faster. He headed back to the list and the safety of the spearmen who guarded its entrance.

Richard could only see ahead of him and felt a jolt as someone bumped into his side. His saddle jerked forwards and up, which meant Solis had kicked out at whoever it was, but Richard kept him racing towards his new lord.

He reached the melee as a horse reared up and threw its blue and white rider onto the ground. Solis dodged to the side and Richard swiped at Guy's back. The sword slashed a wide gash in his surcoat and revealed a hardened leather back plate underneath.

The sword didn't cut through it.

Richard tried again, but a blow rang the very top of his helmet and shook his vision. He blinked and turned his head to his left. He saw the head of a horse next to him, but the face plate blocked his vision of the rider. Another blow crunched down onto the helm and jarred his neck. He wanted to throw up.

'Do you yield?' the invisible knight yelled.

Richard turned Solis into him and the angered horse used his yellow chest to push into the enemy's mount. Wrongfooted, the horse fell down onto a knee. Richard didn't need to tell Solis what to do next. The stallion pushed again and the horse fully fell over onto its side.

Richard heard the knight scream as he hit the ground, but still never saw him.

He turned Solis back towards Guy again, but multicoloured stars danced around his eyes and he felt dizzy. A group of Lusignan knights carved a trio of the Young King's guards away and chased them from the melee.

The Young King matched Guy blow for blow. They were the same age and the same build, with the same training, but one was naturally more vicious and he beat the Young King back.

Count Robert and Adam fought next to him, fending off a dozen white and blue knights, but apart from them, only a single bannerman remained with the Young King.

Richard charged at the Lusignans who buzzed around the red shields to find an opening.

Surprise took everyone when the Marshal and five knights cut into the Lusignans. The Marshal heaved his sword and a foe fell to the ground. Riding with his reins on his belt, he grabbed the reins from another with his left hand and disarmed him with his sword. The Marshal handed the reins to Henry, who cantered off with the captive in tow.

The Marshal forcefully made his way back to his lord, and this time he didn't bother to inquire if his help was needed.

Guy had to leave the Young King to face the Marshal, who had a score to settle, and laid into him with gusto.

Richard reached the Young King, whose helmet was dented and his shield gouged and marked.

'Can we fight our way to the list?' Richard asked.

A blue and white knight attacked Count Robert and split his shield in two.

'I think so,' the Young King said, 'but there are too many of them, and they're all after me.'

Adam broke the arm of an opponent, who wisely broke off and left the fight. 'We'll be overwhelmed soon,' he said.

Guy spun his horse away from the Marshal and disengaged, but shouted at his knights to take out the English knight.

A dozen Lusignans swarmed towards him, which reminded Richard of when the same thing had happened at the Niort ambush. He wondered if these were the same knights who had speared the Marshal and taken him captive.

The Marshal had no wish to repeat his defeat at Niort and sprung back towards the Young King. The knights who pursued him had second thoughts and broke off their attack.

113

The Lusignans regrouped between the list and the royal company, or at least what remained of it.

'Where is everyone else?' the Young King shouted, a tinge of despair in his voice.

Adam spat some blood onto the now very muddy ground. 'Half ran off with that selfish peacock,' he said.

'This is a tournament,' the Marshal said, 'we are here to take prizes.'

'You are here,' the Young King roared like his father, 'to protect your king.'

The Marshal swallowed and looked down at the grass.

Richard unlaced his helmet so he could see who was still with them. The world came back to life and he breathed the crisp air with joy. The light flooded back into his eyes and stung them, which almost made him sick. But Bowman and Gerold were next to him, their horses dripping with sweat and their faces no drier. He could see the wolf-pelt too, on the other side of the group.

'There are twenty of us and forty of them,' Count Philip said, 'we cannot punch through and reach the list, they are preparing for that.'

Guy's company arrayed themselves in two lines of twenty knights.

'We can breach the first line,' the Young King nodded, 'but the second will bring us down to a standstill.'

'And then we're finished,' Adam said.

'Can we just ride out around the rope barrier and get behind it?' Richard asked. 'This is all just a game, anyway.'

The Young King looked shocked. 'My dear Richard,' he said, 'this may be a game, but the stakes are deathly real. Why do you think I am here?'

'To have a good time and spend your father's money?' Bowman asked with a grin.

Everyone glowered at him, and he turned red.

'I'm gaining prestige,' the Young King said, 'I'm proving I'm a king who can be trusted, can be followed, and can be relied upon to act like one. I cannot be captured, but most importantly, I cannot be a coward.'

Richard sighed. He gulped down clean air and his heart sank at the idea of putting the helmet back on.

'What shall we do, Marshal?' the Young King asked. 'This is your mess.'

The knight went to complain, but then stopped himself. 'A diversion, my lord,' he said.

'Like at the nunnery for my sister?' Richard asked.

'Exactly,' the Marshal grinned, 'half of us charge, and the rest take the Young King around the melee and into the list.'

'They will see your ridiculous plan for what it is,' Adam said, 'we are on an open plain and the enemy are only over there. How can we deceive them?'

The Marshal shrugged.

Richard raised his gaze to the limp banner hanging above the Young King. 'What about that?'

'What?' the Marshal asked.

'The banner,' Richard said, 'all we need to do is make sure the banner is with the first charge. In a line and with the banner, the Lusignans will think it is our lord. It only needs to work for a moment, the Young King can gallop around them so fast that he'll be clear before they realise.'

Adam laughed. 'Why not?'

'Richard,' the Marshal said, 'it is your turn to play the distraction.'

'Why me?' he replied. 'I didn't ask you to play the hero at the nunnery, did I?'

'But I did, so you can ride out and save our lord today. My job is to stay by his side.'

Adam and Bowman both burst out laughing.

Richard took a deep breath. He'd had enough of this. 'I'll happily ride into the jaws of defeat myself, but I'm not losing my horse for anyone else. I don't care if he's the king. If I'm risking my horse, I'm going through those ropes and going home.'

The Young King considered Richard. 'Curious.'

'We don't have time for this,' Adam nodded at the white and blue ranks, 'they're going to come for us now.'

'Richard,' the Young King said, 'I pay the ransoms for all my knights and their horses. If you lose yours, I will pay whatever is demanded for him. You have my word.'

Richard looked into the Young King's Angevin eyes. They had nothing of the distrust his father's shone with, and Richard believed he was being honest.

'Fine,' Richard lifted the helmet back up, 'but I'm sick of it, going through all this for a game is ridiculous. My father was right.'

He laced the helmet on and the world went dark again.

'He'd be proud of you,' Gerold's voice came from somewhere nearby.

'I don't want you to come with me,' Richard said, 'I'm going to get battered.'

'We're all here, young lord,' Bowman's voice came from the other side of him.

Richard swallowed and couldn't speak. He was glad no one could see his face because he had expected no one to volunteer to fail alongside him.

'I'm not letting you have all the fun,' Nicholas said from somewhere close by.

Richard could see none of them. 'Is the bannerman here?' he asked.

'He is,' Bowman said.

'The five of you should do it,' the Marshal said, 'we'll ride like we're right behind you, then veer off at the last moment. We'll gallop around, and by the time they've turned to chase we'll be beyond them and safe.'

'God be with you, Richard,' the Young King said, 'I won't forget this.'

Richard clenched his teeth and eased Solis forward. It was a terrible idea.

The Lusignan first line advanced and the two sides neared.

'Once we engage,' Richard said, 'try to stick together and punch through them. Then we'll just ride to the list as fast as we can.'

No one answered because they launched into a canter and the five of them charged the forty.

Guy rode at the centre of his company. He may have been mad, but he led from the front. No one on either side had a lance left, so swords raised into high guards and spurs pressed onto horses.

Solis struck a horse almost head-on, and the smaller horse fell aside like a plaything. Richard struck out but missed everything. Someone hit his shield, and then the five red knights were consumed by a tide of white and blue.

Richard could only see a small part of the battle through his eye slits. The fate of the Young King was unknown, all Richard knew was that blows rained down upon him. Bowman pushed in front of him, jamming his sword into a knight's nose, so Richard followed him.

Richard parried a sword blow and cut backwards into a white and blue knight's exposed armpit, but did little damage.

Guy fought with Bowman, their blows rapid as their blades danced. A dance that ended when Bowman's sword snapped. He threw the useless hilt at Guy and spurred his horse with all his might. The black horse leapt into the air, clambered over the horse that blocked its path, and with an awkward push of its hind legs, got Bowman out of the melee. Guy knew he wasn't the Young King and turned to Richard instead. 'You?' he shouted.

'Me,' Richard flew at him with everything he had. The metal on his head rang and for a moment his vision blurred. At that moment, Guy cut him across his chest and both of his mail shirts compressed under the blow. Richard felt his breath being pulled out of his lungs.

'He's not here,' Guy looked around, then screamed with rage, 'he's gone around us.'

Richard tried to escape. Solis pushed forwards into a Lusignan knight and sunk his teeth into the man's leg. The man went to strike his head, but Richard got there first and drove the point of his sword into the man's chest. The blade pushed into the knight, and metal rings gave way as it pierced his body. Someone grabbed Richard's shield because he felt it being pulled away from him. At the same time a hand grabbed his forearm. Richard tried to shake it free, but he felt another hand clasp his sword-hand and his fingers were peeled from the leather handle.

Something hit the back of his helmet, and then the reins were no longer in his hand. He tried to swear, but his chest still hurt and somebody wrenched the helmet off his head; the lacing dug into his chin, but luckily snapped before his jaw bone could be torn away.

His eyes looked straight up at the sun, that blinded him for a heartbeat.

'A poor replacement for a king, but he'll have to do,' Guy said.

Richard's vision cleared as the breeze chilled the sweat that matted his hair and ran down his face. Blue and White knights surrounded him and the one with his reins led Solis away from the fight. Not that there was much of a fight left. Bowman reached the list just as the Young King stopped safely inside it, but his bannerman was already a captive of the Lusignans, and Richard could see four knights binding Gerold's hands together a short distance away.

Richard twisted in his saddle to look for Nicholas.

The Martel knight was on the ground as three mounted knights chased him. He picked up a lance from the ground and instead of running, he turned and stood firm.

The pursuing knights charged him, but he pointed the iron lance-head at the first knight's horse and he veered away to avoid the risk. The knight next to him pressed his attack, but Nicholas swept the lance over with perfect timing for the knight himself to run onto the point. Nicholas was pushed onto his back by the impact, his lance shearing mail rings and slicing into the man's belly. Nicholas held onto the lance as he catapulted his victim from the saddle. The knight hit the ground and Nicholas sprung to his feet. The third knight took a wide berth and looked to his surviving companion for direction.

As they dithered, the Martel knight ran at them.

One horse saw a wolf coming for it and turned to flee. Its rider pulled the reins to stop him, but the horse's energy had to go somewhere, and the only direction left for it was up. It reared tall on its hind legs, its forelegs flailing through the air with its lack of balance. The wooden war-saddle held the knight in place, but he made the mistake of keeping hold of the reins, and pulled his animal backwards and down on top of himself. The horse landed on its back with a sickening crunch, but the crunch was the saddle breaking along with the bones of the knight.

His companion paled. Nicholas howled up at the sun and charged at him.

'Enough of this,' Guy said, 'we've more captives than anyone else has ever taken in one day, let us store them safely away.'

The band of knights who had taken Gerold took him towards the woods, and the other blue and white knights went the same way.

Nicholas chased them as fast as he could. 'Come back and fight me,' he yelled.

Richard felt pride for him even as they led Solis away from the list.

The Lusignans had to canter to the woods in the end to keep away from Nicholas, but on foot he had no chance to catch them, and no one from within the list ventured out to help him.

A sense of shame swept over Richard as he realised he had been captured. He was worried too, because he knew being a prisoner of Guy of Lusignan was certainly an unpredictable predicament.

The Lusignans arranged their knights to surround the captives, with a large vanguard and rearguard to prevent anyone from the list staging a rescue.

A dozen red-shielded knights stood on the next hill over. They had some captives of their own, but were not strong enough to challenge the blue and white knights, so they stood and waited for them to leave.

The column entered the woods, where a guard of a dozen knights had stood during the entire battle, and where Count Philip stood with some of his company.

'We nearly had him,' the Count laughed.

'Nearly,' Guy said bitterly, 'I've had to make do with this small fish.'

'Ah,' the Flemish Count said, 'I'm sorry, Richard. It's nothing personal, but we are on different teams, you know.'

Richard felt things were intensely personal and looked away from the Count.

'Don't be like that,' Count Philip said as he led Richard into the shade and shadows of the wood. The plain had been warmer, and the narrow path meandered between bushes and trees with low branches. Richard could taste dampness in the air, for the sun didn't reach below the leaves. He could see only a short way off the path on either side, and more than once their party startled a bird, which made a few of the horses jump.

Guy spoke to Gerold, who ignored him, then rode to Richard to try his luck there.

'Your wolf-knight killed one of my knights, did you see?' Guy asked. Richard nodded, but remained tight-lipped.

'Your knight had a crazed look about him,' the Lusignan said.

Richard looked at him. 'You would know.'

Guy laughed. 'Defiant in defeat,' he said, 'a good quality.'

They rode over a clear stream that trickled along a bed of stones and cooled the surrounding air. Richard felt a chill, but that could have been Guy's presence.

'I'm surprised you sacrificed yourself for the Young King,' Guy said, 'I thought you were playing a much smarter game than that.'

'I'm not playing any game.'

'If you say so, although the Young King will trust you now. Was that your plan?'

Richard rubbed his head, which ached. 'There is no plan.'

The Lusignan chuckled. 'No, of course not. I think you are working for the Old King,' he said, 'I think you're worming your way into his son's trust so the old man can indulge in his favourite pastime.'

'What's that?' Richard asked.

'Being paranoid. He thinks everyone plots against him,' Guy said.

'Is he wrong?' Richard asked. 'You plotted to kidnap his Queen at Niort. Simon the Quiet plotted to bring the King down. I wonder, was he plotting with you?'

Guy frowned at Richard. 'How do you know about Simon? But he's dead now, so there's no harm in speaking of it, I suppose. He was loyal to the cause.'

'What cause is that?'

'Freeing Poitou from the Angevin tyrant,' Guy replied, 'and his seed. Their rule is unholy, no man should rule so much of the world.'

'Charlemagne did,' Richard said.

'The boy knows his history,' Guy laughed, 'but King Henry is no Charles the Great.'

Richard almost asked about Simon the Quiet, but thought it better that Guy didn't know it was Richard who had caused him to be executed

Horses snorted as they climbed a gentle hill, crossed another track, and carried on further south. The sun flickered through the leaves above, but the air around Richard was still.

'Are you enjoying your ride?' Guy asked.

'No, not really.'

'It's your last on your horse,' Guy said.

119

Reality crashed into Richard. 'You can't take my horse.'

'I won him,' Guy shrugged, 'he's already not yours.'

Richard looked down at the stallion and the scar down his shoulder. 'No, you can't have him.'

'Finally,' Guy chuckled to himself, 'I've found your weakness. I was beginning to think you didn't have one, other than your sword-work, of course.'

Richard fought to choke back tears, he fought harder than he had in the battle.

'We have arrived,' Guy looked ahead to a wide clearing in the woods that contained a large barn and two square houses. A fence made by bending small trees into a lattice surrounded it, and smoke filtered up and through the roof of one house. They led Richard across the muddy yard and into the barn.

Inside the barn, a knight dragged Gerold from his horse and he hit the earthen floor with a bump.

'Have some respect,' Richard said, 'he's not young anymore.'

The knight laughed and dragged Gerold by his mail over to a pile of straw. The straw was heaped up to the rafters of the barn, but next to the straw stood more captive knights. A pile of red shields at the entrance revealed the allegiance of many, but there were also blue shields, a white one, and some yellow ones adorned with red orbs and chevrons.

Easily twenty knights filled the barn. Gerold's horse was tied up to the wall.

'You can either get off yourself, Richard, or they'll drag you off,' Guy said.

He really didn't want to get off, just in case Solis would be really gone for good, but two knights approached and one grabbed his leg.

Richard kicked it away. 'I'll get off,' he said. Richard tore himself from the wooden saddle with pain in his heart. He lowered himself to the ground and put a hand on Solis's neck. Tied into his mane, there still lived the rolled up parchment with his question over his father's fate. The stallion looked hungrily over at the pile of straw.

'Move,' Guy said, 'leave him.'

Richard felt his horse's warmth through his hand. He was going to lose him.

'However much you want for him,' Richard said, 'the Young King will pay.'

'I think not,' Guy said, 'I saw this horse, I think I might ride him myself later today. I do not need coin, Richard. Unlike those fools who are trampling across the countryside as we speak, I am here for a good reason.'

'What's that?' Richard asked.

'To damage the regime that haunts my land. Without their golden prince, the Angevins will fall. His younger brothers are less of a threat to us, you see. Richard is spoiled and John is too young to even speak, let alone rule. If the Old King dies and the Young King can't rule, the Angevin empire will collapse in on itself.'

'I'm not sure King Henry can even die,' Richard muttered.

Solis was tied up next to Gerold's horse, who he ignored in order to strain over to reach the straw.

Richard wondered what he was doing here. He felt sick to his stomach at the possibility that he was about to lose his horse, but he had children. What would he feel like if he lost them? How would he feel if he'd already lost them? He'd been away from home for so long they could be dead and buried by now.

Guy dismounted and admired his captives. 'Even the great William Marshal would rejoice at such a haul,' he said. 'We will be heading back to our list, but first you will all stand in a line, in the order of the size of your ransom.'

The knights spoke amongst each other.

'What a strange request,' Gerold said.

Richard put his hand on the older man's shoulder. 'Will you be well?'

'It will take more than a few bruises to lay me low,' he replied.

'Come on, get into order,' Guy said, 'we do not have all day.'

The knights told each other their ransom amounts and moved about.

Gerold nodded down to Richard's waist. 'You might want to hide that, I'm surprised they haven't taken it already.'

Richard realised Sir John's dagger still hung at his waist. He slid his hand down the cold and rough iron rings to the dagger, while Gerold stepped across to block Guy's view of Richard.

Richard slipped the belt down and onto the inner mail shirt, then let the outer one fall over the top of it.

'I fear you may need that before the sun sets,' Gerold smiled, but his eyes were sad.

One English knight threw a punch at a Norman who claimed to be worth a higher ransom. Guy's knights broke it up by punching them both in the face until their noses streamed with blood.

'Quickly, please,' Guy said, 'this is important.'

Richard shook his head, Guy's games were tiresome at the best of times. And this was not the best of times.

An argument about who was the poorest knight was snuffed out by the mere approach of one of the blue and white knights.

'I think we can get out of this barn,' Gerold said.

'Are you sure? There's only one door.'

'I've seen a way,' Gerold whispered.

'I can't,' Richard said, 'I can't risk him killing my horse as a punishment. But if you can get out, go.'

Gerold held a hand out to Richard. 'Your father loved his yellow horse, too. I think he would have been foolish enough to die for it. I shall try to escape and get back to the list to bring help.'

Richard nodded and went to stand in the forming line.

'How much are you worth?' a short Breton asked him.

'No idea,' Richard replied.

'Then I will stand on the richer side of you,' the Breton said.

Richard stepped back and allowed the Breton to swap places. Richard didn't really see the point of what Guy was doing, but then he didn't want to be punched in the face, either.

Richard snatched a glance behind to look for Gerold, but the old man wasn't in the barn. At the back of the building, Richard's eye caught the smallest movement and a flicker of a shadow. Gerold had indeed found a way out. Richard allowed himself a smile. The old man was wily.

All twenty captured knights stood in a line across the barn, while a dozen of Guy's knights hung around the entrance with him. One beam overhead creaked. Richard looked up at the old beams, dark knots almost obscured by years of dust and cobwebs. He half wished the whole barn would come crashing down on all of them.

Guy studied the line. 'Where is the division between those who are worth more than a knight's fee and those who are landless?'

The knights looked at Richard.

'I don't know,' he said, 'I've never been ransomed before.'

Guy laughed. 'You have that miserable Norman village, that is one fee. Although barely, I'm told.'

The man to Richard's right stepped forwards. 'I do not have land,' he pointed to the men further to his right, 'but these men are even poorer.'

Guy loomed over him. He sniffed loudly. 'Everyone to the right of Richard, come with me.'

He sauntered away and beckoned for the poorest knights to follow.

'He's letting us go,' one of the five knights said in an accent that sounded quite alien.

Richard felt a peculiar jealousy, for he had been the last in the line to stay and so had narrowly missed being in their group.

'Stop there,' Guy whirled around.

The five knights halted, and two bumped into each other with a clang of mail. One knight turned to complain to the man who had run into him.

Guy flashed his dagger out of its sheath and sunk it down into the neck of the nearest captive. The Norman knight's eyes bulged out as he gasped and tried to grab at the blade.

The other four knights backed away. Arguments over pushing and shoving disappeared and were replaced by disbelief.

'Stand still,' Guy yelled as he withdrew his knife. His victim crumpled to the ground.

'Why?' one captive asked, even as he edged back a step.

Guy's knights stormed forwards and grabbed them before they could try to find a corner of the barn to hide in.

'You can't kill captives,' Richard said, 'this is supposed to be a game.'

Guy held the bloodied dagger up to the throat of a captive being held in place by two of his knights. The panicked man tried to shake them free, but could only shout and turn his head away.

Guy held the man's head still with his left hand, fingers across his cheeks and eyes, then slowly eased the dagger into the man's neck. The prisoner screamed, but Guy twisted the dagger and the noise became a gurgle. Guy left the man to die in the arms of his knights and approached the next captive.

'There are laws against murder,' Richard shouted.

Guy sighed. 'Do you want to join them?' he asked.

Richard wavered. He turned to the knight standing shivering to his left. 'If we charge them, they can't kill us all,' he said.

The shivering knight turned and threw up.

Richard's hand dropped to the dagger concealed between his mail layers. 'Come on,' he hissed to the other knights, 'we can rush them.'

Guy faced the third captive, a man who stood tall and looked the Lusignan in the eyes without blinking.

'Good,' Guy said, 'finally a man who can face his death.'

The man spat in Guy's face.

Guy punched him and he reeled back into the knights who held him. Guy followed up with a blow to his guts and the man almost folded in half. The Lusignan tilted the man's head up and looked down at him. 'Still defiant, I see, good for you,' and jammed the dagger down into an eyeball. It burst open, then the dagger pierced the brain behind it and kept going until it scratched the very back of the man's skull.

'You can't all stand here and let him do this,' Richard whispered.

The knight who'd thrown up righted himself. 'We can if we don't end up like that,' he said, 'besides, they are merely landless knights.'

Richard felt bittersweet relief that Gerold was out of the barn, otherwise he'd be the one having his eye poked out.

The second victim drowned slowly in his own blood, too slowly, and one knight holding him drew a knife and slit his throat.

Guy circled on him. 'Did I say you could do that?'

The knight's face twitched. 'He was going to die anyway, and he didn't offend us. And that knight is right, this isn't a real war.'

Guy thought about striking him, but pivoted on his heels and killed the fourth captive by stabbing him through the ear. The dagger lodged up to its hilt and Guy had to use both hands to prise it back out.

The fifth man tried to drop to his knees, but Lusignan knights held him up.

'Please no,' he sobbed, 'why? Why?'

Guy flung some gore from the dagger onto the floor by the captive's feet.

Richard couldn't take watching any more. He lunged forwards. Before he could draw his dagger, a Lusignan knight punched in the stomach. Another knight pushed him over and the two of them kicked him in the face and ribs. Richard curled up on the cold earth, partly so no one would kick the dagger and notice it, and the blows rained down on him.

'Enough,' Guy said, 'don't kill that one, he could be of use.'

The knights dragged Richard back to his place in the line, where he stayed crumpled on the floor. He spat out blood and wheezed through what felt like a flattened chest.

'To answer your question,' Guy turned to the last landless knight, 'I'm afraid that you are simply not worth my bother. I once held a knight for half a year while I waited for his ransom. The knight was so obnoxious that it felt like a decade. I had to actually lock him up at night to give myself some peace and quiet. And then, after all that, Richard here, lost the ransom for him. That prisoner's ransom was large, but yours is so small that after accounting for your food, you would likely make me a loss.'

'Then just let me go,' tears ran down the knight's face, streaking clean lines through the brown mud that caked him.

Guy nodded. 'I could do that, couldn't I?'

'Yes, let me go, for the love of our Lord above,' the captive cried.

'Christ does preach mercy,' Guy said, 'and what would it matter to me if I let you live? It is such a shame you didn't mention this before I killed those other four knights. We could have avoided all this bloodshed if you'd just spoken up.'

'Atone for it and release me,' the man whimpered.

Guy put his left hand on the man's shoulder, squeezed it firmly, and met his gaze. 'The problem you have,' he said, 'is that I answer to neither lords nor gods.'

He stabbed the dagger into the man's stomach. The narrow blade pushed the rings of the mail into the man, then defeated the taut armour with a snap as the dagger found flesh. With a second shove, Guy plunged the weapon deep into the prisoner's guts.

He cried out in agony, a cry that knotted Richard's stomach.

Guy rotated the dagger around inside the man and it tore through intestines. He pulled it out and pushed the wailing man down to the dirt. The stricken knight clutched his wound and screamed so loudly the two horses in the barn jumped.

Guy stepped over the dying man. 'And no one finish him off,' he said to his knights, even though his gaze was on the remaining prisoners.

Richard pushed himself up to his knees.

'Now,' Guy's dagger dripped blood down onto the ground where it pooled, 'who is the richest man here?'

The knight at the far end of the line briefly thought about trying to swap places with the man to his right.

'You can't hide,' Guy chuckled, 'you put yourself at the head of this table. And that comes with responsibilities.'

The knight's chest rose and plunged, but he held himself upright. He was taller than Guy, and a decade older.

'And who are you?' Guy asked. 'That you judge yourself to be worth more than all these other men?'

The richest knight was broad, dark-skinned, with brown hair. He had a hard face and looked back at his captor with all the courage he could muster. 'My uncle is the King of Scotland,' he said, 'and I am heir to the earldom of Huntingdon.'

'Well, heir to wherever-that-is,' Guy said, 'how loyal to the Angevins are you?'

'Loyal to the bone,' the Scot said proudly in a dialect that was identical to Richard's.

'To the bone?' Guy smiled.

Richard pushed himself to his feet but had to hold his chest. 'Guy, no.'

'To the bone,' the Scot repeated and stepped closer to his captor, defiance in his eyes.

'Very well,' Guy flicked the dagger up and jammed it into the Scot's midriff. Except that it didn't go in. The leather plate under two layers of mail held firm, and the dagger skated off and got stuck between the two mail shirts.

The Scot realised he might as well fight back.

Richard dragged himself up to help, but the next captive knight along held him back.

Guy let go of his dagger just as the Scot grabbed his neck with both hands and choked him. The Scot's bear-like paws closed around Guy's neck and squeezed.

Guy laughed, but his airway was cut off and it came out as a rattle. For a moment Guy did not counter the chokehold, but then he retrieved his dagger from the web of mail that held it, and thrust it up into the Scot's armpit. There was no leather protection there, and even though the second layer of mail held, it broke the Scot's grip. Guy ducked his shoulder and pushed the taller knight backwards.

The Scot stumbled.

Guy rubbed his neck. 'I was rather enjoying that, but I think you might have taken it too far,' he said.

The Scot regained his balance.

'Hold him,' Guy waved at his knights, four of whom swamped the prisoner and held him by the arms.

'You are a monster,' the Scot struggled but four men were too many for him.

Guy scratched his chin. 'I think a simple stabbing might be too easy a method to kill you,' he said.

A captive in the line cried. His composure evaporated, and he sobbed like a frightened child. Richard wondered if Guy was even going to bother keeping any of them alive, and that thought must have been on the minds of the others, for Richard smelt the odour of fresh urine cloud the barn.

Guy sniffed the air and laughed. 'You all looked so brave and magnificent when you were on your horses with your friends,' he said, 'but now look at you, cowering like peasants.'

'Why do you need to kill the Scot?' Richard asked. 'His ransom is whatever you want it to be.'

'Richard,' Guy replied, 'I've already told you that this isn't about riches. But do you see how your fellow captives whimper and piss themselves now they see me kill the most valuable of them?'

Richard did, and that made him hate Guy.

'Now they'll obey my every command,' Guy said, 'these knights won't moan about not being fed enough, or that I won't let them practise their riding. They will meekly submit to me. This is the lesson your greedy, irritating friend taught me.'

Richard wanted to kill the Lusignan, but his words were true, and the visceral and real prospect of a grisly death tempered his thoughts of resistance.

The last landless knight writhed on the barn's floor bleeding to death. His soft moans chilled Richard's heart. Could this be the worst day of his life? Even worse than the day he'd lost his mother, sister, and Keynes?

Guy spent some time in thought, then motioned the Scottish knight over to stand behind the two horses.

'That yellow horse,' Guy said, 'once jumped a barricade I set up to capture the Queen. If it wasn't for that jump, she would not be governor of Poitou now, destroying my family's power.'

'Do nothing to him,' Richard blurted out, then regretted it.

Guy smiled. 'And to control you, it seems, all I need to do is point my dagger at your horse.'

Richard raged inside because he knew the Lusignan was right.

'Stand him behind the yellow horse,' Guy motioned. His knights drew the Scot behind Solis, who was busy munching on the straw.

Guy handed his dagger to a knight and then searched around the barn.

Richard knew what he was looking for.

The Lusignan found a thin stick that was slightly longer than a sword and stood next to Solis.

'Hold him tight,' Guy said to his knights. Then he raised the stick, held it over the palomino's rump, and swatted it down like he was killing a fly. The stick cut through the air with a sharp whoosh and smacked Solis above his tail.

Richard tried to look away, because he knew what any horse's natural reaction to that was. When he was much younger, he'd seen two wolves circle his father's palomino stallion, a year-old Solis, and Solis's mother. One wolf latched onto the mare's rump in exactly that place, and she had kicked it so hard with both legs that it died on the spot.

Solis kicked out just like his mother. The iron-shod hind hooves snapped through the air and broke some of the Scot's ribs with a loud crack. The knights holding him stepped back in surprise, and Solis turned his head around and shot Guy a very dirty look.

'I knew he'd do that,' Guy beamed, 'he could be my execution horse.'

Richard felt sick. He knew any horse could do that, any idiot could train it.

Guy raised the stick above Solis, and this time before he brought the stick all the way down, the stallion kicked out again. His hooves crashed into the Scot's stomach and he cried out in pain.

'That's enough,' Richard cried in the interest of both man and horse.

'Oh, is it?' their captor grinned. 'Good things come in threes, that's what the priests are always telling me, so we'll do one more.'

Guy didn't even need to lower the stick this time, Solis struck out and again kicked the prisoner in his chest.

The knights holding him let him go and he sank to the ground. The Scot moaned once, let out a resounding moan, then blacked out.

'Not so good with pain,' Guy shrugged.

Count Philip rushed into the barn with three of his knights behind him. 'We heard cries,' he froze when he saw the barn strewn with dead and dying men, pools and streaks of blood corrupting the earth. His wide eyes turned on the Lusignan. 'What in the name of all that is holy have you done?'

Guy threw the stick over his shoulder into the straw heap.

'Did they try to escape?' the Count of Flanders looked from one corpse to the next.

'No,' Guy said, 'this is just business, and not yours.'

The Lusignan knights squared up to the newcomers. 'Go back to the cottage,' Guy said, 'sit back down by the fire. Drink the wine, eat the bread. Or not, between you and me it's quite mouldy.' He walked up to Philip and poked him in the chest. 'And keep quiet until we've gone.'

'This is unacceptable,' the Count replied, 'where is your courtesy?'

Guy snorted. 'What good has courtesy ever done me? It is a leash around your neck.'

'It stops murders like these,' the Count raised his voice.

'This isn't murder,' Guy said, 'it's stock management.'

The Count's mouth flapped open. His eyes met Richard's, then found the Scot on the floor. 'You killed Sir Robert of Scotland? What were you thinking?'

'It was quite interesting, actually,' Guy replied, 'you can use horses to execute people. It's much more theatrical than the usual means.'

'Theatrical? This is no play,' Count Philip shouted, 'this is cold-blooded murder. You will go to Hell for this, deep into Hell with the traitors and the heretics.'

Guy sneered. 'With all the best people, then.'

Philip went for his sword.

'Wait,' Guy shouted so loudly that Solis jumped.

The Count hesitated.

'I am not forcing you to stay here,' Guy said, 'and if you consider how many men you have, and how many are behind me, maybe you could also be my prisoner?'

The Count's face trembled, but not with fear. Two of his knights

128

shared a hurried glance, and however enraged the Count was, he could see how things stood. Hand on hilt, he stepped backwards inch by inch until he was in the doorway.

'You can't leave us with him,' Richard shouted, 'he'll slit our throats once you've gone.'

'Let me buy that one,' the Count said, 'I'll pay double his worth if you let him leave with me.'

Richard watched the back of Guy's head with hope.

The Lusignan laughed. 'I have just spent some time explaining to these men that I am not that interested in wealth. I will not repeat myself, so just take my answer as being no.'

'Parole him, then,' Count Philip said, 'I'm sure the Young King will triple his ransom.'

'The Young King,' Guy said, 'is only good at spending money, so I have no doubt that you are correct. However, I am not in the habit of being charitable. Do I look like an almsgiver?'

'There would be no better time to start,' Philip said through gritted teeth, 'a charitable act might be good for your reputation, you could use that.'

Guy narrowed his eyes and tapped his foot. Then his face lit up. 'Why not? That is a grand idea, my dear Count. I will parole Richard, for ten times his worth, with you as witness and guarantor for the full value. I can let him go, it is hardly as if he'll come back with the Young King to fight me today, is it? His men are so broken and ill-disciplined that they will not regroup for hours.'

'I agree to that,' Philip replied.

Richard's heart skipped a beat. Unless Guy was just going to stab him in the back.

'The condition I attach is that you and your black-lioned men go back to the cottage and eat my mouldy bread for a while. You will not take Richard in, nor ride out to help him.'

The Count nodded. 'But give Richard a horse, so you can't just give him a head start and then capture him a second time, leaving me to pay the tenfold ransom.'

A wicked smile snaked across Guy's face and Philip shrank back. 'He'll walk out of here,' Guy said, 'on his own two feet.'

Richard didn't look at the knights to his left, or the lifeless ones on the ground as he walked towards the Count. He couldn't bring himself to look at his horse either, that was too painful a thought.

Richard strode past his captor and braced for a knife to bury itself in his spine. But it didn't come. He turned to Guy. 'Give me my horse, I'll pay a knight's ransom for him myself.'

Guy shook his head. 'You can't have my executioner,' he said, 'and if he tires of his duties, a golden horse is a fitting sacrifice to the God of Battle.'

'Blasphemy,' Philip hissed.

'Oh, nonsense,' the Lusignan replied, 'but go Richard, and you probably will want to run.'

Richard knew time wasn't on his side, so he squeezed past the Count. 'Thank you,' he whispered.

'But if I do re-capture you,' Guy shouted after him, 'that's double your already inflated ransom.'

'Run, boy,' Count Philip whispered, 'as soon as you're out of sight, run.'

Richard didn't need telling twice. In the yard, sixty or more horses were crammed together inside the perimeter. Blue and white knights roamed around them. The Count's horses and shields were over by the cottage that leaked smoke through its roof, but no one paid Richard a second look. He walked to the gate and shut it quietly behind him. He looked back over the fence and swore he'd be back for both the captives and Solis. Birds chirped above him, and he could still see Count Philip in the doorway, so he turned and followed the path back towards the list. The path was slippery after the passage of so many horses, but the green leaves and fresh air gave him a second wind. Once he entered the trees and couldn't see the building behind him, he jogged. Jogging in full mail was no burden if you trained doing it. But Guy was surely playing a game with him. Maybe the Lusignan would come and hunt Richard himself. His ribs hurt and he couldn't take a full breath, but he knew he had cover ground quickly.

Richard's leather soles slipped on the mud and fell flat on his face. The mud was cold, and he pushed himself up and ran along the edge of the path to find better footing. Leaves crunched and twigs snapped underfoot. When he reached the intersection with a second path, he stopped to catch his breath. Maybe it would be worth taking the second path, because if Guy sent pursuers, they would assume hed taken the straightest route back to safety. He looked down and flexed the toe that he had hurt in Ireland. It ached again and he swore.

Hoofbeats drummed on the earth from along the second path. It sounded like a single animal, four hooves only. Richard checked which side of the road had the most cover to hide behind, but before he could dive into the undergrowth, a solitary knight cantered up to him and his horse slid to a halt. The knight wore a red surcoat with a white cartwheel on it and wore a black painted helmet. He had a weathered face that bore no malice, although its stark features had a certain harshness to it.

The knight's horse snorted at Richard and stuck out its nose to sniff him.

Richard looked up. 'Which side are you on?'

'I am from the team Within,' the knight replied.

Richard relaxed. The Within team was based at the larger settlement of Lagny, the Without team the one based at the smaller Torcy. 'You can't imagine how glad I am to meet you,' Richard said, 'there are two companies of the Torcy team down that road, and I think some will come after me.'

'I saw you in the jousts this morning,' the knight said.

'That feels like a lifetime ago,' Richard said, 'would you share your ride and take me back to the list?'

The knight nodded. 'I am heading there myself.'

'God will bless you for this,' Richard said, 'what is your name?'

'I am Otto of Mainz, and Our Lord will bless me for nothing I do here.'

Richard frowned. 'Mainz? Isn't that in the Empire?'

Otto nodded.

'But your French sounds as clean as Count Philip's.'

Otto laughed a rasping laugh. 'We are not the barbarians you might think,' he held a hand out to Richard.

Richard reached up. Hooves echoed from the path back to the barn and cottage. Richard swore, but before he could clasp the German's hand, two riders rounded the last bend and galloped towards the crossroad.

'They have killed captives,' Richard said, 'are you ready to fight to the death alongside me?'

'Captives?' Otto's eyes bulged. 'That cannot stand.'

'Dismount,' Richard said, 'we can't fight them if we're both on your horse, and if you stay mounted, they'll overwhelm you.'

The riders slowed their horses and jeered at them. 'We wagered you would have at least made it to the stream,' one said.

Their horses crabbed sideways as the adrenaline coursing through their bodies tried to find an outlet.

'Attack them on my signal,' Richard whispered, 'and kill.'

'What is your signal?' the knight asked.

'You'll recognise it,' Richard answered.

Otto swung his leg over his black-painted saddle and dropped to the ground with a deftness that defied the weight of his mail and shield.

'Surrender,' the second knight said, 'we'll get nothing from your ransom, so we'd rather not have to fight you.'

Richard stepped towards them and held his wrists up. 'What else can I do,' he told them.

The first knight grinned. 'At least this boy knows when he's beaten.'

Otto left his horse and went to stand next to Richard.

Only the first knight dismounted, which was bad because Richard's half-formed plan needed them both on the ground.

'You look nervous,' the German said out of the side of his mouth.

'I'll think of something,' Richard replied.

'I thought you had already thought of something?'

'Quiet,' the second knight said from his horse. He held his sword ready, the edge glinting in the small amount of sunlight that crept through the slowly shifting leaves.

The dismounted knight approached Richard, and his eyes checked him for weapons.

'If I had a dagger hidden on me,' Richard said, 'Guy would have already taken it.'

'Very well,' the knight stood in Richard's face and a smell of stale red wine wafted over him. The Lusignan knight reached down to a bag on his belt and pulled out a length of rope.

Richard pulled his hand down and thrust it up between his mail shirts. The rings grazed his hand. The enemy knight looked up, but only in time to see the razor-sharp dagger that once belonged to Sir John rush through the air and catch him in the middle of his throat.

'What's happening?' the mounted knight asked from behind his gasping comrade.

Richard shoved his left hand into the knight's eyes and squeezed.

Otto jumped forwards, threw his arms into the air and threw himself at the mounted knight's horse with a blood-curdling yell.

Richard felt an eye collapse under his fingers in a wet mess, and ripped Sir John's dagger sideways so it ripped the knight's throat wide open. For the briefest moment he admired how sharp the old man in Dublin had made the blade.

The knight's throat pulsed bright red, and Richard pushed him aside.

Otto flapped his arms and bellowed at the horse again, which tried to back up with wide eyes and a foaming mouth.

The black stallion slipped on the edge of the path and toppled down onto a tree. A thick branch caught the knight on the back of his helmet, and man and beast both fell to the dirt. His sword spun through the air and disappeared into the foliage.

Otto reached the knight first, but Richard joined him to haul the knight free from the struggling horse. The horse pushed itself to its feet and snorted at them.

'I don't think he's breathing,' Otto looked down over the Lusignan man.

Richard held his dagger over the man, but didn't strike.

The German looked over at him, his lungs working hard. 'Kill him, then. You wanted them dead, yes?'

Richard nodded. 'But this is murder, if I kill him am I any better than Guy?'

'Who?'

'It doesn't matter,' Richard replied, 'and if he isn't breathing we can leave him.'

'Leave him to get help?' Otto shook his head. 'A man must sail a constant course, inconsistency is the Devil's device.'

'What are you talking about?' Richard leant back and lowered the dagger.

Otto reached around to his belt where he kept a variety of weapons.

'He isn't breathing,' Richard said, 'leave his fate to Christ.'

'I find that Christ can be unreliable when it comes to my best interests,' Otto grinned.

The Lusignan knight gasped a loud breath and his eyes sprung open.

'Now,' Otto shouted.

Richard held the knife up, but the man's eyes turned to terror and he couldn't bring Sir John's blade down.

'Did this Guy really kill tournament captives?' Otto asked with quick words.

'He did.'

'Then an eye for an eye,' the German drew a mace from his belt and smacked it down as if he were riveting a nail. The mace-head, golden and inlaid with two blue stones, caved in the knight's nose and mouth, and came up red.

The Lusignan knight wasn't dead. He screamed through his shattered mouth, broken teeth flying out or falling in to choke him.

Richard winced and looked away. When he looked back Otto was watching the man struggle.

'Hit him again, for the love of God,' Richard said.

Otto shrugged. 'Why? He is dead already.'

'You can't leave him, what happened to the men of the Empire not being barbaric?'

The German stood up and shrugged. 'I suppose I lied,' he wiped his mace clean on his surcoat and slid it back into his belt.

The mutilated man pawed at his contorted face and coughed and gurgled.

Richard groaned. 'What is wrong with this world?' He brought Sir John's dagger down into the man's neck, but when that didn't kill him, he had to hold the struggling man's mail shirt off his chest and stab between the ribs to find his heart. The dagger glanced off a rib on the way, but Richard pushed it deeper until the man's breath failed and his body released all its tension and eased to the earth.

'Me barbaric?' Otto glanced down at Richard. 'That was the act of a man who is no stranger to death.'

Richard stood up and pressed his lips together. 'I wish you were wrong.'

Otto looked at the black horse, which had overcome its adrenaline and shock to graze on the undergrowth.

'We should go,' Richard said, 'let's take these horses with us.'

'Good,' Otto replied, 'I could do with something to show for the day.'

Richard pulled some grass up and held it out to the black horse. It sniffed the grass and allowed Richard to take a hold of its bridle.

Otto retrieved the second horse, a bay creature which was rubbing its tail on a tree, which creaked and groaned.

'The bay one is the better horse,' Otto said, 'the black one has three whorls on its forehead. This is a terrible sign.'

Richard knew that was true, so he mounted the bay horse, adjusted the stirrup lengths, and took the reins of the black horse in his free hand to lead it.

The bay horse was wider than Solis, and Richard had to choke down his feelings when he thought about it.

Otto mounted his own horse. 'You are sad?'

'Guy has my horse,' Richard said, 'I need him.'

Otto nodded for a while. 'I understand. I find horses to be better company than men.'

'If I am going to get him back, we need to reach the Young King quickly,' Richard walked the two horses down the path that led to the list.

'Let us fly, then,' Otto pushed his horse into a canter and led the way back towards the list and the stand. The trees rushed by as the horses found their rhythm, and the cool air and the journey gave Richard time to think about what had just happened to him.

But before he could fully gather his thoughts, the woods ended and they rode out into the pasture in sight of the list.

Unfortunately, lingering outside the list was a small company of knights, with white and blue quartered shields.

The Young King and what remained of his company remained in the list, Richard could see their heads above the palisade that protected them.

The white and blue knights blockaded the entrance, as if waiting for the Young King to attempt an escape, but none of the besiegers had an eye on the woods.

Otto slowed his cantering horse so he was alongside Richard. 'Through them or run away?' he asked.

'Through,' Richard clenched his jaw shut and tightened his fingers that held the reins of the spare horse. He could barely feel those fingers now, so cold were they, but he didn't have time to worry about that.

Richard spurred the bay horse for the first time, and it bucked with its hind legs before lowering its head and accelerating into a full gallop. The grass flew by below so swiftly Richard didn't have time to plan anything. He aimed his horse between the ditch and the waiting enemy knights, and prayed they wouldn't see him.

They didn't see him. But they did hear him. The knights turned their heads and shouted an alarm.

Richard was less than a bowshot away when some turned their horses, gathered their reins and fumbled for their lances.

Otto cried a joyous cry and urged his horse on. Their manes flowed, hooves pounded, and Richard's horse made for the gap.

The knights closest to the ditch moved to block the way.

Richard, only a few strides away from them, threw the reins of the spare horse back at it, and it veered off towards the waiting enemy. Richard steered his horse at the ditch and it baulked, then jumped high into the air.

The spare horse swerved to avoid the white and blue knights, but in doing so it distracted their mounts long enough for Richard to land in the ditch unmolested. The bay horse sank into the freshly dug earth up to its fetlocks, but hauled itself up and out of the ditch in a flurry of legs and a loud grunt.

Otto whistled by, smashed his mace into the nearest knight's shield and beat Richard into the list.

He picked up a canter until he reached the friendly infantry at the mouth of the fortification and was allowed inside. The footmen raced back to block the entrance, and the enemy knights could only shout insults in after them.

Richard felt his horse limping and pulled him up slowly to reach the Young King. To his surprise, the black horse that he'd released as a distraction squeezed through the white and blue knights who tried to capture him and made it into the list.

Bowman sat on his horse next to him. 'You took your time,' he said.

'What happened to you?' the Young King scrutinised the blanket of half-dried mud that caked Richard's mail and face.

'Guy murdered some of his prisoners,' Richard replied, 'including a nephew of the King of the Scots.'

'But not the actual king?' Nicholas asked from a horse the Young King had given him.

Richard shot the Martel knight a withering look.

Nicholas smirked. 'We're still special, then.'

'That wasn't during a game,' Richard said, 'Gerold escaped, is he here?'

'No,' Bowman said, 'we've been sitting here like prize fools since you left. Stuck in this trap with no way out.'

Richard counted the knights within the list. 'Surely because we have the mighty Marshal, numbers cannot matter to us?'

The Marshal stood next to the Young King on the grass stretching his legs. 'I'm just recovering my strength,' he said, 'what's the rush?'

'The rush,' Richard locked eyes with the Young King, 'is that Guy has my horse, and if he gets him back to the list at Torcy, I've lost him forever.'

The Young King thought for a moment, his eyes on Richard. 'I think this could be our chance to craft a heroic song for ourselves,' he smiled, 'we ride out, at first against bad odds to escape the list, then against overwhelming odds to rescue a man's horse. Someone could sing an epic about it.'

'It's only fair, Richard lost that horse saving you,' Nicholas rearranged his new red shield.

Eyes turned to the wolf-knight.

'I take no offence,' the Young King said, 'for that is true. It is fitting that I at least risk myself to recover the horse. This could make a wondrous tale.'

The Marshal retrieved his own grey warhorse and almost jumped back up into the saddle. 'I will of course lead the attack,' he said.

'Of course,' Bowman rolled his eyes.

Richard smiled at his new lord, for there was no chance that the Old King would agree to risk so much to rescue someone else's horse. 'The only problem we have,' Richard said, 'is that my horse and the captives are in a barn guarded by all forty of Guy's men, and Count Philip is there too.'

'Why didn't Philip stop the murders?' the Young King asked.

'Guy threatened to take him prisoner,' Richard replied.

'That's outrageous,' the Young King replied, 'and someone bring this man new arms.'

Three servants ran over to the cart to fetch Richard a new sword, shield, and lance. There didn't seem to be a spare helmet anywhere. The Little Lord's sword lay somewhere on the field, Richard hoped he could collect it later.

If no one stole it.

'Well done on capturing a trophy horse,' the Marshal nodded to him as Richard slid the new shield over his head.

'He is worth less than Solis,' Richard replied.

'Is there no room in your thick head for anything other than trophies or prizes?' the Young King asked the Marshal.

The Marshal frowned. 'But that's what we're here for, isn't it?'

The young Angevin raised his eyes to the heavens. 'Give me strength, Lord,' he muttered and turned back to his commander. 'If you abandon me once more today chasing after some worthless knight, I'll replace you. Do you understand?'

'Of course,' the Marshal replied, but his face was a picture of indigence.

'Good,' the Young King said, 'well then Marshal, how should we proceed?'

The swarthy knight studied the white and blue knights outside. He nodded solemnly to himself. 'I have a plan to break out of the list,' he said.

'What is it, then?' the Young King asked.

'We charge out of the list, and smash them apart,' the Marshal held himself tall in his saddle.

The Young King frowned.

'Is that it?' Adam asked. The knight rode his horse closer to the Young King. 'The best plan he can come up with is to charge the enemy?'

'Why not?' the Marshal said.

'We do have the infantry here,' Richard said.

'No one is asking your advice,' Henry the Northerner cried from behind the Marshal.

'Enough,' the Young King shouted, 'there are too many people talking at once. Richard is right, the infantry are our advantage. If we charge and bog the French down, the infantry can rush in and pull them all from their horses. We'll take anyone who doesn't flee prisoner.'

The Marshal put his hand on his hips. 'So now taking captives is acceptable?'

'Silence,' the Young King replied.

'This is a terrible plan,' Adam said, 'is it even a plan? What after that,

137

though? Siege a barn in the woods that's defended by more men than we have?'

'I said enough,' the Young King turned to the Marshal, 'but he asks a valid question. What is our plan to get into the barn?'

'Attack it?' the Marshal replied.

Adam groaned.

Richard didn't think that would work.

Out of the corner of his eye, at the far end of the now mostly empty list, a figure clambered over the stakes on the earthen bank. 'Is that Gerold?' he asked.

'It is, young lord,' Bowman said, 'he doesn't look thrilled, though.'

The older knight pulled a splinter out of his mail shirt and made his way across the list. A few groups of sullen captured knights stood around in groups. They watched the solitary knight who walked through their midst with curiosity, but he paid them no mind.

When Gerold arrived, he stood before the group of mounted knights and let out a deep breath.

'You look terrible,' Bowman told him.

And he did, for his face was purple and sweat dripped down it and onto his mail where it formed a metallic orange beard below his chin.

'It heartens me to see you alive,' Gerold said to Richard.

'Only just, this knight from the Empire helped me,' Richard nodded towards Otto, 'but what happened to you?'

'There's no time for that,' Gerold replied, 'I overheard Guy order his company to prepare to move the captives back to Torcy. I came here as quickly as I could to tell you.'

'Do we have a spare horse for that man?' the Young King looked for a servant.

'I'm afraid not,' the Marshal said, 'except for Richard's lame bay horse.'

'Marshal,' the Young King said, 'you have two dozen captured horses in this list, give him one this instant, you self-centred pig.'

The Marshal pursed his lips and nodded back to Henry. The stocky knight left to find the worst horse from the Marshal's prize collection.

'Thank you,' Richard said to his friend, 'and thank you for helping me get Solis back.'

The anger drained from the Marshal's face. 'I will help you, but mostly because Guy deserves to suffer for murdering my uncle. If they have left their stronghold,' he said, 'then I think I know what we need to do. The last time we were here, we were based in Torcy, so I think I know which route Guy will be taking.'

YELLOW HORSE

The French knights with their white and blue quartered shields lost interest in the Young King at exactly the wrong moment. They casually turned their tails to the list and rode away, bored with waiting for the Young King, and now sure he would not leave their sanctuary to face them.

'Shouldn't we wait for them to leave?' Adam asked.

The Young King's company shortened their reins and shifted their shields around to the most comfortable places.

'Don't be ridiculous,' the Marshal replied, 'we might as well capture a few of them, the rest will break and flee when they realise what's happening.'

Richard took hold of a fresh lance presented to him by a servant. 'I think the Marshal might be right this time, if we ignore the French, they might just circle back behind us. Their retreat could be a trap.'

The Young King laced his helmet back on. It had a thin golden crown riveted onto it. 'See, the war-hero knows his trade. To arms, my boys, let's scatter them.'

The red company streamed out of the list. The Young King and his sole surviving bannerman led the way, the Marshal had to pull his horse back so he was level with his master, but no further.

Richard asked the black horse to move, it ignored him so he had to tell it. His spurs tickled the horse and it joined in with the charge.

Bowman and Gerold charged with him, their hooves thundering out of the mouth of the list as the depleted company poured back onto the field.

The dozen knights caught up with the Young King, who with the Marshal formed the point of a wedge. Richard rode at the far end of the formation. The riders in the wedge pressed together, the mass of all twelve knights and horses focused into a single point.

The wedge closed on the unsuspecting and slowly walking French.

Just before it struck, French heads turned around and a cry of alarm went up.

But Richard didn't hear it, for the air rushed through his hair and he was fighting for his horse.

The white and blue knights didn't react as one to the attack on their rear. Some sped away from the danger, some turned to face it, and some did neither.

Richard sensed victory as they charged. There was confidence in closeness as the wedge smashed into the opposition. The serried ranks of the Young King split apart the white and blue knights as a ship cuts through the waves. The Marshal unhorsed a knight, and the Young King's horse pushed another sideways so that the trailing edge of the wedge knocked him over and then trampled the fallen knight into the mud.

French knights fled away from the relentless force of the wedge as it pushed through their by now shattered formation. The Marshal cried his own war-cry and split off from the wedge to chase the white and blue bannerman.

Richard lowered his lance at a knight who cantered away from him, the point touched his foe's back as his horse strained to escape, both horses racing on at the same speed. Richard shouted at his black horse and it bounded on, which pushed the lance head into the knight's back. The man felt the iron on his spine and twisted in the saddle in an attempt to avoid death. The evasion worked, and the lance-head glanced in front of his body. Richard's point was now useless.

Richard didn't worry, instead he swung the lance across and hooked it under the knight's rein-arm. Richard flicked the lance up and it tore the Frenchman's arm from his reins with a jerk. The horse, now out of hand, dropped its head and bucked out with its hind legs. The knight was catapulted over the front of his saddle, slid down the shoulder of his horse, and fell to the grass.

Iron-shod hooves of the bolting horse trampled its master as he rolled on the ground.

Richard pulled his black horse up with no one else left to chase. The horse sweated and smelled, a different smell to Solis, and its nostrils flared as Richard went to inspect his fallen enemy.

The knight lay on his back, gasping for air, his eyes closed.

Richard could walk him back to the list as a captive, but did he have time?

The rest of the pasture was a scene of triumph for the red company. Infantry rushed over from the list, all too happy to point their spears at the faces of the fallen French knights and haul them back behind the stakes.

The Marshal even reined himself in and rode back towards the

Young King, who stood at the site of the wedge's victory with his banner waving back and forth above him.

That was the sign to return to the flag, and Richard didn't want to waste a moment, so he abandoned his prize and cantered back to the company.

'What a surprise,' Adam said as Richard arrived, 'the peacock is the last to return.'

'I don't think he can help himself,' Richard said.

'Don't defend him,' Adam said, 'not when you left your captive on the earth and the peacock is still bringing his back.'

'I think the war-hero prefers to save his horse than chase wealth,' the Young King said.

Richard blushed but his face was so red from exertion no one noticed.

The infantry herded up the six captives the attack had produced and drove them into the safety of the list.

The Marshal returned, Henry behind him leading a horse by the reins, the French knight on top bright red with embarrassment. Another of the Marshal's knights carried the captured white and blue banner.

'See,' the Marshal said, 'that was perfect.'

The remnants of the enemy company disappeared over the last hill and over the horizon. The only noise on the field came from the crowd in the stands, who all cheered the Young King's victory with whoops and drunken whistles. Richard had forgotten they were there.

'Get rid of that prisoner, Marshal,' the Young King said, 'time is of the essence. Show us where we're going.'

The Marshal grinned. 'We're going south,' he said, 'almost to the edge of the tournament area, to the village of Bussy. No one ever rides that far because the ground is difficult, but if I wanted to get back to Torcy unnoticed, that's the way I'd go.'

The Young King nodded. 'Lead us then, Marshal,' he said, 'and don't spare our horses.'

Richard fell in next to Bowman as the company gathered up and cantered south of the woods. He was putting his horse's fate in the Marshal's hands, which he wasn't keen on, but he didn't have a better plan. They made their way through a meadow of high grass, a few blue and yellow flowers persisting despite the changing season.

The woods to their left rushed by as they made rapid progress towards Bussy.

The trees gave way to more meadow, and the Marshal turned left to follow it, riding with the sun directly above them.

And straight into Count Philip's company.

The Flemings walked south too, but out of the woods, and the Count's knights rushed forwards to form a line when they saw the red shields and banner ahead of them.

The Marshal halted and the Young King caught up with him.

Richard's horse was happy to stop, foam congealed on its chest and its nostrils were speckled white.

'We can't face that many,' the Marshal said, 'do we go back to the list?'

The Young King looked at the Flemish company. 'We can't just give up, and we don't have time to fight them off,' he said.

Count Philip walked his horse forwards alone.

'Although I think he wants to talk,' the Young King said.

Richard glanced in the direction they were supposed to be going. Time was running out.

'My lord,' Count Philip greeted the Young King. The Count's cheeks were hollowed and dark, but his eyes noticed Richard. 'It pleases me that you are alive. I am sorry I could not stop Guy sending those two knights after you.'

Otto chuckled behind Richard. 'Two wasn't enough,' he whispered.

Philip didn't hear. 'Guy set Richard's ransom at ten times his worth, I'm afraid.'

The Young King shrugged. 'I don't care.'

The Marshal leaned in to his lord. 'The Count's ransom would be colossal,' he whispered, 'we could take him here and fly back to the list.'

Horror shot across the Young King's face. 'Where is your courtesy?'

'Well, we can't fight his entire company,' the Marshal replied.

'Maybe we won't have to,' the Young King turned to the Fleming. 'We have heard what happened in the woods. We are riding to recapture Richard's horse and to avenge the dishonourable killing of captives. Will you stand aside? Just as you did when the atrocity took place.'

His last words stung the Count. Richard thought Philip might even cry.

Instead the Fleming backed his horse up a step, his bottom lip twitched, and his hand inched towards his sword.

The Young King stood impassive, his eyes on the Count and his expression hard.

'Very well,' Count Philip said, 'we shall let you pass.'

'You should come with us,' Richard said, 'so you can right the wrong Guy has done to you by dragging you into disrepute.'

Philip wrinkled his nose. 'We are on different teams so I cannot. The tournament is more sacred to me than almost everything else, and I will not act against it.'

The Young King raised his eyebrows. 'That did not stop you from pretending not to take part until we were tired,' he said.

'There are no rules forbidding that strategy,' the Count replied, 'but the teams are sacred.'

'This isn't a game anymore,' Richard said.

'Quite,' the Count said, 'and I wish to get off my horse, out of my armour, and away from mud and blood. You are free to continue, but I will not help you.'

'Very well,' the Young King said, 'and we don't have time to argue. Marshal, off we go.'

After a last bitter look at the Count, the Marshal continued south along the grassy meadow. For a while some in the company turned to check the Flemings were not in pursuit, but they saw nothing but flocks of birds flying from one wood to another.

At a shallow and meandering stream that cut between two low hillocks, the company stopped to water their horses. Flies from the water soon settled on the animals, irritating their eyes and bellies.

'We must walk awhile,' the Marshal said, 'or these animals will not bear up to even a brief fight.'

'Send a scout ahead,' the Young King said, 'find out how much ground we have to make up.'

All the Knights close enough to hear looked away or down at their feet.

The Marshal shook his head. 'Is no one brave enough to be our scout?'

Silence.

Bowman sniffed loudly. 'Are all these cowards afraid of a little ride? I shall scout for you, peacock,' he said.

'Are you sure?' Richard said. 'I think everyone else is worried about riding alone across the tournament field.'

Bowman chuckled. 'It can hardly be more dangerous than riding through the Wicklow Mountains or breaking into castles in Brittany, can it? Besides, we got your horse back once before, young lord, and I'll be damned if we will not do it again.'

Emotion bubbled up inside Richard. He had never had a friend like Bowman before, and in that moment he realised he would never have another like him again.

Bowman turned away and remounted his black horse.

Richard was very glad to have his friend's keen eyes as their scout, but couldn't make himself say anything as Bowman rode away from the stream and eased his horse into a canter. Richard couldn't help feeling nervous as he disappeared from view.

Once the horses had almost drained the stream dry, they remounted and progressed at a slower pace behind Bowman.

The flies stayed with them. Tails swished, and horses shook their heads and manes to throw the flies away. They always came back.

The company walked in silence, apart from the sound of their horses trying to gain a respite from the flies. The Marshal led them into a hornbeam grove which plunged them into shadow and finally left the flies behind. Green leaves screened them from the world, the tall grey trunks of the trees patterned with vertical lines that twisted around their old bodies. Their wood was too hard for using for much other than chopping blocks, and Richard recognised the patterns on their trunks from the chopping block he'd used to sever the Reeve's head from his body back in Yvetot. That felt like a lifetime ago.

They followed a deer track through the grove, a wide track made by hundreds of small hooves over probably hundreds of years. It felt like an ancient place, a peaceful place in the middle of an active tournament field.

Nicholas rode alongside Richard and took in a full lungful of the cool air. 'Did you see how quickly the Young King shrugged off your ransom?' Nicholas said. 'He didn't even complain about it.'

Richard felt a pang of envy over his lord's wealth. He'd gone all the way to Ireland for two shillings a day, and the Young King could spend two hundred pounds on knights without even noticing.

'And yet,' the Martel knight continued, 'my father wouldn't even pay mine, which was probably the same as yours.'

'About the same,' Richard nodded.

'I will not call him my father anymore, not when he doesn't see me as a son,' Nicholas said.

'I'm sorry your life unravelled,' Richard said.

The Martel knight let out another full breath. 'It wasn't your fault. You saved me from Guy at The Pinnacle, remember? And he only wanted to kill me to spite my half-brother.'

'That wasn't his fault either,' Richard said, 'this is all Guy's doing.'

Nicholas's knuckles were white on his lance. 'I'll kill him.'

'As long as you mean Guy and not your brother,' Richard grinned.

Nicholas looked at him for a moment then softened his face. 'I'm free of all of that now, Richard. Bowman is my blood, and it isn't his fault his mother prefers him.'

Richard groaned. He wasn't going to get into that again. 'I'm glad your father didn't pay,' he said, 'I'm glad you're riding with me now.'

The Martel knight smiled. 'Me too, but I do hope we come away from this with a few more ransoms.'

'I know,' Richard said, 'if I had a few pounds I could build the Flying Monk into a real inn, another few more pounds and I could restock the fishpond. Another captured horse and I could rebuild my church.'

'Beware the tale of Midas,' Gerold croaked from behind. 'Greed is a baleful thing, remember your uncle and what it drove him to.'

Richard didn't much want to, he'd rather have a pile of silver to spend. Then he remembered the silver in Abbot Anfroy's tomb and realised he did have a pile of silver. He just couldn't get to it.

Richard sighed.

'Good,' Gerold said, 'let the avarice go. It can only lead to sin.'

'You sound like my priest,' Richard said.

Nicholas laughed.

A sound filtered through the hornbeam trees ahead, and the company readied their weapons in a rattle of wood and iron.

Bowman cantered along the track and collided with the Marshal. Their horses squealed at each other, but Bowman's was lathered and its bloodshot eyes had no lust for a proper fight.

'I found them,' Bowman's cheeks were red.

'How far ahead?' Richard asked.

'Not far,' Bowman swallowed hard, 'I saw their banner at the head of a column a few hills over, he still has forty knights. The captives are being led on horseback and they have a string of captured horses.'

'Did you see Solis?' Richard asked.

Bowman shrugged. 'There was a yellow one. When I left them, they were riding up a hill in a bend in the river.'

'I know the one,' the Marshal said, 'there is a wooden bridge on the other side of the hill, but there's a ford across the river further to the south.'

'We can't beat them to the bridge,' Bowman said.

'No,' the Marshal replied, 'but if we cross the ford, we can lay an ambush once they've crossed. The road over the bridge goes through a shallow valley. There are vines and ditches on the northern slope, and another hornbeam wood on the south side. We can use the ford to reach the wood.'

Richard's eyes lit up. 'Then ambush them.'

'Good,' the Young King nodded, 'we need an advantage to attack forty with twelve.'

'I'll take us to the ford,' the Marshal said.

The Young King's eyes shone with excitement. 'Adam, you and the scout will release the captives. Take Richard's old knight who escaped.

Richard and his wolf-knight can find his horse. Marshal, you take your knights and hold Guy back long enough for the captives and horse to be freed. I will take the rest of the company and attack the Lusignan rearguard, we'll try to give everyone space to retreat beyond us. If we can get back to the bridge and defend it, the Lusignan's numbers will count for nothing.'

Richard was impressed, the Young King might match his father in battle after all.

The Marshal flung his horse around and charged through the hornbeam grove.

Bowman's horse was not thrilled about having to pick up the pace once more, but it also didn't want to get left behind, so it followed along without making too much fuss.

The company surged out of the grove and back into the daylight. Their hooves trampled down the long grass of another long meadow that led them to another wood. The wood rested above the meadow on a raised bank of earth, and they rode close to the trees on the way to the ford.

The bannerman, his horse cantering behind the Young King, ventured too close to the wood and his horse found the holes of a badger set. With a sudden jolt, the brown horse toppled over, causing the knight to be thrown from his saddle along with his banner, which landed far away in the meadow. The horse pushed itself to its feet and looked over towards its rider, who had rolled and flattened a length of meadow by his fall.

Richard stopped beside him and looked down at the young knight. 'Are you hurt?'

The knight rubbed his head and took his helmet off to look at it. A dent had caved in part of the iron.

The Young King came back. 'Can you ride?' he asked.

The knight nodded and pushed himself up. Long grass stuck out of the rings of his mail, but he ignored them and went to his horse.

The animal walked a step to meet him, but did so with an obvious limp.

Richard groaned. 'That horse can't keep up now.'

'No,' the Young King said, 'how far is it to the bridge, Marshal?'

The English knight shook his head in disgust at the knight, who remounted after picking his banner back up.

'That hill over there,' the Marshal pointed, 'is the hill the bridge is on the other side of.'

The Young King nodded and spoke to his bannerman. 'Ride to the bridge, but stay on this side. Hopefully, your horse will recover itself, but we shall bring you a replacement with us.'

The bannerman agreed, but looked unhappy with the idea.

Richard didn't envy him as the company left him and his banner behind, and dashed to the ford.

The river wasn't wide or deep, and they splashed across the stony riverbed with ease. The water that soaked his mail leg armour only reminded Richard that he hadn't drunk since before the jousting, and how dry his mouth was.

As the sound of running water faded behind them, the company rode hard along a track marked with cattle hoofprints. All the horses streamed with sweat, but the riding gave Richard a chance to come to terms with his new mount.

The Marshal dropped to a walk at the base of a wooded hill, and horses snorted throughout the company.

Gerold's horse sweated so much that milky water pooled around its hooves when they stopped for a moment.

'This is the hill,' the Marshal said.

'We need to give the horses a chance to recover their wind,' Adam said.

Richard's horse lowered its head and panted heavily. The saddle moved up and down on his back. 'They won't be fit to fight for a while,' Richard said, 'maybe we pushed them too hard?'

'Better to be on hand with eleven exhausted horses,' the Young King grinned, 'than be late with eleven fresh ones.'

'Well said, my lord,' the Marshal walked his horse up the hill.

Bowman's horse refused to move at first, but Bowman coaxed it up.

Alongside him, Richard's horse laboured to pull itself up the incline. 'Your brother told me he's accepted your mother's preference for you,' Richard said.

Bowman coughed. 'Has he,' he said, 'you should be concerning yourself with your horse.'

'I'm trying to distract myself from him,' Richard ducked a low-hanging branch as the company moved through the track-less wood.

Bowman and Richard took opposite paths around a tall hornbeam.

'Who is that German you've picked up?' Bowman asked.

'Otto?' Richard replied. 'He's just a knight I ran into, he saved me from the Lusignans.'

Bowman grunted to himself. 'Between him and my half-brother, you soon won't need me anymore.'

Richard shook his head. 'Really? That's what you're worried about?'

The blonde man remained tight-lipped.

'No one else will fight for me like you do,' Richard said.

Bowman kept his head forwards as they wove through trees that closed in tighter and tighter.

'Don't trust the German too quickly, young lord, that's all I'm saying.'

'I'm not trusting him at all, it isn't as if he's a part of my household,' Richard replied.

'And my half-brother is still unreliable,' Bowman said.

'I'm not trading you for them,' Richard said, 'let's just concentrate on Guy.'

Bowman almost snarled.

'Quiet now,' the Marshal said as the company reached the crest of the hill and descended the far side.

Downhill required more effort from horses and riders, and more than once a horse slipped on the thin soil that surrounded the old trees.

'Form into our groups,' the Young King said, 'and no one charges until they hear my war-cry.'

Silence answered him as horses snorted and steam from their necks and rumps drifted up into the surrounding leaves. The foliage was thick, and the sun penetrated only a little, and when the ground levelled out and they reached the road, they could barely see it.

But they could see well enough through the silver-grey hornbeam trunks that Richard could tell it was empty.

'Have we missed them?' Richard whispered to Bowman.

'I could tell you if I went close enough to check for tracks,' the blonde man replied, 'but I don't think the peacock will agree to that.'

'The Young King might,' Richard replied.

'No,' Bowman said, 'the peacock is in charge. God help us. But we rode hard, we must be in front.'

Richard hoped he was right. If not, Solis was gone. A pit opened up in his stomach and he felt ill.

'Don't worry,' Bowman said, 'if there is a God looking down on us, he'll give you your horse back.'

'If you say so.'

Bowman didn't reply, instead he peered through the tree trunks at the sunlit road and waited for the Lusignans.

A red squirrel ran down the trunk of a tree and looked straight at Richard. The small animal scurried off almost close enough to touch, but his new black horse ignored it. Solis wouldn't have ignored it, he'd have tried to lick it, and Richard had to fight another unwelcome surge of emotion.

The squirrel looked to his left, paused, then shot back up the tree.

Then the ears of Richard's horse twitched, and his heart allowed itself to hope.

'Bowman,' Richard whispered.

'Quiet,' the blonde man replied, 'I know.'

A horse snorted, and everyone gave the red-shielded knight on top of it an angry look. The knight frowned, he couldn't help his horse.

Voices floated through the trees from the road. Then the first horse made its way into view, and although mostly obscured by the trunks, it was definitely there.

A dozen knights, including the blue and white Lusignan banner, travelled by, and behind them rode the captives. Some of their horses flicked their ears into the woods and Richard swallowed.

Behind the captives came a second group of knights. One of their horses turned its head towards Richard, but received a clout in the face with a lance-butt for its trouble.

Then came the prize horses. Tied together and led by a single knight, over a dozen horses of every colour walked, their valuable saddles still attached for ease of transport.

One of those horses, a thin grey stallion, stopped and pricked its ears at the woods. The horses behind him bumped into his rear and the entire string stopped.

Behind that horse, and through the trees, Richard saw a golden horse. His golden horse. Solis's head sprung up like a startled deer and his eyes scoured the trees.

The knights in the Lusignan rearguard stopped behind the prize horses. They shouted at the knight leading them to get them moving again, but Solis and the grey stallion were unmoved, their ears and eyes locked to the hornbeams.

Solis sniffed the air.

'Which way is the wind blowing?' Richard whispered.

'From us to them,' Bowman answered.

Richard swore.

Solis whinnied. The type of whinny the horse reserved for when Richard approached his stable with horsebread in the morning. Loud and shrill it cut through the trunks.

'Oh, no,' Richard murmured.

The Lusignan rearguard shouted insults at the knight who couldn't get the horses moving. The knights under the banner in the vanguard stopped and turned back to see what the delay was.

The whole column ceased their march.

'That yellow idiot is ruining the peacock's glorious plan,' Bowman said.

149

Solis shouted again, and some knights looked up into the trees.

Guy's voice filtered through the trunks and leaves, rough orders which stirred his knights into movement.

Richard looked through the trees to his left for the Young King. Where was the war-cry? They should attack now before they were spotted.

A Lusignan knight wandered up to the treeline, his horse alert and aware that something lurked amongst the hornbeams.

It wasn't the Young King that began the attack in the end, but the Marshal.

'Dex Aie the Marshal,' echoed through the trees on their right, followed by the hoofbeats of the Marshal's knights.

'Damn the peacock,' Bowman closed his legs onto this horse and turned it towards the captive knights. 'Good luck with your horse.'

Richard touched his spurs and the tired beast surged down the hill. Richard held his lance low to avoid branches and aimed for his yellow horse.

He heard the Young King's war-cry off to his left and the sound of men brushing through leaves and snapping branches.

The black of Nicholas's wolf-pelt flashed by next to Richard as the two of them dodged between the hornbeam trunks and down towards the road.

The Lusignan knight who'd reached the trees realised what was coming and spun his horse around to get out of the way.

Richard's horse tripped on a root, caught itself with a jolting stumble, and emerged on the road.

Solis shouted again, then his ears pinned back in anger when he saw Richard dared to ride another horse.

Richard's momentum carried him up to the retreating Lusignan knight, and his lance drove deep into his back. This was no time for niceties and Richard pushed the lance so far that it burst through his chest until six feet of ash-wood protruded out of the startled knight's front. Richard left the lance in him.

Nicholas tore past and went to attack the knight who led the riderless prize horses.

Richard watched the Marshal and his party crash into Guy's vanguard to his right, and Bowman, Adam, and Gerold attacked those guarding the captive knights.

The fifteen men of the Lusignan rearguard also watched the attack, and with a great cheer rode towards Richard, who suddenly felt extremely vulnerable.

Out of the wood dashed the Young King with his three knights behind him. They caught the rearguard in the flank, lances ripped mail open as the Young King and his knights rode up and over the knights in their path. The weight of horse-flesh crushed the blue and white knights and their horses suffered. But even as the force of the charge wore away, ten of them still stood, and they fought back against the Young King and his outnumbered companions.

With the rearguard engaged, Richard seized his moment. He pushed the black horse into the string of prize horses and drew his sword. He slashed down at the rope that linked them all together and cut them loose. Richard pushed through towards the front of them, where Solis alone stood still, eyes fixed on Richard as the other horses fidgeted and strained against their bonds.

The palomino shouted at Richard again as Nicholas threw his broken lance to the ground. The knight guarding the horses lay defeated on the grass beneath the wolf-knight.

Richard reached his yellow horse and with a surge of energy pulsing through his veins, cut him free.

Solis responded by lunging at Richard's black horse with his teeth, making it spin away in fright.

'Solie, no,' Richard shouted, and the horse backed off.

Nicholas looked up the road. 'Richard. Bowman and Gerold are in trouble,' he shouted.

The Martel knight was right. Bowman, Adam, and Gerold couldn't free the captives because the middle group of Lusignan knights attacked them with war-cries and flashing blades. With three times as many knights, the blue and white shields closed in on the three lonely-looking reds.

Richard joined Nicholas. 'We have to help them.'

'Would he help me?' the Martel knight asked.

'He has done, repeatedly. What is wrong with the two of you? We can argue about it again, or we can charge,' Richard said.

The Martel knight grinned, and before Richard knew it, he'd spurred his horse and stormed towards his half-brother.

Richard followed.

Bowman fended off three knights, using his horse to keep moving and not quite letting any of them get close enough to strike him decisively.

Nicholas used his horse to collide with a blue and white knight, which pushed the unsuspecting enemy out of his saddle.

Richard raised his sword in a high guard above his head and aimed at a knight who tried to get round the back of Bowman.

Richard flashed the blade down and it sliced a shallow gash into the

Lusignan's shoulder. The knight dropped his sword and cried out. He wheeled away, his arm too damaged to continue to wield a weapon.

Bowman, finally one against one, faced his foe and thrust his sword up into the man's face. His sword entered through the young man's mouth and dealt him his death blow.

The three of them turned to Adam and Gerold.

A knight with a mace cracked Gerold on his shield and it split down its centre. The old man reeled in his saddle as he barely parried a sword aimed at his head.

'Help Gerold,' Richard shouted.

'I'll save Adam,' Bowman said between gulps of air.

Before they could argue about it, Gerold bolted towards them, three blue and white knights on his tail.

Nicholas charged straight into them. All four horses came together in a tangle of hooves, shields, and men.

The Martel knight tumbled from his saddle as his horse went down on both front knees.

Richard swooped on the stalled Lusignans. One was dazed in the saddle and one crawled on his knees on the road, struggling to get back to his feet. Richard went for the third.

That blue and white knight whirled an axe around at Richard, who parried it away and swung backwards on his way past, the backswing of his sword clanging into the back of the knight's helmet.

Bowman, riding behind Richard, finished that knight off. 'You just can't stay on your horse, can you?' Bowman said to his half-brother.

The Martel knight, back on his feet, lunged at the crawling knight, kicked him in the face, then jumped on top of him.

Richard knew what would happen next, so turned his attention to the dazed Lusignan knight. That man, with a bushy grey beard, looked up with wide brown eyes that pleaded with Richard for mercy.

Richard peered at him and couldn't blame the knight for his master's deeds. Enough blood ran along the ruts on this road already. 'Go,' Richard shouted.

The bearded knight pulled his horse around and spurred it away up into the vines on the hill on the other side of the valley.

Bowman rushed towards Adam, who danced his horse from one opponent to another, dealing strikes to all three while somehow evading too much damage himself.

Gerold kept fleeing as far as the captive knights, who he went through one by one to cut the bonds that tied their hands.

The freed horses ran in groups up into the vines on the far side of the road, jumping the ditches or getting distracted and eating the grapes that hung in deep purple bunches, only days from being harvested.

Distracted by the horses helping themselves to the grapes, at first Richard didn't notice half of the Lusignan vanguard bearing down on them.

Bowman engaged the knights Adam had so far staved off, but only Nicholas stood between him and the six fresh enemies. Their horses dashed across the ground.

Nicholas's horse had strayed too far to remount, so the wolf-knight picked up a lance from the ground and pointed it at the oncoming knights. He wedged the butt of the lance against his rear foot on the ground, locking it in place, and aimed it at the lead knight, the knight who raised his sword to cut down at him.

Richard couldn't leave Nicholas alone. His black horse found a second wind and bounded at the Lusignans. Solis was behind him, swishing his head in excitement and trying to bite the tail of Richard's horse.

The lead Lusignan ran straight into Nicholas's pike. It sunk into his horse, but the force pushed Nicholas over and onto his back. The horse rolled over, but Nicholas hit his head hard on the ground. Lying on the ground, he avoided the attacks and hooves of the other knights as they rushed by above him.

They rushed into Richard. His sword parried an incoming lance and ran down the shaft. The sword ran to the blue and white knight's hand and sliced right through his thumb, instantly taking him out of the fight.

A second Lusignan knight locked swords with Richard, but their horses bumped into each other and both swords came together and locked. Neither man yielded, and both lost their weapons.

Richard could hear Bowman mocking him in his head.

Nicholas was on his feet again, his eyes clouded over. With a broken lance in his hands, he sprinted towards the four Lusignans that circled Richard.

A sword glanced off Richard's rein hand, which made him drop his reins, and another hit him in the shoulder, which made him cry out. Richard went to draw Sir John's dagger, but it was still in between his two layers on mail, and on horseback, he physically couldn't get to it. Another sword aimed at his face, but Richard blocked the attacking arm at the wrist with his hand and deflected it away.

A Lusignan behind Richard cried out as a broken lance thrust up between his mail leggings and his mail shirt, right into his kidneys. Nicholas pulled the lance out. The wounded knight broke off from the combat, the act of riding now excruciatingly painful for him.

Nicholas dropped the lance and grabbed another blue and white knight's leg. The Martel knight pulled with all his might before his victim knew what was happening. The next thing the knight knew, he was face down on the ground. He never got up.

The two remaining knights backed away from Richard, unsure what to do about the crazed wolf that stalked them.

'Yield,' Richard shouted, more in hope than expectation.

The knights actually thought about it.

Then Nicholas ran at them with no weapons in his hands, and one of their horses reared up in fright. The Martel knight didn't stop, reached the horse which seemed to be suspended in the air on its two hind legs, and pushed it over backwards. The grey horse fell onto the other Lusignan horse and brought it down too.

Nicholas sprawled over the belly of the writhing beast, ignored a flailing hoof that caught him in the chest, and flung himself at the two knights who were temporarily trapped under their mounts.

Adam and Bowman rode over, their opponents retreating towards Guy and the vanguard who were battering the Marshal.

'What kind of devil is he?' Adam watched as Nicholas used one knight's own axe to hack his hand off.

'Leave the last one,' Richard shouted, 'he's done for today.'

The Martel knight left the first knight to clutch his stump and scream, and set about the second despite Richard's command. That knight had a leg trapped under his horse, but still waved his sword at Nicholas, terror in his eyes.

'Leave him,' Richard shouted.

The Martel knight took a blow from the sword on his upper arm, which his mail saved him from, and tore the knight's jaw off with his bare hands. He held the jaw up to the sun and his eyes cleared.

'Find a horse,' Richard shouted.

Nicholas blinked and looked up at the jaw in his hand, then at the two screeching knights below him. Theirs would be long and painful deaths.

'The peacock isn't winning,' Bowman said.

Adam's horse pawed at the ground. 'I can't believe I'm saying this, but we might need to break him out of that melee.'

Gerold's captured horse, now freed, found Solis and the two of them arched their necks to sniff each other's noses as if they'd never seen each other before.

'We've got what we came for,' Richard said, 'let's rescue the Marshal and get away from here.'

Adam grinned. 'I'll do it just so I can say I rescued him.'

'I can't wait to tell him that,' Bowman kicked his horse on.

Richard urged the black horse onward for one last charge, and with Adam they charged at Guy.

The melee between Guy's vanguard and the Marshal's handful of knights was not going well for the red shields.

Through force of strength the Marshal held at bay the wolves that circled him, riding with his reins hooked onto his belt and brandishing a sword and a mace in opposite hands. His grey warhorse turned left and right with the movement of his hips, and he smashed shields and parried blows.

But he hadn't unhorsed a single Lusignan knight.

Henry the Northerner succumbed to attack from a cluster of blue and white knights, and one snatched his reins away from him. He squealed out in anguish as the three of them rode off with their new captive.

Richard couldn't help but laugh to himself as his horse flew up the road, because one way or another, Henry had taken three opponents away from the battle.

Guy tried to push through his own knights to get at the Marshal, so Richard tried to cut him off.

He squeezed between two Lusignan knights who hadn't seen him coming, and grabbed one's shield. Richard pulled at it and the knight almost fell into his lap. Then he grabbed the man's mail coif and asked his horse to jump away. The horse obeyed, and with a fist full of mail, Richard strangled the knight with his own armour. He dropped his sword as Richard dragged him off his horse and he hit the ground head first.

Guy spotted Richard, his face hardened, and he stopped chasing the Marshal.

As the Lusignan leader glared at him, Richard's right hand suddenly felt very empty.

Adam cut his way through the throng of blue and white knights and reached the Marshal. 'Break out,' he shouted, 'we can go now.'

'Go?' the Marshal's face was alive and grinning. 'I've only just begun to fight.'

Bowman slammed into an enemy knight and cracked some teeth out with the hilt of his sword. 'The rest of us are going, peacock, but stay if you like,' he said.

The Marshal frowned as he blocked a sword attack with his own and countered with a swing of his mace.

Guy rode at Richard with fury. 'This was you, wasn't it?' he cried.

Richard went to rotate his horse away from Guy as if he was dodging a boar, but it wasn't Solis underneath him and nothing happened.

Guy smiled, missing tooth and all, and Richard had to roughly pull his horse to the side to escape. Except that it didn't quite work.

Guy's sword cut across Richard's chest and ripped a gash in the first of his mail shirts. The mail didn't stop his chest, already battered from earlier in the day, from exploding in pain.

Bowman and Adam hastened back towards the Young King, Lusignan knights in pursuit.

The Marshal was only a single horse's length behind Guy, but as he retreated he veered over just far enough to hammer his mace into Guy's left shoulder.

It was enough to stop his second attack from slicing through Richard's unprotected head.

Richard broke out of the chaos towards the vines where the freed horses still grazed on fat grapes. The black horse leapt the boundary ditch and the horses all looked up, purple smears around their faces. Richard found himself between two lines of vines and had to retrace his steps. Luckily no one had bothered to chase him.

The scene down on the road was carnage. Everyone headed towards the battle between the Young King and Guy's rearguard. Fallen horses and men littered the road everywhere in between, most wounded, but a few lay quiet and still.

Some of the freed captives struggled with wounds, some had found weapons and joined in the fight against their captors, but most galloped past the Young King and made for the bridge.

Richard felt anger at their flight, that was no way to show gratitude for being rescued.

Solis had followed him, and the stallion bit Richard's horse again. 'You could try being more grateful, too,' he said.

Richard jumped over the boundary ditch to leave the vines and cantered back down the road. He couldn't see Nicholas, hopefully he'd found a horse.

Richard, still without a weapon, rode towards the convulsing mass of horses and men. Before he reached them, the red shields peeled off from the fight one by one and streamed away towards the bridge. Hopefully this was the planned retreat, but even if it was, Richard would reach the bridge last, and find himself behind all of Guy's men. Panic seized him and he galloped the black horse as fast as it would go.

The ambush became a horse race. A race for the bridge.

Powered by adrenaline and fear, the Young King's beleaguered company beat the Lusignans to the bridge. Richard watched them charge over the wooden structure to regroup around the bannerman on his lame horse, who waited on the far bank.

Richard still had to breach the Lusignans if he was going to rejoin his company.

Otto was the last red man to reach the bridge, and he turned around to check his pursuers, saw Richard, and stopped as the rest of the red shields crossed the river to safety.

Guy held his men, wary of making an opposed river crossing, and they stopped a few horse lengths from Otto and the bridge.

Richard kept riding because something told him that Otto was making a distraction for him.

The German twirled his mace above his head and challenged Guy to a duel.

Guy walked his horse forwards and said something to Otto.

Richard, followed by Solis, who literally had the black horse's tail in his mouth, spurred his horse one last time. He made to squeeze between the two enemy knights who he could see the most daylight through. Guy slung his shield onto his back and hooked his reins onto his belt, accepting the challenge.

Otto looked less sure of himself, and did not, or could not, do the same.

Guy's men cheered, which was just enough noise to shield Richard's approach.

To protect his knees, he pulled his feet out of his stirrups and lifted them out and up alongside his horse's neck.

The black horse charged through the gap, and there was a loud crash. Richard's wooden saddle rammed into the knights on either side of the gap and pulled both of their legs away from their bodies. One dislocated with a pop. Their horses baulked at the sudden noise and impact, and suddenly Richard was through. His saddle was broken, but it wasn't his so he didn't care. He swung his legs back down and streaked past Otto and onto the bridge. Solis was still attached to the black horse's tail.

Guy charged at Otto, but the German turned tail and fled over the bridge behind Richard.

Their iron hooves rattled the wooden planks, but they reached the other side and the Angevin company welcomed their return with a great cheer.

Guy didn't follow.

'Is this your horse, Richard?' the Young King asked. Half of his golden crown was lost, the silver helmet beneath it dented and his face black and bloody.

Richard had to catch his breath before he could answer that it was.

Solis let go and immediately threw his head down to graze.

'I think he's letting you ride other horses now,' Bowman laughed.

The Young King nodded. 'This story will be told in castles across the realm,' he said with a wide grin. 'For my part, I cannot believe we have all come out of this alive.'

'We lost Henry,' the Marshal said.

'No loss there,' Adam sneered, 'if anything, his loss makes this more successful.'

The Marshal wasn't bothered enough to argue. 'Did you see me fight them all off?' he asked.

'Do not count your blessings so eagerly,' the Young King said, 'we aren't back at our lodgings yet.'

Guy stared at the bridge, his captives gone and half of his men dead or badly wounded.

'Can I duel with him?' the Marshal asked.

The Young King spat blood onto the green grass. 'This is not about you, not this time,' he said, 'and we still need to reach our list. Guy still outnumbers us, and will cross the bridge as soon as we're too far away to defend it.'

'I have a score to settle,' the Marshal complained.

'Not today,' the Young King said, 'your vendetta can wait. You may yet have your chance when he chases us back to the list.'

'Let him duel,' Adam said, 'see if Guy can prune a few feathers from him.'

'Let our horses catch their breath,' the Young King ignored Adam, 'then we speed towards the list and pray our horses have enough in them to win the race.'

'At least we're safe while we stay here,' Richard said.

'I'm not so sure,' Bowman looked up the hill behind the company.

A banner appeared over the top of it, a banner that drew nearer.

'Whose banner is it?' asked half the company.

Richard said a silent prayer to make it a banner from the Lagny team.

The banner fluttered in the breeze and lifted for a moment. It was yellow.

'Are they friendly or hostile?' Bowman asked as a column of knights joined the banner.

Jeers floated across the river as Guy's company recognised the banner as Count Philip's.

The Flemings poured over the crest of the hill and formed a line, a line far longer than the Young King's company could muster.

Guy rode halfway across the bridge, his knights behind him. 'Yield now and save yourselves the humiliation of defeat,' he shouted.

The Flemings finished forming their line and charged down the hill.

'What's he doing?' the Marshal asked. 'I thought he was standing aside for us?'

The Young King remained resolutely silent.

'Can someone give me a sword?' Richard asked.

Otto handed him his mace. 'From what I hear, this may suit you better than a sword.'

'Where did you hear that?' Richard asked.

'While you jousted. You're the knight who drops his blade.'

Richard's pride stung, but he still grabbed the mace. It had a heavier feel than a sword, but the jewelled and bloodied head felt satisfyingly solid.

'What do we do?' Adam asked his lord.

The Flemings swept down the hill as it bottomed out towards the river and the red company.

Lusignan knights made their way further over the bridge, their confidence restored. Guy was nearly across.

'Count Philip gave me his word,' the Young King watched them with disdain.

Guy's horse stepped onto the muddy area around the mouth of the bridge. His knights yelled and they accelerated.

'No, I trust Philip, follow me,' the Young King turned away from them and raced off parallel to the river.

The Marshal looked at Richard. 'The Count will crush us.'

'Not everyone thinks like you, try trusting others,' Richard followed his lord.

The red company turned and galloped along the river, showing their backs to the Flemings.

The Lusignans spewed out onto the meadow, and as one they turned to follow the Young King.

Except that the Flemings did not do the same. Count Philip aimed his company directly at the Lusignans.

Richard's hair cooled as the air rushed through it, he looked back and saw the Flemings swamp the depleted blue and white company.

'I suppose he doesn't care about the sanctity of teams as much as he thought,' Richard shouted over the sound of galloping hooves.

The Young King laughed and eased his horse. The bannerman with the lame horse lagged behind, but he caught up as the company fell to a walk and turned back towards the list.

'Do I have permission to join in the fighting?' the Marshal asked.

The Young King whirled round in his saddle. 'Rein yourself in, you prancing idiot. Do you not listen to a word I say? Your disloyalty to me is overcoming your prowess, do not let it reach a tipping point.'

'My loyalty,' the Marshal reddened, 'is beyond doubt.'

'No, it's not,' the Young King stopped his horse so his Marshal could draw level, 'you confuse loyalty with self interest. You will ride in your company and seal your mouth shut. Do you understand?'

The Marshal locked his jaw and booted his horse in the ribs. The animal lurched forwards, and the company walked behind him.

Sounds of iron clashing on iron rang out with ferocity from the bridge, but Richard looked for Nicholas.

The wolf knight rode at the other end of the company, on Gerold's freed horse, his pelt slashed and torn. Mail was now visible through it, but at least he'd made it over the river alive.

Richard relaxed, everyone was safe and Solis was behind him. As they retraced their path back towards Lagny, the palomino repeatedly stopped to graze until nearly out of sight before cantering to catch up. Richard reflected on having so very nearly lost Solis. Maybe, if a career as a tournament knight was his future, he would have to ride the black horse into them instead.

Exhaustion dimmed the excited post-fight chatter by the time they reached the hornbeam grove. The company rode between the grey trunks in single file, each man alone with his own thoughts in the crisp shade.

Through the meadow they went next, reversing their path over the long grasses their hooves had flattened down on their hurried earlier journey.

'Keep the mace,' Otto drew alongside Richard as they rode past the woods of the massacre.

'Really?' Richard said. 'It looks valuable.'

The German nodded. 'Not as valuable as the tale I can now tell back home,' he said, 'besides, I shall ask the Young King for a place in his company for a short while. It will make me rich, and that is thanks to you.'

Bowman snorted up ahead. 'Finally something you do ends well, young lord,' he said without turning his head.

'Don't be jealous,' Nicholas said, 'you'll be rich, too.'

'I didn't ask you,' the blonde man replied, 'keep your demonic rampages and opinions to yourself.'

'Enough bickering,' the Young King said from the head of the short column. 'And Richard, we shall have to speak about the rampant bloodletting.'

Richard didn't reply, the bloodletting had seemed largely justified.

Some spectators in the stand had left by the time the company returned to the pasture that contained the fortified list. Those who remained cheered at the Young King's return, oblivious of the task they'd embarked on out of sight. The young Angevin waved back at them as the company crossed the threshold of the list, and the musicians who had gone to sleep started up again.

Hundreds of captive knights sat or slept in the list while their horses were corralled together for easy keeping. Yet more hundreds of servants and squires ran back and forth organising captured equipment and trading prisoners between captors, some of whom remained while others sallied out in search of more victims.

The knight Richard had rescued from his captor earlier in the day, Count Robert of Meulan, welcomed them back. 'Your return gladdens my heart,' he said to the Young King.

'We have had quite an adventure,' the young man replied, 'and we shall drink long into the night with Count Philip.'

'Have you heard what happened in the woods?' Count Robert asked.

The Young King's smile faded. 'I am very aware, that is why Count Philip broke the code of the tournament to fight for me.'

Count Robert nodded. 'I see. They have brought Sir Rob the Scot into Lagny, he is awfully battered and has been taken to the care of the monks in the abbey. The monks protested, saying today's deaths were God's vengeance for taking part in a tournament, but they took Sir Rob in for care. Eventually.'

'I should go to him,' the Young King said.

'There is plenty of daylight left,' the Marshal said, 'we should ride out as a stronger company now.'

The Young King narrowed his eyes. 'I have little wish to furnish your reputation any further today, Marshal. You may do whatever you please, but I will already have to hear the ladies proclaim you as the tournament champion again tonight.'

The Marshal turned his back on his lord and went to inspect his prizes and arrange the ransom for Henry the Northerner.

Richard felt weak. His limbs ached and felt empty, and he still had not drunk. 'I think I should come with you to see Sir Rob,' he said to the Young King, 'it was my horse that Guy used to break his ribs.'

The Young King raised his eyebrows. 'Very well, I shall be glad of the company. Don't tell my priest, but quiet abbeys tend to unsettle me.'

EYE OF A NEEDLE

Sir Rob's mail shirt lay in a corner of a grey-walled chamber in Lagny Abbey. Its monks had taken some time to find a smith able to cut the armour away from his body, for they knew with his injuries it would be unwise to lift the metal garment off over his head. The smith they'd dragged over from the tournament stand had cut over a hundred rings in half, one by one with a pair of iron shears, until they could slide it away underneath him. The smith had easily been able to saw apart Sir Rob's leather breastplate, and the monks had paid the smith handsomely for his time and care.

Richard and the Young King stood over the fallen knight in that dim chamber as a monk inspected the yellow, black, and blue marks on his body, then had to rush away to be sick.

Brian rolled his eyes at the fleeing monk, then felt rib after rib of his patient, calling out which ones had broken and which held firm. The other monks obeyed him when he called for incense and certain balms, and soon the chamber smelled of sweet things that reminded Richard of Christmas.

'Will he live?' the Young King asked Brian.

The Irish monk shrugged. 'It is for Our Lord to decide these things, we can only do our best and pray.'

'Why are the monks listening to you?' Richard asked.

Brian grinned, his face far too happy for the situation. 'These monks treat illness and disease, and it has been decades since any of them hunted with their families as youths. They do not leave the abbey and as such are now squeamish.'

'So they're just letting you do the horrible task they don't want to,' Richard said.

Brian's grin only widened. 'It is God's task to heal. And after leaving my homeland I am quite glad to heal rather than harm,' he said.

Two monks lit a fire in a brazier and the dark grey walls flickered to reflect its yellow light. Others found some dried plants to burn to improve the air and set those to smoulder. It smelled like a herb garden.

'Did you know this is an Irish abbey?' Brian moved his fingers down to the knight's stomach, which had the clear imprint of a horseshoe on it.

'Irish?' the Young King said. 'I thought they were all pagan?'

Brian shot a glance at him. 'Do I look pagan to you?'

The young Angevin shook his head.

'This is the chapel of Saint Fursey,' Brian said, 'he was Irish and founded a monastery here. It's an abbey now.'

Sir Rob moaned, and his eyes opened for a moment before they closed again.

'Fetch him something for the pain,' Brian ordered, 'if he wakes up fully he will be in agony.'

Some monks rushed past the grey stones and thin carved columns of the chamber. Stonework protruded from one wall, an arch with biblical figures carved into the limestone and a wooden shelf in the centre holding a golden cross and some of the burning herbs.

'He's bleeding inside, isn't he?' Richard asked.

Brian's expression fell, and he nodded. 'The black under the skin is a terrible sign. His whole belly is the wrong colour. But if he was a pious man, God may still save him.'

'I don't know if he was pious, but he was rich,' Richard said, 'that's why Guy did it.'

Sir Rob's eyes opened more fully this time, and he looked about the chamber. He screamed and tried to get up.

Brian held his arms down, and Richard had to join in. 'Stay still, Rob, you're in the abbey,' he said.

'What abbey?' the Scot asked.

'You are in Lagny,' the Young King said, 'at the tournament. Now you are in the abbey being treated for your wounds.'

Rob looked down at his body as the pain reduced him to gasps. He shivered.

'Put a log on the fire,' Brian nodded proudly, 'he has fallen into phlegm, so we must raise his yellow bile with fire.'

A monk tossed a log into the brazier, which for the moment only reduced the heat it threw out into the chamber.

Richard couldn't believe Brian was having so much fun, it was the most alive he'd seen him since they'd landed in England. Maybe even since he'd landed on that sandy beach in Ireland where Brian had welcomed the invasion.

Richard leant over the stricken knight. 'I must apologise to you,' Richard said, 'it was my horse that kicked you.'

Sir Rob's breathing had been rapid, but he had enough strength to collect himself. 'The fault lay not in your horse, but in the man who wielded the stick,' Rob said.

'We made him pay for it,' Richard said, 'we cost him many knights.'

The Scot still shivered. 'What good does vengeance do me?'

Richard shrugged but said nothing.

'Do you know who I am?' the Young King asked.

Rob nodded, which strained the muscles running down to his chest and he flinched.

'I will give you the best care money can buy,' the Young King said, 'and I will pay for a hundred monks to pray for you day and night until you recover.'

'Your generosity is admirable,' the Scot's voice wavered, 'but I fear my time is short and I am not headed to heaven.'

'Nonsense,' the Young King said, 'do you hear mass, confess, and pray to Christ?'

'I do,' Rob replied, 'but I am too young, I have nothing to show for my life.'

The Young King, who was younger than the Scot, looked to Richard, but he could offer no support.

Brian stood back and sighed as the brazier cast brighter yellows across the walls.

'I am wealthy,' Rob coughed, which caused a spasm of pain, 'but wealth does not grant me a spot with the angels above.'

Brian shook his head. 'It is easier for a camel to go through the eye of a needle than for a rich man to enter the kingdom of God.'

'That's the first time I've ever heard you quote scripture,' Richard said.

'It is the first time in the company of you and your friends that it has ever seemed relevant,' Brian replied with some satisfaction.

The Young King went to laugh but then remembered the man before him whose life hung in the balance. 'This is the proper time for piety,' he said instead.

'My life has been pointless,' Rob said, 'I have wasted my years and now the Lord punishes me.'

'You must have done something virtuous?' Richard asked.

Sir Rob coughed and this time blood came up. 'What is the life of a warrior? We eat what others grow, we sleep by hearths others have built. We kill those who others nurtured. I never took the cross. I never did the one thing that could forgive my sins.'

The Young King frowned. 'God's will is mysterious, but he judges everyone fairly, so if you have not committed a serious sin, you should not fear death.'

The Scot cried out in pain. A tear ran down his dusty face. 'Do not waste your life as I have mine, my King,' Rob said, 'you are richer than I and surely will be judged more strictly than the poor.'

The Young King knelt down by the wounded knight and took his hands in his own. 'If this is your end, you can go to it with confidence that your soul is safe.'

'I'll find a priest to hear confession,' Brian left the chamber.

Rob's breathing rattled and Richard was sure his face was paler than before.

'I forgive the man who did this to me,' Sir Rob whispered in broken words.

'I don't,' Richard said.

'Forgiveness is all I can do now,' the Scot mumbled but his words trailed off. He writhed and spasmed from the torment of his shattered body. The knight cried out, but his cry was cut short as his lungs ran out of air. His body convulsed and more blood fell from his mouth. Rob's breathing failed him and the Young King gripped his hand and started praying in Latin.

Richard froze on the spot, unsure what to do, but before it mattered, Rob died with a final rasping exhale of air.

The Young King held his hand for a while longer in prayer, until eventually he let go and stood up. His face was ashen.

Richard shivered. A cold shadow swept over him as Brian returned and walked in front of the brazier.

'Oh,' the monk realised he was too late.

'It's curious,' the Young King said, 'no death on the tournament field has had this power over me.'

'You are no stranger to death,' Richard said.

The Young King nodded. 'But in Sir Rob I see myself.' His eyes were full and shone in the brazier-light.

'You are young,' Richard said, 'you have time to avoid his fate.'

The Young King turned away and wiped his eyes. 'Why would Guy do this? What was the point?'

'Guy wanted to make sure the captives wouldn't give him any trouble,' Richard said.

'Trouble?' the Young King turned back, his eyes red. 'Why would any of the captives give him trouble?'

Richard scratched his neck. 'He wanted to make sure no prisoner ever gave him as much trouble as the Marshal did.'

'The Marshal? You mean to say the massacre in the woods was his fault?'

Richard shook his head. 'I wouldn't say it was his fault. You can't really blame him directly,' Richard said, 'although he was a terrible prisoner.'

The Young King wrinkled up his face. 'He may be the greatest knight in the company, but he has rankled me of late.'

A pair of monks entered the chamber and cleared the incense away.

'The man is still warm,' Brian told them, 'have some compassion.'

One monk held up some of the herbs. 'The ones we can't grow are very expensive.'

Brian frowned.

'It may be time to thin the peacock's wings out a little,' the Young King said to himself. He gazed down at the body and sighed. 'Richard, you don't know how lucky you are.'

Richard creased his brow.

'You're poor,' the Young King said, 'wealth and power do not curse you.'

'I wouldn't mind a bit of wealth,' Richard said, 'I don't need to be a baron, I just want enough wealth to make my family happy and my village respectable.'

The Young King put a hand on Richard's shoulder. 'We are all doomed to see the fortune of others but to overlook their afflictions,' he said.

Richard couldn't see how his wants were so bad. Or why the Young King envied his pennilessness. 'If your wealth is so burdensome, I would be happy to look after some of it for you,' Richard said.

The Young King half smiled. 'You earn so much a day that you will have your chance,' he said.

'How can you afford to hand out so much money for knights?' Richard asked. 'Your tournament winnings cannot cover a quarter of the cost.'

'No,' the Young King chuckled, 'and to begin with we lost a lot more than we won.'

Brian said something in Latin over Sir Rob's body.

'Why does your father keep sending you money?' Richard asked.

The Young King held his hands up to the brazier and orange light danced on his palms. 'He will not give me land, so he gives me coin to keep me quiet.'

Richard thought about his own father. He would trade a fortune just to spend an evening with him. 'I've lost count of the number of times I've almost died chasing after a few pounds. But what choice do I have?'

'There is always choice,' the Young King said.

'That's easy for you to say,' Richard said with much more force than he should have to a crowned monarch.

Brian spun around with wide eyes to watch for the Young King's reaction.

The young Angevin ran his hands through his hair, hair which matched the colours of the fire. 'Do not grow too familiar with me, Richard,' he said, 'but some men are born to toil, others to fight for their whole lives to provide for their families, and others to lead. We cannot choose our lot, but you have it within yourself to look at me and not be jealous.'

Richard sighed. He walked over to the dead Scot and couldn't keep his eyes from the hoofprint. 'The thought of the good things I could do with ten or twenty pounds hurts me to my bones,' he said.

'Jealousy is a sin,' Brian said.

Richard ripped his eyes from the hoofprint. 'I know that.'

'The ache you feel for ten pounds,' the Young King said, 'is the same ache I feel for the kingdom I cannot have. I was born to rule it, but rule I cannot until my father gives me land or is himself buried beneath it. I look at every castle, and maybe even yours, and wonder what I could do with lordship over it. How could I improve the defences, the pasture, the workshops, the horse breeding? This ache follows me everywhere, Richard. You do not suffer alone.'

Richard went to look at a figure carved into the stone archway above the shelf. A hint of incense still hung in the air. He rather thought that it was a lot better to be a rich king with no land than a knight with one paltry village, but thought better than to say it.

Brian approached the Young King. 'You should donate some of your vast fortune to the church, it might save your soul if you were to suffer a premature death like our poor knight here.'

The Young King looked offended that a lowly monk dared to speak to him, but his sour expression faded. 'I have time,' he said, 'and once I rule there will be plenty more of it to see to the church and my soul.'

'What keeps you?' the Irish monk asked.

'You forget yourself, monk,' the Young King raised his voice. 'All monks leave the chamber.'

Brian looked to Richard.

Richard shook his head, and the Irish monk left with the rest, leaving Richard alone with one of his two kings and a corpse.

'I know he's Irish,' the Young King said, 'but a monk cannot just speak to a king.'

'I know,' Richard said, 'he is just excited to be in this abbey.'

'His question annoyed me because it was pertinent,' the Young King left the fire to peer down at the cooling body. 'If I died today, I would be as unprepared as this poor soul.'

The two men stared at the Scot for a while as the last log in the brazier burned down into ash.

'The priest never came,' Richard said.

'He did not,' the Young King said, 'and this only adds to my ache. We have precious little time in this life, and sometimes I worry I squander it.'

'I don't think you do,' Richard said because it sounded like the right thing to say.

The Young King snorted. 'Don't be a sycophant like Henry the Northerner, I have plenty of those.'

'Very well,' Richard said, 'then I don't understand why you spend so much time going around the tournament circuit.'

The Young King smiled. 'That's better,' he said. 'You see, Richard, the wealth I am given is material, impermanent, and not mine. I spend it to gain other things, things that will be useful to me once I am the only king. You see the hundreds of knights who have served me on the field?'

Richard nodded.

'They will serve me again when I face the French in battle, or ride to the Holy Land for the sake of our church. The counts and dukes of France prefer me to their own king, and all those who rebel and plot against my father, they flood to me. They will not rebel once my father is gone. I am building a reputation that will secure my throne. When we ride to secure our borders, enemies will bend the knee before fighting because they have heard of my prowess and my generosity.'

'So you play at war now so you might avoid fighting real ones in the future?' Richard asked.

'Indeed,' the red-haired man replied, 'with a united land, imagine what we can accomplish?'

Richard thought he might understand.

'These things will outlive me, and unlike the coins themselves, they will accompany me into the next life.'

'Thoughts like that must be a weight,' Richard said.

The Young King's eyes softened for a flicker of the fire. 'I see no malice or unbridled ambition in you,' he said, 'unlike so many of the others who clamour around my feet and fight for scraps.'

Richard blushed. 'I'm just trying to help my family.'

'They all say that,' the Young King said, 'but with you it might actually be true. They are all jealous of me, jealous of those whom I favour, but you can at least admit it.'

Richard looked down at the blue ribs of the dead man.

'I think we have both learnt something here,' the young Angevin said.

Richard swallowed.

'But,' the Young King said coldly, 'I have not forgotten the circumstances of your arrival at my court.'

Richard had forgotten about that.

The Young King looked him in the eyes. 'I have decided to trust you. Fully, with all my heart. My father would pry and spy and suspect, but I shall do the opposite. I will welcome you in and treat you as equal to my other knights.'

'Thank you,' Richard said.

'But do not forget,' the Young King said, 'that if betrayed, your betrayal will then cut me all the deeper, and once wronged I am quite as vengeful as my father.'

Richard gulped.

The stare from his lord was both warm and cold, and Richard wasn't sure if things had changed for the better or worse. Something about Young King Henry drew him in.

'I'm very sorry,' Richard blurted out, 'I thought I could keep your father happy and be true to you at the same time. I just can't lose Yvetot, my family would die on the road. I never wanted to be a pawn in a royal game, I've never wanted to betray anyone.'

The Young King's face softened. 'He is old and a bully, but you always have a choice.'

'I just want to be loyal to the crown,' Richard said, 'my father was, and it's all I ever wanted to be, but how am I supposed to do that when there are two crowns?'

'Pick one.'

'It's unnatural,' Richard sniffed and fought back tears of anguish, 'why should I suffer for another family's squabble?'

'We all suffer what we must,' the Young King turned towards the door. 'But I will rebel against my father again. This time I shall force concessions and land from him, but you should know what I intend. How you navigate that is up to you.'

The Young King turned back from the door, the light from outside shone around his frame. 'But that news cannot reach my father's ear. Do you understand?'

Richard nodded.

'Anything else you can pass on if you feel you must,' the Angevin said, 'but that plan must remain secret.'

'I understand,' Richard replied.

'Come,' the Koung King stepped out, 'we must return to our hall where the knights and rich merchants will queue to see me. I must slip the mask back on, you will see that mask tonight. Do not envy my wealth, for it is not mine. I own nothing I can touch, Richard. My wealth will be the loyalty and love that my people will show me when my time finally arrives. The glory that our realm will stamp on the memory of the world. When I am the sole king, we will enter a golden age of peace. I may drink wine all night and laugh all day, but it is with this in mind.'

'Thank you,' Richard said.

'What for?' the Young King asked with a straight face.

'For sharing this with me. You shoulder a great burden.'

'And none can shoulder it with me. So be glad of your poverty. It shall make your death easy to bear when it comes for you. My death will be pain and anguish, for even if I die old and infirm in my bed, I will have left half of my plans undone.'

The Young King left the chamber.

Richard didn't want to be left alone with the dead, for that was known to be risky for your soul, so he followed his king out and back into the world of the living.

Richard left the abbey and Brian with soaring spirits. He had glimpsed the world of the Young King, a rare privilege, and had been truly honest with him. Spying for the Old King had knotted Richard up, and he felt as if that evening the knot had unravelled. He'd survived his first tournament too, and rescued his horse. The only thing he'd lost was the Little Lord's sword, but that had a maker's mark of a spur rowel stamped into the blade and he would ask Gerold to look for it in the morning. It would be speckled with rust, but that could be cleaned.

The sun sank below the horizon toward Paris and the looming darkness made the road back to Lagny difficult. Richard's black horse stepped in more than one puddle he hadn't seen, but even as night fell Richard felt like celebrating.

He followed the Young King past the still empty gallows, and into the festival that was Lagny. Everyone who had spent their day in the stands had drunk so much they wobbled around the streets, hanging off each other's shoulders. More than one lay comatose up against a wall. A farmer ran down the torch-lit street clutching a fur lined hat that was worth more than ten of his fields. Two friends ran with him, all laughing loudly. Somewhere over the rooftops the rhythmic tones of a drum sounded, and street sellers operated here and there selling pasties of every kind. Men walked around with barrels of wine, offering free samples and then directing satisfied tasters to where more of it could be purchased.

The Young King rode by unrecognised, Richard assumed because he didn't have a large retinue or a banner, until they reached the merchant's house.

The party within the Young King's lodgings spilled out onto the street, and to get his black horse into a stable, Richard had to push through a group of celebrating Flemish knights. The knights told each other rapid and tall stories of their deeds, or asked after friends they hadn't yet seen and might need ransoming.

Richard followed his lord into the hall, which was so warm and loud he almost had to leave.

Nicholas lay asleep against the far wall, his pelt over him and the feet of drinking knights a hand's width from his oblivious snoring head.

Bowman sat in a corner by the hearth with the black dog in his lap. The blonde man's eyes were glassy, and he'd probably fall over if he tried to rise. The dog was too big for his lap and his hind legs drooped down towards the floor. He opened one eye when Richard neared and wagged his tail.

On the table nearest Bowman, Gerold and Otto sat on a bench. They squeezed apart and made room for Richard.

'You look like the soberest men in the hall,' Richard told them.

Otto grinned awkwardly. 'Drunkenness is a sin, and it loosens one's tongue too much.'

Richard laughed and reached for a cup. 'Have you got secrets you don't wish to tell us?'

'Of course,' the German said, 'who doesn't have any secrets?'

'I don't,' Gerold yawned, 'and I'm getting too old for this. Back in my day, we took tournaments seriously, there was far less of this excess. It is little wonder the church seeks to ban them.'

Richard found wine to pour and drank for the first time since dawn. The wine soothed his parched throat but made him cough.

'Too strong for you?' Otto chuckled.

Richard shook his head. 'My throat's just dry. And that incense in the abbey stuck in there. Sir Rob died.'

Gerold raised his empty cup. 'To the Scot.'

'To the Scot,' Richard and Otto echoed.

Richard finished his second cup, and a wave of relaxation swept over him.

'Slow down, my lord,' Gerold said, 'you should eat before you drink so much.'

There was no food yet, indeed a few enthusiastic knights still roved around the tournament field to snap up any lost or wounded knights who hadn't made it back to their lists yet. Two servants carried a square table out into the hall and laid carving knives onto it.

Richard liked how he felt, so poured a third cup.

When he later needed to get up to let the wine out, Richard's legs wobbled their first few steps. He pushed through knights in bright red, yellow, or blue tunics until he reached the crisp, cool air. On his way back in, Richard staggered through the door but had to rest on a window to steady himself.

He burped, which surprised himself, but no one seemed to pay attention. A storyteller began a long rhyming poem near the Young King, whose face was happy and bright. Richard searched for any sadness in his eyes, any crack in his mask, but saw none.

A figure appeared in front of Richard and blocked his view of the Young King. The young woman noticed Richard and smiled at him. Her long brown hair was topped with a silver circlet and her bright blue dress triggered Richard's memory.

'You?' he asked. 'Why did you throw a favour at me earlier? And why did you pretend to be Count Philip's niece?'

The woman who was not Count Philip's niece laughed. It was a carefree laugh with a freedom to it.

'Men like you live by robbing others of their lives. Women like me live by robbing them of their wealth,' she smiled, 'I think I know which is worse.'

'I am no thief,' Richard frowned, 'but why did you throw the favour?'

'Because your horse was a pretty colour,' she said.

Richard groaned. 'You can leave me alone,' he said, 'I am one of the poorest men here.'

'I saw you win your joust,' the woman said, 'so you are not so poor anymore.'

'I don't have the coin from that yet,' Richard said, 'and knowing the Marshal, he'll find a way to weasel out of paying me.'

The woman stepped closer and placed her hand on the plastered wall. 'The Marshal,' she said, 'he is a distasteful man.'

Richard sniggered, which was unexpected, and for a split second the room spun. 'He is not my easiest friend,' he said.

'This is your first after-tournament party, isn't it?'

Richard nodded.

'What do you like doing?' she asked. 'When you aren't robbing men of their lives.'

'I sit in my castle and wish I could leave it,' Richard burped again, but caught it this time.

The woman frowned. 'That sounds like a woman's lot,' she said, 'you must do more than sit and brood?'

'I read,' Richard said, 'although I only have one book. I know it by heart.'

The woman's eyes lit up. 'Which book? I love to have stories read to me.'

'Eric and Enid,' Richard said, 'the martyred archbishop gave it to me.'

'How exciting,' the woman drifted closer and Richard could smell something sweet on her. 'You will have to tell me the story of how you got the book, too. But I'd love to hear you recite its story,' she said.

Richard's heart skipped a beat. Sophie had listened to the story once, then dismissed it as a fantasy. The real world was a much more boring place, she had told Richard, and he shouldn't distract himself with such trivial stories. Not when he had a family to provide for.

'You could recite it to me now?' she asked softly.

Richard went to begin but stopped himself. 'Are you trying to rob me?' he narrowed his eyes.

'You are so drunk I could rob you without you knowing I was here,' she replied, 'besides, you have nothing I desire but Eric and Enid.'

'I need to get back to my bench,' Richard said, 'and I need to eat something.'

The woman frowned and made a show of bowing to Richard and freeing his path. 'I will be waiting for you, my lord,' she said.

Richard pushed himself off the wall and then pushed his way through groups of knights until he reached his bench.

Otto nudged him with his elbow. 'Make the most of it,' he said, 'the tournament circuit is a world within the world. The doings on the evening of the event stay within that inner world.'

Gerold cleared his throat. 'I recognised her, Richard, and you would do well to avoid her. Ignore this German also.'

'I know,' Richard thumped his hand onto the table and his empty cup rattled. 'I want nothing to do with her.' His eyes found her in the hall and followed her around the room.

Bowman clapped a hand on his shoulder. It gripped quite hard. 'You have a wife, young lord.'

Richard swallowed. 'I don't know what you're talking about.'

Bowman relaxed his grip. 'I only meant that you have a wife, so you should at least try to be discreet.'

Richard looked up at the blonde man. 'What?'

Bowman laughed. 'Every count and duke here has women hidden

away.'

'Like your mother?'

Bowman's face flashed with anger, but his face was already red from the wine. 'That was uncalled for.'

'Sorry,' Richard said, 'that just came out.'

The black dog appeared under the table and scavenged for scraps that weren't there yet.

'I would ignore that woman in particular, young lord,' the blonde man said, 'find one we know isn't a thief.'

'She had a good argument about that,' Richard said, 'but I can't remember what it was.'

'There are plenty of others here,' Bowman said, 'just take one outside if you need it.'

'Your father never took another woman,' Gerold said.

'I hope not,' Richard said.

'But your drunk friend is right, it is the done thing. Even your grandfather thought your father was damaging himself by having eyes only for your mother.'

'Ha,' Bowman slapped the older knight on the back, 'I bet you had some fun when you were young.'

'I'm not that old,' Gerold shrugged Bowman's hand off.

'If you thrill for the chase, young lord,' Bowman said, 'we shall not tell your wife.'

The woman floated around the hall to speak to another group of knights. Richard watched the silver circlet.

'I don't see you finding another woman,' Richard said.

Bowman nodded with a straight face. 'You know my heart belongs to a woman in a faraway land. We will be reunited, and until that day I need no one else.'

'You're an idiot, you know that?' Richard replied.

Four servants appeared to a great cheer, for between them they carried a whole roasted boar. The knights cleared the way for them to reach the side table where the carving began.

Richard's mouth watered as the smell of hot roasted meat saturated the hall. Boar was the least flavorful of the animals they could have prepared, but it was a warlike prey for warlike men.

The black dog shot out from under the table and pawed at the servants carving the boar.

The merchant's wolfhounds were not close behind, and Bowman left to offer unasked-for advice on how to carve it properly.

The storyteller paused his story as attention turned to food, trays of cooked fish were brought out and served to the Young King and those near him.

Richard watched the woman take a drink and thought about Sir Rob's unfortunate fate. A bit of fun at a tournament might be expected, but that didn't stop it being a sin.

'Either take your eyes away from her,' Otto said, 'or go and take her. Sitting here like a dithering merchant accomplishes nothing.'

Richard ate some bread that a servant threw onto their table with little care.

The woman with the silver circlet spoke to two knights, one of whom had a bandaged right hand.

His companion slapped him in the face. A cheer went up as the bandaged man swung a punch at his assailant, but he hit him with his wounded hand and cried out in pain.

The woman pushed him away, and he tripped onto the floor where jeering knights laughed at him. The victor of the brief encounter grabbed the woman by the arm and dragged her out of the hall.

Richard jumped up from the bench and left Otto chuckling behind him as he surged through the crowd. He pushed a surly Breton knight aside as the woman disappeared through the door and out into the courtyard.

The courtyard was no less busy than the hall, but in the night it was far cooler. A few braziers had been borrowed or stolen from somewhere to provide light, and knights celebrated the day's action just as loud as those inside.

Solis whinnied at him and kicked his stable door.

Richard nearly slipped on the mud in pursuit of the woman, but her rough companion actually did and landed on his rear with something between a thud and a splash.

She pulled her now free arm away from the fallen knight. 'That's what you deserve, a roll in the filth.'

The knight got to his feet and looked round at his soiled tunic. 'I look like a farmer,' he complained. His accent was southern, like Richard had heard in La Rochelle.

'You behave like one,' the woman replied.

Richard arrived and bunched his fists at the knight. 'Let her go,' he said.

'And you are?' the knight half ignored him and looked at the woman.

'My saviour,' she replied and nodded at the knight.

He backed away with his hands up to Richard. 'I'll leave her to you, you have frightened me away.'

Richard frowned and kept his eyes on the knight until he'd left the courtyard toward the street.

The sound of dogs barking floated over the courtyard from the town.

'Thank you,' the woman said, 'there are many unpleasant men at tournaments.'

'And many unreliable women,' Richard replied.

She put her hands on the tight-fitting hips of her blue dress. A thin fabric belt lay around her waist. 'Do you like it?' she asked.

Richard raised his eyes. Then shrugged. 'I don't know your name, what is it? Your real name.'

'I am Alice,' she said.

'Why are you here?'

'To find a decent man,' Alice replied, 'however much it pains me, a woman needs a man to prosper outside of the church.'

'I'm married,' Richard said, 'so I'll be of little use to you.'

'What makes you think I'm after you?' a wry smile crept across her lips.

Richard's cheeks warmed. 'Because you threw your favour at me.'

'Oh, that,' Alice said, 'don't think too much into it.'

'I wasn't,' Richard sighed, 'I think I should go back inside.'

He turned to leave, but Alice reached over and caught his wrist. The touch tingled.

A shadow blocked the light from the nearest brazier and a familiar rodent-like face peered up at Richard. 'Holding hands with a woman who isn't your wife?' Brother Geoffrey asked. 'The tournament spirit has overtaken you quickly.'

Richard pulled his hand away and felt the need to rub it. 'No, I was just rescuing her,' he said.

'I hardly needed rescuing,' she smiled.

'It isn't proper,' the monk said, his black robe looking extra black under the moonless and cloudy sky.

'Is it proper for a monk to be here?' Richard asked. 'In the middle of all this drinking.'

'And whoring,' Brother Geoffrey stepped closer to Alice and squinted up at her.

'She's not a whore,' Richard snapped.

'Oh,' the monk raised his eyebrows at Richard, 'is she not?'

Alice slapped the monk across his face. He lost his balance, knocked a knight's drink from his hands, and fell flat on his back in a shallow puddle.

The partygoers howled and mocked him.

Alice sneered. She clapped her hands together and nodded at Richard. 'I'm not welcome here, come and see me when there are no monks to ruin everything.'

'Ruin what?' he asked as Alice stomped past the monk, which served only to splash more dark water onto his robe.

Brother Geoffrey cursed her and scrambled to his feet. 'You,' he pointed at Richard, 'do not know with what you play.'

'I'm not playing with anything,' he replied, 'or anyone.'

'Spare me,' the monk said.

'What do you want?' Richard watched the blue dress exit the courtyard.

'Something for the king,' Brother Geoffrey said.

'We aren't supposed to be seen together,' Richard whispered, 'we had an agreement.'

'I need information,' the monk said.

'No wonder Sir Wobble knew what you were,' Richard mumbled to himself.

'What?'

'Never mind,' Richard said, 'I have nothing for you, I've been fighting all day.'

'So you don't know where the next tournament is?' Brother Geoffrey asked.

Richard's shoulders sank. 'Of course not, the current one is still going on. There are still knights out there fighting in the dark.'

'You can't avoid telling me something useful forever.'

'Leave me alone,' Richard turned his back on the monk and went back into the merchant's house, hopeful that however stupid the monk was, he wasn't so stupid that he'd follow.

Richard burst back into the hall, where Henry the Northerner stood on a bench near the Young King, regaling everyone with his story of the day.

'And then the valiant Marshal swatted the knight to the ground, seized Count Robert's reins and rescued him.'

Richard blinked twice. He was quite sure he had rescued Count Robert himself.

'The Marshal then beat away three other knights, manfully capturing one while the others fled for their very lives,' Henry's loud voice boomed over the tables and through the knights packed into the chamber.

The Marshal sat on a chair beside the Young King, grinning and eating some of the roast boar.

Adam pushed his way towards the door and nodded at Richard. 'I know who rescued the Count,' he said, 'and I'm not staying to hear what other nonsense he's going to spout.'

Bowman left behind Adam. 'The peacock is now happy to display feathers in his tail that belong to others,' he said.

'For you, that's almost poetic,' Richard said.

Bowman belched and pushed his way out of the door.

The black dog had followed him this far, but sniffed Richard and sat down by his feet, looking up at him with dark pleading eyes.

Richard didn't follow Adam and Bowman out, instead he picked his way back to his bench with his dog close behind.

'The Marshal battered Guy with his sword,' Henry continued, 'and dealt the evil Lusignan many foul blows. Soon his foe withered under his force, melted before his prowess, and fled over the river and to safety. He left behind his tattered reputation, and his glorious conqueror in possession of the field.'

Richard remembered things quite differently. He slumped down on the bench and Otto winked at him. 'Nothing wrong with being quick,' he said.

Richard groaned. 'Don't be stupid.'

Brother Geoffrey appeared in the entrance to the hall.

'Speaking of stupid,' Richard said under his breath.

The monk stood in the doorway, searching the packed hall for Richard.

A newly arriving squire shoved him out of the way so the monk crashed his forehead on the door frame. The squire paid him no mind and ran into the room waving a roll of parchment above his head. 'The Young King,' he shouted, 'where's the Young King?'

'What do you want?' the young Angevin shouted back as the noise in the hall died down.

'The next tournament,' the squire stopped to catch his breath, 'has been announced.'

'Well, then, where is it?' the Young King asked.

'Corbie,' the squire replied, 'near Amiens.'

Conversations restarted as knights discussed the merits of the tournament site at Corbie. Apparently it was smaller.

Richard locked eyes with the monk.

Brother Geoffrey looked back at him, mostly with annoyance.

Richard shrugged and mumbled under his breath. 'There you are, monk, you've got what you wanted, we're all going to Corbie.'

WOLVES AT THE DOOR

Lagny Abbey wasn't the only one to have suffered damage from fire. Flames had destroyed Corbie's abbey a generation ago, but the monastic complex the Young King took up residence in had been rebuilt on a grander scale. How Brian knew all this, having never set foot out of Ireland until recently, Richard didn't ask. The Irish monk spent most of the ride north from Lagny telling Richard all about the famous Corbie scriptorium, and speculating on which famous works he might find within its hallowed walls.

Richard hadn't seen the monk since they had arrived and laid their possessions out along the walls of the abbey's refectory. The monks who would normally eat their meals there grumbled and cast angry looks at the knights as they trudged off to their dormitories to eat there instead.

The Young King would sleep alongside his knights in the refectory, and a servant busied himself checking his master's mail shirt before wrapping it up in two layers of oxhide. Richard watched him as the Young King finished speaking to Count Robert.

'You asked to see me?' Richard said to catch the Young King's attention.

'Ah, yes,' the Young King sat on the abbot's own chair in the cold chamber. There was no fire or hearth, only a dark long room that almost seemed to have been built around the long, thin wooden table that was its centrepiece.

A small mouse ran along the edge of the room, scuttling from one set of bedding to the next. The black dog gave chase in a flurry of claws on stone.

'I want to know if Guy of Lusignan is at this tournament,' the Young King said, 'I am concerned that he never came to request your ransom, and wish to know if I need to worry about the Marshal's lust for revenge.'

Richard scuffed the stone floor with his shoe, a shoe that had very thin soles now.

'I know you don't want to,' the Young King said, 'but you know what he looks like, and you know Count Philip, which gives you a place in the Without village to go to.'

'You want me to visit the Count and then look to see if Guy is there?' Richard asked. He'd been hoping for a good night's sleep. They had stayed for a week at Lagny, waiting for muscles to stop aching, bruises to fade, and cuts to seal up. Richard had wanted to sleep more than usual since the tournament, and he still didn't feel ready for the next one.

'Yes,' the Young King replied, 'you can be at Franvillers and back before midday. It will also give you a chance to see the tournament area.'

'Do I have to go on my own?' Richard asked. 'Is there anyone who knows the way?'

The Young King looked to his side, where Adam pulled a woollen hood over his angular head.

'As Adam is dressing for the cold, he can be your guide.'

Adam groaned. 'I'm dressing for in here. I hate abbeys, they only ever have one fire outside the kitchen.'

'The warming room is small and for the monks,' the Young King said, 'we will show them we can endure the cold just as gladly as they do.'

'Speak for yourself,' Adam said.

The young monarch grinned. 'I'm not asking you to walk there on your own feet. Stop complaining.'

Richard tried to make Bowman come with him, but the big man raised his eyebrows and ignored him. Richard hadn't asked Nicholas, his skill set didn't seem to match the job, and he didn't want to take Gerold, who had come down with a sickness and lay shivering in his blankets.

The black dog had tried to follow, but Richard had sent him back to Bowman on his way to saddle the black horse. Solis was too recognisable.

The early morning mist clung to the green rolling hills to the north of Corbie. The grey-shrouded horizon was impossible to see, and Richard could taste the moisture in the air. Adam led him between clumps of trees and hedges, along a track with two ruts dug by decades of ox-drawn carts. A ditch ran alongside the track, clogged with dirt and smelling stagnant.

Richard pulled his hood tighter around his face.

Adam chuckled. 'I don't know why I complained, it's actually warmer out here than in that abbey.'

They rode without mail, their cloaks and hoods keeping the wet air out. Adam had borrowed another knight's simpler clothing instead of his own, but Richard hadn't needed to do the same. His old tunic was sun-bleached, but not as badly as his cloak, which was torn and in one corner, moth-eaten.

The track climbed a long shallow hill that culminated in a prominent ridge that commanded all else in sight, at least as far as the mist allowed.

'This is the very middle of the tournament area,' Adam said, 'Corbie is in a bend in the River Somme, and the river is obviously the southern boundary. The plains here up to Franvillers are great riding.'

Richard nodded. The whiteness of chalk showed up through the various grasses on the hillside, and they soon reached a flatter plain with a small tower protruding from it.

Poplar trees lined the track, and through the mist, Richard noticed a small wooden tower coming into view.

'Franvillers is a small place,' Adam said, 'a squire was the lord the last time we were here. It's probably only worth a quarter of a knight's fee.'

'How can it be worth a quarter of a fee?' Richard asked. 'Do they send a mailed leg when their lord summons them?'

Adam cocked an eyebrow. 'You country boys, I can't tell if you're being serious or not. No, they don't send a quarter of a man, they just send money worth a quarter of the fee. King Henry mostly receives bags of silver from English lands when he calls on them now, he spends them on mercenaries. He'd rather do that anyway, which suits the English as only the greater men of the realm happily cross the narrow sea.'

Richard assumed that was partly because King Henry didn't trust his own lords all that much.

Franvillers made Yvetot look well developed. A collection of long fields stretched out from the village to the east, and to the west lay a large common area fenced off with hedges. A temporary village of small tents grew up to the south, interspersed with horse corrals and parked carts. The tournament goers and their assistants numbered several times more than the actual villagers, who had made themselves scarce. Banners drooped from poles across the campsite.

'Blue and white, isn't it?' Adam asked.

'Yes, but I don't see Guy's,' Richard said, 'although it's hard to tell with no wind.'

'We'll ride around a bit to be sure, then find the Count,' Adam said.

As they walked their horses from banner to banner, they did not spot the Lusignan colours, only glum men huddled around inadequate fires. Horses stamped their feet from boredom or cold and slept with their heads hanging down. Richard knew some of them would still be recovering from Lagny, just like their riders.

'This tournament will be smaller than Lagny,' Richard said.

Adam laughed. 'Lagny was the greatest tournament of all time,' he said, 'we might never see another like it.'

'It wasn't all that great,' Richard mumbled.

'Not for you,' Adam said, 'but they will sing about it for a hundred years, long after tournaments like this one have been forgotten.'

'I don't care as long as I'm paid,' Richard checked a blue and white banner, but it was quartered and not striped.

'The yellow banner with the black lion flies from the tower,' Adam said, 'we can warm up there and return to the abbey as late as possible.'

Franvillers's tower was three storeys tall and ringed with a wooden palisade that was more of a glorified fence. Scorch marks scarred parts of it, and the tower looked like a recent build. It had a well and a storehouse, but little else.

Count Philip's Flemish banner hung out from a top storey window horizontally. The lion was unfurled and stretched down towards the ground, the black beast on its side, as if attacking the earth.

Flemish tents dotted the local area in clusters, and they left their two horses by a pile of hay and went inside to find the Count.

Count Philip sat by the hearth in a hall that was even smaller than Yvetot's, a grimace on his face as he lost himself in the flames. His face changed when he saw Richard. 'Ah, someone interesting. What are you doing here?'

'We got cold in the abbey,' Adam said.

The Count smiled. 'This might be a demeaning hall for me, but at least it has a hearth,' he said, 'and why should we be cold? We're not monks, are we?'

Adam shook his head. 'I don't see the point of being cold when the Lord provides us with forests to burn.'

The Count motioned at a servant who stood waiting. 'Find these men something to drink.'

'Thank you for intervening at Lagny,' Richard said, 'when Guy crossed the river after us.'

Philip snorted and threw an apple core into the fire. 'He shamed me, insulted me, and threatened me,' the Count said, 'and that does not come without consequences. I am a count.'

'Either way,' Richard said, 'our horses were not fresh enough to outrun them, so we owe you.'

'You owe me nothing,' the Count's lips pressed together, 'I was in that barn.'

No one spoke as the hearth crackled and a log popped. The servant presented wine, which Adam downed. 'The monks have hidden their good drink,' he grinned.

'Of course,' the Fleming said, 'but why are you really here? You could find wood to burn and wine to drink in Corbie if you wished it.'

Richard looked over at Adam, who shrugged back.

'The Young King wants to know if Guy is here,' Richard said, 'we don't know if he's travelled here or gone home.'

The Count sniffed loudly. 'He's not here. I have a man watching the track for him. I'm in this tower because I wouldn't be surprised if he came for me at night to knife me in my sleep.'

Richard would not be surprised either. 'Can we stay here for a while to see if he arrives?'

'You are my guests, and you are welcome as long as you wish,' Philip said, 'I'll be glad for the company. No one here is much in the mood for talk, this tournament is happening too soon after Lagny, and the weather has dampened everything, including our spirits.'

Richard and Adam took their chance and sat down in the hall that was otherwise devoid of people.

'What is being said about me in your court?' Count Philip asked.

Adam took his cloak off and put it on the bench next to him. 'There is little love to be found for the Lusignans anywhere, everyone approves of your actions, wrong team or not.'

'Not all of them, I'm sure,' the Count pushed some of his long straggly hair out of his face.

'No one blames you for the massacre,' Richard said, 'and almost no one is talking about it. The Scottish company was furious, but they haven't come to Corbie.'

'As long as no one is speaking ill of me,' the Count said.

Richard shook his head.

'They are all speaking about the Marshal and how he drove Guy back in single combat,' Adam said, 'the man is a leech.'

Count Philip jumped out of his chair. 'What do you mean? I drove Guy back, the Marshal had nothing to do with it.'

'We know,' Richard said, 'it's that knight who follows him around that's spreading the story.'

'The Marshal allows it,' Adam brushed some dust off the table.

The Count kicked at some straw that covered the floorboards. 'Why did I even bother?'

A man wearing a thick woollen cloak burst into the hall. His face was red from the cold. 'My lord,' he said, 'a company is approaching.'

'I told you to only report the Lusignans,' Count Philip said.

The lookout had mud over his leather shoes and left dark brown footprints behind him. He nodded. 'The blue and white banner, my lord, horizontal stripes,' he said.

The Count kicked another clump of straw, but it was hiding droppings from the tower's cat and he swore as it got stuck in the mail that covered his toes. 'Now I have to sleep in my mail and with half my men on guard,' he shouted.

'And we have to go back to the cold abbey,' Richard said.

'I'm not in any rush,' Adam said.

Richard would have been far happier if Guy wasn't at Corbie. 'What if he comes into the tower?'

'What if he does?' the Count said. 'I'll invite him in and offer him some wine with one hand while I hold my dagger ready in the other.'

'We probably shouldn't be here if that happens,' Richard said.

'Scared of Guy?' Adam laughed.

Richard looked the knight in the eyes. 'Yes. And you should be too.'

The coldness of Richard's reply stopped Adam's laugh in its tracks.

The lookout took his chance to speak again. 'My lord, they arrived with another company, one I do not know.'

'What colours?'

'Red and yellow.'

'What pattern?' Richard asked, his heart quickening.

'Small squares,' the lookout replied.

Adam frowned. 'It's strange for Count Robert of Meulan to be riding with Guy,' he said, 'he's in our company.'

Richard put his head in his hands.

'Who else has those colours?' the Flemish Count asked. 'No one from the Low Countries does.'

Richard kept his face hidden behind his fingers. The Count noticed his missing finger and stared at the stump.

'I lost that to pay for the Marshal's ransom from Guy,' Richard looked up.

'That's ironic,' Adam grinned, 'I wouldn't lose a hair off my head for him, let alone a finger.'

'It's not important,' Richard said, 'but I think the new company is the Martels.'

Count Philip folded his arms. 'Geoffrey Martel once broke a trade agreement with me over wool imports. He left me with a shipload of spoiled fleeces and never refunded me. But he is English, what is he doing coming to Franvillers? He should be in Corbie.'

'It is widely known that he is King Henry's man,' Adam said, 'presumably he therefore wishes to ride against his crowned son.'

'I want to leave,' Richard said, 'but I need to know if it's really the Martels.'

'Why do you care?' the Count asked.

'I have unfinished business with them,' Richard said, 'or they do with me. When we last met, we didn't exactly part on good terms. I think I stole one of their dogs.'

'Go then,' Count Philip said, 'I'll fortify myself in this tower and see you when the tournament begins.'

Adam got to his feet with a groan and flung his cloak around his shoulders. The waft of air made the fire twist and turn.

Richard led the way out of the tower. He felt sick, sick from the uncertainty of not knowing if Eustace was here. He needed to know.

Richard almost ran down and out of the tower and back into the damp air. The sun hinted at its presence above, a yellow disc shining through the haze, but so dimly it was safe to look at.

Richard reached the road and looked down it. Riders with banners above them were entering the tent village, and soon they'd reach the wooden one.

Adam caught up. 'So, do you want to spy on them or get out of here?' he asked.

'I need to know if it's them,' Richard pointed at the nearest farmer's house, 'let's hide in there.'

Richard rushed over to the single storey wooden house with a flaking cob wall of soil, water, and straw. He pushed the door open and went inside.

It was dark, but there was a fire. Six knights sat around it, a few more lay in beds along the walls.

'Where are the farmers?' Richard asked.

'Out,' a knight replied with a heavy accent that Richard assumed was some sort of Flemish.

'They've kicked the farmers out?' Richard asked.

Adam grinned. 'Knights are more important, of course they have,' he said.

'Fine,' Richard half closed the door behind them, but left enough open that he could see out.

The Flemish knights motioned to shut the door, but Adam swore at them and they didn't bother to continue their complaint.

Richard heard the horses of the new arrivals long before he saw them. He had a good view of the gateway, which Count Philip's men had shut behind them, and four horsemen appeared and stood in front of it.

One was Guy, and another bore his blue and white banner.

They shouted inside, but no one opened the gate for them. Guy ordered some Lusignan knights to dismount and break in.

'They can't just break in,' Richard whispered, 'who is the lord here?'

'No one who cares much about it. The lord probably doesn't know he owns it,' Adam replied. He went to sit by the fire.

Richard swore. Eustace Martel strode into view, in his mail, and inspected the gate. There was a small hatch to communicate to those inside, and his arm shot through the hole and grabbed something.

'Open the gate or I'll rip your clothes apart and keep going until there's nothing left,' he shouted.

He threw the guard away and left the hatch.

Guy shared a joke with Eustace.

'Those two should hate each other,' Richard said, 'Eustace stole the ransom meant for Guy, and then Guy stole Eustace's castle. What are they doing laughing together?'

Adam groaned. 'Who cares?' he mumbled.

Soon after, the gates opened and Count Philip appeared fully armed and with half a dozen of his men at his back.

'Who are you?' Eustace asked.

Guy scowled as Philip answered.

'We need this tower for our lodgings,' Eustace said.

'I've already taken it,' Count Philip said, 'you can stay in the village if you want, or even better, in some tents far away from me.'

Richard shut the door even further.

'I'm not staying in some rotting hovel,' Eustace said, 'do you know who I am?'

'Not a count,' Philip snorted, 'so leave me and my tower in peace.'

Eustace walked up to the Count and looked down at him. The two largest of the Flemings together would still not have been as wide as the Martel knight.

'I have enough men to lay siege to this tower,' Eustace said, 'hand it over now and none of your men need to get hurt.'

'This is absurd,' the Count replied, 'this is a tournament, not a war.'

'I don't care what it is,' Eustace said.

Geoffrey Martel entered Richard's view and put a hand on his son. 'Speak to the Count with respect, he is a friend to our King. You do not threaten our friends, only our enemies, and Count Philip is not one of them.'

'Why have you brought an army to a tournament?' the Count asked.

Geoffrey, in dazzling civilian clothing, clasped his hands behind his back. 'We have a hundred crossbowmen because we are in the service of our king. But that is none of your concern. Tell me, where is the monk?'

'In Corbie,' Count Philip replied, 'and do not think to bully me with your vulgar show of force.'

'It is no show,' Geoffrey said, 'and it is not aimed at you. My tent is grander than this tower anyway, so I will leave you alone. What Eustace chooses to do with his infantry, however, is up to him.'

Richard could only see his back, but he knew Eustace grinned.

Geoffrey left the gateway with Guy.

Eustace gave them a moment to leave then turned to the Count. 'I'm laying siege. My tent is also better than this tower, but I don't like being disrespected.'

'Disrespect? You disrespect me,' Count Philip backed up and turned to his men. 'Bar the gate.'

The gate slammed shut in Eustace's face, but the Martel knight laughed and ordered his men to loose crossbow bolts at any man they saw through a tower window.

A party of Martel spearmen set up by the gate, and as quickly as that, a private war had started in Franvillers.

The Flemings in the hovel with them spoke between each other, but seemed to resign themselves to sitting by their fire instead of helping their lord.

Richard waited for the sound of the column's hooves to go back south before opening the door.

'Can we go back to the Young King now?' Adam asked.

Richard shook his head. 'I need to know what Guy and Eustace are doing together.'

'Why?' Adam asked. 'Haven't we done enough here?'

'Guy was after the Young King at Lagny,' Richard replied, 'I'm sure he sought to kill him. If he is working with Eustace, then they might now have enough knights to manage it.'

Adam coughed. 'Fine, I suppose I've got nothing better to do.'

Richard left the hovel and the Martel spearmen swiftly lowered their spears at him.

Richard held his hands up. 'I'm not a Fleming,' he said, 'and we're leaving.'

The spearmen cautiously relaxed, and Richard noticed two dozen crossbowmen fanning out around the palisade. The Flemings inside the farmer's hovels still declined the opportunity to challenge the Martels.

The main part of the Lusignan and Martel companies rode back out to the edge of the tent village, which their rumbling carts had only just reached.

'We need to get amongst them,' Richard said.

Adam laughed as they walked away from the spearmen. 'Isn't that a dangerous idea?'

Richard picked his way through canvas shelters, tents, and fires until he found a cluster of parked carts. Most had sheets covering their loads, and out of one protruded a full load of saplings that had been cut into tent poles.

'This will do,' Richard said.

'You want to steal a cart?' Adam said.

'No,' Richard said, 'just borrow it.'

Adam looked around the sea of tents and depressed men. All were hooded and huddled, and none paid them any attention. 'We don't have a draught animal,' Adam said.

Richard grinned. 'If we act like we belong, no one will pay us a second glance,' he said, 'the oxen are corralled over there, let's just take one and harness it up.'

Adam chuckled. 'You're mad. Mad enough for it to work.'

Richard hadn't handled an ox before, but he retrieved one from their corral and treated it like a horse. The lumbering beast was twice as wide as Solis, white and mustard coloured, and was almost as tall as Richard's chest.

Richard harnessed it badly, but it was functional enough to drive the cart down the track. He halted in the middle of the mixed company as they unloaded sheets of canvas from their own carts.

'You sell the poles,' Richard said to his companion, 'and I'll walk around.'

'You want me to play a merchant?' Adam asked.

Richard nodded.

'Only if you promise not to tell anyone, especially Sir Roger. He'd never let me hear the end of it.'

Richard nodded with a grin, but when he next saw de Cailly, he knew the first thing he'd do was tell him all about it.

Richard left de Cailly's knight with a bundle of poles in his arms. The two companies seemed to be camping amongst each other, which was a worrying sign of cooperation. With the horde of infantry, it felt more like a campaign camp than a tournament one. He followed the two banners into the heart of the burgeoning campsite, one that would house hundreds of men. But there was at least one woman too, and Richard recognised her blue dress and the silver circlet in her hair.

Alice sat on her horse next to Guy, who dismounted and pointed something out to one of his men. What was Alice doing there? Richard remembered that the first time he'd seen her at Lagny, she'd been on Guy's arm, but he'd assumed that was just chance. This meant it wasn't, and he felt worry and sadness that he had no reason to feel.

Geoffrey Martel barked orders for where his grand tent should be pitched, and four carts full of canvas and long staves of wood were drawn up. An army of servants and squires laid out piles of wooden pegs. Richard could see that the canvas had gold woven or painted onto it, and marvelled at how large it would be. With his hood still up, he wandered amidst the bustling company with his ears straining.

'I detest tournaments,' Geoffrey told Guy.

The Lusignan nodded. 'Lagny was my first, and I failed to see what the excitement was about.'

'Only because you lost all your captives like some wet-behind-the-ears junior knight,' Geoffrey scoffed.

Anger flashed in Guy's eyes, but to Richard's surprise, he did nothing about it.

'Now we are here,' Geoffrey continued, 'you are less likely to fail.'

'I had better not,' the Lusignan said, 'I am trading something of great value to you for this.'

'The Pinnacle was our castle to begin with,' Geoffrey snarled, 'it is only my generosity that allows you to trade it at all. I had half a mind to take it back by force just to make a point.'

Guy looked up at Alice, who shrugged back. 'We have a deal,' he said, 'don't try to intimidate me.'

Geoffrey snorted at him. 'My very existence should intimidate you. Once the Young King has fallen, our business will be concluded. If we meet after that, I will put you down, too.'

Richard bumped into a servant who dropped a sheet of canvas into the mud.

Geoffrey whirled around. 'Pick that up right now, and clean that filth off before you dare erect my tent. Lick the mud off if you have to, useless swine.'

The servant shot Richard a harsh look but scurried away from his master.

Richard walked the other way and hoped no one had looked too closely at him. He walked a slow circle around Guy and Geoffrey, staying in earshot.

'Trust me,' the Lusignan said, 'I have no wish to stay this far north, I want nothing more than distance between myself and the Old King.'

'The Old King is your true king,' Geoffrey said, 'and once the young one is dealt with we can go back to standing on opposing sides. You reek of treason.'

Guy spat onto the ground. 'All the Angevins can rot,' he said.

The Martel patriarch drew a dagger and had it held under Guy's chin before the Lusignan knew what had happened.

'Let him go,' Alice shouted.

Geoffrey smiled in Guy's face. 'Do not forget your place. Who are you, anyway, are you a king? No, are you even a duke? No. Not a count either, and who here has the larger force?'

It was clear that the Martels had more infantry alone than Guy had knights.

Geoffrey pushed Guy away and sheathed his dagger. 'I am the lion here, you are the bastard cub.'

The Lusignan rubbed his neck, a scowl etched on his face.

The senior Martel turned his back on him, which Richard thought was brave, and strode off to shout at those dealing with his tent.

Guy turned to Alice, looked up at her, and they exchanged words Richard couldn't hear. He'd heard enough though, the Martels and Lusignans were working together, and the Young king was their target. He took one last look at Alice, felt jealous of Guy, then carried his bundle of poles back towards the cart.

Which was now empty.

Adam stood grinning next to it. 'Give me those poles,' he said, 'I've got buyers for them.'

Richard handed the damp wood over, and Adam swapped them with a squire for a couple of dark-coloured coins. He slipped them into a pouch inside his tunic.

'I thought being a merchant was a terrible thing,' Richard said.

Adam grabbed the pouch through his tunic. 'But look at all this. Anyway, what did you find out?'

'They've joined forces,' Richard told him, 'and they want the Young King to fall, whatever that means.'

'Fall as in kill him, or capture him?' Adam asked. 'His capture would be an event for the ages, but it wouldn't exactly be treason. This is a tournament after all.'

Richard remembered how they'd spoken to each other. 'I don't think they're after money. I think they want to kill the Young King, and probably everyone near him.'

'I wouldn't mind if the peacock got poached,' Adam said, 'it would make the court much simpler.'

'He's not that bad,' Richard said.

'Not that bad?' Adam said. 'You heard the tall tales his lap dog has been spinning. And you lost a finger for him. From what I've heard, he has never even thanked you.'

Adam was right. Richard sighed and felt the frigid chill of water around his toes. Water soaked through the seam between his soles and the rest of his shoes, and Richard knew he'd now have cold feet until he could hang his shoes up by the fire in the abbey's warming room.

'What more would you lose for the peacock?' Adam asked in a serious tone.

Richard flexed his four fingers. 'Not any more of those,' he grinned.

Adam nodded, but he didn't smile.

Richard assumed Adam was having a joke. 'As long as you aren't planning on killing him,' he kept his grin wide.

Adam's face didn't change. 'No, I'm not planning on killing him,' he said, 'but I think we should go now.'

Richard turned the ox around and drove the cart back to where they'd found it.

'How much did we make?' Richard asked.

'Four shillings,' Adam replied.

'Not bad,' Richard said, 'but we probably should leave it on the cart for whoever owned the poles.'

Adam frowned. 'But I did all the work.'

'Did you cut the poles?' Richard asked.

Adam sighed. 'Fine, I'll leave it here.' The knight counted out some coins and left them under the cart's canvas. Richard was quite sure he only left two shillings, but didn't see the point in complaining about it.

They retrieved their horses and Richard was glad to get up off the ground. His shoes had dark patches where the water had soaked in, and his toes might as well have been touching ice, so cold were they.

The ride back south didn't help his discomfort. With his toes unmoving in the stirrups, Richard only felt the chill spread back along his feet and up his ankles.

Adam rode in silence as the mist lifted, and the land appeared greener in the haze as the sunlight grew in intensity.

The sun reached its peak as they spotted the tower of the abbey below them in the bend in the Somme.

Richard went straight to the warming room, a small chamber with a hearth, and left his shoes under it. Once he warmed his toes a little by holding them up to the fiery flames, he made his way barefoot to the refectory.

The Young King frowned when he saw him. 'Adam has told me,' he said.

Richard's feet cooled already on the bare stone floor, and the toe that had ached in Ireland throbbed again.

'We should leave,' Count Robert said, 'we can find an excuse and let their unholy alliance fall apart without a target.'

The Young King looked at the Count with a sour expression. 'We shall not flee with our tail between our legs just because we face a larger enemy. Maybe we could send to Amiens for their militia, however. Their numbers could maintain order. They love me there.'

The Count nodded and ran his fingers through his curly brown hair. 'Whatever you wish.'

'I don't wish to be seen as a coward,' the Young King said.

Richard found it surprising that the Marshal was not there. 'Did Adam tell you they want to kill you?' he asked.

The Young King shook his head. 'He said fall, they want me to fall. It doesn't mean they plot treason. It just means they seek a king's ransom.'

'You know what Guy did in the woods,' Richard said, 'he hates your father and I think he said at Lagny he would kill you.'

'It changes nothing,' the Young King smiled, 'we will stay here and fight in the tournament. We may add a few more men from Amiens to garrison the list and the town, which is normal practice, but nothing else changes.'

'Just make sure the Marshal doesn't slip his leash and run off after glory again,' Adam said.

The Young King said nothing in reply.

'I think we should take extra precautions,' Count Robert said.

'Let the matter lie,' the Young King replied, 'my father drives his subjects away by his paranoia. I will not make the same mistake. I will act as though all are loyal until they act as if they are not. Words do not hurt me.'

'They can,' Count Robert muttered.

The Young King let out a deep breath. 'If they capture me, so be it. If they try to kill me, it shall not go unanswered. My father will hang both of them like common criminals.'

'Geoffrey Martel thinks he's doing your father's work,' Richard said.

'My father doesn't want to kill me, just keep me quiet,' the Young King said.

'My lord,' Gerold croaked from his sickbed.

Everyone turned to the other side of the narrow chamber to where the older knight lay under every blanket he'd been able to find.

'Yes?' the Young King replied.

'I had the displeasure of the Martel's company for years,' Gerold said. His face was pale, although it was hard to tell in the glow from the candles that lined the long table. 'Geoffrey thinks himself loyal to King Henry, but thinks he knows better how to serve the King than the King himself.'

'Arrogance,' Adam sneered.

Gerold shivered. 'Geoffrey almost went to kill the Archbishop for the King. He went as far as to ask Richard's uncle to gather some men together for it.'

'But someone beat them to it,' the Young King frowned, 'when I was in Becket's household I always found him kind and generous, although I was so young I barely remember it now.'

Richard nodded and remembered the book the martyred archbishop had gifted him.

'Be that as it may,' the Young King said, 'it still changes nothing for me. I will stand my ground and face them, whether or not they mean me harm.'

'Did you tell him about Count Philip?' Richard asked Adam.

The Norman shook his head.

'Eustace has surrounded the tower in Franvillers with infantry and wants to force the Count out.'

'What?' the Young King jumped up from his chair. 'That is an outrage. What is the cause of that?'

'Eustace wants to sleep in the tower,' Richard said, 'and the Count won't move out.'

'Quite rightly,' the Young King said, 'I've half a mind to ride out and relieve him.'

'The Martels and Lusignans outnumber us,' Richard said, 'and they have many spearmen. And crossbows.'

'The Marshal would agree to it,' the Young King dropped back into his chair and folded his arms.

Adam grimaced. 'And the Marshal would get you killed.'

The news Richard had brought into the refectory dampened the mood that afternoon. There was no party, instead the knights spent their time resting or rolling dice on the table.

Servants brought in drinks and set up their carving table in the gloomy chamber in silence.

Richard asked around where Otto the German had gone, but no one knew, so he settled down with Bowman and the black dog, who was almost invisible in the refectory, so dark was his coat.

Adam sat opposite Bowman, and they rolled a pair of dice on the candle-lit table.

A portly monk with a golden shawl draped around his neck entered the refectory and approached the Young King, who dozed in his chair.

The Young King sensed his presence and woke up. 'Abbot Hugh,' he said, 'how can I be of service?'

The abbot's belly swung underneath his robe as he faced the Young King. The churchman's face was pink, but pink in a way that looked like it was always that colour.

'Move some of your knights out of here,' he said, 'I have nowhere to sleep and my monks are packed together in their dormitory now that Baldwin of Hainault has moved in there with his band of ruffians.'

'Cousin Baldwin is here?' the Young King's face lit up.

'I don't care that he's your cousin,' Abbot Hugh said, 'he's filled up my dormitory and now I've got monks sleeping in the kitchen. It is a disgrace.'

'Count Philip's his cousin, too,' Adam rolled two sixes and Bowman groaned.

'You Angevins are all the same to me,' Abbot Hugh cried.

'Count Baldwin is not an Angevin,' the Young King replied.

The Abbot grabbed his own grey hair. 'I don't care. I want somewhere to sleep, and then I want you all gone.'

'Sleep here if you wish,' the Young King waved his hand to show the refectory.

'Here?' the Abbot strained himself. 'You offer me a spot to sleep in my own abbey? Your generosity really is as bountiful as they say. Next you'll be allowing me to remain in my own clothes.'

The Young King shook his head. 'There is no need for hysterics, go and sleep wherever you like, and we'll be out of your abbey in a day or two.'

'Is he lying?' Richard whispered to Bowman.

'Aye,' the blonde man rolled two ones and sighed.

The abbot stormed off with fists and teeth clenched. 'I'll sleep in the warming room, then, that's the only place you vermin haven't touched.'

Richard's cold toes reminded him of his shoes and where they were.

The abbot returned from the warming room as quickly as he'd stormed away. He held Richard's damp shoes up. 'Whose are these?'

Richard thought about not answering, but that risked him losing his only pair of shoes that were not the leather soles sewn into his mail leg armour. 'Mine,' he raised his hand.

The abbot threw them across the refectory at Richard, except that his aim was so bad they landed on the sleeping Nicholas instead.

Who woke up and swore at the abbot.

'You dare blaspheme in a holy place?'

'Enough, abbot,' the Young King said, 'you did throw some soggy shoes at him. Please come back later in the evening and I will speak to you over food.'

Servants entered with a silver platter of venison to be carved on their little table.

'You can't eat meat today,' Abbot Hugh watched them and their roasted cargo drift by. He licked his lips.

'Robert,' the Young King gestured to the Count, 'please take the abbot to the warming room and help him settle in.'

Count Robert nodded, but his face showed his distaste. He grabbed the abbot and pulled him out of the refectory.

The evening's food and festivities were subdued. Servants served, a musician played, and the abbot returned once to complain about their noise.

As the night drew near its end, Nicholas, who had been quiet, grabbed his wolf-pelt from his bed. 'Richard, I am going to equal things with the abbot.'

'What do you mean, equal things?' Richard asked.

Bowman had given up on dice and turned to drink instead. 'Whatever he's about to say or do, young lord, stay out of it.'

'I'm not asking for help,' the Martel knight said, 'I just thought you'd like to watch.'

Richard was bored, so he decided he did want to watch.

Nicholas left the refectory, and they walked a short way through the murky corridor to the warming room. The chamber was square and small, but a fire lit the back wall and a chimney took the smoke away. The warmth lured Richard in. The abbot slept on his back in front of the fire where he snored deeply.

'You won't kill him, will you?' Richard asked.

'That would be a bit much,' Nicholas said, 'who do you think I am?'

'The man who smashed a king's face in with a golden cross,' Richard replied.

Nicholas nodded. 'I suppose that's fair.' He grinned and tiptoed into the warming room.

The fire roared away but Richard hovered near the doorway, unsure he wanted to be even this close to whatever Nicholas planned.

The Martel knight, pelt over his shoulders and the head of the beast over his, stood over the abbot and waved at Richard. 'Light a stick in the fire, it'll be better if there are flames reflecting off me.'

'You're going to stop his heart,' Richard tiptoed to the fire anyway. He stuck a dried piece of long kindling into the hearth and pulled it away once it had caught.

'This is a bad idea,' he whispered.

The Martel knight grinned. 'Nothing fun is ever a good idea,' he put a leg either side of the abbot and stooped over his pink face. 'Hold the torch below me so the fire shines on the wolf.'

Richard crouched down and waved the torch next to Abbot Hugh's head. The yellow glow blazed back in the wolf's empty eyes.

The heat also cooked the churchman's cheek. He awoke to a hellish vision. He could feel the very fires of hell on his face. Above him, with flame casting reds and oranges onto the wall behind, loomed a creature of the devil. A black mass of fur with pointed ears and evil eyes. There was fire inside them, too, bright yellow eyes straight from the depths of hell. This, Abbot Hugh knew in his bones, was the end of times, the rapture. Finally, the world was to end.

Then the wolf burst into laughter, the fire by his cheek vanished, and he was lying in his warming room with his heart racing so fast it was surely about to burst.

Nicholas tilted the wolf's head back and straightened up. 'The book you like to read from says an eye for an eye,' he said, 'and I think this is exactly equal to your throwing of some shoes at me.'

The abbot clutched his chest.

Richard threw the stick of kindling into the fire. 'If he dies,' he said, 'we're going to Hell, you know that, don't you?'

Nicholas shrugged. 'At least it would be warmer than here.'

Abbot Hugh calmed his breathing and furious eyes looked up at Nicholas. 'Throwing shoes is not the same as making me think I was about to be torn limb from limb by a monster.'

'The shoes were wet,' the Martel knight replied.

Richard laughed. A laugh that caught him unawares, but the Abbot shot his angry eyes at him. 'I was aiming the shoes at you, why do you boys torment me?'

'We've just explained that,' Nicholas said.

The Abbot rolled onto his side and tried to push himself up. 'You'll be punished for this, I'm going to have grave words with your lord.'

'I don't think he'll do much about it,' Nicholas yawned.

The Abbot's face grew a darker shade of pink. 'Then forget that prancing youth. I excommunicate you.'

'You can't do that,' Richard said, 'can you?'

'I just have,' the Abbot glared back.

'But it is such a big thing,' Richard said, 'surely casting us out of our religion must take more than shouting some angry words.'

Abbot Hugh rose to his feet and pointed a bony finger at Richard. 'Your soul is done. No sacrament or death-rites for you.'

Richard couldn't believe it. This was worse than dying. 'Surely you have to say something in Latin?' he asked. 'Or at least write something down.'

'Shouldn't someone have to witness it?' Nicholas asked. 'Like a charter?'

'The Lord is my witness,' the Abbot hissed, 'he sees all.'

'But no one can ask him to vouch for you, can they?' Nicholas asked.

Richard would have laughed at that, but he'd just been cast out of the church, which was no laughing matter.

'You should really find a witness,' Nicholas said.

The Abbot howled with pent up rage. 'I lay a curse down on you.'

'Isn't that blasphemy?' Nicholas asked.

'I think only pagans can do curses,' Richard nodded.

'You will both die here,' Abbot Hugh raised his voice, 'upon all that is holy, the church will kill you both.'

Nicholas sniffed. 'I'm done, Richard, we can go back now.'

The Abbot's mouth gaped open. He lunged at Nicholas with clawed hands.

The Martel knight unthinkingly batted him away, but the holy man tripped. His face hit the seasoned log pile and his neck jerked back as he crumpled to the floor.

Richard stared wide-eyed. 'What did you do? This is like King Dermot all over again.'

Nicholas shrugged. 'He attacked me.'

'Is he dead?' Richard asked.

The Martel knight prodded the Abbot with his foot.

The Abbot groaned.

'Oh, thank God,' Richard said.

'I don't think you're allowed to say that anymore,' Nicholas said.

He was probably right, but Richard wasn't sure about anything now.

Abbot Hugh rolled over and felt his mouth. A finger came up red. 'I've lost a tooth,' he whispered.

'That's what happens when you attack innocent people,' Nicholas said.

'I think we should go,' Richard said. He left the warming room as quickly as he could and returned to the refectory. Luckily Nicholas did the same before he could do any more damage.

Bowman looked up from the table. 'So, how did it go?'

Richard sat down beside him. 'You might have been right,' he said.

'I told you, young lord, but you never listen.'

'This time I should have,' Richard said, 'I think I've just been excommunicated.'

Bowman spat out some of the wine he'd drunk. Then he laughed. 'Never boring,' he shook his head.

'I don't know what it means,' Richard put his head on the table.

'Not much,' Bowman replied, 'although I know you care about all that. Who cares what some louse-ridden monk says? I assume it was the Abbot?'

Richard groaned. 'Nicholas knocked his tooth out.'

Bowman almost choked on some half-swallowed wine. 'I told you he's trouble, send him back to his family before he gets you killed.'

Nicholas wandered in and sat at the long table. Candlelight from a dozen candles bathed him in a warm glow. 'Who is going to get who killed?' he asked.

Bowman raised his eyebrows. 'Are you really asking or are you just stupid?'

Nicholas threw the unused dice at his half-brother.

Bowman parried them but sprung to his feet. 'What is wrong with you?'

'Me?' Nicholas replied. 'You're the one with the problems.'

'Did you get excommunicated, too?'

The Martel knight yawned again. 'I don't think it really matters,' he said, 'why would you care, anyway? You would be happy if I died.'

Bowman paused, even for him death was only sometimes a laughing matter.

'See,' Nicholas said, 'you had to think about it, and even then you couldn't deny it. Our mother would be ashamed of you.'

A vein on Bowman's forehead pulsed.

'He didn't mean it,' Richard said, 'neither of you meant any of it.'

Bowman got to his feet in silence and looked for the black dog. 'Come here, dog,' he shouted, 'we know when we're not wanted.'

The dog appeared from underneath the long table, its ears pricked.

Bowman stomped over to the door. 'Come on,' he said.

The dog whined and looked over at Richard.

'No?' Bowman said. 'After all I've done for you, you're choosing them? Judas.'

The dog shrank back underneath the table where there was no candlelight.

The blonde man whirled around and left.

'I think Judas would be a good name for him,' Richard grinned.

'The Abbot would be angry about that name,' Nicholas grinned back, 'so I like it.'

The Young King sat on his chair with his greater men around him deep in their own conversations. Their heads only turned briefly to see what Bowman shouted about before they lost interest.

Adam returned soon after Bowman's departure, his hand shepherding a young man into the refectory and towards the Young King. Richard was the only person who watched their entrance, but when the young man reached the Young King, he spoke to him in words Richard couldn't hear.

'What?' the Young King shouted. 'That cannot be true.'

'It sounds very plausible to me,' Adam said.

'It surely is slander,' Count Robert of Meulan said, 'the Marshal doesn't even know what a woman is.'

'Apparently he does,' Adam replied.

'That's enough,' the Young King shouted, waking up some in the rectory who had dozed off. 'Find the Marshal. Bring him to me now, and I don't care what he's doing or what excuses he comes up with.'

Adam bowed, a little too quickly for Richard's liking, and dashed out into the dim corridor.

'I'll have his head,' the Young King shouted to no one in particular.

'I beg you,' Count Robert said, 'see him in the morning when you have had time to calm down.'

'Calm down?' the Young King raged. 'They're talking about my wife. She is a queen.'

'These are unfounded allegations,' the Count replied, 'how well do you know this boy? He could be spreading rumours on someone else's behalf.'

'Nonsense,' the flame-haired monarch replied, 'he has been overstepping for months. That war-cry of his, my father would rip his tongue out for that.'

Count Robert nodded. 'The matter of his war-cry should be addressed, but that is very far away from what he is being accused of now. You should speak to the Queen first.'

Richard whispered to Nicholas. 'Do you know what they're talking about?'

The Martel knight shook his head. 'No, but I expect the Marshal is guilty. He thinks too much of himself.'

Richard rubbed the stub of his missing finger.

Nicholas watched. 'He's not worth that finger, let alone any more. Just keep quiet. We all know that if you try to help, you'll only make things worse.'

'You sound like your brother.'

'Half-brother. In which case, speak up for the peacock, see if I care,' Nicholas said.

Richard grinned. 'I'll see what he is being accused of first.' He approached the Young King, who Adam whispered to.

'What has the Marshal done?' Richard asked.

'It does not concern you,' the Young King said.

'Sit back down,' Adam's gaze almost pushed him away.

'I might be able to help,' Richard said, 'he'll talk to me, but he won't speak here in public. I know him. If he is innocent, he will think that mounting a defence is beneath him, and if he's guilty, he won't think whatever he's done is a crime. In his head he's perfect.'

Adam scoffed. 'Pride comes before a fall.'

'Yes,' the Young King pointed at the Norman, 'and there has been an abundance of pride from the Marshal recently. His lap dog's tall tales have grated me. It must stop.'

'But what is he accused of?' Richard asked.

Before the Young King could answer, the Marshal and Henry the Northerner entered the refectory.

'You asked for me?' the Marshal asked, his tone happy.

'You've been found out,' the Young King said with venom, 'your sinful dalliance with my Queen has been unearthed.'

Richard laughed, was that the charge? His friend would never even dream of such an act. Would he?

The Marshal did nothing but blink once. A long blink.

Henry jumped out from behind him. 'Who is making such wild accusations?'

'It hardly matters,' the Young King said.

'I think it rather does,' Count Robert said.

'I didn't ask you.'

The Count sighed. 'The function of a counsellor is to advise. My advice is to avoid haste. The Marshal is being accused by some boy who does not claim to have seen the act itself, merely heard about it from someone else. Caution would be wise.'

'Caution be damned,' the Young King pointed a finger that gleamed with a red-jewelled ring at his Marshal. 'Your war-cry is a cynical copy of mine, you steal that from me. Then your pet Englishman steals my victory and covers it with your name, and to finish the insult, you steal my Queen.'

The Marshal remained still as stone as the Young King's breath rushed past his unmoving face.

'I was just telling a story,' Henry shrank back behind his master, 'I meant no offence.'

'You caused it,' the Young King said.

'That story put Count Philip out, too,' Richard said.

'See,' the Young King's pointed finger swept around to Henry, 'your lies are not unnoticed.'

Henry winced, and his bottom lip trembled.

'Have you nothing to say for yourself?' the Young King asked the Marshal.

'I will not speak on the matter,' the knight replied, 'I am deeply offended that your trust in me is so much shallower than I had believed.'

The Young King gripped his chair tightly. 'All you have to do is deny it and tell me how ridiculous the accusation is, and I will believe you,' he said.

'I should not have to,' the Marshal replied, his expression still set. 'Loyalty works both ways.'

'Loyalty?' the Young king coughed on the word. 'You question my loyalty? Where would you be without me? A poor landless knight with a Tancarville shield.'

'I would still be your mother's knight,' the Marshal replied.

'Yes, yes, it all makes sense now,' the Young King's voice echoed off the black walls, 'you started with my mother and now you move to my wife. God help me if I ever have a daughter.'

The Marshal's lips didn't move, but they clenched together and his lungs heaved even though his body stood impassive.

'Your silence is a confession,' Adam said.

The Marshal glared at him. 'Who asked you?'

Adam stepped back with his hands up. 'I'm just saying what everyone knows to be true.'

'Enough, Adam,' Count Robert said, 'this matter is between them, stay out of it.'

Adam looked at the Marshal, a wry smile on his face.

'Adam is right, though, isn't he, Marshal?' the Young King stood up. 'Why will you not respond to the accusation? You are famous for never lying, which is another boast I might add, and if you never lie, then silence can only mean guilt. Answer me, damn you.'

'My lord,' the Marshal said slowly, 'I will not dignify the matter with a single word.'

'If you have taken my Queen, then you cannot stay here,' the Young King's face glowed red.

'If you believe this could be true, then I do not wish to stay,' the Marshal spun on his heels.

Henry ducked out of his way, then followed his master out of the chamber.

'Go then, find someone else who will tolerate you,' the Young King shouted.

'I will,' the Marshal replied as he strode down the corridor, 'the people of Amiens will appreciate me. They will not treat me like this.'

Richard let out a breath he'd been holding. Surely his friend would not abandon his lord?

Count Robert sighed and rubbed his forehead. He went to speak to the Young King but gave up.

Adam looked around the room, his grin still in place, and wandered back along to the table where he took a seat and poured a drink.

Richard didn't know what had just happened. What he did know was that Guy and Eustace had Count Philip penned up in a tower, and now the Marshal had left the Young King. The tournament was going to be deadly.

THE ABSENCE OF ENVY

Richard and Nicholas mounted their horses as the sun peeked over the abbey outbuildings to the east. Solis snorted clouds of steam into the brisk morning air as the two men arranged their cloaks around themselves and began their journey to Amiens to find the Marshal.

Lay brothers scurried around the abbey even at this early hour, already well into their daily tasks, but Richard paid them no mind. He had to find a way to bring their friend back to the Young King's company before the next day's tournament, or their hands might soon be stained with another king's blood. The task already seemed hard enough. Bowman had refused to help, instead trudging off to find Adam, muttering that the peacock deserved to face the hounds that hunted him. Gerold lay ill, his condition not improving, and Otto was still nowhere to be found, so the task fell to the two of them alone.

The black dog ran around the heels of their horses and tried to urinate on the leg of a monk who was busy lowering a bucket down into the well.

'Judas, no,' Richard shouted.

The monk spun around looking for Christ's betrayer, but saw nothing other than an intimidating dog and two strutting tourneyers on their frivolous horses.

Judas sauntered back over to Richard with his tongue out.

'Come on,' Richard said, 'we need to go. The Marshal could be anywhere in Amiens, the last thing we need is distractions.'

Nicholas yawned. 'I never seem to sleep enough anymore,' he said.

They rode out of the abbey gate and onto the road that ran west to Amiens. The grass and scrubland outside Corbie glistened with dew that twinkled when the weak sun's rays caught it. The air was still, but the mist was far lighter than when Richard had ridden north to Franvillers the day before.

From that direction, a rider galloped towards them.

Richard squinted as the figure grew more detailed.

'Oh no,' Nicholas said.

'Who is it?' Richard asked.

'A distraction,' the Martel knight said, 'let us ride on quickly. She'll never keep up, her horse is already lathered.'

'She?' Richard's heart skipped a beat.

Alice's ermine-lined cloak covered her body and draped part way down her chestnut gelding.

Judas bounded over and barked at her, his paws splayed out and his black hackles raised as he growled.

'It's alright,' Richard shouted and the dog's growl dropped to a low rumble.

Alice approached, and Judas lurked closely behind as if stalking prey.

'What are you doing here?' Nicholas asked.

'Franvillers is frightfully boring,' Alice replied, 'there are no women there and the men are all damp and dull.'

'So you thought you'd ride over to the other camp?' Nicholas asked. 'At this early hour?'

'Why not?' Richard asked his friend. 'I wouldn't want to be in their camp. Franvillers is even smaller than Yvetot.'

Alice cocked him a questioning look. 'When have you ever been to Franvillers?'

Richard licked his lips and looked at Nicholas. 'That's just what I've heard,' Richard said.

'I see,' she placed her horse next to Richard.

Solis sniffed the chestnut horse and went to nibble its nose.

'I would be glad of the company,' Richard told her.

Nicholas sighed deliberately loudly. 'She will not help us.'

'Why?' Alice asked. 'What are you doing?'

'Don't tell her,' the Martel knight said.

'It's fine,' Richard said, 'and we're just going to Amiens to find the Marshal.'

'Him?' Alice said with distaste. 'He is such a bore.'

'We need him to come back.'

'Don't tell her,' Nicholas said, and Judas barked at Alice again.

'Quiet,' Richard shouted, 'both of you. He's just having a tantrum and we need to bring him back, it's not a secret.'

He rode off down the trackway. The River Somme lay to the left far away at the end of some low-lying marshland. Trees lined the other side of the road.

'I'll ride with you,' Alice said, 'Amiens must have some civilised people and I have never been there before.'

Nicholas sulked behind them as the sun warmed their backs, and said nothing until trees flanked them on both sides and blocked it out. They tracked the course of the Somme until they reached the town of Amiens. Alice asked Richard to tell her the story of Eric and Enid, which he was pleased to, and he finished his summarised version just as they passed through the town walls.

Amiens remained quiet, for it was Sunday and all the trades that practised within its walls were prohibited from doing so on the holy day. Distant dog barks were the loudest sound, and each one drew a terse reply from Judas.

Nicholas broke his silence and rode up next to Richard. 'You know what she's doing, don't you?' he asked.

Alice laughed, a carefree laugh. 'I'm seeking entertainment,' she said, 'and Richard is providing it.'

Richard puffed his chest out and grinned. 'I didn't know I could tell stories.'

'You can't,' Nicholas said, 'you missed out one entire part and your attempt at speaking in different voices nearly made me sick. She wants something from you.'

Alice put her hand on her chest. 'Me? What could I want from him?'

Richard frowned. 'I have a lot to offer.'

'You're married,' Nicholas said, 'so you have nothing to offer.'

Alice smiled sweetly. 'Marriage is not so much of a barrier.'

'To what?' Nicholas asked loudly. 'Richard, get rid of her.'

Richard didn't want to. Alice looked at him with eyes that no one else ever had, certainly not his wife. 'She's harmless,' he said.

Alice raised her eyebrows. 'Your man is depressing me, can you dismiss him?'

'See,' Nicholas said, 'she's after you, don't let her. She isn't even that pretty.'

'Speak for yourself, you ugly halfwit,' Alice scowled, her tone changing in a heartbeat.

Richard looked at her with confusion. 'He's not a halfwit,' he said.

'Thanks,' the Martel knight said, 'so I'm just ugly?'

'You knights are all so prickly,' Alice said, 'and your man is jealous of me.'

Nicholas snorted. 'Long ago I might have cared for your looks, but I haven't felt that care for a while now,' his face almost looked sad.

'A broken man, then,' Alice sneered.

'Enough,' Richard weighed up his knight's words. 'Nicholas might be right, there is no good reason for you to come all this way. What are you really here for?'

Church bells rang out from around the town. Their clang sent a flock

205

of pigeons flying overhead.

Alice sighed. 'Guy wanted me to find you,' she said.

'Guy?' Richard felt a stab of worry. 'What does he want me with? How did he even know to find me in Corbie?'

'The Young King is in Corbie,' she shrugged, 'so you were in Corbie.'

'Tell me,' Richard said flatly.

'He wanted me to spend some time with you, he wishes to know what sort of man you are.'

'But why?'

'Go and ask him,' Alice said, 'but he also has a message for you.'

A man and woman approached on expensive horses and wearing expensive cloaks. Richard couldn't tell what furs lined them, so he couldn't tell if they were nobles or from the trades. The world was becoming a confusing place.

'What's the message?' Nicholas asked. 'You can deliver it and go back where you came from.'

'He awaits your ransom,' Alice said, 'and is angry that he has not yet heard from the Young King about it. Apparently the terms of your parole were that you cannot fight in a tournament until it is paid.'

Richard almost choked. 'He said nothing about that, he's making it up.'

Alice's eyes followed the richly dressed couple as they rode by. 'That's your business,' she said, 'but if I were you, I wouldn't tourney tomorrow. If Guy catches you and you haven't paid his ransom yet, I think he'll take more fingers from you.'

Richard tried to hide his missing finger.

'I have seen that,' Alice smiled, 'and I quite like it.'

'Richard,' Nicholas shouted, 'she is as subtle as an axe to the face. Can't you see?'

Richard could see, and plainly, but he couldn't help himself. 'She means no harm,' he said.

Judas growled at a townswoman who strayed too close.

'My brother had another message for you,' Alice said.

Richard slammed Solis to a halt. 'Wait. Brother?'

Alice laughed so hard it became a cackle. 'You didn't know?'

'I told you,' Nicholas nodded, 'you can't trust her, she's one of them.'

'Them?' Alice shot a sideways glance at the Martel knight. 'And I know who you are, bastard. You should be back at Franvillers with your family.'

Nicholas spat onto the ground. 'The only family I have is Richard,' he said.

Richard looked at his friend with suprise.

'Children,' Alice waved a dismissive hand out of her cloak.

Richard was stuck. Alice surely couldn't be trusted now. 'What was the other message?'

'I don't really understand it,' Alice said, 'he wants his executioner back. Apparently you stole him.'

Solis snorted and tried to snatch his reins down to drink from a brown puddle.

'I reclaimed him fairly,' Richard said, 'Guy is trying to manipulate me.'

'Obviously,' Nicholas said.

'You're not helping,' Richard said.

'You actually have an interest in me, don't you?' Alice smiled at him.

Richard's cheeks warmed. 'You are too forward with your words.'

'For God's sake,' Nicholas said.

'Mind your language,' Alice snapped.

'I think I'm allowed to say it now,' the Martel knight almost grinned.

Alice didn't understand, but Richard now felt conflicted and wanted to be left in peace. 'I've got something you can take back to your,' he shuddered, 'brother.'

Alice waited for him.

'Do you know your father's fate?' Richard asked.

'What do you know about that?' Alice asked. 'He is lost in the Holy Land.'

Richard nodded to himself. It was better that Guy still didn't know. 'Tell him to ask Geoffrey Martel about him.'

Alice frowned. 'What are you talking about? That uptight prude cannot know anything about our father.'

'Can't he?' Richard asked. 'You know he is a crusader?'

Alice froze. 'If he knows and hasn't told us,' her words trailed off.

Richard smiled. 'Just tell Guy.' He walked Solis off towards the centre of Amiens.

'I underestimated you,' Alice followed, 'I thought you were just a boy, but maybe you are smarter than you look.'

Richard shifted his fingers on his reins.

'I will tell this to my brother,' Alice said, 'but then I'm coming back. For you.'

Richard held his breath.

'His wife,' Nicholas said.

'I know,' Alice said, 'you keep telling me he's got a wife.'

'No,' the Martel knight said, 'his wife.'

Richard frowned and looked at his friend.

Nicholas groaned, then pointed to a raised horizontal wooden beam that was used as a tying up point for horses. 'No, Richard. Look, your wife.'

Richard stopped in his tracks because lashing her horse to the beam, the palfrey that had been her wedding gift, was Sophie.

Her delicate face turned nervous when Judas ran at her, his black paws brown with mud. She backed into her horse to get away from the advancing dog, but he didn't bark at her. He stood, his tailing wagging and his tongue hanging out, looking up at her with happy eyes.

'Sophie?' Richard asked.

The Lady of Yvetot looked up from the black dog and into her husband's face. 'Richard,' she gasped.

'What are you doing here?' he asked.

Sophie's face, for a moment elated, dropped. 'I was hoping for a nicer greeting,' she said.

'I'm sorry,' Richard said, 'I just wasn't expecting to see you here.'

'I received your letter,' Sophie said, 'and a herald with the news of the Corbie tournament passed through Yvetot on the way to Castle Tancarville, so I thought to find you at Corbie.'

'That's very clever,' Richard said.

'Don't sound so surprised,' his wife replied, 'but I needed to see you. I've just been inside the mayor's house, and I bumped into young William. His clothes are much finer now and he's so much bigger.'

'We're looking for the Marshal,' Richard said, 'you've saved us some trouble.'

'That's not why I came, though,' Sophie said, 'I have a year's worth of news from Yvetot for you, but I came to tell you I am glad you're alive and am not upset at your leaving.'

'You're not?'

Sophie shook her head, and the black dog sat down by her feet. She scratched its head. 'No,' Sophie said, 'I've spent a lot of time talking with Sarjeant and the Priest, and I've come to understand some things I didn't before. But who is that woman who rides next to you?'

Alice leant towards Richard and put an arm around him. Their legs touched and Richard wasn't sure if he wanted to be closer or to push her away.

'I am Richard's tournament companion,' Alice looked down at her rival.

'Companion?' Sophie's face whitened.

Richard shrugged off Alice's arm. 'She is nothing of the sort.'

'Oh, don't be like that,' Alice said, 'you aren't like that at night.'

'At night?' Sophie's face trembled. 'Richard?'

'I don't know what she's talking about,' he replied.

Nicholas moved closer to Sophie. 'This woman is a parasite, she's making it all up.'

'You would say that,' Sophie looked over at Richard. 'How could you? So close to home. In Ireland I could have forgiven you, but here?'

'I have done nothing,' Richard said, 'I barely know this woman.'

'Oh, Richard,' Alice said, 'you know me very well.'

Sophie's eyes filled, but it wasn't obvious how much was sadness and how much was rage. She snapped round to the tying post and released her reins. 'I should have never come. I should have stayed at home like a good wife and not tried to be kind.'

'Wait,' Richard said, 'don't go.'

'Don't go?' Sophie threw herself up into the saddle. 'Is that all you have to say to me? After lying with this young tart.'

'Who are you calling a tart?' Alice's tone sharpened.

'Spare me,' Sophie pulled her horse around, 'are you even old enough to be called a woman? Don't answer that.'

'Wait,' Richard cried.

'I'm going back to the mayor,' Sophie said, 'but don't think of coming to see me, or coming back to Yvetot. Don't you dare show your face.'

'But,' Richard groaned as his wife kicked her horse back up the road and deeper into Amiens.

Nicholas sat quietly on his horse beside Richard.

'Say nothing,' Richard said.

'I wasn't going to,' the Martel knight said. 'If you want sarcastic replies, you should have brought my half-brother.'

'Why did you do that?' Richard turned on Alice.

The Lusignan woman smiled. 'Now you can be mine.'

'Why would you want that?'

'Because my brother was worried enough about you to send me here,' Alice said, 'which means you're interesting.'

'That doesn't justify driving my wife away,' Richard said, 'what am I going to do now?'

'Find the peacock,' Nicholas said, 'which is what we came here for. I think the Lusignan should leave. The Marshal won't trust us if she's with us.'

'That's how you know the Marshal,' Richard said.

'Of course,' Alice said, 'and someone of sharp mind would have realised it long ago.'

'You should go back to Guy,' Richard said, 'remember to tell him about Geoffrey Martel.'

Nicholas coughed and cleared his throat.

Alice looked up to the heavens. 'Very well,' she said, 'but you will see me again.'

'I've been a fool,' Richard said as she turned her chestnut horse and left them.

Nicholas nodded. 'You have.'

Judas walked up and whined at Richard. 'Not you, too,' he said to the dog.

'Sophie went that way,' Nicholas pointed, 'so we just need to follow her and we'll find the Marshal.'

'If she's with the mayor, should I try to speak to her?' Richard asked.

Nicholas laughed. 'How should I know?'

Richard asked Solis to follow his wife, and they rode into the centre of Amiens to find the Marshal.

The mayor's house stood on the corner of a crossroads where the gutter had blocked up causing a foul brown stream to trickle across the street. Solis sniffed it and at first refused to cross, but he followed Judas when the dog jumped it.

The four-storey house had its lowest levels made from fine stone with arched windows, and a set of overhanging upper storeys made from wood. They tied their horses to a series of iron tie rings set into a wall behind the house. Other horses were there, including Sophie's, and some that looked like tournament horses.

A middle-aged member of the town militia stood guard at the doorway, dressed in a stained padded jacket and wearing an iron helmet. He leant on his spear. The guard glanced at the spurs on Richard's feet, and the wolf-pelt on Nicholas's back, and stepped aside.

The mayor's house had a roaring hearth in what was purely a reception chamber, bright tapestries on one wall and painted patterns on another. The back wall had a battle scene painted across it, knights in mail rode at dismounted men-at-arms who fought back with long teardrop-shaped shields. They seemed to be losing.

The Marshal descended a staircase and frowned at Richard. 'Why has your wife just run upstairs in tears?' he asked. The Marshal had for once forgone his mail, but still wore his tattered green knighting cloak over a blue tunic.

Richard explained what had just happened, although he left out the part where he had failed to discourage Alice.

The Marshal folded his arms. 'You are making a poor show of being a husband,' he said, 'I will be a far better one.'

'We're not here to talk about rich heiresses,' Richard said, 'we're here to get you back into the Young King's company.'

The Marshal turned his nose up. 'You know I haven't seen the Queen since England, and surely you know that I have no interest in her.'

Nicholas chuckled. 'We believe you,' he said, 'and I don't think the Young King even really believes it himself.'

'It sounded like he did,' the Marshal's eyes cast down.

Richard sighed. 'You can argue as long as you want about why you had no reason to lie with the Queen.'

'It's not as if I could marry her and become king,' the Marshal unfolded his arms and pointed at his face, 'all I would gain is the loss of my head.'

'I said we didn't need to talk about that,' Richard said, 'what we need to talk about is what you're going to do about it.'

'I'm going to find another company,' the Marshal went over to the hearth and peered into its glowing heart, 'did you know that in the past Count Philip offered me the rents of a quarter of the city of St-Omer to join his company?'

Richard shook his head. 'Obviously not.'

'Do you know how much that is?' his friend asked.

Richard closed his eyes. 'Obviously not.'

'It's more than my father ever made in a year from all his lands in England. It's even more than Lord Tancarville can muster from his.'

'Maybe we should just let him go,' Nicholas said, 'let everyone carry on thinking he's guilty.'

The Marshal turned away from the fire and looked at the Martel knight. He stared as the fire hissed and the smoke dyed the plaster nearest it yellow. 'Reputation is everything,' he mumbled.

Richard grinned. 'You need to answer the accusation. Return to the Young King.'

'I will return to the company,' the Marshal said.

Nicholas let out a sigh of relief.

'If,' the English knight said.

Nicholas groaned, took one look at him, and walked out of the house shaking his head.

'If,' the Marshal repeated, 'the Young King apologises.'

Richard rubbed his chin. 'He might need some convincing, but I'd wager less than his father would,' he said.

'If he announces he made a mistake to the company, then I will gladly rejoin,' the Marshal said.

'Can you prove your innocence, then?' Richard asked.

A pair of men entered, gave the knights a distasteful look and ascended the stairs.

'Of course not,' the Marshal said, 'how can I prove I didn't do something? It should be up to whoever made up the accusation to prove it.'

Richard didn't have an answer for that because it sounded entirely reasonable.

'My lord should trust me, he should place his faith in my honesty and integrity,' the Marshal stomped away from the hearth.

'Sometimes you have to swallow your pride,' Richard said.

'My pride?' the Marshal said and for a moment he looked like Sir Wobble again. 'I have no pride. I have loyalty, and my lord should always assume my innocence.'

'I don't think it's as simple as that,' Richard said.

The Marshal inspected the battle scene. 'It should be.'

'We need you back,' Richard said, 'you might have to overcome your pride and show what a true and wise man you are. Guy and Eustace are planning to kill the Young King tomorrow, so we need you on the field to protect him. With you there, we might have a chance.'

The Marshal snorted. 'If he needs me back so badly, he would apologise himself.'

Richard tried to steady his breathing. 'This isn't all about you,' he said, 'but actually, what if it was? What if the Young King is killed tomorrow, killed while you're living like a merchant in Amiens? Imagine if that happens?'

The Marshal did. For a moment his face paled, but then his lips hardened. 'I cannot serve a lord who does not have unquestioning faith in me,' he said, 'look at your men, Richard. They followed you across Brittany for no reason, then invaded Ireland with you. What was there to gain for them against the risk? It was so foolish as to be suicidal. Their loyalty and trust in you drove them, and I want that same loyalty from my lord.'

'I think you've got most of that the wrong way around,' Richard scratched behind his ear and fought the urge to remind the Marshal exactly why Richard had gone to Brittany in the first place.

'That's not the point,' the Marshal said, 'I would follow the Young King anywhere, so he should support me against anything and everything. If men can have that steadfast faith even in you, how can they lack it in me?'

Richard fought an urge to reply to the insult, but instead took a moment. 'Don't envy me, you're the most famous knight in the north of France. Most landed knights would kill their own fathers to be you. You have a reputation that surpasses even some barons, not that I understand how you've got it.'

'What good is reputation if your lord doesn't trust you?' the Marshal flicked some dust off his sleeve.

'It's not just the story about the Queen,' Richard said, 'the Young

King is furious about your war-cry. What were you thinking?'

The Marshal shrugged. 'It's a good war-cry, I just made it work for me.'

'It is the royal war-cry, you idiot,' Richard grabbed his own hair, 'turning it into yours sends messages, can't you see that?'

The Marshal looked confused.

'I've had enough of you,' Richard said, 'you can't see what's right in front of you. Come back to Corbie, apologise about the war-cry, and I think the Young King might forget about the Queen.'

The Marshal crossed his arms. 'I will not apologise, I've done nothing wrong. There is no law against using that war-cry. My lord must apologise to me.'

Richard sighed. This was getting nowhere. 'Maybe we can do something about the accusation,' he said, 'the young man who made it, I think he's a squire, was brought in by Adam.'

'Him?' the Marshal raised his voice. 'All he ever does is try to belittle me. He's so green with envy he might as well be a tree.'

Richard nodded. 'I think you are right. I think this is Adam's plot to cut you away from the Young King.'

'He's been jealous of me since I arrived,' the Marshal said, 'he sneered at me for having been a Tancarville knight. Adam thought he was going to lead the company one day, and when I took on the role of marshal, he must have decided to bring me down.'

'So you replaced him?' Richard asked.

The Marshal shook his head.

'Are you sure?' Richard asked. 'If I ask the others, will they agree with you?'

'Of course,' the Marshal said as defiance flashed in his eyes.

Richard raised his eyebrows. 'I suppose it doesn't really matter,' he said, 'but I'd bet good money that he's got a decent enough reason to dislike you. He's not an unreasonable man, and I was growing to like him.'

'Don't side with him,' the Marshal said quickly, 'but whatever his reasons, they aren't enough to make up tall tales. Where is his honour?'

'No,' Richard said, 'and I think we need to clear that up. Then you can come back. We need the militia of Amiens, too, just in case the Martels use their infantry. We'll just get peppered with crossbow bolts otherwise.'

'They can't use infantry tomorrow, it's a tournament.'

Richard shrugged. 'I think Guy and Eustace play by their own rules.'

The Marshal marched towards Richard. 'The mayor here is a

friend to both me and the Young King, but I have told him of my mistreatment. He is as shocked as I am, and I am quite sure that he won't want to be involved in a tournament squabble.'

'The planned killing of your lord is just a tournament squabble?' Richard shook his head.

'It is also the Lord's day today, and he is a pious man, he cannot issue a muster until tomorrow,' the Marshal said.

'I thought you just said the mayor is a friend to the Young King?' Richard asked.

'He is,' the Marshal said, 'everyone in Amiens is, but he has also heard that the Martels are here, and they are famed for their savagery. Not to mention Guy and his treasonous Lusignans. They have never been this far north, and the stories from the south are well known here. They heard about Niort, and I don't think the mayor wants to lead his militia towards such an enemy. He isn't a noble like us.'

'Can't you convince him?'

'Me?' the Marshal laughed. 'I need to convince myself. He isn't supposed to use the militia in tournaments, anyway. They are only for defending the walls of the town. They are not a battlefield company, and the mayor is right, the Martel infantry will cut them to pieces.'

'They'll cut your lord to pieces if you insist on finding excuses not to help him,' Richard said.

The Marshal shrugged. 'You can leave now,' he said, 'I'm going to console your wife.'

'Don't change the subject. But can I see her?' Richard asked.

'That fact that you're asking me means you know you shouldn't,' the Marshal walked up the staircase and left Richard feeling very alone.

So he left. The skies above Amiens had cleared of clouds, although the smoke from a hundred fires twisted up into the air and merged as a thin, dark smog above the rooftops.

Richard found Nicholas hauling Judas back by the scruff of his neck from the crossroads.

'What did he do this time?' Richard asked.

'You don't want to know,' Nicholas let the dog go. 'Is the peacock coming back with us?'

Richard shook his head. 'What do you think?'

'At least we tried,' the Martel knight said. 'But now what?'

'We're going to find the squire who spread the lies that have caused all this mess,' Richard said.

'What about your wife?'

Richard exhaled. 'I don't think she wants to see me, but I might ask Brian to write a letter for her later. But she can wait a day, we need to get the Marshal back into the company first.'

They found the squire in the marketplace that had sprung up between the abbey and the small town of Corbie. Traders of every kind manned tented temporary shops in much the same way they had done at Lagny. However, there were fewer of them, and the knights inspecting their wares were less willing to spend money.

The squire was at a shieldmaker's stall, going through a stack of freshly made shields with unpainted faces. The squire asked how much it would cost to have a shield painted, and it was before the trader could answer that Richard found him.

'You,' Richard grabbed his shoulder, 'there you are. We need to talk.'

The squire was shorter than Richard, and maybe a year or two younger. His straw-coloured hair topped a suddenly nervous face.

'Looking for shields?' Nicholas asked. 'Have you recently come into some wealth?'

'No,' the squire stammered.

'You could get one for free from the Young King, so this looks odd to me,' Nicholas said.

'That's a nice new tunic you're wearing,' Richard said, 'the sun hasn't faded it even slightly yet, has it?'

'My lord is generous,' the squire replied.

'I suppose that lord is Adam Yquebeuf,' Richard kept his grip on the man tight.

The squire nodded.

The shieldmaker was a burly man. 'I'll have no trouble here, my lords,' he said.

'Don't worry, we're going to go somewhere quiet,' Richard whispered to the squire, which made him flinch.

Nicholas grinned right in his face, and the squire trembled. At the sight of the black dog that stood by the Martel knight, he trembled more and any thoughts of resistance he might have fostered evaporated.

Richard pushed him away from the stall and, with his hand wrapped around the squire's shoulder, guided him out of the town.

'Why are we going towards the marsh?' the squire asked. 'Shouldn't we be going to the abbey?'

'People will hear us in the abbey,' the Martel knight grinned.

Richard couldn't tell if he was just acting menacing or looking forward to the prospect of some mild torture, but the wolf-knight had the squire shaking in his suspiciously clean shoes.

They dragged the young man down the incline that led towards the

Somme, the mud soon caked the new shoes. Richard let the squire go under a dead tree with bare branches that reached up into the sky like outstretched fingers.

Birds chirped in the distance and flew overhead. A crow settled in the dead branches above them and cawed.

Judas chased a bird off into the bushes, leaving a trail of cracked and snapped branches behind him.

'Do you know who I am?' Richard asked.

The squire's eyes darted between the two knights. He nodded. 'You are the king killers.'

'Is that all we're ever going to be known for?' Richard asked.

Nicholas grinned. 'It does make torturing people easier,' he said, 'if they know we won't spare royalty.'

'Please don't hurt me.'

'I think my friend would quite like to,' Richard said, 'maybe you can delay your confession until he's at least broken a few ribs?'

'No, no,' the squire held his hands up, 'mercy, I beg of you.'

'Why did you do it? Apart from obviously a handful of coins.'

'Sir Adam threatened me,' the squire said, 'he said I'd never be a knight if I didn't do as he ordered. He said he could make sure Sir Roger never even knows my name.'

'De Cailly?' Nicholas asked.

Richard nodded. 'Sir Roger is a good lord, you should have trusted in him. Do you see my spurs?'

The squire peered down, but the spurs were covered in brown sludge. 'No,' he said.

Richard sighed.

Nicholas chuckled. 'That ruins the effect of your point,' he said.

'I know,' Richard turned to their victim, 'my spurs might be familiar to you if you had ever paid attention to Sir Roger's own pair.'

'I don't understand?' the squire wanted to back away.

'Have you ever noticed what spurs Sir Roger wears?'

The squire nodded quickly. 'Iron spurs,' he said, 'everyone knows that, he's famous for it. But no one knows why.'

'Those iron spurs were once mine,' Richard said, 'as my golden spurs were once his.'

The squire's eyes widened.

'You may fear Adam,' Richard said, 'but maybe you should fear me a little more. I have more sway with Sir Roger than Adam does.'

Which was probably untrue, but the squire might not know that.

The squire's bottom lip quivered. 'I didn't know.'

'Well you do now,' Richard said, 'so now's the time to tell us your

216

story.'

The squire sobbed. 'I didn't want to do it,' he said.

'We don't care,' Nicholas loomed in his face and the wolf-eyes caught the squire's attention.

'He got me drunk,' the squire blurted out, 'in a room full of men I hadn't met before. They told me all the rumours about the Marshal. I don't really remember what they said, exactly. Or what the men looked like. I think some are in our company.'

'Good,' Richard said, because part of him had wondered if the Marshal somehow believed the Queen was rightfully his, and that the accusations might be founded in truth.

Judas sauntered through the undergrowth with blood around his muzzle. The dog stalked up to the squire and sent him recoiling backwards.

'Stand,' Richard said, and the dog halted.

The squire sniffed and tore his eyes away from the hound. 'In the morning my head ached so badly I thought I was dying. My stomach churned like a stormy sea, and Adam came and pushed me in front of the Young King. I was terrified.'

'We won't feel sorry for you,' Nicholas said.

'No,' Richard put his hands on his hips, 'you don't know the trouble you've caused. The Young King could be killed because of you.'

'God have mercy on my soul,' the squire howled and dropped to his knees. Mud soaked up his legs. 'Anything but that, I'd give my life for the Young King.'

'That seems to be the effect he has on people,' Richard shook his head.

Nicholas grinned. 'You might get your chance to die for the Young King tomorrow, we all might.'

'I tried not to tell him,' the squire bawled, 'I tried to say no. Then Adam told me he'd tell Sir Roger how at Lagny I ran at a horse with a lance, frightened it and opened a hole in the line.'

'That was you?' Richard asked.

The squire cried.

'Idiot,' Nicholas said, 'you shouldn't ever be a knight, you aren't up to it.'

Richard shook his head and looked over at the waterway that he could see in the distance. The air tasted of cold, muddy water, he thought, and it was cooler down here than in Corbie.

'Come on, Nicholas,' Richard said, 'it's time to put this right. Drag the fool back to the abbey.'

Nicholas dropped the squire onto the icy stones of the refectory in front of the Young King. A dozen knights, including two counts, sat around him, and all looked up at the hapless squire as he picked himself up with red and skittish eyes.

'What is he doing here?' the Young King asked Richard.

'This squire has something to tell you,' Richard replied.

Nicholas let him go and stood back with a proud look on his face.

'I thought I said I never wanted to see this boy again,' the Young King shuffled in his chair, his face dark even in the poor light of the refectory.

The squire could only hold his head in his hands and cry.

Richard grabbed his head up and held it up so he could see the Young King. 'Tell him what you told me.'

The squire did. In between sobs, sniffs, and apologies, he told the sordid story of Adam's plot.

Count Robert threw a bone across the chamber and Judas scrambled after it. 'Envy is the root of all of this,' he said to the young Angevin, 'all the wealth and prestige of your court attracts wicked men, and draws out the worst of the good ones. Jealousy has poisoned Adam's soul, but he isn't a wicked man. I can speak to him quietly now that this charade has been exposed, things do not have to escalate, and we need both the Marshal and Adam on the field tomorrow.'

The Young King drummed his armrest with his fingers. 'I would rather the Marshal stewed for a while in his exile. It might teach him something.'

Some knights around him snorted or laughed.

'I'm not sure he thinks he's in exile,' Richard said, 'he thinks he's the wronged party. Which, if I may say, he partly is.'

The Young King blinked at Richard. He stopped drumming his fingers. 'Do not presume you know the Marshal better than I. And do not forget his war-cry and his list of other slights. He needs to learn that such behaviour cannot stand.'

'We need him tomorrow,' Richard said, 'could he be punished after the Martels and Lusignans have been seen off? His presence may cancel out Guy's.'

'I'm sure in his mind he could carry the field on his own,' the Young King said.

'He hates Guy,' Richard said, 'his captivity at his castle wounded his pride. Not to mention how Guy murdered his uncle in front of him.'

'He has never spoken about his time in Guy's gaol.'

'They locked him away at night and didn't let him ride or fight during the day,' Richard said, 'and he thinks they denied him the proper amount of food.'

The Young King laughed. 'A lack of food would quickly drive him to madness. It doesn't sound like he was mistreated to me, but I can see how that pig-headed oaf would be offended.'

Richard wondered if he should mention the Marshal's demand for an apology. 'If the Marshal was to return without Henry the Northerner, would you accept him back?'

The Young King nodded slowly. 'I can forget the matter of this squire, but the Marshal needs to apologise to me in person, in front of everyone, for overstepping his bounds. That war-cry of his would be enough for my father to execute him for treason. He's killed men for far less.'

'The Marshal may be too proud to apologise, this split can only be resolved if both sides give something,' Richard said.

'Do not tell me what I should give,' the Young King said.

'This boy is right,' Count Robert said, 'this is a chance for you to display the clemency and trust you like to tell everyone you have.'

The Young King turned to his advisor. 'There is free-speaking, and then there is what you and Richard are doing.' He sighed and scratched his forehead. 'It pains me to forgive the Marshal his grandiosity. Who is he anyway? He's nothing more than a landless knight with some skill with his sword.'

'My King,' Richard bowed, 'I would advise you to be empty of envy over his prowess and fame. His popularity is great, but it is but a shadow of yours. Do not let his celebrity, which can never rival yours, block his return.'

'You're my advisor, too, are you?' the Young King asked.

'If it saves your life, I am,' Richard said, 'if you cannot bring yourself to recall the Marshal, you could die tomorrow.'

'Scandalous,' a knight stood up being the Young King, 'to even speak of the death of our lord is treason.'

'Oh, sit down, John,' the Young King said, 'and I'd rather you spoke of my death in order to avoid it than remain silent and let it happen.'

'Quite right,' Count Robert said, 'and this isn't your father's court, this can be a place of honesty.'

The Young King thought for a moment. 'What is your name, squire?'

'Maynard,' the squire snivelled, his face puffy and red.

'Well, Maynard,' the Young King said, 'I absolve you of your guilt on this matter. Go.'

'Thank you,' Maynard staggered towards the door.

'And Maynard,' the Young King added.

The squire paused and looked back at his monarch.

'Next time you run at one of our horses with a lance, I'll hack off the hand that holds it,' the Young King smirked.

The joke caused a ripple of laughter that saw Maynard flee out of the refectory.

'Richard,' the Young King said, 'there, I have done my part, and if he apologies for the rest he can take his rightful place alongside me.'

Richard looked down at the black dog which sat beside him panting. 'I don't think the Marshal will bring himself to apologise, he is the proudest man I have ever met.'

'This is my one chance to teach him some humility,' the Young King said, 'it is the only lesson I think I can teach him, and we shall all be better for it.'

'If he doesn't come, then what of tomorrow?' Richard asked.

'We shall do without him,' the Young King said. 'Which would teach him another valuable lesson.'

'Even if it kills you?' Richard shook his head.

'Even if it kills me.'

THE HIGH BATH
OF HONOUR

Shafts of red light from the east heralded the new dawn. The new day arrived, but the Marshal did not.

The Young King's company took no part in the preliminary jousting, instead they prepared in the abbey's yard as if they rode to war. Knights in stony silence adjusted shield straps, found rust to work out, and looked all the while over to the abbey's main gate for their war-leader to appear.

The red-shielded company, a hundred men smaller than at Lagny, left Corbie behind them and formed up before midday. They left Gerold too, who still could not leave his bed. Richard was concerned that the old man wasn't recovering, but he had more pressing problems to contend with.

Three hundred knights and horses are a substantial number, and it took some time for them all to muster and crest the small hill that separated the abbey from the Corbie list. Unlike at Lagny, there was no stand, and the palisade of stakes was modest and had no ditch around it. No infantry guarded it either, that job would fall to the squires of the participating knights.

'This is a connoisseur's tournament, not one for the masses,' Otto said to Richard as they waited for someone somewhere to do something. Richard hadn't bothered to ask him where he'd been.

'It feels different here,' Richard said. Solis didn't paw the ground or fidget, instead the stallion had his head up and ears pointed northwards.

The German watched a company of thirty knights ride out from Corbie. 'It will be smaller, too. But you are right. The air has a coldness. It tastes like death.'

Richard frowned. 'Everyone's already on edge, don't say things like that.'

The Young King glanced to the west road more than once, but it remained empty.

Adam rode up to him and said a quiet apology, which the Young King merely nodded back to. The crestfallen knight swore to defend his lord and rode away.

Count Robert took command in the Marshal's absence and ordered the line to be formed. The Corbie team stretched out facing away from the town along the ridge of a green hill. The Franvillers team appeared and fanned out across the crest of the next rise. It looked like the two sides would meet in the valley between.

'There aren't many of them,' Bowman said.

'Three hundred, I reckon,' Nicholas replied.

Bowman scoffed. 'Three hundred and fifty, more like.'

'Fewer than we are, either way,' Richard said, 'but I don't see any Lusignans, Martels, or Count Philip.'

'Half the Martels will still have the Count walled up,' Bowman said, 'which suits us.'

'Does it?' Richard asked. 'The Count has helped us before, and things are even more serious now. How do we know he wouldn't change sides again?'

Bowman grimaced. 'Let us just hope we can start soon, young lord, and scatter those who are here already,' he said.

Richard shifted the weight of his two mail shirts on his shoulders and looked over at Bowman with envy. The blonde man wore a new leather breastplate he'd purchased with the Young King's credit. Richard was sure the Young King had granted no permission.

The Young King and his four bannermen stood in the centre of their line, this time their horses were barded with leather armour on their chests, rears, and heads. The Young King's horse wore full mail barding over the leather, and Richard marvelled at the expense of all that metal. He wished he could cover Solis in all that protection and promised to do so if he could ever afford it.

The Young King checked the west road for a final time and then instructed Count Robert to begin. The Count bellowed the order to advance, and the tournament began with no fanfare or cheering.

Three hundred and more knights, grouped in their coloured companies, swept down the opposite hill to meet them. It was a glorious sight, the concentration of wealth, prowess, training, and courage charged towards the larger team from Corbie.

The company Richard lined up against displayed colours of yellow and blue diagonal stripes.

Richard rode knee-to-knee with Bowman, but Nicholas lagged half a horse-length behind. However much practise a company had, a solid line was never inevitable.

The yellow and blue company's formation broke up as the keener horses raced the others.

Richard lowered his lance at a knight just before the two lines came together. What no one had noticed, however, was that the shallow valley between the two hills was significantly wetter than the higher ridges.

Solis pushed on as his hooves sank into the mud, but Richard's opponent slowed to a walk, and as such his lance uselessly skated off Richard's red shield.

Richard's lance pushed the yellow and blue shield backwards and the knight reeled in the saddle, but stayed in it.

Knights all along the valley floor ground to a halt, their horse's hooves mired in boggy grass that only grew more boggy with each urgent hoof step.

Richard urged Solis to turn, and he found his previous target righting himself in his saddle. Richard lanced him in the shoulder from behind and the knight cried out, dropped his lance, and winded himself on the front of his high war saddle.

Otto grabbed the knight and hauled him from his horse.

'They're running already,' Nicholas grinned beside Richard, his lance already broken in half.

The yellow and blue knights scrambled back up their hill, their horses splattered with brown mud up past their fetlocks.

Otto took the surrender of the unhorsed knight, a wide grin on his weathered face.

Red knights streamed up the hill after their fleeing enemy, Richard saw the red banners amongst them so followed.

Solis had to fight to push himself up the hill, but Bowman's horse was ahead and the palomino stallion wasn't happy being behind.

A gust of wind almost blew Richard's lance out of his hands as they crested the hill, a crest that revealed a far-reaching wood that seemed to promise sanctuary for the retreating knights.

Victory scented, the Young King's company, or the half of it that wasn't still fighting in the boggy valley, charged after them.

Clusters of knights chased different groups, and Richard and his companions pursued six yellow and blue knights in the middle of it all.

Both sides covered the ground in a flash, and then they were in the dark of the woods. There were no tracks, and as the leaves had only just started to fall from the trees for the year, it was impossible to see far ahead as foliage rushed by.

A damp branch slapped Richard in the face as they burst through the hazels and elms. His lance got tangled in an older elm and had to let it go. Richard drew the jewelled mace instead and tried to keep up with the enemy knights who he could only catch fleeting glimpses of.

The trees gave way to a wide clearing that stretched to their left and right, with a raised bank on the far side. The yellow and blue knights made it halfway up the bank before the red company reached the clearing. Shouts of jubilation rang out from the Young King's company, they were gaining on an enormous set of ransoms.

The ground beneath the high bank was wet under the surface, and it slowed Richard down. Bowman's horse overtook again as the enemy knights clambered up the mound and disappeared over it.

Richard would always remember this moment as the moment everything went wrong.

Along the full length of the bank appeared knight after knight, knee-to-knee and with lances ready. Richard pulled Solis up, but some of the Young King's men didn't, or couldn't, stop.

'Eustace,' Bowman hissed as he tried to turn his horse around, but the mud slowed him down and his horse left two long skid marks as he slammed to a standstill.

The banner that flew over the centre of the new company was the familiar Martel red and yellow chequerboard pattern.

'This is a trap,' Nicholas found Richard.

'A gold coin to the wise man,' Bowman sneered.

'The rout wasn't a rout,' Nicholas said as the Martel line descended the bank in good order.

'What do we do?' Bowman asked.

Some of the red company attacked, some pulled back, and some dithered in between.

'No one is giving orders,' Richard said, 'where are the banners?'

Bowman pointed his lance far to their left. 'The Young Fool is charging,' he said.

Richard turned Solis toward the far-off banners. 'That's where we're going then.'

Nicholas followed. 'I don't like this, this is bad,' he shouted as their horses found their speed.

Eustace's company found its speed too, and they hurtled down the bank in a terrifyingly coherent line.

The red and yellow tide consumed the fragmented bands of the Young King's men who had continued their chase, but that at least broke up Eustace's formation as knights surrounded the pockets of red shields.

As Solis flew over the ground, and wet earth flew into the air, Richard marvelled at the perfection of Eustace's plan. The red company scattered over the clearing, with only the group around the banners big enough to provide any meaningful resistance.

Eustace himself now aimed at the Young King, and they crashed together near the bank. Horses tumbled down and men fell from their saddles. One red knight fell headfirst, but before he could raise his soiled head, a Martel lance speared him in the back.

One of the four red banners went down.

'Come on, Solie,' Richard shouted and whirled the mace through the air as if it would make his horse go faster.

Another banner half fell, was righted, then dropped out of view behind the melee that drew in knights from both sides.

'The Young King is running,' Bowman cried.

He was right. The remaining two red banners fled north, along the clearing under the bank. The Martel knights went after them, and quickly Richard could only see their backs as they chased his lord into the woods.

Bowman threw down his lance before they crashed back into the dense undergrowth, and again Richard could no longer see ahead of him. Solis kept going, but Bowman was in front, and his black horse took them after the Young King and the Martels.

They emerged onto a track, now covered in hoofprints and all churned up, and raced along it. The track led to another clearing, but this one had a forester's compound nestled in it, a cluster of wooden buildings surrounded by a boundary of impassable thick and thorny hedging.

The Young King's company, or the few dozen men of it that remained with him, sought refuge inside.

Eustace stopped his men outside, a long bowshot away, and Bowman called a halt before they got close enough to be noticed.

'There are over forty of them,' Bowman said, 'and four of us.'

Solis panted and steam rose from all their mounts.

The Young King and his men dismounted and formed a defence around the gateway with some unbroken lances held as spears.

'Eustace can't charge in there,' Richard said, 'he'll have to wait for the Young King to come out.'

'We need to gather the rest of our company,' Nicholas said, 'we can bring them here and strike those bastards from behind.'

Bowman laughed. 'Bastards? That's rich coming from you.'

'Quiet,' Richard said, 'but if we ride back there, we'll have to fight through the rest of the Martels, and spend half the day rounding up our company.'

'What do you suggest, then?' Bowman asked. 'Charge in there and cut our way through? Because that won't work.'

Richard slid the mace back into his belt. 'No, it won't,' he said, 'but I know where we can find a fully formed company.'

'Where?' Bowman asked.

Richard grinned and looked up for the sun so he could tell which way east was. 'We're going to Franvillers.'

Martel infantry still ringed the tower of Franvillers. The tent village was almost empty, only a handful of squires and servants wandered around waiting for their masters to return or to keep the scattered fires going. The breeze that swept over the forest of canvas made their job harder. Richard took his small party around Franvillers, so they entered from the opposite side that knights from the tournament would be expected to. It took longer, but meant they could ride straight into the village without being challenged.

'The Flemings are still here,' Nicholas nodded over towards a paddock where a few dozen horses grazed.

'Should we get rid of these red shields?' Otto asked.

'Not a bad idea,' Bowman chuckled.

'If we throw them off now it'll look suspicious,' Richard said, 'we just need to kill the infantry blocking Count Philip from leaving his tower.'

'We can charge them,' Nicholas flashed his sword for effect.

Richard shook his head. 'Put that away, we'll tie the horses here, and go on foot.'

They secured their horses to the paddock fence containing the Flemish mounts and left their red shields in a stack beside them.

'Try to look happy or bored,' Richard said and led his men to relieve Count Philip's siege.

A few Martel crossbowmen huddled around a fire on the far side of the tower, but they were a long way away, and it was the group of mostly spearmen who had lit a fire near the tower's gate that Richard headed for.

Laughter, dull and unenthusiastic, sounded from the fire. One man leant his crossbow against the nearest house and walked off to relieve himself.

Bowman made for the crossbow.

Richard approached the fire and counted the infantry. Seven, plus the one walking away. More than he'd hoped for, but they at least had the element of surprise.

Bowman picked the crossbow up and a rough-looking spearman with large ears that stuck out of the side of his head turned to look at him.

'That's not yours,' he said in an accent from the Midlands of England.

Bowman admired the stock of the crossbow and the groove that ran along it. A bolt sat in the groove. 'This rail isn't straight,' he said, 'you'll never hit anything with this thing.'

Otto and Nicholas reached for weapons.

Bowman turned the crossbow around and shot it. The bolt sunk deep into the big-eared man's belly and his companions looked around at the unexpected noise.

'I suppose I was wrong, it will hit something,' Bowman thrust the crossbow at the next nearest man's face.

Richard slipped the mace from his belt and swung it at a spearman who fumbled to lower the spear he'd been resting on. The mace crunched into the side of the man's head with a loud crack.

Nicholas stabbed a man in the neck, and Otto cut into an arm.

One of the three remaining men couldn't draw his weapon before Bowman got to him, but the last two went for Richard.

Richard parried a spear thrust with his mace, but the next spear ran up the outside of his arm and put him off balance. The spear flew around to stab at Richard's face, but a black wolf jumped on him and bundled him to the ground where he died with a muffled scream.

The final spearman backed away from Otto, but only into Bowman, who slit his throat from behind.

The crossbowman who had left returned in time to scream out and run away at the sight of his slaughtered comrades.

'Knock on the gate,' Richard said, 'we haven't got long.'

Otto banged the hilt of his long knife on the gate once, and it swung open before he needed to do so again.

Count Philip stepped out, mailed and with his yellow surcoat gleaming. 'I was expecting the Marshal, but you will do,' he grinned.

'Eustace has the Young King trapped in a forester's compound in the woods,' Richard said, 'we need your company and we need them now.'

The Count's face dropped. 'How dare those bastard Martels desecrate our sacred tournament? I should have guessed, their low cunning is devil-sent.'

'Muster your men,' Richard said, 'they have been cowering in the houses like children. They could have broken you free themselves.'

Count Philip shrugged as the four men who had been trapped inside with him left to rouse their comrades. 'No one gave them an order to, so they didn't, the halfwits.'

The Flemings, once incited to action, had themselves and their horses ready in no time.

Count Philip mounted first and his horse tried to kick Bowman's. 'Where is the Marshal then?' the Count asked.

Bowman snorted. 'Sticking peacock feathers up his arse,' he said, 'and watch my horse.'

'The Marshal will not help us. We are doing without him,' Richard said, 'apparently.'

Count Philip shouted at his men to hurry and some formed up on the track behind him.

The more dithering of the Flemings hoisted themselves into their saddles and Count Philip nodded to Richard. 'Let us rescue my nephew. He'll never hear the end of it.'

Richard didn't share his optimism as the company rode straight out of Franvillers and back onto the tournament field. Some of the Martel besiegers raised the alarm, and one crossbow bolt even sailed overhead, but most ran towards Geoffrey Martel's towering golden tent.

That was the simple part done, Richard thought. On their way to the woods, they passed a pair of opposing knights leading three captured horses, but there was no sign of their riders. Count Philip greeted them but neither looked twice at the red shields amongst his yellows.

'We need to go faster,' Richard said, 'if more Martel knights find Eustace they might force a way in.'

Count Philip nodded as the treeline came into view over the next hill. 'We are close enough to go faster.' He turned to his company. 'We fight to capture, but only seek prizes once the Martels flee.'

The company broke into a canter and covered the last hill quickly. Richard hoped it was quickly enough.

Once again they plunged into the darkness of the woods and the Flemings retraced the hoofprints that Richard and his party had left on their way out.

Tall weeds flanked the track as Count Philip thundered along it. The Fleming rode well, Richard thought, he didn't seem to move in the saddle as his muscled stallion surged along the track with never ending power.

Solis laboured now and Richard knew they should look for a stream when they had the chance.

The forester's compound appeared before Richard felt ready to fight, and the Flemings yelled a war-cry Richard didn't understand and lowered their lances without slowing.

The Martels had spread out around the boundary hedge searching for a weakness, but those who remained mounted near the entrance spun around at the clamour surging along the track.

The yellow knights slammed into their supposed teammates and cut into their loose and unprepared ranks.

Richard swung his mace and it split a shield open, but he rode on towards the Young King as the Flemings laid into the Martels.

Bowman and Otto forged on behind him.

Under the red and yellow banner just ahead, the enormous figure of Eustace turned towards the fight. He found a Fleming and sent him out of his saddle with two quick blows.

Bowman angled at Eustace, fury in his eyes, and clashed with a Martel knight who got in his way.

Richard heard Nicholas howl somewhere, but took a sword cut on his shield and couldn't see his friend.

Eustace thrust his sword into a Flemish knight's face and Richard lost the last hope he had that this tournament could remain just a game.

Nicholas pushed his way beside Bowman and the two half-brothers cut a path towards Eustace. Richard wasn't sure the two of them would be enough.

The Young King's war-cry sounded from inside the forester's compound and the Martel knights near Richard looked in their direction with jittery eyes. One glanced back to the track and Richard took the chance to shatter his shoulder with the jewelled mace. The crunch of bone should have sickened him, Richard thought, but instead it spurred him on, and he brought down the mace again to ensure the knight would never use the arm to wield a weapon again.

Other red and yellow knights turned and left the melee, which became a static slugging match.

Eustace looked back at the Young King's advancing banners, seemingly undecided on which way to go. He chose retreat, but that put him directly in the path of his half-brother, who swung his sword at him.

Eustace blocked Nicholas's attack, but Bowman got on his other side and hammered down on his shield.

The big Martel shrugged it off and flashed his blade at Nicholas. 'I'd wondered when you'd turn up,' Eustace said as Nicholas parried.

Richard tried to join in, but couldn't get past Bowman or Nicholas.

Bowman cleaved a chunk of wood from the shield, relying on brute force to reach the man below.

Eustace hit Nicholas so hard that his horse had to stagger sideways to keep his rider in the saddle. Eustace took the chance to dart into the gap, escape them, and make for the track. Most of his knights got there before him as their retreat turned to flight. Cheers rose from the Young King's company, although Eustace unhorsed another Fleming on his way to safety. The Martel knights fled into the trees or down the track, and Count Philip called for a halt before his men left the clearing.

The Young King led his company to meet his cousin. 'They were about to cut through the hedge,' his face had a bruise on one cheek, 'you arrived just in time.'

'Thank Richard,' the Count said, 'he came and found me.'

'See,' the Young King grinned, 'who needs the Marshal?'

Some men laughed, but Richard frowned. 'He would have helped, but don't anyone tell him I said that.'

'We need to be away from here,' the Young King sheathed his sword, 'the Martels will regroup soon, and they outnumber us as it is.'

'This tournament has not been the quiet affair I'd looked for after Lagny,' Count Philip said.

'Tournament?' the Young King coughed and took a deep breath. 'This is an attempted assassination.'

The Count shook his head. 'What has become of our beloved tournament?'

Richard approached them and Solis sniffed the Young King's horse who squealed back at him. 'We still don't know where Guy is,' Richard said.

The Young King sighed. 'Back to the list, then, we need to regroup. We have shown the faces of our shields on the field, so we can retire now with honour.'

Count Philip, who knew the tournament field well, led the company back to the ambush site. A few dead horses littered the ground beneath the bank, but only a few human casualties lay with them.

'Where did everyone go?' Nicholas asked. A red mark ran across his forehead below the rim of his iron helmet.

The clearing was eerily quiet. The area of battle, so recently so full of noise and blood now only contained the sound of rustling leaves.

'Scattered into the wind,' Otto looked up at the tall trees as orange leaves were torn from their branches and floated down to the damp grass.

Richard found the clearing unsettling, and he checked over his shoulder for signs of a red and yellow banner on their tail. There was no sign of Eustace, but neither did any more of their company appear either. They left the woods the way they'd entered, and rode out over the last few hills back to Corbie.

Bowman let out a sigh. 'I feel much better being out in the open ground, young lord, it felt like being back in the Wicklow Mountains in those trees.'

'What mountains have woods like that?' Otto asked.

Bowman locked eyes with Richard, and they shared a knowing chuckle.

'You had to be there,' Richard said.

Bowman looked over his shoulder this time. 'But Eustace is more dangerous than the Irish,' he said.

The two companies rode in a loose column, the Young King's company now in the lead and the Flemings behind them.

Richard allowed himself to close his eyes for a moment and thought of how sitting around a cosy fire would smell. The seasoned wood in his nostrils. He opened his eyes, and they refocused on something that moved on the horizon.

'Lances,' Bowman said, 'a lot of lances.'

'Whose are they?' Nicholas asked.

'That's a stupid question,' Bowman snapped, 'what do you think banners are for?'

'I was just asking,' the Martel knight replied, 'and had you killed Eustace while I distracted him, we could be safe now.'

'Me?' the blonde man raged. 'You're blaming me for not killing Eustace?'

'Stop it,' Richard said.

'I am,' Nicholas replied, 'he couldn't have blocked you, and you wasted your time smashing his shield apart.'

'There's a banner,' Richard said.

Bowman cast his eyes to the horizon and the banner that came over the hill. He groaned.

'Lusignan.'

'Hold,' the Young King ordered and the joint company stopped. The wind chilled Richard's neck as it blew over them. It seemed to strengthen.

Blue and white knights filled the horizon, an equal match for the Young King's force. The Angevin's red hair stuck out from under his helmet and through his mail coif, and it wafted in the wind. 'Can we go around?' he asked.

'Who are you asking?' Adam said. 'The Marshal is sulking and Count Robert isn't here.'

The Young King frowned. 'Their horses will be fresh and ours are not. If we go around, they will catch us,' he said. 'I am looking for someone with a better idea.'

Hushed conversations revealed no better ideas.

'Going round will cost us dearly in ransoms,' Bowman muttered, 'but I suppose the Old King will be the one paying.'

'I can't be captured by Guy again,' Richard said, 'he will not let me or Solis get away from him this time.'

'But we'd get the Young King to safety,' Nicholas said, 'that is our job, isn't it?'

'Charge them,' Richard said, 'we can punch through. It's got to be better than trying to gallop around them and showing our flanks.'

The Young King looked over to the west but caught himself. He searched the faces of the surrounding knights. 'All ransoms will be paid,' he said, 'attack them head on and we don't wait for anyone. Most of the company will get bogged down, but if we stay together, half of us might make it through.'

A chorus of sullen nods were his only reply.

Richard drew the mace out of his belt again, a smudge of red on his mail where the blood on the mace had dripped in between the iron rings.

'This is exactly what we did at Lagny,' Richard said, 'it worked quite well for everyone other than me and Gerold.'

'We did lose you, though,' the Young King frowned.

'But we didn't lose you,' Richard replied.

The Young King chewed on his tongue. 'Guy will not have forgotten it, either. He may expect it.'

Count Philip rode through the red company. 'Do we attack or go round?' he asked.

'Attack,' the Young King rode his horse forwards a step and raised his face to the heavens. 'Where is the god-damned Marshal,' he roared, 'where is the cursed Marshal and his damnable knights?'

Count Philip turned to rejoin his company and Richard watched him go. Except that, pouring out of the woods they'd just come from, was a mass of infantry.

'Bowman,' Richard said.

The blonde man followed his gaze and squinted.

'I don't need to look to know who that is,' Nicholas spat onto the ground. 'I'm going to kill him.'

The Young King realised what was happening. 'Martels? The infantry? This is a bloody war. This is treason.'

Richard nodded. 'But what do we do about it? If we get stuck fighting Guy, then the infantry will have time to reach us. Then we're all dead.'

The Young King screamed in rage and for a moment looked like his father. His red surcoat was no longer brighter than his face. 'I'll have them all killed,' the Young King cried, 'no, I'll kill them myself.'

Five knights rode ahead of the infantry that had just appeared, but their banner was the familiar pattern and their leader could only be Geoffrey Martel.

'I'm not done with him, either,' Bowman swore and drew his sword.

'Finally something you can both agree on,' Richard said. He wasn't sure if he'd meant it as a joke, but neither half-brother bothered to reply. A lingering thought in the back of his mind told him that he'd led Geoffrey here, but he squashed away.

Adam put a hand on the Young King. 'You showed me a kindness after I let you down,' the knight said, 'and now we must act quickly. We must put distance between us and the spears of those infantry. Whatever action you choose, it must be chosen now.'

Bowman gritted his teeth and sighed as if letting go of something. 'I'll lead a few men to hold the infantry off,' he said. 'And I'll cut the head off the snake while I'm at it.'

'You'll die,' Nicholas said.

Bowman shrugged. 'If I take him with me, then that is the best service I can perform for this world.'

'No,' the Young King said, 'we must fight as one, we cannot afford to separate any more than we already have. We take on the Lusignans.'

'Forwards,' Adam ordered and the red company pushed off.

Richard gripped his mace and swallowed, his throat rough and dry, the smell of warm horses in his nose.

The Lusignans drifted towards them only slowly, aware that the infantry was on their side and that time favoured them.

The Young King's company walked only two steps when Adam stopped and his face lost all colour. He pointed to their left.

Richard followed his gesture.

'We're dead,' Adam said. 'We're all dead.'

An icy fear grabbed Richard's heart and twisted it. Icy shards stabbed at his guts and he felt weak because, charging over a rolling green hill, were Eustace and his company.

Bowman sniffed. 'Aye, he's right. We're all dead men.'

'We can't fight through them as well,' Richard said.

'No, young lord, this is no romance.'

'I know that,' Richard pressed his lips together and the Lusignans, smelling blood, burst into a canter.

Nicholas turned his horse to face Eustace. 'I want my father, but I want to hurt Eustace more. I'll hold him off.'

'You and who else?' Richard asked. 'You'll last no time on your own.'

'Silence,' the Young King shouted. 'Company, through the Lusignans and to the list. Into a wedge and charge, let's show them how we can fight.'

'We'll form the tip,' Richard shouted, 'this is a war now, this is what we do. Let us lead it.'

Adam laughed and kicked his horse forwards. 'The most noble at the front, that's how it's done. So you're at the back.'

The Young King pushed alongside Adam as the two of them surged forwards, followed by the two surviving bannermen. Red shields swarmed and formed a wedge, although it wasn't as tightly pressed as the Young King might have liked.

Rushing horses all around him, Richard joined the Flemings as the two companies rode into battle.

Consumed by knights on both sides as they struck out across the plain, Richard couldn't see Eustace to their left, or Geoffrey Martel to their rear.

War-cries reverberated all around and those knights who still had lances lowered them. Richard braced. He tensed and locked his legs into his saddle, turned his core into a solid mass and readied for the impact.

The Young King's company scythed into the Lusignan line, but unlike at Langy, this one was three ranks deep.

As the wedge ground to a halt the horses behind crashed into each other and pushed the whole formation deeper into the enemy. Solis rammed his head into the flank of a horse he bumped into, and Richard's legs jarred against the knights on both sides of him. His sore toe erupted in flame as another man's pointed spur stabbed it.

The blue and white banner flew directly ahead, and the two red banners pushed towards it, but the Young King was a long way from breaking through.

Shouts of alarm sprung from the Flemings behind and Richard snapped his head around to see movement outside of the formation.

'They're surrounding us,' Bowman shouted.

Richard tried to urge his horse forwards, but the Young King's company was a solid mass in his path. Count Philip's company pressed from behind and only added to the crush.

The red-shielded knight on Bowman's left defended himself from sword blows over his shield.

'To the left,' Bowman shouted and tried to turn to face the incoming threat.

Richard wheeled left as the red-shielded knight had his reins cut and a Lusignan knight dragged him away from the struggle.

A blue and white knight wielding a hand-axe filled the gap he left. He swung at Bowman but the blonde man got in first and shaved the knight's fingers from his axe handle.

Nicholas swooped in and jammed his sword into the now axe-less knight's eye. He tried to turn his horse to flee, but Bowman slashed at his neck and he slumped in the saddle.

Richard forced his way next to Nicholas as a Lusignan mace rattled the wolf-knight's helmet. He cried out and his eyes came up cloudy. Nicholas lashed out at his assailant and knocked the mace from his hand.

Solis bit the man's thigh in a crunch of metal rings, which cleared the way for Richard to use his own mace to knock the knight's helmet clean off his head.

Nicholas careered past and into the throng of blue and white knights who swirled around the two battered companies.

Richard followed in his wake, the wolf-knight carving a path with blow after blow from his gore-covered sword.

Richard's shield was almost hewn in two by an axe strike, but then they were out of the melee and in open ground. He spun Solis around. The red banners were next to the blue and white one.

'He's nearly through,' Richard said.

'But we're in trouble,' Bowman pointed his dented sword north to where Geoffrey Martel led his infantry into the fray.

'He's going to slaughter Count Philip,' Richard said.

Otto appeared, his horse foaming at the mouth and someone else's blood on his mailed arm.

Bowman looked at Richard. 'I'll stop them,' he said.

'You can't, you'll never survive,' Richard said, 'we could ride around the press and free the Young King. Before the Lusignans even notice we've got out.'

The blonde man shook his head. 'I'll never have a better chance to kill him, young lord. And Count Philip deserves our help. You save the Young King, I'll give the Count a fighting chance.'

'No,' Richard said.

Bowman spurred his horse and rode towards the advancing Martel infantry.

'Don't worry,' Otto grinned, a smile that showed blood on his gums and teeth, 'I'll look after him.'

'Idiots,' Richard shouted after them. Two of them against five knights and a hundred spearmen. They didn't have a hope.

'We have a bigger problem,' Nicholas rushed his words. 'Eustace is coming.'

The other Martel company galloped over the hills and towards the battle.

'He's going to cut the Young King's escape off,' Richard said, 'Eustace will overwhelm him.'

'Shouldn't we help my brother first?'

'Brother?' Richard cocked an eyebrow. 'Bowman's chosen his battle, our duty is to the Young King. We'll come back for your brother.' Richard asked his horse to leap straight into a canter, and the stallion obliged.

Eustace rode under his red and yellow banner and charged toward Corbie. One of the Young King's banners fell, and the other tangled with the Lusignan standard and still hadn't broken free. What he and Nicholas could do to stop Eustace's twenty knights, Richard wasn't sure, but they had to try.

The Martel company got behind the melee and wheeled to face it. The jaws of the trap were about to slam shut, and Eustace was the teeth.

Nicholas homed in on his Martel half-brother and pulled ahead of Richard.

Eustace ordered the attack before he'd noticed the two knights heading for him, and his company bounded towards the melee.

The first knight Nicholas reached wasn't sure whose side the wolf-knight was on, and it cost him his life.

Richard used his mace to smash the neck of a knight from behind as he dodged his lance on the way by. He had to turn sharply to find Eustace, who had spotted Nicholas and turned to face him.

'I'm glad you returned,' Eustace raised his sword.

Nicholas blocked the first strike, and their horses wheeled around each other. 'You made me into a monster,' Nicholas replied.

'You added the animal skin yourself,' Eustace parried his half-brother's thrust.

Richard got close enough to land his mace on the red and yellow shield, but it did no damage other than crack the paint.

'You as well?' Eustace laughed. 'I'll send you to hell alongside your father.'

'Did you kill him?' Richard spun Solis around and used the mace to bat aside Eustace's sword.

The big Martel knight grinned. 'He caused his own death. And you should have died long ago.'

Nicholas attacked from the other side and his blade flicked Eustace's coif, splitting some rings but missing the flesh.

'A wolf and a dog,' Eustace laughed.

Two knights with red shields broke through the melee and raced their tired horses towards Richard. A handful of Martel knights turned and chased them on much fresher mounts.

The first red knight's horse wore full mail armour.

Eustace spotted the Young King as Richard did and pushed Richard's next attack dismissively aside. The Martel Knight rode straight for the Young King, whose surcoat had been cut and torn.

The other knight was Adam, and he threw himself in front of the Young King. Eustace struck at him with such force that Adam's parry saved his life, but not his eye, and the Martel blade dug into Adam's eye socket and the eyeball popped.

'An eye for an eye,' Nicholas laughed as he attacked his half-brother from behind and cut with enough skill that the mail on Eustace's back tore open.

The big Martel knight cried out in surprise more than pain, but locked on to the Young King. Richard jumped in front of his lord and hammered down towards Eustace's head, but the knight somehow raised his shield to block the mace.

Adam regained his senses, and even missing an eye battered one of the Martel knights that chased the Young King. Another of those fell to the mud as his horse slipped and went down.

'I'll hold him,' Nicholas forced his horse between his half-brother and the Young King, and took a blow meant for him. The clang of sword on helmet rang out as Richard kept hammering the red and yellow shield. It had to break eventually.

The Young King had to fight off a Martel knight who caught him, and with a deft stroke relieved the knight of his front teeth.

'Go,' Richard said, 'we can give you enough time.'

'Ride with me, Richard,' the Young King shouted as he pressed his legs onto this horse, 'we can both escape.'

Richard hammered down with the mace, and the shield cracked. 'No, I'm staying with Nicholas, and then we're going back for Bowman.' His own words sounded like someone else's, and Richard wasn't sure how he'd make good on them.

Eustace pushed his horse into Nicholas's and it stumbled away.

The Young King's barded horse put its last reserve of energy into a sprint to the abbey, its armour not heavy enough to inconvenience it.

Richard pointed Solis at Eustace, and the stallion went for his horse's neck. It put Eustace off balance enough for Richard to smash a chunk of his shield away, but the big Martel recovered and his sword flashed down onto Richard's helmet. The blow had so much power he saw stars.

Adam clashed with a knight, but an attack came from his blind side and almost knocked him from the saddle.

Two other red knights arrived from the melee, but a chasing Lusignan knight felled one.

Richard snatched a glance towards the abbey, but the Young King was still in view. Eustace hit Richard again and the lacing under his chin loosened. The helmet slipped over his eyes and Richard had to dart away in order to rip the helmet off his head.

A Lusignan knight took his chance to attack.

Richard threw the helmet at him halfheartedly and the knight had to deflect it away with his sword. Richard didn't chase him, instead he went back for Nicholas, who circled with his half-brother trading blows. But the bigger man was stronger.

'You'll die here,' Eustace sneered.

Richard charged in, swung the mace and hit Eustace on the upper arm. The big Martel knight merely grunted and flung out his sword at Richard. It flicked his ear and caused it to sting sharply.

A red knight unhorsed a blue and white knight, but was thrown from his own saddle by another foe.

Nicholas caught Eustace on his bicep as Richard tried to target the big Martel's rein hand.

Eustace's next blow sliced the end off Nicholas's sword, and Richard could only harmlessly hit his opponent's wooden saddle.

Eustace slashed out at Richard's unprotected head and he raised his mace to block it. He missed his parry, but the sword caught the bottom end of the mace. The sword ran up the wooden shaft and pain exploded from his little finger.

Nicholas thrust his jagged sword into his half-brother's face. It gashed a hole in his nose which erupted in a spray of blood and skin, but the big Martel jerked his head out of the way before it went deeper.

Eustace, anger burning in his eyes, aimed a great cut at Nicholas.

The wolf-knight did the same, and neither knight made any attempt to block the other.

Nicholas's broken sword cracked Eustace's jawbone, but Eustace's sword was unbroken and pierced the wolf-knight's skull.

Richard's heart missed a beat.

Eustace pulled back his blade and felt his jaw. Blood seeped from the wound and the jawbone looked out of place.

But Nicholas collapsed in his saddle, and as his horse spun away, his body toppled down from it.

Grief wracked Richard. 'No,' he cried and hurled himself at the big

238

Martel knight. Eustace went to grin, but grimaced in pain instead and pushed Richard's attack aside.

Tears streamed down his face. Richard hadn't felt this feeling since Eustace and his uncle had come to Keynes. Richard's muscles strained as he whirled the mace down onto his enemy's head, denting his shield and smashing shards of wood from it. Eustace could only weather the storm.

But all storms run their course, and Richard's strength ran out before he could defeat Eustace. Richard mustered the last of his strength, and with a howl of anguish the mace drew down, but Eustace caught it with his sword. The jewelled mace head detached from the shaft and crashed into Eustace's already damaged jaw.

The big Martel cried out, but before Richard could fumble for his sword, Eustace had recovered. His eyes bore into Richard.

Eustace spat red onto the ground. 'You're next.'

Richard's hand found the hilt of the Little Lord's sword, the blade recovered from Lagny by Gerold but not yet cleaned of rust. Richard gripped the handle, but he also knew he couldn't best Eustace with a sword, especially now his strength was gone. He glimpsed the wolf-pelt on the mud, but choked down his loss as that had to wait.

Red knights and Flemings streamed back through the melee, the wedge had finally ground its way through the Lusignan knights.

Richard backed Solis up away from Eustace.

'Running again?' Eustace laughed, but had to check his glee when his jaw caused him pain. 'You ran at Keynes and you ran at the bastard's mother's castle. If you run here, I'll just find you again,' he shouted.

The running battle that was the melee caught them up and swallowed them. A red knight ran into Eustace and Richard was shocked to see infantry wading through the mud towards him. He kicked Solis on, but there were suddenly horsemen all around and he had nowhere to go. A moment of concern for Bowman flashed through his mind, but then he felt Solis move sideways and glanced back to see a spear strike his rear quarter. The stallion kicked out so fast the spearmen never comprehended his death and fell to the mud with a mangled face.

Solis limped his next step, which meant he'd been struck deeply. Richard's stomach felt as if it was in freefall. He couldn't lose his horse. Not like this. The Lusignan banner approached, and if Guy was under it, Richard knew he'd die next to his friend. A tear blocked his vision for a moment, but it mixed with blood for Eustace had cut him above his left eye and running blood stung it.

'I'm sorry,' he whispered and dug his spurs into Solis to get him to safety. He knew the horse was wounded and knew it could kill him, but he had to run. Solis grunted and cantered off with an unsteady wobble.

They would not get far, and certainly not fast enough.

Everyone raced towards Corbie.

Solis slipped on the ground and nearly went over. Richard knew if he did, he'd never get back up.

The stallion groaned a deep bellowing roar and pushed on, but he wobbled even more and Richard had to let him walk. His heart beat rapidly as red-shielded knights barreled past him.

A blue and white knight pulled his horse up next to Richard. 'Do you yield?' he asked.

Richard's face, tear-streaked and blood-soaked, gave the knight pause. Richard used the pause to throw the mace shaft at him, then leapt from his saddle at the Lusignan knight.

They collided in a tangle of shields and mail, but Richard had fury on his side and he pressed a thumb into the knight's eye until it gave way, then pulled his helmet backwards to throttle him with the lacing under his chin. Richard put all his grief and rage and sorrow into it and the knight's neck snapped with a pop and a crunch. Richard's chest heaved and with what he had left of his might, he pushed the knight off the horse.

Richard settled into the unfamiliar saddle with stirrups that were too long, and called to his horse. 'Come on, Solie.'

The stallion pinned his ears back at Richard's new horse, who at least obeyed his command to canter towards the abbey. The yellow horse followed, freer without a rider's weight.

The Martel and Lusignan knights knew their quarry had slipped their trap, and their exhaustion tempered their lust for captives.

Richard and a handful of the Young King's knights made their way back to the abbey in a sorry state as their pursuers abandoned the chase.

Count Philip stood next to his horse by the gateway, seeing the survivors in. 'Are you the last of them?' he asked. Red stains smeared Count Philip's yellow surcoat.

Richard nodded and a tear ran down his face.

The Count sighed. 'Did you lose men? I wept the first time I lost men, our brotherhood is tighter than blood,' he said softly.

Solis bit Richard's new horse on the leg, but the palomino stood with a hind leg held in the air.

Richard cried at that as much as Nicholas. And Bowman, what about

Bowman? 'Why didn't the Marshal come?' Richard snarled. 'This is his fault.'

The Count held Richard's horse on the bridle to calm it. 'There will be plenty of time for blame,' he said, 'but I do not think it's over yet.'

Richard wiped tears and blood from his eyes and turned around. Martel and Lusignan knights still approached. At a walk, and not in great order, but they were coming.

'I think they still mean to kill the Young King,' the Count said, 'you best get inside the abbey and get off this horse. We need to build defences.'

Richard dismounted, but when he hit the short grass, his legs wobbled. His body was drained. He led the new horse inside and put it into Nicholas's stable. Which made more tears flow. He put Solis away and went to inspect his wound. Blood poured down the stallion's back leg. Bright red and terrifying it dripped onto the straw.

'Come on, Richard,' Count Robert shouted from the abbey compound's yard, 'there's no time for horses, we have to block the gates and the streets of Corbie.'

Richard swore at the world for its cruelty. What was the point of all this suffering? He left Solis with a heart wrenching pat on the neck and went to help wheel carts out of the abbey to barricade the road that attached the abbey to the town.

'If we block this road,' Count Robert said, 'we can keep access to the town.' The Count's helmet had its nasal piece missing, and half of his red surcoat hung torn from his body.

Knights, squires, and servants ran back and forth to reinforce the barricade, or bring lances up to the main gateway into the abbey to use as pikes.

Richard could see over the compound wall, and he could see the enemy gather on the hill above the town.

The Young King strode over and nodded at Richard. 'Thank you,' he said, 'you saved me and I won't forget it.'

'He killed Nicholas,' Richard said.

The Young King paused on his way and turned back. 'Your friend fought and died for his king and his friends. He fought and died in sweat and blood and with the taste of iron in his mouth. He attained the high bath of honour that only those who fight can understand.'

Richard would have cried, but he was out of tears.

The Young King nodded. 'We will lose more good men before this is over, they are surrounding the abbey,' he said. 'We are under siege.'

CORNERED

Wind howled over the top of the abbey's inner courtyard, but the air between the four walls was peaceful and unmoving. The gnarled and twisted trunk of an old yew tree grew in the centre of the square, thick limbs reaching up towards the darkening sky.

'It's ancient,' the Young King said to Richard when he entered. 'Or so the Abbot said before he stopped talking to us.'

Richard remembered that Nicholas had died excommunicated and had to sit down on the bench where the Young King sat in his armour. Richard had entered the abbey searching for something to distract himself from the loss of his friend. A loss that felt futile and pointless.

'I blame myself for this,' the Young King said, 'you were right when you said I should swallow my jealousy and invite the Marshal back. A quiet apology would have stung less than the regret that stabs me now.'

Judas walked up to Richard and licked blood from his hands. Richard was numb to it.

'Count Robert is organising a defence,' the Young King rested his elbows on his knees and dropped his head into his hands.

'I know,' Richard said, 'I helped move some carts to block a street.'

'The traitors will pay dearly if they wish to break in.'

'But they will get in,' Richard said.

The Young King groaned. 'They will. Or tomorrow they may organise themselves enough to fire the town and burn us out.'

Richard looked up at the grey clouds that rushed overhead. 'I think the town might be too wet to catch by then.'

Judas licked the stub of Richard's little finger, and he flinched back in pain. The dog jumped away and whined.

'You shouldn't let them taste blood,' the Young King said, 'once they have, they lose their respect for men. You should probably kill him before he hurts you.'

Richard looked into the dog's yellowed eyes. 'He won't hurt me, and I'm not killing any animals unless I'm going to eat them.'

The Young King snorted. 'You provincial knights never fail to amuse me. You countryfolk prefer animals to the company of men. The Lord gave us animals for our use, not our pleasure.'

'Animals don't try to kill me,' Richard stroked the black dog's head. 'Usually.'

'We are like rats trapped in a bucket here,' the young Angevin said, 'just waiting for a new puppy to be thrown in to learn its trade.'

'Then we need to get out of the bucket,' Richard said.

'How?' the Young King stood up and gazed up at the dark yew tree. 'If we could get out, don't you think I would? We're outnumbered and have too far to run.'

A litter carried by four monks crossed the courtyard on the way to the infirmary. A knight lay stricken on it, screaming from a bone-deep cut on his forearm.

Richard covered his ears until they were inside.

The Young King watched him. 'If the screams still bother a war-hero, then I shall never grow used to them,' he said.

Richard didn't hear but eventually uncovered his ears and looked at his lord. 'I'm not staying in the bucket,' he said, 'I'm going to get out of the bucket, or bring an army of rats to overwhelm the dogs.'

'I think we've stretched that word-game far enough,' the Young King smiled faintly, 'but if you have an idea, then do not keep it to yourself.'

Four of the Young King's servants found him and rushed over with a basin of water and a silver cup of red-coloured drink.

The Young King shuddered at the liquid but washed his hands in the basin. Brown mud clouded the clean water and mixed with blood from a cut on his wrist.

'Let him wash next,' the Young King said, 'his finger should be washed. I think that's what they recommend now, until there's puss to rub into the wound.'

Richard dipped his right hand into the water, which stung. 'I want to bring the Marshal back,' he said, 'Eustace and Guy nearly killed you, and we are fewer now than we were.'

'That's your plan?' the Young King waved the servants away. 'Why do you think he will come now?'

'Because he can play the hero,' Richard said, 'he can add to his fame and his importance. And today is now Monday, so the mayor has one less excuse to muster the militia.'

'What good will they do against four hundred knights?'

Richard shrugged. 'I'd rather have them than not.'

'Very well, the Marshal is more likely to listen to you than anyone else in my company. But do not go alone. This is a task for two, you should not leave until dark, and men should not be out alone in the wild at night.'

Richard's eyes filled. Bowman hadn't come back at all, and he along with any knights still on the tournament field would be blocked from returning now. 'Who is there?' Richard asked.

Adam looked around a doorway, linen wrapped over one eye, and nodded when he saw the Young King.

'You will be rewarded for your actions,' the Young King said when the knight bowed to him.

Adam shook his head. His mail was thick with mud, and like Richard he had lost his helmet. 'I paid my debt to you with my eye,' he said, 'who could argue that it was not God's plan and judgement.'

The Young King nodded.

'But I cannot fight properly,' Adam said, 'I cannot tell how far away things are. I shall need to relearn both lance and sword.'

'Then I have something useful you can do,' the Young King said.

Richard looked at the mess that was Adam. 'I'm not sure the Marshal will want to see him, although he might just so he can kill him,' he said.

The Young King smiled. 'If the man who concocted the plot falls to his knees in tears before the Marshal, and gives him my apology too, he may yet come to our aid. Tell him I put your eye out as a punishment if it helps.'

Richard stood up. 'That might work. Although, it's also all we've got.'

'Will you do this for us?' the Young King asked his knight.

Adam nodded. 'My life is yours.'

Richard went to check on Solis first, and it was at the large stable building that he saw a familiar head of blonde hair emerge from a water trough.

Bowman shook his head and water flew everywhere. He gasped for air from the shock of the almost freezing water and noticed Richard. 'Oh, thank the lord,' Bowman said, 'I was worried about you.'

Otto stood behind him, his entire body covered in mud with sticks and leaves poking out from his mail.

Richard noticed Bowman looked the same. 'What happened to you, did you crawl through a tree?'

Bowman nodded. 'Ever since the battle,' he said, 'we lost all our weapons and had to let the horses go.'

Richard swallowed, and his eyes itched and reddened. 'Your brother,' he said.

'My,' Bowman stopped and narrowed his eyes at Richard. 'What? Where is he?'

Richard tried to speak but the next word hung in his throat and only tears came out.

Bowman shook his head as water ran down his face. 'Maybe he's still out there? There were others,' he said.

Richard shook his head. 'I saw him fall.'

Bowman blinked for a moment, shook his head, then roared a cry of grief. 'What if I could have saved him? Maybe if I'd been kinder to him?'

'It was nothing to do with you,' Richard said, 'it was Eustace that killed him.'

'Him?' Bowman shouted, his eyes burning.

'Nicholas broke his jaw, I think.'

'I'll rip it off and cram it back down his throat,' Bowman shouted, so loudly that servants nearby found reasons to leave. 'He's taken everyone from me I cared about, I'll ride out and face him. German, fetch me a horse.'

Otto gestured at the stables. 'We have not got our horses, or even a small blade between us. I know you are large, but you can't fight him with your bare hands.'

'There's plenty of weapons lying around,' Bowman walked towards the refectory. 'Weapons belonging to men who no longer live. I'll give them a use.'

Richard caught his arm and the blonde man scowled down at him. 'Step out of my way,' he snarled.

Richard looked up into his friend's hatred-filled eyes. 'Not now,' he said, 'we all want to kill Eustace but you can't do it now. He won't indulge you with a duel, he'll send men to swarm you and your gesture will be for nothing.'

'But then I won't feel what I feel,' Bowman whispered, 'do you know why you ran into me in that alleyway that wasn't an alleyway?'

Richard shook his head.

'It was because I ran away from everyone I had left,' Bowman said, 'away from anyone close enough for me to feel their loss, because Eustace either killed, kidnaped, or crushed my whole family. I ran away so I couldn't feel that again. '

'I'm sorry,' Richard said.

'I wasn't supposed to care for anyone ever again,' the blonde man's face grew red, but it could have been the cold water, 'then you came along and ruined everything. If it wasn't for you I'd still be hating my brother instead of hurting for him.'

'Riding out to get yourself killed is not the way to deal with it,' Richard said.

'You'll tell me to wait,' Bowman said, 'be patient. Wait for the Marshal to come and rescue us. But that doesn't help me now.'

Richard looked over to Otto for help, but the German shook his head vigorously with wide eyes.

Bowman's eyes overflowed with pain. Disbelief and grief cracked his expression apart, and Richard couldn't think of any words that would help.

So he slapped him in the face.

The blow shook the broad man and caught him by surprise. He rubbed his cheek and stepped back.

'If you go out there and die, how will that make me feel?' Richard asked. 'You're the only one who has been with me the whole time, everything I've been through, you've been through with me. Don't you dare leave me here.'

Bowman scratched his neck and his hand came back with a twig.

Richard took a breath. 'Before you go and kill yourself,' he said, 'do you remember Eva? Do you remember how certain you are that you need to live to look after your child?'

Bowman shut his eyes for a heartbeat and colour returned to his face. He nodded as if defeated.

'I'm going into Amiens with Adam to get the Marshal back,' Richard said. 'You're going to stay here and help build defences. I never give you orders, but I'm giving you one now. Stay inside the barricades.'

Bowman exhaled a long breath.

'Did you kill Geoffrey Martel?' Richard asked.

Bowman spat. 'A crossbow caught me as I went to strike, but my new leather breastplate held it up. Then the spearmen came, and we had to retreat. We piled up our saddles and shields under a tree near the river. What happened to your ear?'

'Nothing,' Richard touched it and it stung.

'You've lost the top half,' Bowman looked down at Richard's hand, 'there'll be nothing left of you soon, young lord.'

Richard thought he was more right than he knew. 'Go and build up the barricades,' Richard said, 'and stick with the German. We're all suffering but maybe there's something I can do about it.'

Richard's plan of sailing up the River Somme had sounded good in the still air of the courtyard, but as he peered over an upturned cart at the southern edge of Corbie in the fading light, its major drawback dawned on him. 'Adam, do you know how to sail?'

The knight shook his head. His hand on the cart, he peered into the bushes that grew only a few paces outside the town. 'Do I look like a seaman?'

Richard shrugged. 'The townspeople have all gone, so if there's a boat with a sail, we'll have to sail it ourselves.'

'I might not be a seaman,' Adam grinned, 'but this isn't the sea. If there are oars, I can row.'

'So you do know of the water?'

'Do you remember Sir Roger's colours?' Adam asked.

'Blue at the bottom with a green top and a yellow line in the middle,' Richard said.

'What do you think the blue means?'

Richard sighed. 'I suppose water, you don't need to show off.'

'What do you think the yellow represents?'

'I don't know,' Richard tested his footing on the cart, 'and I don't really care.' Richard clambered up the obstacle and dropped down the other side.

'It's sand,' Adam followed him.

The black dog crawled under a wooden table stacked against the cart and joined Richard.

'We can't bring a dog,' Adam said.

'I don't think we can stop him,' Richard replied, 'come on, we need to be quiet now.' He made for the bushes that covered the gentle slope down to the waterway. Dusk cast shadows amongst the vegetation and Richard thought he heard a horse snort in the distance.

'This way,' Adam whispered as they crouched low and picked their way parallel to the track. Tall trees towered over them and Richard had to squint to focus on anything.

A waterbird flew away from them, and they stopped to listen for anyone who might come to investigate. Judas looked between the bird and Richard, who signalled the dog to lie down. To his astonishment, he did.

A few tense moments later they continued to edge south, the air freshening and clearing away from the town's fouler odours. They reached the end of the foliage and the riverbank at the same time. A wooden platform ran along it like a dockside, many flat-bottomed barges moored off it and bobbed up and down on the river.

Judas let out a low growl at a barge, and Richard hesitated. A boatman with grey hair popped his head up from the side of his barge and considered how dangerous he thought the creeping knights were to him. He said something to a companion and the two of them unmoored their barge.

'Wait,' Richard hissed, 'take us with you.'

They used a pole to push their barge away from the bank, and then to propel themselves up the river.

'Cowards,' Adam sneered.

Richard sighed. 'You can hardly blame them,' he replied, 'which one of these do you want to take?'

Adam's selected barge was the smallest they could find, the others were larger and normally all pulled by horses. Judas wobbled on the shallow deck as it cast off, his eyes set longingly on the bank.

Richard wasn't any more comfortable and he crouched down in the hull as trees and bushes slunk past in the encroaching night. But the undergrowth drifted by far too slowly and it soon became clear their current mode of transport would take the entire night to reach their destination. When they came across a sleeping hamlet of four houses by the waterside, they therefore ran the barge up the bank and tied it to a weeping willow.

They crept around the houses until they reached a paddock. It was small, set against one house and contained a shaggy grey horse.

'I'm not riding that,' Adam said, 'my legs will brush the ground.'

'Fine,' Richard climbed through the wooden fencing, 'you can walk beside me.'

The grey horse came over to investigate Richard, although it snorted at the black dog when it appeared from the chilly night wagging its tail.

Richard gently stroked the grey's neck and looked around for a rope. At the entrances to paddocks everywhere he'd been, halters and ropes for horses would be found tied to fences or on the grass, and sure enough, slung over the gate was a length of rope, knotted in two places to make a halter than could slip over the horse's head.

'I think it's a barge-horse,' Richard said.

'I have a hunting dog that's taller,' Adam said with disdain in his eyes.

That was probably true, the horse came up to Richard's midriff, but riding would still beat walking. He mounted it by simply swinging his leg over and then hoped the horse had been broken to ride. He pressed his thighs and the grey pony walked on.

Adam trudged along behind. 'I'm not walking the whole way,' he complained once they were out of earshot of the hamlet.

'I'm not making you,' Richard said, 'the Templars ride two to a horse, so can we.'

'Their horses are bigger,' Adam grumbled.

Halfway to Amiens, along a tree covered lane so dark he couldn't see the ground, Adam relented. He climbed onto the rear of the horse and just about balanced on it without a saddle.

The plodding pace of their mount and the darkness around them gave Richard's mind space to wander. For the first time since the tournament, he could take a breath, but the relaxation just let in thoughts that made him clench his teeth and wipe tears from his eyes. Nicholas had been his brother-in-arms just as much as Bowman still was, and Richard didn't know how to deal with his loss.

Yellow dots in the blackness appeared to break him from his sadness.

'Those are the watch fires on the town wall,' Adam said. If he'd sensed Richard's inner turmoil, he didn't let on.

A huge wooden beam locked the town gate shut because of the late hour, but Adam shouted up and invoked the Young King's name to gain an entrance. Four militiamen escorted them at spearpoint to the mayor's house, where Richard tied the shaggy pony up to the tie-rail.

'He won't be happy being woken at this hour,' one of the town guards said, 'we try not to wake him, so his foul mood will be on you.'

'Just wake him up,' Richard said.

An owl hooted somewhere, and Richard started to make the sign of the cross. He stopped himself halfway through and sighed. The owl hooted again and Richard swore because with Nicholas dead, the owl had already claimed its victim for the day.

A while later the door on the corner-house swung open and a bleary-eyed servant carrying a horn lantern appeared. He squinted in the dim light at the knights. 'He'll come down to you,' he said, 'wait here.'

'We were already,' Adam groaned as the servant walked slowly up the creaking stairs.

Footsteps thudded on the ceiling above. A black cat slunk in from the street looking for mice. Judas exchanged a look with it but stayed still, and Richard wondered if Eustace had beaten the poor animal until it left cats alone.

'Get that out,' one guard waved a spear at the feline. 'I don't need more bad luck, my sister lost a child last week.'

The cat meowed and escaped just as the mayor swept down his staircase, his best robe around his shoulders.

The mayor groaned. 'You again.'

'We need your help,' Richard said.

'Everyone needs my help. Most of them are polite enough to wait until daylight.'

'The Young King is besieged at Corbie, and we need your aid,' Richard said.

'What can I do?' the Mayor scrunched his face up at the sight of Adam's bandage.

The stairs creaked heavily as the Marshal descended. He beamed at Richard. 'You didn't die without me then.'

Richard trembled. 'Many did,' he said, 'and the Martels and Guy have surrounded Corbie. They're going to kill your lord.'

'So he lost the tournament without me?' the Marshal asked.

'That's your reaction?'

The Marshal reached the ground and folded his arms. 'Serves him right for ignoring me,' he said, 'and now he's sent you crawling over to apologise for him, has he?'

'He didn't ignore you,' Richard replied, 'he needs you back. We lost too many knights to be able to defend him from the next attack.'

'Just agree parole and get them back,' the Marshal shook his head. 'Can nothing be done without me?'

'We can't parole the dead,' Richard let his words hang in the air.

'Two tournaments in a row with deaths?' the Marshal asked. 'That is terribly bad luck.'

'Bad luck?' Richard laughed. 'We didn't lose one or two, we lost dozens.'

'I doubt it,' the Marshal said, 'tournaments aren't so violent, they are merely a game.'

'A game?' Richard shook his head.

'Does this look like a game?' Adam pointed at his empty eye socket.

'An eye for an eye,' the Marshal replied, 'and if I was not so dulled from the sleep you interrupted, I might have taken the other one already.'

Richard sighed. 'If I hear an eye for an eye one more time.'

Adam's remaining eye looked down at his feet.

'William,' Richard said to the Marshal, 'it was no game, and the losses are no story. We lost Nicholas.'

The Marshal paused. He frowned. Then he shrugged. 'He was a Martel, wasn't he? They are the enemy. At least they are your enemy if I remember your story correctly?'

'He was my friend,' Richard felt anger and sadness and was caught between the two.

'I don't understand why you insisted on keeping him around,' the Marshal said, 'I always thought he'd stab you in the back.'

'I didn't keep him around, it was his choice,' Richard said, 'and he proved men can change. Don't you want to believe that?'

'Why would I want to change?' the Marshal's dark face looked confused.

Richard shook his head. 'You're an idiot.'

'You're not doing a very good job of convincing me to come and help you,' the Marshal said.

'I shouldn't have to,' Richard said, 'if you love our lord as much as you tell everyone you do, you should come running to save him.'

Adam stepped up to the Marshal. 'I have come to apologise for what I did to you,' he knelt down on one knee and bowed his head.

'I don't know why you've bothered. Does apologising make the accusation go away? Will everyone who heard it now forget it?'

Adam looked up. 'If that were in my power.'

'You tried to destroy me,' the Marshal said, 'you know what Count Philip did to the man who was adulterous with his wife?'

'He beat him to death,' Adam said, 'and if that's what you need to do to me, then do it. Sate your revenge and then do your duty to your lord.'

'You've only got one eye,' the Marshal said, 'I don't want to be known as the knight who beats useless cripples.'

Adam held back whatever he wanted to reply. 'The Young King needs your help, and I am sorry for what I did. It was a mistake, and I will prostrate myself in front of you if it will make you come and save our lord's life.'

The Marshal rubbed his chin. 'It might, actually.'

'What?' Richard asked.

'Lie on the floor,' the Marshal ordered.

'That's too much,' Richard said, 'he means what he says, and he and you are both of the same rank. There's no need.'

The Marshal glanced at Richard. 'You lost your friend because of him, why are you protecting his dignity?'

'Thank you, Richard, but I have no pride to defend,' Adam lowered himself down onto the floor that was covered with Somme rushes. Face down and flat, he spread his arms out as if he honoured a king.

'William,' a sharp female voice sounded from the staircase. Sophie stepped down with tired-looking eyes. 'That is quite enough. You are being petty and vindictive and it does not suit you. Adam, rise.'

The knight pushed himself up and looked up at the Marshal, who kept his arms folded and avoided looking at Sophie.

'Up,' she reached the bottom of the stairs.

Adam got to his feet.

'You are boys playing at being men. You, William,' she stabbed a pointed finger into his back, 'are the reason my husband abandoned me for half a year, and why he has a scar across his face and fewer fingers than he should. Maybe you should kneel before me and ask for my forgiveness?'

The Marshal glared at Richard as if he could help.

'You won't even look at me, will you?' Sophie had to walk around to the Marshal's front. 'Avoiding me like a scolded child. All this posturing, all this loud and pointless talk that woke me from my sleep.'

'Can we?' Richard started to ask.

'Don't,' Sophie said, 'I'll get to you.'

Richard swallowed.

'You,' Sophie stood a hand's width from the Marshal and had to look up to meet his gaze, 'will prepare yourself for battle. Gather the knights you brought here, and you will damn well go back for your lord. Because if my husband loses any more parts of him...'

Richard felt his ear and thought not to mention it.

Sophie stood on her tiptoes to get closer to the Marshal's face. 'You will have to answer to me, and that will be worse than facing King Henry himself.'

An alien expression crept across the Marshal's face. It might have even been fear.

Sophie snapped round to Richard. 'Where is your whore, then?'

'I don't have one,' Richard replied, 'I never have, and Nicholas is dead.'

Sophie paused. She looked into his eyes. 'How is his half-brother taking it?'

'Bowman is calling him brother now.'

'I see,' Sophie said, 'he must truly be in great pain.'

'I'm worried about him,' Richard said.

His wife's face softened, and she looked at his ear. 'You really need to be more careful.'

'I wasn't planning to have part of my ear sliced off,' Richard clenched his right hand so the bandaged tip of his little finger was out of view. 'It was Eustace.'

Sophie pushed some hair out of her face. She hadn't brushed it. 'He ruined our wedding,' she turned to the mayor. 'Eustace Martel was at my wedding. He cursed us, he killed a man on our wedding day and I have been cursed ever since.'

'That is indeed a tragedy,' the mayor said, 'have you considered finding a skilled churchman to exorcise your marriage?'

Sophie's eyes twitched. 'Those churchmen have no power over such things. A death must answer the death. While Eustace is alive, I shall be cursed.'

'Of course,' the mayor bowed to her, 'you are correct.'

'Then you'll send your militia to ensure it,' Sophie wasn't asking.

The mayor rubbed his fingers together. 'I could consult with the town council.'

'Could?'

'Yes, I could. I mean, yes surely I will,' the mayor said.

'When?' Sophie tapped a foot on the rushes.

'I will send for them and raise the matter,' the mayor nodded. He didn't wait for Sophie to say anything else and shouted for some servants before disappearing upstairs as fast as he could shuffle.

'I want an explanation,' Sophie turned back to Richard, 'I came here to tell you that you had my support. That your children were well. Then you threw that tart in my face. How would you like it if I arrived here with a new knight on my arm?'

'That woman was just causing trouble,' Richard said, 'she is Guy's sister, and he is playing a game with me.'

Sophie frowned. 'But William, you should have known who she was. Surely you would have seen her when you were a prisoner of Guy's?'

The Marshal shrugged. 'This does sound like something Guy would do, nothing is beyond his evil. I don't remember her face, though. When we met her on the road before Lagny she didn't seem familiar. She may have been at Castle Lusignan, but I never noticed her.'

Richard couldn't help smiling. 'That's how I know you never misbehaved with the Queen.'

The Marshal gritted his teeth. 'You should have known my innocence, regardless.'

'Do not start this again,' Sophie snapped. 'I can believe William was oblivious to a woman, he lives in the world of men and was almost certainly too self-obsessed during his captivity to look outside his own struggles. However, I will not be made a fool out of, husband, if I so much as hear that you have been alone with her, I will go to the bishop and your marriage will be over. Remember who the legitimacy of rule flows through in Yvetot.'

Richard did remember, although he wasn't sure the village was worth the trouble it caused him. 'I will avoid her if I can, you have my word,' he said.

'If you can?'

'Fine, I will,' Richard said, 'but we need to reinforce the Young King. I need to see to that first. Without both the Marshal and the militia tomorrow, he will be lost.' Richard turned to his friend. 'Just leave

Henry the Northerner here.'

'Why?' the Marshal asked. 'He's done nothing wrong.'

Adam groaned. 'The Young King does not see it that way. And nor does anyone else.'

Richard stepped in front of the one-eyed knight. 'If you leave Henry here, the Young King will apologise to you. You don't need to do anything else, certainly nothing undignified. '

Richard thought he could put off mentioning the issue over the war-cry until later.

'I'll think about it,' the Marshal said.

'What is there to think about?' Richard asked. 'If you stay here, by the time the sun sets tomorrow, we could all be dead. It might already be too late.'

The Marshal grunted. 'Don't watch the road for my arrival.'

Sophie coughed, and the swarthy knight looked at her out of the corner of his eye.

'I told you to prepare to leave, why are you still here?' she asked. 'Go.'

The Marshal glanced at Richard for a moment, then beat a hasty retreat up the staircase, his heavy footfalls echoing down from the ceiling when he reached the upper storey.

'This is all his fault,' Richard glanced at Adam, 'and yours.'

'What if the mayor is a coward, or his council declines to help?' Adam asked.

'Sophie,' Richard said, 'we must go back, my place is beside the Young King, but if the mayor tries to weasel out of helping, pressure him.'

'Me?' she replied. 'This has nothing to do with me. What sway does a woman have? Neither the mayor nor William have any reason to listen to me.'

Adam chuckled. 'I think you've sent them both upstairs with their tails between their legs,' he said, 'you have as much chance as anyone.'

'Tell the mayor that we just need a body of his men who won't run, and are armed with spears and crossbows. They just need to march to Corbie, their arrival will be enough to scatter the Lusignans.'

'Will it?'

Richard shrugged. 'Tell him whatever you need to. Tell him of the stories he'll be able to tell his merchant friends. How jealous they will be. Tell the Marshal how famous he'll be if he were to lead the militia and triumph.'

Sophie shook her head. 'This is madness, all of it. If you men poured all your energy into useful things rather than this nonsense, imagine what the world would look like?'

'I will pray tomorrow will be my last battle,' Richard said, 'I can't watch more friends die.'

'You're a knight,' Adam scoffed, 'it's what we do. We fight and we die.'

'I'd rather there was less of the dying,' Richard said.

'You could stay here,' Sophie said, 'stay in Amiens where it's dry, warm, and safe.'

Richard shook his head. 'I can't leave Bowman in that abbey, his mind is so black he may seek death in battle if I'm not there to stop him. And Solis, he was speared. I can't leave him, either.'

'Is it bad?' Sophie asked. 'I know you love that horse more than yourself.'

Richard didn't answer but his eyes watered.

'Is it always like this?'

'What do you mean?' Richard asked.

Sophie walked up to Richard and held out a hand. He hesitated as if the hand contained a cursed relic.

Sophie nodded and smiled faintly. 'Your adventures,' she said, 'are they all this dangerous? This desperate?'

Richard placed his hand in hers. She closed her fingers around his and looked down at the recently damaged little finger and frowned.

'Yes,' Richard said. 'Pretty much.'

Mist lay thick on the ground by the time they moored their barge outside Corbie, two bends before the mooring point from where they'd borrowed it. Richard had returned the shaggy grey horse to his paddock first, and then moored the barge amongst some rushes on the north bank of the Somme. The sun had not yet risen, so their return was still covered by darkness.

Judas leapt from the barge before it reached the bank and disappeared into the shadowy foliage.

'That dog's going to get us killed,' Adam whispered.

Richard felt exposed without either of his mail shirts, having just his cloak to keep the cold or any enemies away. He rested a hand on Sir John's dagger as he pushed through the trees that hung their low branches into the dark green river.

Richard crouched down and waited for Adam to catch up. The one-eyed knight bumped into a tree and shook some branches. Droplets of water showered down on them and Richard swore under his breath. The water was freezing cold on his head but he pressed on in the hope the abbey was near. It wasn't long before the rushing noise of the flowing river faded behind them.

255

Richard's foot sunk into the cold earth and moisture cooled his feet. He looked up and saw Judas ahead of him with his black hackles raised. The dog stood motionless, his head low and yellow eyes peering ahead into the bushes.

Adam bumped into Richard and almost knocked him over. 'What are you doing there?' Adam asked.

Richard clapped his hand around the knight's face to silence him. He pointed to the dog.

Rustling leaves drew Adam's attention. There were voices ahead. Richard couldn't tell how many people there were, or who they were.

The sound grew louder, and the dog growled.

Richard reached out and put a hand on his back. The fur was slick with water, but Richard gripped him and the dog quietened.

Richard pulled his feet out of the mud and slowly pushed through the next bush. The voices were even louder. Through the undergrowth Richard could see a path or track. Drops of water spattered from the clouds onto the leaves above. He couldn't see much and everything was cold and black.

A shadow darkened the track, and Richard froze. He retreated carefully into cover as two men made very slow progress down the path.

'I told you it would rain,' one man stopped walking.

His companion sneezed. 'I don't see the point of this, these woods are too thick for horses.'

'Ground is too wet for horses, too,' the first man said.

'I don't see why we had to come north. It's a frozen wasteland up here.'

'We could just go back and sit by a fire, no one would ever know,' the first man said, 'who would be mad enough to be here at this ungodly hour?'

Mud squelched further up the path. More footsteps from someone else. A loud voice rang out from the murk. 'How would you know that? Are you privy to the enemy's plans?'

It was a voice that Richard knew.

'I'm sorry, my lord,' the first man said, 'we didn't know you were there.'

'Of course you didn't,' Guy said, 'or you wouldn't have dared to say it.'

In the night Guy was just another shadow as the rain started to patter down thickly onto the trees. He approached the men and punched one. His victim reeled back into a tree clutching his face.

'You fools are not here on a whim,' Guy said, 'you are here because you need to be.'

'We didn't mean to complain,' the other man backed away from his lord.

Guy grabbed him by the throat. 'Keep your eyes open or I will have you thrown into the river,' he flung the man back.

The first man untangled himself from the tree. 'We'll keep a good lookout,' he said.

'I'm sure you will,' Guy replied. 'Just because we expect them to strike out towards Amiens doesn't mean you can shirk your duty. If we defang the Angevin snake here, then they may cease their interference in my affairs. Which means you sorry idiots won't have to leave home again.'

The two guards stood motionless as the first of the raindrops infiltrated through the leaves and branches and landed around them.

'I'll be back,' Guy said, 'and if I hear you before I see you, then I'll take a finger from you both.'

They nodded.

Guy continued on the path, Richard presumed to find the next set of lookouts to terrorise.

He stayed perfectly still until he couldn't hear the Lusignan's footsteps in the rain anymore.

One man let out a deep breath and rubbed his nose. 'I think it's bleeding, Matthew.'

Matthew pulled his cloak further around himself. 'I was speaking to one of the Martel squires yesterday, I think their lord is nearly as bad as ours.'

'I dream of stabbing him in the throat,' the first man said.

'Do you remember what he did to Ralph the Breton?' Matthew asked.

'I'll be sick if I do.'

Adam crept up to Richard so he could whisper in his ear. 'What if they stand here all night?'

'We'll creep around them,' Richard said, 'I think Judas knows to be quiet.'

'What sort of man names their dog after Christ's betrayer?'

Nicholas, Richard thought bitterly, but he never said it because Adam sneezed.

The one-eyed knight froze and looked at Richard with shock on his face.

'What was that?' Matthew asked.

There was no time for thought or hesitation. Richard drew Sir John's dagger and leapt through the thicket.

The man called Matthew was a squire, for he wore only a padded jacket and leather helmet. An axe hung in his belt, but Richard attacked before his hand could retrieve it.

The black dog sprang at the other man and latched onto the arm of his thick tunic.

Richard brought his dagger down with everything he had and it easily pierced the fabric armour. His left arm caught the wrist of the axe-hand before it could be drawn, and Richard pushed Matthew backwards.

The other man windmilled his arm around, swinging the dog through the air, but the animal's jaws were latched on. The man fumbled his free hand to draw his knife.

Richard forced Matthew to stumble, and he landed on his back on the path with a squelch. Richard fell on him and his knee landed on Matthew's groin. He never had a chance to scream because Sir John's dagger stabbed through his gaping mouth and burst out of the back of his head. The tip of the blade dug into the mud. Rain washed down Richard's face as he pulled the dagger out and struck again. His grief drove the blade again and again into Matthew's face until it no longer resembled one.

Adam belatedly appeared on the path with his knife as Judas's victim had his back turned. Adam sank his weapon into the squire's neck and he collapsed in a heap. Judas released the arm, barked at the man, and lunged at his neck.

Richard stood up from Matthew and wiped water from his face with the back of his sleeve. He took the axe for himself and slid it into his belt.

Adam got out of the black dog's way as Judas shook the dead squire's neck in his snarling jaws.

Watching the dog savage the now dead squire cleared the rage from Richard's mind.

'Stop him,' Adam hissed, 'someone will hear.'

Richard shook his head. The rain grew harder and puddles formed on the path.

Judas ripped chunks of flesh from the corpse's neck until he snapped the head free. He threw the severed head from side to side in his jaws until something else tore away and the head flew off and crashed into a tree trunk. It left a red smudge on the bark.

Adam put a hand down towards the dog.

Judas bared his red teeth and growled.

'Let him,' Richard said, 'the rain's so loud now we don't have to whisper. He can tear these bodies to pieces, when Guy finds them he might think a wild beast is stalking his men. Let them spend the rest of the night in fear.'

'That's devilry,' Adam said, 'savage devilry.'

Richard, dripping dagger in hand, went back to Matthew. 'Come on, let's help the devilry.' Richard butchered the body, pretending it was Eustace he stabbed, until he felt tired. Judas tore the squire apart with Adam's help, until bite marks surrounded a severed arm, and his bloodlust waned.

Blood and gore covered the path, it was as if the two men had exploded.

'We're going to Hell for this,' Adam wiped his blade clean.

Richard shrugged. 'I already am.'

Judas sauntered by with a hand in his mouth.

'Leave that here,' Adam said. 'Drop.'

The dog shook it, dropped it into a brown puddle, and barked at it.

The sound of men walking came from down the track.

'I think someone heard,' Richard said.

'I told you,' Adam replied, 'I bloody told you.'

Richard ducked into the hedge on the other side of the path and struck out in the direction he hoped the abbey was.

Adam followed close behind, but the dog wasn't with them.

Richard looked back for Judas and heard him bark. A ferocious series of barks that made the back of Richard's neck tingle. Maybe the Young King was right and he shouldn't have let the dog taste human blood.

Shouts and a scream came from the path before the dog burst through the foliage and came to a stop by Richard, his tongue hanging out and his breathing heavy.

Richard grinned, and his uncertainty faded. 'They saw him,' he said, 'now they think a dog did it.'

'A dog did do it,' Adam mumbled, 'can we go now? I'm soaked through.'

Richard nodded, and they pushed through the woods only a short way until they found the town of Corbie.

A considerable amount of open space separated the edge of the woods from the town, and there were pairs of Lusignan men using the treeline to shelter from the rain.

'Should we run for it?' Adam asked.

Richard shook his head. 'Then it's obvious who we are. Walk slowly.'

'They'll have crossbows,' Adam said.

'It's cold, wet, and dark,' Richard said, 'if they loose a bolt, then we can start running.'

'You're mad,' Adam said.

Instead of replying, Richard walked calmly out of the tree cover and towards the houses ahead. Smoke rose into the stormy sky and light from fires dotted Corbie. Out in the open, the wind tugged at his cloak and blew his hood from his head, but he kept walking. The rain chilled one side of his face.

Adam followed but kept looking behind him.

'That's suspicious,' Richard said through a powerful gust of wind.

'What?' Adam shouted.

'That's suspicious,' Richard repeated at the top of his voice.

A cry rang out from the treeline. Richard looked back as the twang of a crossbow cut through the raindrops. The bolt whistled past.

'Now we can run,' Richard spun on his heels, slipped on the short grass, and made for the nearest street.

Another bolt sank into the earth near him as he ran, and a third flew overhead and buried itself in the wall of a house on the outskirts of the town.

The road he aimed for had two upturned carts barricading it, and spears appeared through gaps as a challenge was shouted from inside.

'We're with the Young King,' Richard said as he crashed into the cart. A bolt buried itself into the wood by his head with a dull thud.

'Who are you?' someone asked from inside.

'Richard and Adam, we've been to see the Marshal,' Richard climbed over the cart without waiting for a reply.

Count Philip greeted him when Richard landed next to two knights and a trio of squires.

'You made quick work of the journey,' the Fleming said, 'although we didn't think you'd make it back. I owe one of my knights some coins.'

Richard caught his breath. 'I wouldn't be too happy, our journey was not a shining success.'

Adam crawled under a cart, Judas right behind him.

'Does your dog have blood all over it?' Count Philip asked.

Richard grinned but his limbs were weary. 'Don't ask.'

Richard left his cloak to hang by the fire in the warming room of the abbey. He took his shoes off too, which were wet through again, but luckily this time the Abbot was nowhere to complain. Richard made his way into the gloomy refectory and shivered in the cool air when his eyes rested on Nicholas's empty bed. He looked away quickly. Snores filled the long chamber and a single candle flickered on the extended table.

Gerold sat up in his bed with difficulty when he saw Richard. 'Thank the Lord,' he said.

The hour was very late, but the Young King stirred in his bedding and got up to greet Richard. 'I prayed for your survival and your success,' he said.

Richard brushed some water from his face, which still felt raw. 'Truthfully I don't know if it was a success or not. The Marshal is thinking about helping us. The mayor is almost convinced, if the Marshal comes to our aid, he might follow.'

'Cowardly merchants,' Adam entered the refectory behind Richard.

The Young King rubbed some sleep from his eyes. He wore nothing but a linen undershirt. 'Do not blame the mayor,' he said, 'it isn't his fault. A life of hoarding wealth can only set him up to fear death. You see, because all he values will be lost when he leaves this world. If you prize wealth and what it can bring you, you can die but a small man, so the longer you live the better. We who prize our reputation and deeds above all else have little to fear from death. Do not blame the merchants for their fears, and I will order the monks to pray for their arrival.'

'We've tried praying before,' Richard said, 'and it only works if you do something to help it work.'

'That's why I sent you to Amiens,' the Young King's eyes twinkled.

'We overheard something you might like to hear from some Lusignan men on the way back into Corbie,' Richard said, 'Guy is expecting us to attempt a breakout towards Amiens.'

The Young King nodded. 'That is the only sensible course to take. And at dawn our horses will be fresh enough to attempt a breakout.'

Richard frowned. He could feel Nicholas's empty bed behind him even though he faced the other way.

'There were only a few guards around the town to the south, but the ground and undergrowth would slow us down,' he said. 'If they expect a breakout along the Amiens road, Geoffrey Martel surely would have most of the Martel infantry there. Guy blocked a road with a tree when he captured the Marshal, they could do that here and block our way.'

'If you are our strategist now,' the Young King folded his arms, 'what would you suggest?'

'The Somme blocks the south and east, so their mounted forces will block the open tournament field to the north. We can ride around any infantry in the wide open plain, and concentrated, we might break through their knights. It's a longer ride to Amiens after that, but it might be clear.'

The Young King rubbed his chin. New ginger stubble sprouted from it and he looked tired. 'If I were the Martels, I would place my mounted

261

reserve on those northern plains to block us,' he said. 'With mounted messengers all around to alert them to wherever we attack. Even if we do go north, I expect we'll run into their whole mounted force. Which is larger than ours.'

Richard sighed. He rubbed the hilt of Sir John's dagger. 'What if we could get them to move away from the plain?'

The Young King's eyes brightened. 'A diversion.'

'Precisely,' Richard said, 'we can either attack along the road, which they expect, or down towards the moored barges, as if we were trying to get you away from harm. Once you were a way down the river on a barge, you would be safe, so they may believe it.'

'Both might be believable,' the Young King said, 'but I will not slide away on the water and leave my company to be dismantled behind me.'

'Of course,' Richard said, 'I would attack the infantry we think are guarding the Amiens road.'

'Are you offering to lead the diversion?' the Young King asked.

Richard swallowed because he hadn't.

The Young King laughed. 'Worry not,' he said, 'I was having fun with you.'

Adam sneezed. 'Richard wanted to lead the wedge, I remember him saying something about he and his men being the ones to fight a real war.'

Richard winced at the memory of his own bravado. He turned to Adam. 'I spoke up for you when the Marshal made you prostrate yourself, and this is how you repay me?'

Adam shrugged. 'You did say it.'

The Young King grinned and ran his hand through his tangled reddish hair. 'I will find you and your men the fastest horses in the company, and give you every servant we can find a crossbow or spear for. You can ride along the road until you run into the enemy, then feign surprise. Bring up the crossbows to start a fight and hold there as long as you dare. The servants will fight for a time, and we only need long enough for them to send a messenger to draw their mounted forces in. Then flee in any way you can.'

Richard's face dropped, and he couldn't hide his horror.

The Young King pushed his bedding aside and approached Richard. He placed his hands on Richard's shoulders. 'The Marshal would have had this task, and with one eye Adam cannot lead, so I am asking you to serve your king. Once I am the sole king, I will reward you with the full set of Martel estates.'

Richard's mouth went to speak but only a gasp came out.

Adam raised a hand. 'Do not be rash, my lord,' he said, 'Richard is a poor knight, you cannot raise him that far.'

'Why not?' the Young King asked. 'Others have risen further. The Marshal is already far above his birth. I will be a king who rewards loyalty and sacrifice.'

Richard felt Nicholas's absence again. 'How many more do we need to sacrifice? How much more blood needs to be spilled? Nicholas survived the whole Irish invasion only to be killed on a game-field.'

'I did not ask for this,' the Young King said, 'we cannot choose what happens to us, only how we react.'

Richard exhaled, but he wanted to scream. 'I'll do it,' he said, 'but I don't want to fight after that.'

'What do you want, Richard? What do you really want?'

'I want my wife to trust me and to watch my children grow old,' he replied. 'I want to see an end to death and mutilation.'

The Young King smiled. 'I think you have seen your fair share, and as you keep losing fingers I think you might be right.'

Richard failed to see the joke.

'There will be more lost fingers tomorrow,' the Young King said, 'but I will pray that yours remain attached. We shall lose many good men.'

'I have an idea to avoid that,' Richard said.

'You are full of ideas,' the Young King went to pour himself a drink.

'We face an enemy that is two separate parts,' Richard said, 'their alliance is unnatural. Maybe we can divide them.'

'The Martels are the driving force of this plot,' the Young King took a drink, 'so you have an idea to pull Guy away from them?'

Richard nodded. 'Geoffrey Martel thinks he does your father's work, but Guy is only here for himself. Offer him something he prizes more than your death. The concept of loyalty is alien to him, we just need to make him the right offer.'

'And what would that be?'

'Promise him that when you are the sole King,' Richard said, 'you will leave him and his family alone in Poitou. He is only here to weaken your family's ability to suppress him. I think he actually just wants to be left in peace.'

'If I leave him alone, he'll stab me in the back,' the Young King said.

'Probably,' Richard replied, 'but this way it won't be tomorrow.'

The Young King sniffed. 'Your suggestion is nothing short of an immense loss to my family's possessions,' he sighed, 'but I'd rather be alive to deal with him later.'

Weariness seeped through Richard, and he sat down on the nearest bench.

'How do we communicate our offer to Guy?' the Young King asked. 'He is somewhere outside the town and we only have a short while before sunrise in which to reach him.'

Richard shrugged.

Gerold coughed and hauled himself to his feet, which took two attempts. He staggered over and dropped onto a bench. 'You need a man who you can spare,' his voice was rough and laboured. 'I cannot aim a crossbow or swing a sword.'

'No,' Richard said, 'Guy will recognise you from Lagny and cut your throat.'

'I need some clean air,' Gerold said, 'I've been stuck in this damp room for days. I may die anyway, so I may as well be of some use first.'

'I can't lose you, too,' Richard whispered.

'My lord,' Gerold said, 'do not cling to this world. I do not.'

'Give him a monk's robe,' Adam said, 'tonsure his head and Guy won't look closely enough to recognise him.'

'That's not a bad idea,' the Young King said, 'and the monks here will have a mule for him to ride.'

'Write me a message to hand over,' Gerold said, 'then even if a crossbow finds my chest, Guy may still receive the offer.'

Richard groaned with the realisation that he would change no one's mind about using Gerold. 'I'll find Brian,' he said, 'he can write it.'

Brian slept with the monks. Richard tiptoed barefoot into their dormitory but still awoke monks who shushed him and tried to wave him out.

Richard shook Brian until his eyes opened. He dragged the monk from the dormitory until they were in the cloisters outside. 'I need you to write a letter,' he said.

Brian yawned. 'Can't it wait until the morning?'

'No,' Richard said, 'don't you know what's going on here?'

Brian nodded and yawned again. 'Yes, but it seems like a time for lances, not quills.'

'It's exactly the time for quills,' Richard said, and then told him what he needed to write.

'Oh,' Brian said, 'the monks won't like me using their writing equipment. They are protective over their scrapers, parchment, and ink.'

'Write it before they wake, then,' Richard said.

'There is no need to be terse,' the monk said, 'trust in God and we shall be saved.'

'I can't be saved,' Richard said, 'the Abbot excommunicated me and Nicholas.'

'He can't do that,' Brian said, 'abbots do not have the power.'

'Are you sure?'

Brian nodded. 'Although maybe it is different here? But even so, if people think you have been cast out of the church, I can hardly have anything to do with you.'

'You'd leave me just for a fake excommunication?' Richard asked.

Brian looked away.

'We don't have time for this,' Richard said, 'write the letter and give it to Gerold. I've got things to do.'

'You look like you haven't slept all night,' Brian said, 'and you look terrible.'

'It hardly matters at this point,' Richard said, 'I need to go and be bait.'

BATTLE OF THE SOMME

Richard's diversionary attack would comprise all the non-fighting men of the Young King's company. The sullen collection of clerks, servants, grooms, drivers, farriers, cooks, falconers, and huntsmen all marched out of the abbey towards Amiens at first light. Sunbeams illuminated the clouds faintly even if the sun itself had not yet breached the horizon behind the abbey. The assortment of men, some old, but most young, armed themselves with the last of the brightly painted and unused red shields, and took lances from the carts to wield as spears. Most were unarmoured.

'I don't fancy their chances,' Bowman glanced over his shoulder as Richard led them out of the abbey on a black horse. Otto and Adam rode beside him, while Brian trudged along at the head of the infantry with a spare royal banner grasped tightly in his hands. The infantry marched in silence, their expectations of success little better than Bowman's.

'We don't have to rout anyone,' Richard said, 'just let the huntsmen shoot crossbows at them for a while.'

'I have never seen common men so willing to risk themselves for their lord,' Otto said.

'I don't think they're planning on dying,' Richard said, 'although they do love the Young King, there's no denying that.' He adjusted Matthew's axe in his belt and wished he still had the jewelled mace.

'The sun will be in the bastard's eyes soon,' Bowman grunted, 'they may not see your company for the bunch of servants they are.'

'It's not my company,' Richard said.

Otto laughed a laugh that was more of a cackle. 'You are the leader here, are you not?'

Richard did not want the responsibility, for either their lives or their success. He wanted to hide somewhere quiet. He wanted to go home.

The company marched along the western road until trees flanked them closely on both sides. The sun appeared over the abbey buildings behind and warmed Richard's neck through his coif. He'd found a leather breastplate to strap over his partly compromised double-mail, as well as a shiny new iron helmet, but as the undergrowth closed in, he still felt vulnerable.

'What if they're in the trees?' Bowman asked.

Richard pursed his lips.

Otto squinted into the woods, which were darkening as they thickened.

Richard sighed. 'We'll go slowly and stop occasionally to listen for sound. If they get around us, we'll not get back to the abbey, so I'd rather avoid it.'

He turned in his saddle to look down at Brian's dour face. The monk held the banner with two hands, disapproval of their mission written across his face. Some grey clouds overhead started to spit water down on them.

'Great rains,' Brian said loudly, 'that's bad.'

'Why?' Richard asked.

'Great rains fall after great battles,' the monk continued, 'Plutarch said so.'

'Who is Plutarch?' Richard asked.

Brian shook his head. 'Pray it doesn't rain any harder.'

Richard turned around as the water landed on his helmet and hit some puddles already on the road. 'I'm hoping this will just be a skirmish,' he mumbled to himself. His mail coif rubbed on his cut ear and the helmet pressed down on the raw skin to cause constant pain. He could feel the scab had been rubbed off already.

'Young lord,' Bowman said. 'Up ahead.'

Richard squinted. 'You'll have to tell me.'

'Men blocking the road,' Bowman said.

'That is good, is it not?' Otto asked.

'That depends if there is anyone in the surrounding trees,' Richard looked but saw no movement.

Bowman looked too. 'The Martels would be foolish not to,' he said, 'stay as far back as we can.'

'Let's put our show on,' Richard said, 'with me.' He cantered his new black horse towards whoever blocked the road. Their hooves splashed in brown puddles and threw dirty water up onto their horse's bellies. They closed quickly on the enemy, whose shields were red and yellow.

Richard halted his horse, which didn't obey instantly. 'This is close enough,' he struggled to stop it racing.

'No banners,' Bowman joined him later as his horse avoided all the puddles. 'But there's at least fifty of them.'

The Martel infantry formed a tight row of shields, ten men wide, across the road. They stood several ranks deep, but even from horseback Richard couldn't tell how many. A few riders stood behind the infantry, but only a few.

Richard waved his hand around and pointed at the blockade. 'Try to look like we're surprised or arguing,' he said.

Bowman spun his horse around a few times for effect. 'This is ridiculous, can we just get out of crossbow range?'

The first bolt flew along the path and sailed into the trees off to one side.

'Yes,' Richard turned his horse and cantered back out of range. He got as far as Brian and the approaching company of servants. 'They have crossbows. We need the first rank of spearmen to make a wall with their shields, your huntsmen can shoot over them.'

The cooks and clerks in the front rank edged forwards with their shields raised up to their eyes. They reached the spot where Richard had reached, and rested the bottoms of their shields on the road.

'Close those shields up,' Richard shouted from behind them.

A cook dropped his shield in the mud, and his companions jeered at him.

A Martel bolt whistled through the air, skidded off the road and hit the bottom of the red shield next to the scrambling cook. The servant holding it was pushed back a step and the bottom of the shield smacked into his shin. The rest of the formation quietened and their movements became jittery.

The Young King's huntsmen had a handful of crossbows and some normal bows with them, and they loosed arrows and bolts steadily towards the Martels.

The red and yellow line hunkered down behind their shields, and the huntsmen hit them again and again.

'They are better shots than the enemy,' Otto chuckled.

'I'd hope so,' Richard said, 'the Young king would hardly employ poor hunters. These are the best shots in the realm.'

A bolt cut through the air overhead, and Richard ducked instinctively.

'Less ducking, young lord,' Bowman said, 'you have to set an example.'

'What, by getting shot?' Richard pulled his shield round more to his front.

Adam, who had ridden behind the infantry as a rearguard until now, rode up. 'Is it working?'

'Maybe,' Richard said, 'but we can't see if they've sent a messenger or not.'

A huntsman scored a direct hit to an enemy's face, and the red company cheered.

Adam sneezed. 'Do we have enough ammunition for this?'

Richard shook his head. 'We're equipped for hunting, not war, but they are shooting slowly.'

A bolt clipped the shoulder of a cook, and he cried out in pain.

'They're nervous,' Otto said.

'They aren't trained for it,' Richard said, 'but while the enemy is this far away, they'll stand.'

The Martel shieldwall stepped forwards.

'That's your fault,' Bowman said with a grim face.

Richard waited for Nicholas to reply, but nothing was said. Bowman locked eyes with Richard and both men nodded to each other.

The wounded cook stepped back.

'Plug that gap,' Bowman shouted.

A clerk Richard recognised as an Englishman called Wigain stepped into the gap. The clerk recorded the Marshal's tournament winnings and was paid handsomely for the task. He was a small man, but lithe, and spirited.

Another cook shuffled out of line but Wigain hauled him back into place by his shoulder.

The Martels closed the distance, and the huntsmen now shot at them as fast as they could.

Richard dismounted. 'Come on,' he said, 'we need to stand in that front line, we can't leave it to a clerk to lead the fighting.'

Bowman groaned. 'If I lose an eye to a spear, I won't be pleased.'

'Adam hasn't complained about it,' Richard turned to the one-eyed knight, 'hold our horses.'

Adam nodded as Otto and Bowman followed Richard on foot through the ranks of the ragtag company.

The Martel infantry shouted a war-cry and the sound chilled Richard's bones. He might not flinch at a block of men shouting, but he smelled urine in the air and those around him had never been in this much danger before.

The water in the air turned into real rain, and shoulder to shoulder with the servants, it reeked of damp wool.

'We'll fight them off,' Richard said, 'and retreat slowly when I order it. Not before.'

'Liking your taste of command, are you?' Bowman asked from a few men along the line. They stood at the front, three knights spread between seven servants, but backed by many more.

Against professional soldiers.

Richard drew his sword. The ten Martels in their front line drew close enough for their faces to be clear. Except only their eyes and one-handed spears showed above their red and yellow shields. Spears with wickedly sharp iron points.

The cooks and clerks lowered their spears.

'Don't close your eyes,' Richard said, 'and don't duck.'

The enemy advanced and their spears fenced with the red company's.

Wigain lunged with all his strength but his spear only found the top of a red and yellow shield. A Martel struck back and ripped his tunic.

'Don't take any risks,' Richard said.

The clerk grunted and fended off a strike that aimed at his neighbour.

The spear fight sounded like twenty people knocking on twenty doors. Iron rarely hit iron, rather the wooden shafts of the weapons swept and parried and blocked each other.

It sounded like a practice field for boys until the cook on Richard's left screamed out. A spear nicked his face and blood ran down his cheek.

Richard realised that with his sword he was doing nothing useful, and worse, was leaving his own side outnumbered by spears. He darted two steps forward on his own and past the points of the Martel spears to close with their owner's.

The enemy cried out and tried to shorten up their weapons, but with one-handed spears this took more than a moment.

Richard only needed a moment to cover the last two steps. He crashed his shield into the man in front of him and arced his sword over their locked shields. His victim cried out. Richard lashed over again at the shoulder of the spearman next to him and gave him a serious wound.

An enemy spear gouged along his leather armour so Richard jumped backwards. The Martel spearmen tried to lance him as he retreated, but he got back to his own line where he was greeted by a half-hearted cheer.

Otto copied him. The German dodged the spears and used a mace to knock a spearman unconscious. Bowman ran out and the confused Martels weren't sure who to aim at. Bowman killed two spearmen before one bashed his helmet with a spear shaft and he ran back to the safety of the line shaking his head.

Richard sheathed his sword and drew Matthew's axe instead. The axe needed less room to swing.

The opposition advanced. They had been trained and drilled, for they all stepped at the same speed, shuffling towards the bakers and farriers.

Some of the red company took small steps back and Richard sensed their line might not hold for long. Not once they took casualties. Men are often brave until their neighbour is cut down.

'Bowman,' Richard shouted, 'now.'

They both attacked. Otto went too, but a spear found the middle of his shield and stopped the German in his tracks.

Richard hooked the axe over a shield and pulled it forwards. The spearman lurched with it and Richard brought the axe down onto his neck. The fabric protection half split, but the force cracked something, and the man dropped to a knee. Wigain's spear found his exposed chest.

Richard hooked another shield, but he felt the owner brace so he rammed the axe forwards and the end of the shaft smacked into his opponent's nose and broke it. A spear tore a chunk from Richard's shield from his left, and on his right another iron point flew in and painfully glanced off his shoulder. Richard disengaged and returned to the red line.

Behind the enemy line horsemen congregated in a swirl, men shouted, and hooves churned up the road.

'We should go back,' Bowman said, 'on our own terms.'

Richard wasn't sure, for one step might too easily become full flight, and suddenly the whole plan seemed stupid.

Wigain thrust his spear into a Martel's face, and the Young King's company cheered, but not nearly as enthusiastically as before.

'One step back,' Richard decided to try the managed retreat while matters seemed hopeful.

The company bumped backwards into its rear ranks but eventually ended one step back closer to the abbey.

Three Martel spearmen advanced out of their line and one thrust his spear with force into the face of a cook who lost his eye with a scream. The man wailed and his comrades dragged him out of the battle.

The Martels pushed into his space. Bowman cut one down, but other enemies moved in behind and threatened to split open Richard's wavering formation.

'Move back to the abbey,' Richard said, 'one step at a time.'

Clerks bumped into falconers, and servants slipped past drivers to get back quicker.

'Slowly,' Richard cast an enemy spear aside with his axe.

'Martel knights,' Bowman shouted.

More horsemen rode behind the spearmen than before.

'Back, but hold the line,' Richard cried, but the Martel spearmen had driven a wedge into them, and the line's cohesion was gone. He heard running feet behind him, the servants were breaking.

'Defend the abbey,' Richard shouted, 'bar the two entrances. Let no one in or I'll kill you myself.'

The cooks fled.

An enemy spearman grew too brave and as Richard pushed his spear up into the air, Wigain speared him under the armpit.

The Young King's company retreated at pace. Some realised that an organised retreat would keep them alive longer, and the huntsmen took close range shots through the melee that often found their targets.

Richard needed to find out if the Young King was using his chance to escape. 'Wigain, can you keep them defending the abbey gates?'

The clerk nodded as he back-pedalled with his bloody weapon always pointed at the foe. 'Aye,' he said, 'we know they'll kill us if they get in.'

'Good man,' Richard pushed back through his men. 'Bowman, Otto, to horse.'

Adam threw the reins back to the knights when they found him. A crossbow bolt protruded from his shield.

Brian held the red banner aloft in the centre of the company. The rain fell harder even as clouds drifted in front of the rising sun. The mixing of ran and sunlight drowned the road in a cold golden haze.

Richard hoped the monk would make it, but he didn't pray. Instead, he turned his new horse around and they tested the speed the Young King had promised. Judas had waited next to Adam, and he joined the three horsemen as they abandoned their company to search for their lord. Richard felt a tinge of guilt and pity, but promised himself he would return for them.

Richard led the way back to the abbey, then they turned north and towards the plains of the tournament field. Cool air stung his face as they let their horses race. Rain made the grass slippery on the chalky earth, but Richard needed to know if the Young King had reached safety. If the diversion had been worth it.

'Horse tracks,' Bowman pointed his horse in the direction the tracks went.

Richard hoped they were today's, but knew Bowman well enough not to ask.

They rode up a long but gentle incline, the rain now heavy enough to reduce visibility of the horizon into a white mist. The horses were as fast as promised and the muscled animals propelled their riders up the slope and over its ridge.

Where they found the Young King.

Two red banners flew above a marching column of a hundred knights. A short way behind them Count Philip's Flemings rode under their yellow and black flag. There were only two dozen of them.

'Over the next hill and they'll be beyond the tournament boundary,' Bowman shouted through the rain. The boundary meant safety because the terrain closed in and the reduced visibility would hinder anyone chasing the Young King.

Richard eased his black horse out of its gallop but the sweating beast fought him and wanted to charge on.

The Young King and the Flemings moved at a gentle canter, trying to get clear of the plain as fast as they could whilst saving some of their horse's stamina.

A squall of rain buffeted Richard's party and coated their bodies and shields in water.

'We have a problem,' Bowman shouted. 'Look.'

Over the next hill, and directly in the Young King's path, a mass of shadow darkened in the mist.

The mass moved like infantry, and they were so far away that Richard couldn't tell if there were horsemen with them.

The Young King's company halted, seeing the danger at the same time.

Richard's overly keen horse took him thundering past the Flemish company and into the back of the red.

Horses and riders swore at Richard as his enthusiastic mount crashed into them when it had nowhere left to go. It snorted and sweated in the rain, and Richard had little love for it.

'Make way,' Richard cried as he pushed his way to the two red banners.

The Young King rode under them. 'Richard?'

'We held as long as we could,' Richard said, 'but the Martel infantry attacked and pushed us back. Your company of servants is defending the abbey.'

'It may have worked,' the Young King said, 'I think only infantry are approaching us ahead.'

Count Robert was at his lord's side. 'Infantry are irrelevant, we shall simply ride around them. If we ride at speed, we can get off this plain and out of danger briskly.'

'Give the order,' the Young King nodded to the Count.

Count Robert barked a command, and the column lurched into a walk and turned right and away from the approaching Martel infantry. The rain lashed the right side of Richard's face and he felt it seep through the mail on his arm. Brian was getting his great rain.

Richard felt far safer amid armed knights and squires than he had on the Amiens road. Knee to knee with armed men always made him feel invincible.

A cry of alarm rang out from the front of the company, but Richard couldn't see through the mass of mailed backs and cloaks in front of him.

'What is it?' he asked.

Bowman tried to look through the knights ahead of them. He swore. 'There is someone ahead of us,' he said.

'Is it Guy?' Richard asked.

'I can't see their banner through the rain,' the blonde man said.

Richard swallowed. It didn't matter who it was, Guy, Eustace, or Geoffrey, because it meant the diversion had not worked and a body of enemy knights remained on the field to face them.

'Ride east to the river,' the Young King said, 'there are trees around it we can lose them in.'

'There's marshland, too,' Count Robert said. 'And it's raining.'

'Do you have a better idea?'

The Count ordered the two companies to ride east at a canter.

'It feels like we've been here before,' Richard said to Bowman.

His friend said nothing in return and there was nothing to do but ride with the red company towards the Somme. Unfortunately, that meant riding straight into the oncoming rain. It drove into Richard's eyes and the wind made it hard to catch a breath. The company moved at speed, which put distance between them and the Martel infantry, but whoever the newly appeared mounted company was, they matched the Young King's speed and direction.

Richard's new black horse pulled up the incline of a rolling hill. They reached the brow and plunged down a steeper slope on the far side. Richard leant back in his saddle to help the horse balance and the company fought to maintain control of their mounts as some rushed or slowed down.

Battered by rain, Richard's rein-fingers grew stiff in the cold.

The horse in front slowed, and Richard's ploughed into the back of it. There was a squeal and a quick tangle of hooves. Other horses collided all around.

The black horse stopped moving and instantly sank into the soft earth. Richard looked down at the long-stemmed grass but the company moved forward and his horse went along with them. It raised its feet high to move and Richard knew that as a sign of deep ground.

'We've found the marsh, then,' Bowman said.

The company bogged down. Tufts of longer grass grew in clumps and the earth was darker than up on the plain.

'We need to turn around,' Richard said, 'it won't get any better if we keep going towards the river.'

Dark mud caked the legs of all the horses as they struggled on.

'About turn,' Count Robert shouted. The command relayed around the company.

'Finally,' Bowman pulled his horse around.

Richard's horse bumped into a brown animal as it turned. Stallions kicked and bit each other. Men shouted and tried to pull horses apart. Richard's earlier sense of safety rattled and he wished he hadn't proposed the diversion in the first place.

Richard pointed the black horse out of the marsh, nearly ran over Judas, and looked up at the hill they'd just cantered over.

Lance tips rose above it, as if growing out of the ground. They didn't belong to the royal company, but to whoever pursued them.

Richard stopped feeling the rain, stopped being annoyed at the numbness of his face, stopped cursing the toe that had started to ache again.

A banner joined the spears, and it was red and yellow.

The line of spears became a line of Martel knights who crested the ridge, and cheered when they saw the Young King's men mired in the mud. They spurred their horses.

Richard knew they had no way to evade them. Count Philip's Flemings now stood between the Martels and the Young King, and being on firmer ground, the Count shouted his war-cry and charged back up the hill. At best his futile attack might buy them enough time to get out of the worst of the marsh.

The Young King caught up with Richard. 'Where is the damned Marshal?'

Richard didn't answer. He had no answer.

'It's Eustace,' Bowman shouted.

The Martel line flowed down the hill towards the yellow and black knights. The Martel line was three times as long, and behind it came a second wave of knights that stretched out as wide as the first.

'Where is the Amiens militia?' the Young King cried. 'They've doomed us all.'

Count Robert's horse pulled itself free from the marsh. 'Charge,' he shouted, 'charge.'

Richard sighed, took a deep breath, and followed.

The Martel front line crashed into the Flemings, lances driven by the momentum of the descent threw the yellow and black knights from their saddles and flipped their horses over backwards. The black lion banner went down and was trodden into the earth by many sets of hooves.

Their resistance didn't even slow the Martels.

Richard withdrew Matthew's axe from his belt and spurred the black horse. Speed was this horse's virtue, and it bounded up the slope to meet the enemy charge. A Martel knight flew down at Richard, but he parried the lance tip with the shaft of his axe. As the horses crossed Richard ran the axe down the lance and flicked it up at the last moment to chop into the man's shoulder.

The second wave of Martels bore down on him, over some fallen Flemish horses, and lowered their lances. Richard aimed to ride between two of them. The knight to the left lanced Richard's shield and jarred him in the saddle as the lance shaft snapped.

The knight to Richard's right lowered at Count Robert, which left Richard free to swing the axe at his head. The axe connected just below the iron helmet of the knight and caved in his skull above his eye.

Richard was through. He tried to haul his horse back to turn, but it fought him and tried to keep going. Richard had to use his right hand to grab the reins and overpower the beast by asking it to circle, which he accomplished only as it reached the top of the ridge. From there he could see over the hill back across the tournament field, and out to the northwest where the Martel infantry marched on and on in their direction. Richard could make out the banner even in the squall and mist. Time was running out.

Richard pulled the obstinate horse around to point back down the hill, which was a scene of chaos. The Martel banner and the two red banners clustered together at a standstill near the edge of the marsh. Knights from both sides fought running battles in all directions, and only when he saw their shields could Richard tell who was who. But those running battles didn't matter, what mattered was getting the Young King away from the Martel banner, because otherwise Eustace was going to kill him. Richard didn't dare spur the black horse down the hill in case it bolted, so he eased it into a canter and aimed at the knight Bowman fought.

Richard's axe chopped into the knight's raised forearm as he was about to strike, and Bowman took his chance to stab him in the throat.

'Get to the Young King,' Richard said.

Bowman turned his horse and followed Richard.

Shouts, screams, and iron clashing with iron rang in Richard's ears as the rain made the slope slippery. His horse, instead of taking more care, rushed over the uncertain ground and Richard thought it was going to fall with every careless and slipping step.

But it reached the flat ground still on all four feet and took Richard into the beating heart of the melee.

He went to strike a knight but saw his red shield just in time and pulled the blow. The red banners were ahead of him. Richard spurred the horse now, and it pushed between two fighting knights, one of whom battered Richard's helmet with his sword on his way through. His ears rang, but he pressed on, swung the axe at the back of a Martel helmet, and heard the black dog barking somewhere behind him.

Bowman pushed into Richard and the blonde man's shield jammed into the back of Richard's knee. He looked down to untangle them and something cut through the air above his head. Bowman stopped, which freed Richard, and he found himself with red shields on all sides. He pushed on behind the Young King's knights and found his lord and his bannermen catching their breath.

The Young King's helmet had a fresh dent.

'The Martel infantry is still approaching,' Richard said.

Count Robert burst back into the company and grinned at Richard. 'That was a fine blow,' he said.

Richard couldn't remember what he was talking about.

'I'm glad you are so cheerful,' the Young King looked worried.

Count Robert caught his breath and looked around at the battle that raged on three sides of them. 'We need to get away from this marsh,' he said, 'on hard ground we can at least race.'

'This is the Marshal's fault,' the Young King said, 'all of it.'

'We just need to kill Eustace,' Richard said, 'there are enough of us and he only has two arms to fend us all off.'

'We aren't winning this fight, and we'd never reach Eustace in enough numbers,' the Young King said, 'it would be prudent to retreat.'

The red and yellow chequerboard banner pressed the red-shielded knights who defended the Young King.

Adam found his way into the company. 'We don't need to kill Eustace, just occupy him long enough for the company to get away,' he said.

The Young King looked to the heavens but rain just flooded his eyes. 'I don't want to lose more good men on account of my safety.'

'You'll lose more if you stand and fight,' the one-eyed knight said. A red smudge stained the linen over his empty eye socket.

'I'm not ordering men to die for me in a tournament,' the Young King shook water from his face and waved his sword through the air. 'I'll fight him myself.'

'No,' Count Robert grabbed the raised arm and lowered it. 'You are a crowned king, you cannot die here. Your death would throw the question of succession back open and hurl the entire empire into chaos.'

Adam placed his horse in front of the Young King. 'I have chosen poorly in the past and paid a heavy price for it,' he said, 'but all I have ever done, good and bad, has been for your sake. I can hold Eustace off long enough for you to escape, you don't have to lead them by much to win a race.'

'You'll die,' the Young King said.

'At least I'll die for a reason,' Adam spun his sodden horse around. 'Do not waste my offering.'

'You are redeemed in my eyes,' the Young King shouted.

'Tell Sir Roger I died well,' Adam spurred his horse toward the Martel banner.

Count Robert punched the Young King in the shoulder. 'Peel your eyes away and use whatever time he can give us.'

'Go to God in peace,' the Young King said, then turned to the Count, 'and leave one red banner here.'

Adam's mailed back disappeared into the melee as a red knight was clubbed to the ground by a mace-wielding Martel knight.

Bowman walked his horse after Adam.

Richard caught him just in time. 'Where do you think you're going?'

'His fall from grace was the peacock's doing,' the blonde man said, 'I can keep him alive. And I owe Eustace for my brother.'

Richard had to spit out rain that had run into his mouth. 'This isn't over,' he shouted above the din of battle, 'we will kill Eustace. But not here.'

Bowman clenched his teeth.

'Think of Eva and your daughter.'

'Don't keep throwing that back at me,' Bowman said, 'not when you don't believe I can be with them.'

'Prove me wrong, then,' Richard said, 'by surviving to look after them.'

Bowman grunted and turned his horse in the direction the Young King and Count Robert had already gone. They'd ridden south, skirting the edge of the marsh.

'We need to be with them, come on,' Richard said.

Otto flew past with a broken sword in his hand.

Richard asked the black horse to go, and it did. The stallion grunted and did what it loved. Mud flew into Richard's face as the red company peeled away from the melee in ones and twos after their lord. Richard gained ground on the Young King and Count Robert as they pushed aside the Martel knights who had been trying to outflank them. They turned up the slope to escape back onto the plain.

Otto raced ahead and Richard was glad that the Young King had been true to his word and given them his quickest mounts.

Richard snatched a glance over his shoulder before they crested the hill. Red knights strung out behind him, but the Martel and the other red banner were still locked together in a dense press of mail, horses, and swords. Loose horses picked their way through the marsh or bolted north up the hill in the other direction. Wounded knights scattered the ground amongst the dead men and broken lances. A crow landed on an unmoving body.

Richard reached the top of the slope and rode down the long incline on the far side.

Where the Martel infantry stood with lowered crossbows.

Richard pulled at the reins of his black horse when the more refined methods to ask for a stop failed. The horse responded simply by lowering its head and finding another turn of speed.

The Martel infantry stretched out before him in a line of red and yellow, the colours on their shields almost mocking Richard by their existence. He'd had enough of that family.

Otto charged ahead of Richard, and he tried and failed to turn his horse away from the wall of spears that blocked his path.

Richard marvelled at the speed with which the infantry had reached them. They must have run, which would at least mean they'd be gasping for air and their muscles tight and burning.

The first of the crossbow bolts whistled by, sounding like giant summer bees as they whizzed past his ears.

The Young King charged at the head of his disorderly company, but instead of trying to go around the mass of footsoldiers, he realised the quickest way to get away from the infantry was through them.

The infantry realised they were under attack so they locked their shields.

A bolt knocked a red knight from his saddle and Richard's horse had to leap over him. It jarred Richard's back because he was more focused on the infantry line that was only a few strides away.

The red company clattered into the infantry. Some horses half-jumped it and their hooves and chests sent spearmen flying. Other horses ran onto spears but still carried away whoever clung on to them.

Richard tried to steer his horse into the gaps created by the company already, but it disobeyed. The black horse's flat-out gallop took Richard into the Martel line as fast as he'd ever been atop a horse. Three spearmen tried to aim their weapons at him while a fourth broke and ran.

The black horse ran straight onto the middle spear, but ran right over its bearer and knocked him to the grass. Bravery was often fatal. One of the other spears glanced Richard's mailed thigh, but the third spear tangled up in the horse's front legs.

Richard never remembered the fall.

He opened his eyes and rain landed on his face. He blinked the water away as the black dog leapt over his body and savaged a screaming spearman's neck. Richard rolled over and looked up. Bowman rode towards the Martel banner and the cluster of horsemen that probably contained Geoffrey Martel. Bowman was fighting his own private war.

A crossbowman not four paces away tried to reload his weapon, his eyes on Richard. He was just a boy, fresh-faced and sweating in the rain, but he slid the wickedly sharp bolt into the groove all the same.

Richard had to reach him first.

The boy pressed too hard with the bolt, and it slid from the groove.

Richard picked his axe up from the grass, and even with a wet handle he could grip it well enough to clout the youth around the head with it. The unfortunate crossbowman's head jerked to one side and Richard looked down at his mangled red ear. He was too young to be here.

Two spearmen attacked Richard.

His shield still hung from his shoulder, and although his left arm was not in the straps set up for fighting on foot, he swung it round to his front. One spearman's shield had a muddy hoof print on it, and he was covered in slimy soil.

Richard knew he had to get close to them quickly, so he ran at them. Both men expected just that and made stabs at his head. Except that Richard slipped on the slick grass and stumbled forwards, underneath their spear tips. He part fell and part ran shoulder-first into the first spearman and knocked him backwards. Richard righted himself, hooked the muddy spearman's shield with his axe and tried to pull him over. The spearman didn't move, his weight greater than Richard's, and he grinned back with the look of a man confident of victory.

Richard cared little about victory. He cared about keeping Bowman alive, so he turned away from the large spearman and ran towards the

Martel banner. The spearman tried to give chase, but a man used to running in mail is no slower than anyone else.

A bannerman held the Martel banner in the middle of twenty knights, knights who headed towards the red banner as it broke through their infantry.

Geoffrey Martel rode a horse caparisoned in his colours, and Richard made for him. The black dog appeared beside him, his tongue hanging out of a red muzzle.

Bowman crashed into the Martels as they caught the Young King and stopped the Angevin's charge before it could become an escape.

Richard kept going, but his leather soles kept slipping on the grass. Bowman took on two Martel knights with great swings of his sword.

More red knights crashed into the infantry, but those who weren't engaged looked around and slowly flocked to their young lord's banner.

Richard had to get Bowman away from there because he was on his own amid the enemy.

A crossbowman loosed a bolt at a mounted knight, and Richard hacked down at his weapon. His axe snapped one of the bow's limbs so he left the terrified man alive.

Judas had no such clemency and his jaws clamped down on the crossbowman's hand and dragged him to the ground.

Richard didn't have time to worry about it, and a Martel knight riding around the melee spotted Richard running towards him. The knight had an unbroken lance, and in Richard he saw a ransom opportunity. He spurred his grey and brown-coloured horse and clods of mud flew up from its hooves. Richard felt the ground tremble through his cold feet.

His axe was at quite a reach disadvantage, and Richard could hardly outrun the horse, so he stopped running. The Martel knight charged him and Richard gritted his teeth and hurled the axe with all his might. The axe spun through the air, flew over the horse's lowered head, and clattered into the knight's midriff. It didn't make any difference.

Richard drew the Little Lord's sword as a rush of air almost knocked him off his feet. Otto raced towards the Martel knight who had only eyes for Richard, and he noticed Otto too late. The German's mace hit his chest with the same sound Solis's hooves had made on Sir Rob's ribs.

The Martel knight's heart stopped, and the lance fell from his armpit.

Richard stepped aside as the now directionless horse cantered away.

He picked up the dropped lance.

Otto kept charging towards the red banner.

Richard clutched the lance in two hands and ran after Bowman.

The blonde man tried to reach the red and yellow caparisoned horse, but he was a lone red shield amongst the enemy and they noticed he was there.

Richard had too much ground to cover and the remaining Martel infantry were moments away from swamping the Young King.

Richard couldn't help Bowman and couldn't save the Young King. What's more, he wasn't even going to die on horseback, he thought, but that only made him angry.

The Martel knights who approached Bowman peeled away and their heads turned to the west.

Richard took his chance, and his feet pounded along the grass, his eyes followed their gaze and spotted a company of horsemen to the west. They could be Lusignans coming to attack the Young King despite Richard's letter, but he didn't have time to think about it.

He rushed at the distracted Martels and drove his lance into the back of a knight who fenced with Bowman. The lance got stuck but Richard pushed it in further, and the horse under the knight had to take a step to balance Richard's thrust. Bowman's sword finished what Richard's lance started.

Richard used the lance to lever the knight from his saddle, then he stole his horse. The knight had been shorter than Richard and the stirrups were too short to use, but then Richard didn't have time to slide his second foot in anyway, because a sword struck Bowman on the arm.

The strike came from his potential father-in-law. Geoffrey Martel struck again, but Bowman hunched his shoulders so the sword found only his shield.

'If it wasn't for you,' Geoffrey cried, 'Nicholas would still be alive. Alive, obedient, and useful.'

Bowman lashed out with his sword but Geoffrey batted it away. 'What am I supposed to tell his mother?'

Richard waded in, but was on the Martel's shield-side and couldn't stab at his polished iron helmet.

'His mother?' Bowman said. 'She's my mother, and you took her from me.'

'I raised her up,' Geoffrey snarled and cut down. Bowman parried the sword and the two blades locked together.

Richard pushed his new horse into Geoffrey's. He hooked his pommel over the rim of the Martel's shield. He pulled it back, and the shield came towards him along with Geoffrey's neck.

Bowman pushed his enemy's now flailing sword away and slashed down across his opponent's chest.

Ring's burst open as Richard tried to move his horse away and drag Geoffrey off his horse.

Geoffrey's bodyguards finally became aware of his danger and they charged Richard.

Bowman struck again before he had to block a fresh attacker.

A Martel knight thrust a sword at Richard and he had to disengage his sword to parry it.

Geoffrey clung on to the neck of his horse and rode out of the melee. He pushed his way free and rode away from the battle.

Bowman turned to chase him and Richard had to distract a Martel who nearly cut across his exposed back.

Bowman broke free of the melee before Richard, but the Martel knights didn't follow. The Young King was their concern now that their lord no longer required protecting. They ignored the paltry ransom potential of Richard and Bowman, their eyes on a royal prize.

Richard pulled his horse up. 'Bowman,' he shouted, 'you can't catch him and he's not worth it.'

The blonde man swore and stopped his pursuit. His eyes looked back over the high ground that blocked their view of the marsh.

Richard looked, too, and his mouth dried and his heart thumped in his chest.

Because Eustace Martel was coming.

He wasn't alone either, and two dozen knights cantered over the hill beside him.

'This is about survival now,' Richard said, 'we don't have time for revenge.'

'Damn you,' Bowman shouted, 'but either he or I will die today.'

'We'll worry about that once the Young King is safe,' Richard wheeled his horse to face the battle around the red banner.

Luckily Bowman did too, but it didn't look like they'd free the Young King before Eustace reached him. The Martel knights Geoffrey had left behind almost matched the red company, but the Martel spearmen brought down their horses one by one.

Richard, no alternative or clever plan coming to mind, stormed back towards the red banner. Rain stung his eyes and horses slipped on the grass that now was crisscrossed with running streams of rainwater.

The company riding from the west closed. Richard couldn't see them through the melee as they lowered their lances, but he heard their war-cry.

'Dex Aie the Marshal.'

Richard laughed the laugh of a condemned man. The peacock hadn't even had the humility to change his offensive war-cry.

The Marshal's dozen knights dashed at the Martel infantry just as it mustered into a coherent unit, and he led a charge that broke deep into their ranks. Behind his new face-plate helmet, the Marshal drew his sword and cracked skulls and severed shoulders as his men drove right through the infantry. His knights slashed and their horses trampled, and a moment later the shattered footmen broke and fled.

Richard caught them as they ran and sent a few of the fleeing men crashing down to the earth. Bowman sent a few more, fully aware that fleeing men can rally and rejoin the fight.

The Marshal led his men to rescue his lord.

Richard reached the mounted combat just behind him and saw Henry the Northerner clout a Martel squire in the back of the head with a mace.

'You can never be wrong, can you?' Richard shouted at the Marshal.

The Marshal looked at who shouted at him. 'I'm happy to be wrong,' he smashed a knight's nose, 'I'm just not wrong now.'

'You should have left Henry behind,' Richard fended off an attack.

'He's helping,' the Marshal battered a young knight's fingers so hard his sword fell from his hand.

'You're arrogant,' Richard swatted a thrust away.

The tide turned as the Marshal cut his way through to the Martel banner and prised it from the grip of its bearer, who wisely yielded.

'Eustace is coming,' Richard said.

The Marshal turned his horse. 'An equal contest,' he said, 'this will be a true match. It's a shame no spectators can witness our glories.'

A handful of red-shielded knights surrounded the Young King. Many of their number lay strewn on the saturated earth nearby, stabbed to death by infantry. Many others were being chased away by marauding Martel knights.

Count Robert had lost his helmet, but nothing else apart from his breath, which he tried to catch next to the red bannerman.

Bowman shook water from his eyes. 'We'll never get a better chance. We can't run again.'

Count Robert shook his head. 'We have a clear path back to Amiens. We should take it, that was always our intention.'

Blood dripped down the Young King's chin, and a dark mark surrounded his eye. His crown, half dislodged previously, was now completely gone. He surveyed the surrounding field, littered with his fallen company, and an iron look filled his eyes. 'Richard's rude knight is right, we kill him and end this.'

Eustace and his company charged.

Richard thought of home. The children he hadn't seen for months and the village he almost cared for. The wife who had come to support him, and the yellow horse that bled in a stable. The image of the black wolf-pelt lying in the mud, near to where they fought now, was the last straw.

'The devil can take everything else,' Richard said, 'they killed my friend and probably my horse. I'm with Bowman, Eustace dies here.'

'For Adam,' the Young King shouted.

'Adam?' the Marshal said. 'What happened to that traitor?'

The Young King's harsh face turned on his Marshal. 'He died so I could live. Because you weren't here.'

The Martels rushed over the corpses and wounded men.

Richard put his horse next to Bowman's, ready to charge as the survivors of the red company poured forwards in attack around them shouting the Young King's war-cry.

'For Nicholas,' Richard said.

'For my brother,' Bowman spurred his horse.

Eustace held himself back when he saw the red company organise to meet his charge. His knights lowered their lances and rammed into the Young King's men.

Richard was knocked so hard by a lance that he fell out of his saddle and onto Bowman's shield. The blonde man pushed him back upright, but it slowed them down and Count Robert surged ahead of them.

The Count of Meulan reached Eustace first, or rather the end of Eustace's lance reached him. The Martel knight's blow was so hard that the back of the Count's winged saddle snapped and propelled him backwards off his horse.

Eustace wore his coif loose around his chin, the flap of mail untied because of the damage Nicholas had done to his jaw. His nose was still bloody and he no longer had a full set of teeth. But there was fire in his eyes and nothing wrong with his sword-arm.

Otto careered in at an angle and his horse made Eustace's swerve out of the way. That put Maynard the squire directly in his path and he collided with the Martel knight.

Eustace punched his shield at the squire who struggled to control his horse and didn't have a chance to defend himself. The iron dome at the centre of the red and yellow shield connected with Maynard's face and he dropped both his reins and his weapon. Eustace's horse flashed his teeth at the squire and he overbalanced as his horse shirked away from the Martel's foaming stallion.

Otto turned his horse while Eustace dealt with Maynard, and the German clouted the Martel shield with his mace.

Richard urged his horse on and Bowman charged with him.

Eustace ignored Otto's blow and struck down on his helmet. The sword dented the helmet once, twice, three times, mangling its shape and rocking the head beneath it. Otto swung his mace again but less forcefully than before.

Eustace battered the helmet two more times and Otto swayed in the saddle. A final swift strike sent him to the ground.

Richard clenched his teeth. How many men could Eustace kill in two days?

The last thing Richard saw out of the corner of his eye before he reached the Martel knight was the Marshal leading a string of captured horses away from the fight. Rage flowed through Richard's veins. If the Young King didn't kill the Marshal for his shocking disregard for his duty, Richard would do it himself.

Eustace probably grinned when he saw Richard and Bowman, but his jaw was so deformed it was hard to tell.

Richard clashed swords with him and despite his anger the Martel's blade pushed his own back and dragged across the two mail layers on his upper arm. Neither layer gave.

Bowman clipped Eustace's helmet with the tip of his sword, but the Martel knight didn't notice. He turned his horse to chase Richard.

Richard tried to spin his horse to match, but the black beast wanted to run off, moved too quickly, and took him out of reach.

Bowman thrust at Eustace's back but missed.

The big Martel knight turned his attention to the blonde man and hammered his shield. 'You'll see your brother again soon,' he snarled.

Bowman's face was bright red. His eyes bulged and channelled everything he had left into frantic cuts aimed at his opponent's face.

Eustace parried them all and laughed. 'Come on, you must have more than that?'

Richard hauled his unhelpful stallion around and came to his friend's aid.

Eustace swung at the head of Bowman's horse and Richard realised this contest wouldn't follow the normal knightly rules. Bowman pulled the horse's head out of danger and jabbed his sword at Eustace, cutting a few rings from his forearm.

'Close,' Eustace flicked his blade back and cut Bowman's nose, 'but not close enough.'

Richard lunged but only caught the red and yellow shield.

'And you,' Eustace brought his sword over and jarred Richard's arm when he blocked it, 'I will make you suffer. I'll burn your village.'

'Someone already did that,' Richard aimed at the Martel knight's rein-hand, but dug into the wooden saddle instead.

'I'll have your wife, she's a pretty little thing,' Eustace snarled.

Bowman rammed his horse into the Martel's and their legs tangled.

Richard took what he thought would be his best chance and slashed at Eustace's face.

The Martel knight lifted his shoulder and the shield hanging from it took the blow.

Even with two of them they couldn't get through his defences. Richard's anger faded as no one else came to their aid. The Marshal could have ended this already.

The black dog barked. He ran under the legs of Richard's horse, which made it jump, and sprung up at Eustace. Judas's teeth clapped around his mailed foot and his former owner cried out.

Eustace tried to shake him loose, but the dog clawed at his horse and the animal spun around in a vain effort to get away from the predator that swung under its belly.

Bowman tried to get close to strike, but his horse wouldn't go near the snarling hound.

'That's my dog,' Eustace shouted, 'the disloyal swine. I'll chop this bastard Judas's head off.'

'How do you know he's called Judas?' Richard's horse wouldn't go near the growling hound, either.

Eustace flung his foot through the air and the black dog slipped down to the ground, where he darted away from the stamping hooves of the angered horse.

'What?' Eustace frowned. 'I don't name my hunting dogs.'

Bowman's horse finally obeyed him and leapt at Eustace. Distracted, he didn't see the crossguard of Bowman's sword punch into his cheek. Eustace's horse snapped round at Bowman's and pulled a clump of black mane away in its mouth.

Bowman's horse shook its neck and sprung away from its attacker.

Eustace spat blood, except that he couldn't spit properly and it dribbled down his chin and onto his mail shirt.

Richard was running out of ideas. His horse now approached Eustace, but the Martel knight kept Richard on his shield side and attacked Bowman.

The blonde man raised his sword to parry, but the end of the sword snapped as Eustace cut through it. His sword kept going and sliced down into Bowman's shoulder. The blade missed the protective leather that covered his chest and Bowman almost dropped his sword as he winced from the blow that mangled and cut his mail. When he tried to raise his sword again, it stopped short.

Crimson ran down from Eustace's mouth, and Richard could smell iron in the air.

Bowman tried to swing his broken sword but Eustace batted it away without even looking. His eyes were on Richard.

Richard feigned an attack at his head and instead pulled the blow to again cut around at Eustace's rein-hand.

The Martel knight shifted his shield to block it and swung back at Richard, hitting him across the helmet and sending a burst of bright colours across his eyes.

Richard couldn't see, so waved his sword around in case he could block something, he felt the sudden pressure of it hitting Eustace's weapon.

The colours cleared from his eyes just as the point of his enemy's sword arced down and scratched a new line in his helmet. Eustace did it again and Richard remembered how this method had felled Otto.

Richard flashed the Little Lord's sword out hoping he could distract Eustace long enough for Bowman to do something useful. The two men exchanged undefended blows, but Eustace kept his horse circling so Bowman couldn't reach him. Even when he closed for a moment, the blonde man couldn't swing his sword with enough force to trouble his foe.

'You're finished now,' Eustace spattered blood from his mouth as he spoke.

Richard blinked fresh blood from his eyes and they stung and wanted to close.

Richard's arm struggled to raise his sword high enough to strike again. He may as well have been trying to lift a horse.

Eustace raised his arm, but it was half-drained and slower than before. Nevertheless, his sword still cracked down and almost knocked Richard off the black horse.

Bowman howled in an effort to summon the last of his strength and crashed his horse into Eustace's.

The Martel knight turned his body to face him and his sword cut a long cut on Bowman's cheek. 'I'll have your eye next,' he said, 'just like that one-eyed knight. He died blind.'

Bowman may have been exhausted, but he was still angry. He thrust the jagged edge of his sword at his enemy's face and a sliver of iron stabbed Eustace in his already bleeding nose.

The Martel knight flinched away. 'You'll die like that pathetic brother of yours,' he shouted. 'Face down in the mud like a commoner.

Like the commoner you are. Like the commoner your mother is.'

Richard used the pommel of his sword to hammer Eustace's shield. Richard's body glowed with heat from exertion. Sweat covered every part of him as the mention of the wolf-knight's name mustered the very last of his energy. Richard hammered down again, but it merely pushed the shield harmlessly into Eustace's helmet. He could taste blood on his tongue.

Eustace had more strength to give. He ignored his weary attackers and brought his sword down onto the head of Richard's horse. The blade landed between its ears and forced its head down to its chest.

The horse wobbled under Richard, and fear surged through him. He was going down.

Judas, who had been spitting mail links out of his mouth, flew at Eustace's horse and buried his big teeth into the horse's left hind leg. The stallion kicked out it him, but missed as the dog dug its claws into the haunches of the animal.

Eustace went to attack the dog with his sword, but he was on his left side and Eustace couldn't reach. His horse tried to kick again, but slipped on its other back leg and its rear end fell to the mud with a tremendous thud. Eustace gripped his saddle to stay on, but dropped his sword in his desperation.

Richard, sick at himself for having to do it, brought the Little Lord's sword down onto the neck of Eustace's horse. It felt like the Reeve's neck.

Bowman thrust his sword again at his opponent's face, but Richard couldn't do anything else as his own horse buckled to his knees. Richard, his feet having never been in the overly short stirrups, jumped away from his horse and rolled on the ground, the bottom of his shield snapping off as he landed.

Eustace's horse pushed its back end up and stamped down on Judas, who whined and jumped away from the danger of its kicking hooves.

Eustace threw himself from his stricken horse, sensing that it was becoming unstable.

Richard got to his feet, mud down the side of his body, and picked up his sword from a murky puddle.

Eustace sprung up even quicker, and his dark eyes found Richard.

Richard stood his ground. The battle raged around them, horses slipped and men fell, but still no one came to their aid. What was the Marshal doing?

Eustace stepped over the earth their horses had churned up and drew his shield to his front.

Richard did the same, but he knew he couldn't hide behind it for long. Bowman struggled to control his horse which spooked away from Eustace's as it erratically struggled to stay on its feet.

The Martel knight advanced and Richard stepped backwards without meaning to.

Eustace's sword flashed out from behind his shield. Richard tried to parry but missed and his shield took the brunt of it. He staggered backwards and his foot slid on the grass. If he fell, he'd be dead.

The Martel knight cut down and Richard brought his sword up to meet it. The Little Lord's blade was pushed down onto his shield and it jumped from Richard's wet hands. It bounced off his shield and the flat of the blade hit him in the nose as it dropped to the earth.

Eustace laughed. The same laugh as when he'd ruined Richard's wedding.

'The stories really are true,' Eustace said, 'you can't keep a hold of your sword.' The Martel relaxed his stance as Richard's ability to strike him vanished.

'Maybe,' Richard didn't retrieve the sword, instead he brought his hand back behind his shield.

'And now you'll die,' Eustace said, 'it's time to join your father.'

Richard thought of Nicholas. 'I might drop my sword,' he said, 'but I've never dropped my dagger.'

Eustace frowned, but he was experienced and knew what that meant.

Richard flashed the pointed blade of Sir John's dagger out of its sheath, but this wasn't Eustace's first knife-fight.

The Martel knight lowered his shield to give himself room to sweep his sword round to catch Richard before he could get close enough to use the dagger.

Except Richard didn't try to close the distance. Instead he raised his shield-arm up so the broken shield was horizontal, and stabbed the jagged bottom of it at Eustace's face.

The Martel knight, fearing for his already torn jaw, used his swinging sword to push it away, but that gave Richard the time to step in. He plunged it into Eustace's right forearm. The dagger pierced the single layer of mail, then it slid through two layers of wool and split open the Martel knight's skin and muscle. His grip released and his sword tumbled.

Richard withdrew the knife and pressed up against his enemy so closely that blood from Eustace's broken jaw sprayed into his face. His second strike buried the dagger into his bicep. The muscle was a large target, and the dagger split it apart until it scraped bone.

Eustace's left arm shot over and grabbed Richard's wrist. His enemy was so strong that Sir John's dagger stayed right where it was and Richard couldn't move it to attack again.

'Not good enough,' Eustace growled, and with the strength of a bear, pulled Richard's wrist back and slid the dagger out of his own bicep.

Richard fought against him but Eustace was going to turn the blade and bury it in Richard's neck. He didn't have the strength to do anything other than delay the inevitable.

But he had another hand. His left hand pushed around Eustace's shield and fumbled about his midriff. The rivets on the mail rings scuffed his knuckles and flayed his skin. One of his nails caught in the mesh of metal and was ripped off. Agony flared in his hand, but Eustace turned Sir John's dagger around and Richard for the first time could see it pointing at him, straight at his eyes.

Richard's bleeding and torn left hand found something that wasn't mail. His hand clenched around whatever it was and Richard pulled it free. It felt like a handle. Hopefully a knife. He stabbed up towards Eustace's left arm and a blood-covered blade erupted from Eustace's left arm. The Martel knight howled.

Richard withdrew the knife and stabbed up again. This time it caught in the mail and Eustace jerked his arm back, twisting the knife out of Richard's hand.

But Eustace had let go of Richard's right arm, and now free, he thrust it at the Martel's neck.

Somehow Eustace brought an arm up to catch the attack and pushed the dagger out of the way.

'Won't you die?' Richard made to jump at Eustace as a last resort.

Judas grabbed his ankle, but he missed the mail and his teeth tore into the flesh where the leather lacing tied the armour tightly around his leg.

Eustace kicked the dog in the face with his other leg. 'Disloyal mut.'

Judas took the kick and bit down harder.

'He's not disloyal,' Richard said, 'you kicked him for no reason back in England, remember?'

Eustace kicked the dog again.

Richard scowled. 'Get off my dog,' he drove Sir John's dagger up into Eustace's armpit as the knight turned to fend him off. The dagger punched through armour and skin and then penetrated a lung. Air escaped with a sucking noise.

One of Eustace's huge hands clawed at Richard's face, trying to get to his eyes. Richard pushed the hand away and placed his leg behind his enemy's. Then he pushed.

Eustace fell on his back with a crash as his shield smacked him on his mangled nose.

Judas shook the leg, then let go to reveal white bone.

Eustace took a breath, but it was a wheeze and he lay on the ground, his arms half in the air.

Richard swallowed and caught his breath.

The Martel knight tried to push a leg around to support himself but he slipped and fell back to the earth. Yet more blood poured from his shattered jaw, but now it flowed from his lungs, too.

'You'll drown in that,' Richard said. He looked at his left hand, which was red and black from the oil that coated the mail. His missing nail burnt as if held in a fire.

Bowman's horse now let him ride close, but he stopped and looked down at his fallen adversary. 'No more jokes left, eh?'

The Young King's armoured horse arrived with its rider missing his shield and helmet. 'Is that him?' the young monarch asked.

Richard nodded and went to retrieve the Little Lord's sword. It lay in another brown puddle, chipped and dented.

'His men are leaving, Richard,' the Young King said, 'when he was unhorsed they lost heart. It seems to me that none of them desired all that much to save him.'

The rain that soaked Richard to his skin caused him to shiver. Judas lay in the mud licking his own back. So much mud and blood covered him you could hardly tell he was a black dog. Richard just hoped not all the blood was his own.

Eustace tried to roll onto his side, but he could only flap his right arm. Blood trickled out of his left armpit into a puddle of rainwater. His breathing rattled.

'It would be a mercy to put him out of his pain,' the Young King said.

Richard shook his head. 'I'm not doing it,' he said, 'if it wasn't for him I'd still be at home with my mother and sister. My uncle would never have dared to take Keynes on his own. I'd still be searching for what happened to my father, and I wouldn't be missing one and a half fingers, half an ear, and probably by tomorrow, my horse.'

'We will reform the company,' the Young King said, 'the Lusignans have not yet shown themselves.' He rode towards where Count Robert had fallen to see if he lived.

Bowman rotated his right shoulder but couldn't quite manage it. 'Dying in peace on the ground, shattered or not, is too easy for him.'

Richard looked down at his foe but didn't pity him. 'Have you anything to tell me about my father before you journey to the next world?'

Eustace spat blood up at him but it only landed on Richard's foot.

The Martel knight tried to laugh, but it turned into a rasping cough.

'Do whatever you want,' Richard said to Bowman, 'I've avenged myself and I don't feel any better about anything.'

The blonde knight placed his horse at Eustace's feet. 'I'm going to kill your father,' he said, 'you should know that. And what I'm about to do to you is for what you did to my own father.'

Eustace tried to speak but his words were bubbles of blood and nothing more.

'But most of all,' Bowman pressed his calves into his horse, 'this is for my brother.' His horse stepped forwards and an iron shoe landed on Eustace's leg. The Martel knight cried out. Another hoof landed on his groin as Bowman kept the horse walking even as its hooves slipped off body parts. The stallion landed on his soft stomach and Eustace tried to curl up around it, but the horse kicked him over and another iron-shod hoof cracked and collapsed three of his ribs.

Richard looked away for a moment, but looked back in time to see the horse's hoof rise and flick Eustace's jaw clean from his head.

Bowman completed his walk and looked down at the devastated and unmoving figure of his enemy. He sniffed. 'I don't know why you don't, young lord, but I really do feel better,' he said.

The odour of the Martel knight's ruptured bowels made Richard gag. 'I need to find a horse,' he went to Judas first, and the dog licked him in the face. Which made Richard retch.

The Marshal returned to the field after a short pursuit of the Martels, a prize horse following by the reins behind him,

'You,' Richard shouted at him and his nausea evaporated, 'I saw you ride off when we fought Eustace. He nearly killed us and you could have helped. You were supposed to come back to help us defeat him, not to enrich yourself while we did the dangerous work.'

The Marshal lifted his new helmet off to reveal an almost red face. 'You are alive though, aren't you?' he asked. 'So everything worked out for the best.'

'The best?' Richard shook his head. 'Give me that horse.'

The Marshal frowned. 'This one? I just took it, it's the best horse I've captured here all day. It's the same sort as our King's.'

'You owe me a horse, or have you forgotten that?'

The Young King returned. 'I was going to ask you to donate that horse to Count Robert, he is very unsteady, but Richard is right, you do owe him a horse.'

'But this one?' the Marshal said. 'Look at its colouring.'

'I know, a blue roan,' the Young King said, 'and now it's Richard's blue roan.'

Richard approached the stallion. It had an enormous black head, but its colouring changed down its neck and body into a greyish blue. 'From the Italian States,' Richard said.

'The war-hero knows his horses,' the Young King almost grinned but his eyes were sad, 'we'll find something else for the Count. Richard has earned this prize.'

Richard snatched the reins of his new horse and mounted the brand new war saddle on its back. Rain had soaked into the leather side flaps, but Richard was already wet-through so it hardly mattered.

The Young King ordered the captured Martel banner to be carried next to his own as a trophy, and discussed how they could prove Eustace was dead if they met Guy.

Bowman answered him by dismounting. He picked up the Martel knight's jawbone and remounted with it in his hand. 'This should do,' he waved it at the Young King.

'That is barbaric,' the young Angevin shook his head, 'we aren't in Ireland.'

Richard ignored them and looked for Otto amongst the fallen and wounded of the battlefield. Crows landed and pecked at eyeballs and brains.

The German sat on the ground when Richard found him, rubbing his head and the back of his neck. 'I have run out maces,' he looked up at Richard, 'but that is a fine horse.'

'It is,' Richard said, 'the Marshal has more you can borrow.'

It took some time to reorganise the company. Count Philip and five of his men walked over on foot, the only survivors of the entire Flemish contingent, all muddied and bruised. The Count carried his sodden banner aloft, where the rain washed the mud from it.

The Young King greeted his cousin happily as the two dozen survivors of the engagement formed up to march. Otto was loaned a prize horse, but two of Count Philip's knights had to share the last one.

The wind died and the rain ceased, but the plains were soft under hoof and the company's progress was slow.

Exhaustion overcame them, and conversation was sparse because the danger was not over. Guy remained at large.

Maynard the squire found Richard. He shivered and had a gaunt, sunken look to his face. 'I heard Count Philip tell the Young King that Adam is dead,' he said.

'He fought a rearguard so we could flee the marsh,' Richard said, 'as his man you should have gone with him.'

Maynard grimaced. 'He betrayed my loyalty, I don't think I would have followed him to death even had I known what he did.'

Richard shrugged, it hardly mattered now. 'Go back to Sir Roger then, go back to Castle Cailly. My home is that way, you can ride part of the way with us for all I care.'

Maynard scratched his neck. 'That's why I'm speaking to you,' he said, 'I want to ride all the way.'

Richard looked at the young man, although he was only a few years younger than Richard himself. 'Why?'

'I saw how you fought Eustace Martel,' Maynard said, 'as I tried to get up and my head spun, I saw you face him even though he was stronger than you.'

Richard frowned. 'If you are trying to pay me a compliment, you are missing the mark.'

'I need a new master,' Maynard said, 'and you have no squire.'

Richard glanced at Bowman.

'I'm not your squire,' he replied, dark shadows around his eyes and blood streaming from his cuts.

'You can ride with us as far as Yvetot,' Richard said, 'then we'll see.'

Otto rode behind Richard. 'You are getting ahead of yourselves speaking of home,' he shouted.

'He's right,' Richard said, 'Guy is no less dangerous than Eustace.' He scanned the horizon but saw only the spire of the abbey under grey clouds. Richard thought he saw smoke rise from it, blacker than from a hearth. They rode towards both smoke and spire.

'I thought we were riding for Amiens,' Richard said.

The Young King heard. 'All my clerks and servants are in the abbey, fighting for their lives,' he said, 'that's what you told me. And I leave no one behind.'

Richard was happy with that because Brian was there, and so was Solis. Hopefully they both still lived.

His face dropped when they crested the final hill and were greeted by flames licking the sky, the blaze roaring from a wing of Corbie Abbey. A great plume of billowing black smoke darkened the air as Martel infantry stood around a large fire some distance from the complex, using it to light torches to hurl over the compound wall. The fire that raged was in a row of buildings next to the stable. Richard's heart skipped a beat. He had to get Solis out of there.

A handful of Martel knights commanded the infantry and pushed one group of spearmen towards the main gate of the abbey. A hedgehog of spears resisted their attack from inside the gateway.

The Young King called a halt, however, because another company of knights stood near the abbey watching the attack. Their unbroken lances pointed at the clearing sky and the newly shining sun glinted from their clean mail. The breeze ruffled their banner and revealed blue and white stripes.

'I suppose your plan didn't work in the end,' the Young King raised his voice so Richard could hear.

'He hasn't attacked us yet,' Richard said.

'Then why has he got a noose around Gerold's neck,' Bowman said.

'What?'

'Your man is right,' the Young King said. 'Is Guy waiting for us to appear so he can hang Gerold in front of us?'

Richard closed his eyes. He had nothing left to fight Guy with, and nor did most of the men surrounding him.

The Lusignan company wheeled to face the red company, who reached for weapons and looked to their lord.

Count Robert, filthy and bruised, coughed. 'We can still ride away,' he said, 'they outnumber us.'

'I can see they outnumber us,' the Young King said, 'and their horses are fresh too. We might have been able to outrun the winded Martel knights, but these men and horses shall be too quick.'

The Lusignans approached as glowing embers from the abbey floated up into the sky.

Gerold rode a few men along the line to Guy's left, still in the monk's robe, but now with a length of rope hanging from his neck. His hands were bound. But on Guy's right, Alice rode in a bright blue dress wrapped in an orange cloak.

'Allow me to lead the attack,' the Marshal said from next to his lord, 'Guy wronged me and I will capture him for you.'

'There are two of them for each of us,' the Young King said, 'and have we not had enough violence for one day? Raise the captured banner and show Guy the jaw.'

Bowman pushed his horse out in front of the company and held the severed jaw aloft. Flesh hung from it and the teeth that jutted up from the bone shone white in the sun.

Guy stopped his company when he was close enough to see what it was. 'And who have you taken that from?' Guy asked.

'Eustace Martel,' the Young King said, the two companies faced each other with fidgeting horses. A few pawed the turf.

Guy studied the jaw. 'You would think I would know if that was his,' the Lusignan said, 'but it is amusing how I cannot even picture his face.'

'You can find the rest of it near the river to remind yourself,' Bowman said.

The Lusignan snorted a laugh. 'I didn't think you had it in you. Did you do it?'

Bowman shrugged. 'I finished it,' he nodded at Richard, 'but he's the one who jammed a dagger into his lungs.'

Guy nodded in appreciation. 'Geoffrey Martel was supposed to be unstoppable because of his son.'

'Apparently not so unstoppable,' the Young King said, 'and now the Martels are broken, your cause is finished.'

Guy looked at the captured red and yellow banner. 'My cause is not their cause,' he said, 'and my cause is very much alive.'

'So you want to fight?' the Young King asked. 'To kill an anointed king?'

'What we want,' Guy said, 'isn't your head. We want an end to Angevin interference in our lands. Your younger brother claims to rule us, and your mother organises our repression.'

The Young King avoided looking at Richard, but Richard saw a flicker of a smile.

'You read my offer, then?' he asked. 'Despite the loss of your allies, it still stands.'

Guy rode forwards. 'You're only saying that because we still outnumber you, and your horses are foaming and their energy drained. You'll say anything to save your skin.'

The breeze chilled Richard, and all eyes glued to Guy and the Young King.

'I made the deal before today, the matter is as simple as that. Do you accept it?'

Guy looked at Richard, and it made him uncomfortable. Then he looked at the Young King and smiled. 'I do. I accept your offer. Independence for my family's current lands, and anything we gain between now and the death of your father is also safe from you, once you hold power.'

'Those were not the terms,' the Young King said, 'do not push me.'

'I think I can afford to push a little,' Guy sneered, 'or would you like a trial by combat between our companies?'

The Young King pursed his lips but remained quiet.

'How dare he speak to a king like that,' Count Robert said, 'it cannot stand.'

'Silence,' the Young King whispered to him while trying not to move his mouth.

'Do we have an agreement?' Guy tilted his head. He smiled to show his missing tooth.

'If,' the Young King rode his horse forward until it was close enough to sniff Guy's, 'if you atone for the treason you were a part of here.'

'Treason?' Guy laughed. 'When did I lay a hand against you?'

'You tried to kill me yesterday.'

The Lusignan shrugged. 'It was a tournament, I never tried to kill you.'

'Do you agree to atone?' the Young King asked.

'You haven't told me what I'd have to do,' Guy said.

'Take the cross.'

Guy almost choked. When he recovered he laughed, then Alice laughed, and then his company laughed. Guy wiped away a tear. 'What makes you think I would leave my lands and toil in the sun for Our Lord? Your mother will swoop in and I'll come back from the Holy Land a landless knight. What makes you think I would ever accept that? You think me a simpleton?'

The Young King walked his horse next to Guy's and spoke quietly to him. Richard strained his hearing, but he heard nothing, and it served only to remind him that his ear stung and the reopened wound was bleeding down his neck.

The Young King wheeled his horse around and showed his back to the Lusignan. He rode a few steps then stopped and turned in the saddle. 'Oh, and release the monk,' he said.

Guy sniffed. 'I know he's not a monk, do I look like the village fool? I only kept him alive because he was so sick I didn't want to get close enough to kill him.'

Richard was relieved when Gerold rode forwards on his horse, Guy having swapped out the borrowed mule presumably so Gerold could keep up with them. The old Keynes knight had a pale face and dark patches under his eyes. Richard wondered if he still had all of his fingers.

Guy waved Gerold away and went alone to the Martel knights who still besieged the abbey. They took little convincing to abandon their work and plodded back towards Franvillers as if they'd been defeated.

Servants and huntsmen from the abbey gate watched them go, but they didn't cheer their victory. Wigain stood amongst them, Richard could make him out in the distance, but he couldn't see Brian.

'We need to put that fire out,' Richard said, 'before it reaches the stables.'

The Young King, the day's worry etched into his face, agreed, and only as he ordered his company to see to the abbey, did the mayor of Amiens and his militia finally arrive. The mayor rode a chestnut gelding and was the only man in his column wearing mail. He shifted his shoulders about as if the mail weighed him down, and looked nervously after the retreating Martels. Beside him, and on the only other horse in the column, came Sophie.

LOOSE ENDS

The Abbot of Corbie Abbey refused to let all the fallen knights be buried on its consecrated grounds.

'It's as if he dislikes you all,' Brian said to Richard as the wind pushed dark clouds across the sky. The abbey's graveyard had two fresh pits dug under the far wall of its fenced area, and around them gathered a large crowd. Water pooled in the bottom of the graves.

'Thank you for tending to Solis,' Richard said.

'Packing his leg was of little trouble to me,' the monk said, 'at least not once I'd let him drink so much wine he could barely stand on his feet.'

'He looks miserable at the moment,' Richard grinned, 'he's suffering the morning after like we do. He didn't even care when I stabled the blue roan next to him.'

'Your horse did bite a monk,' Brian said, 'and he kicked another who won't walk again for some time.'

Richard chuckled. 'If he's kicking people, then he's not feeling too sorry for himself. At least I can ride my new horse until he's better. If he recovers.'

The Abbot and an assortment of churchmen stood around the graves and sprinkled blessed water over the two linen bundles half submerged inside. The Abbot declined the opportunity to speak and instead pushed a priest forwards. Richard stood at the back of the crowd with Brian where the Latin from the front fought a losing battle with the wind. The priest did not have a powerful voice.

'Do you think anyone would notice if I slipped away?' Richard asked.

Brian nodded. 'Bowman would,' he said, 'and I would not want to displease him today.'

'I'm not ready to say goodbye,' Richard swallowed.

'Who ever is?' Brian asked. 'Thank God that we found a way for Nicholas to be buried here. At least the monks can speed his soul to heaven with their prayers.'

'Heaven?' Richard shook his head. 'How can any of us who live by the lance reach it?'

'He died defending his lord,' the monk said, 'there must be piety in that?'

'You're scrabbling around in the grass looking for green thread,' Richard said, 'and you're not being clever enough to make me feel better. I know he's not been thrown into the unmarked graves on the plain, and I'm thankful for that. But just because he's being buried in the abbey grounds, doesn't mean I'm happy.'

'We all die.'

'You're not helping,' Richard said.

The monk's hood blew off his head and he slipped it back on. 'At least the abbot relented on the matter of his excommunication,' Brian said, 'both Nicholas's soul and yours are safely back in Our Lord's flock.'

'I'm no one's sheep,' Richard pulled his cloak closely over his tunic.

The priest said Adam's name, and Richard was not sure how he felt that Adam and Nicholas would be buried next to each other.

Otto threaded his way out of the crowd. Richard stepped over and put a hand on his shoulder to block him. 'Where are you going? If I have to stay here, then so do you.'

The German had a solemn look on his face. 'My time here is at an end. No one will notice my absence,' he said.

'You're not just leaving the funeral, you are going to leave the company?'

Otto nodded. 'I am not from these lands and I have duties I must attend to. Remaining in the company was a foolhardy thought. I became carried away being so near to the Young King. My order is expecting me to arrive somewhere far away from here, and one can only be so late without arousing suspicion.'

'Your order?'

'I am a knight of the Hospital,' Otto said.

'A Hospitaller?' Richard frowned. 'But you fought in the tournaments. The Holy Orders don't do that.'

'We all have our vices,' Otto said, 'and nothing keeps a warrior's edge sharp more than use.'

'In my experience, use tends to chip and blunt edges.'

The German smiled and drew closer to Richard. 'My use of words might be crude, but my meaning is clear. My time at tournaments this season has been more dramatic than I had expected, but my body is stronger and faster than before. Although I shall need to replace my maces before I reach Pisa.'

'Pisa?' Richard asked. 'Where is that? No, never mind, just come back to my castle with me.'

The German's eyes widened. 'You, a Norman knight, wish for my company?'

'Apparently I'm not really Norman,' Richard said, 'but I would be happy for you to stay with me for a while.'

Otto shook his head. 'Be your offer trick, joke, or real, I must decline. I am no replacement for your dead friend.'

Richard looked away.

'There is no shame in mourning,' Otto said, 'and I liked your friend, but don't seek for someone to replace him. He was a good man.'

'Thank you,' Richard said.

'If you ever journey to Pisa, ask for me at the Church of the Holy Sepulchre,' Otto smiled at Richard and walked away from the funeral.

'Where's Pisa?' Richard said after him.

Two knights at the back of the crowd hushed him for his noise.

'Do you know where Pisa is?' Richard whispered at Brian.

The monk shrugged.

'You're going to leave me, too, aren't you?' Richard asked. 'If I go back to Yvetot now and stay there, then you'll leave me like Otto. There is nothing for you in Yvetot is there?'

The monk sighed. 'Today should not be about you, but about honouring the dead.'

'So you *are* leaving.'

'I have not thought about it,' Brian said, 'yesterday I was fighting for my life and didn't think I'd see another sunrise. I have no desires on where my destiny leads. God will take me where He pleases.'

'Would you come to the Holy Land with me?'

Brian's eyes lit up. 'Every Christian should make the pilgrimage once, of course I would grab such an opportunity.'

Richard scratched his cloak where the cross was sewn onto the tunic underneath. The linen of the cross was yellowed and spotted with old blood, and the crosspiece was long gone, but the promise Richard had made to take the cross still stood. 'Good,' Richard said, 'I need to find the Templars of Jerusalem.'

'Your horse will have a cross shaped scar if he lives,' Brian said. 'It is a sign from Christ.'

'I don't think he's blessed by anyone,' Richard said, 'and I expect the monk he crippled agrees with me.'

'Perhaps it is a sign,' Brian said, 'of the urgency of your call to the Holy Land.'

'It could be,' Richard scratched his chin. Signs after all were everywhere.

'Or,' Brian grinned, 'your horse has taken the cross.'

Richard raised his eyebrows. 'I know horses can be tried for murder, but I don't think they can be crusaders.'

The monk shrugged. 'We live in a changing world. Normans rule in Ireland and all human knowledge is being committed to parchment. The scriptorium here is a true wonder. You should see it.'

'In another life,' Richard said, 'I would be happy to read everything they have here.' He sighed and a gust of wind brought the awkward Latin words of the priest to his ears. 'Bowman will sulk if I don't stand with him for some of this.'

'You should do that,' Brian said, 'the loss of kin is difficult.'

'I'm aware of that,' Richard gripped the hilt of his sword and twisted his palm across the rough and frayed leather. His damaged finger caught on it and ripped the half-formed scab off. He groaned and tentatively pushed through the crowd and towards the droning Latin.

Bowman stood next to the Young King with wet eyes and the black dog sitting at his heel.

Richard nodded to Bowman, who sniffed back.

The priest ended his eulogy and looked to the Abbot for assurance that he could leave. None of the monks liked the knights who had invaded their abbey, and all were keen to see them go.

The Abbot closed the funeral and Bowman stepped forwards and threw Eustace's jaw, still a tangle of bone and flesh, into Nicholas's grave.

'Take that out,' Abbot Hughes pointed into the pit.

'Make me,' Bowman snarled, then unrolled the wolf-pelt from beneath his cloak and threw it in on top of the bone.

'This is a Christian abbey,' Abbot Hugh said, 'not some pagan outcrop in the savage east.'

Bowman squared up to the Abbot, who despite his smaller size held his ground and looked up at the blonde man with angry eyes.

The Young King put himself between the two men. 'This knight is grieving, the fallen knight was his relation. I am sure that Our Lord will understand that his intentions are to honour his brother and are not heretical.'

Abbot Hugh flared his nostrils and stomped off towards the main abbey complex. His monks followed him, and so did most of the knights. The few who either served or knew Adam stayed a little longer.

The Young King ruffled the black dog's head and his yellow eyes looked back up at the young Angevin. 'Guy told me about the Black Wolf of Corbie,' he said, 'and how some demonic beast tore two of his men to pieces. Do you know anything about that?'

Bowman shook his head and Richard realised the only other witness to that attack apart from himself lay in the ground beside Nicholas. 'No,' Richard said, 'maybe it was Nicholas's ghost.'

'Who knows what lurks in the dark?' the Young King gazed down at the graves.

Bowman looked up at the blustery clouds. 'I need to tell our mother,' he said.

'You can't go in person,' Richard said, 'Geoffrey Martel will expect that, and there will be more than one guard on the castle gate next time. Besides, he will tell her himself.'

'He won't tell her the truth though, will he?' Bowman said. 'He'll blame me and break my mother's heart twice over.'

'Write a letter,' Richard said, 'Brian loves to scribble things onto parchment.'

Bowman nodded. 'Fine. I need to tell her what those bastard Martels really did here. She needs to know the truth about the man in whose bed she sleeps.'

The Young King raised his eyebrows to ask what he meant, but Richard shook his head back at him.

'Good,' Richard said to the blonde man, 'I'll speak to Brian, but we're going to Yvetot not England.'

'It's always about you, isn't it,' Bowman sniffed, 'and this is your fault, anyway. If you hadn't wanted to make some money, we wouldn't be here in the first place.'

Richard held his tongue.

The other knights left the graves and some lay monks heaped dirt back into the pits.

'What do you want?' Richard asked. 'In this life.'

Bowman watched the linen bundle disappear under the light coloured earth. 'No idea.'

'I'm sorry,' Richard said, 'for bringing you and Nicholas here.'

'If you hadn't, I'd never have stopped hating him,' Bowman said, 'I suppose I should thank you for that. But I don't want to feel this ever again. Don't you dare die before me, young lord.'

'I don't intend to,' Richard replied, 'I don't intend to be anywhere near any more tournaments or wars. We'll find a way to survive in Yvetot with what we've won so far. We'll stay where it's quiet and safe.'

Bowman snorted. 'It's not that safe,' he said, 'but we still have a hoard to recover, don't we?'

Richard turned back to the abbey, out from which Sophie approached. She greeted the Young King.

'You're right,' Richard said, 'we should recover the silver before someone else does. But do you want to spend it on drinking, or getting to the Holy Land?'

The corner of Bowman's lip almost curled upwards. 'Both?'

Richard smiled. 'That's the spirit,' he grabbed his friend's shoulder then went to speak to his wife.

The Young King bowed to Sophie and walked back to stand next to Bowman, who was the sole knight still standing by the graves.

Sophie held a hand out to Richard. 'I'm sorry about Nicholas.'

Richard took her hand.

'He was less vulgar than his half-brother,' Sophie said, 'and I will miss him. But I have never seen such devastation as the carnage around this abbey. On our way along the Amiens road we rode over bodies, Richard, bodies.'

'That was partly my doing,' Richard scratched his neck.

His wife frowned. 'How can men fight around a sacred building?' she asked. 'Is there no regard for Christ here?'

Richard shook his head. 'God and Christ often seem to come second to man's desires.'

'I thought this was supposed to be a tournament,' Sophie said, 'where is the festival, the rules, and prisoner taking? I might not approve of them but they should be safer than war.'

'This was a battle dressed as sport,' Richard said, 'but we didn't know it would be this bad.'

'The smell,' Sophie rubbed her nose as the memory of it made her flinch, 'of all those bodies outside the abbey.'

'You didn't have to be near them,' Richard said, 'and each fallen man had a priest speak words over him. None have been denied a Christian burial.'

'Tell that to the spearmen and servants who are being rolled into the big pit,' Sophie mumbled.

'Since when did you care about them?' Richard asked. 'It's those kinds of people who have more than once tried to burn you out of your castle.'

Sophie took a deep breath and tucked her hands inside her blue cloak. A heron flew overhead with a long silver fish in its long beak.

'Brian told me the Abbot tried to excommunicate you. Brian seems nice, by the way.'

'The Abbot is a hateful man,' Richard said, 'you should have seen his face when Nicholas…' Richard had to stop.

'Don't worry,' Sophie smiled and nodded, 'we can go home now.'

Richard glanced at the Young King.

'Can't we go home?' Sophie frowned.

'You certainly can,' Richard said, 'I don't know if I need to ask his permission.'

'I'll ask him,' she said, 'he can't argue with me.'

Richard caught her before she moved a step. 'Let me speak to him, you'll make me look like a child if you try. Wait for me inside.'

Sophie rolled her eyes but left Richard alone at the graves with Bowman and the Young King. Richard knew he was very lucky that she wasn't holding on to the Alice issue, but in the same thought he reminded himself that he kept thinking about Alice and her silver circlet. He just hoped he wouldn't see her again.

The Young King spoke to Bowman. 'But if you were me, you would have to contend with the Marshal. For all his talents and uses, he is a spoiled child. He spent half of this morning berating me about the deal I made with Guy, even though he doesn't know what the deal was.'

'What was the deal?' Bowman asked.

The Young King smiled. 'The deal is a private matter.'

'You can't trust Guy,' Bowman said, 'the Lusignans tried to kill your mother.'

'You sound like the Marshal,' the Young King said, 'but I am the king and I can handle that brood.'

Richard could sense the damp taste of rain in the air. 'Guy has no respect for anything or anyone,' Richard said.

'Do you trust me?' the Young King asked.

Richard nodded.

'Then trust in my actions,' the Young King said, 'I have had enough arguments today with the Marshal as it is. I had to make him swear on his own soul that he would refrain from abandoning me in the future for his own profit. What would have happened had the two of you not defeated Eustace?'

'He would have found you,' Richard said.

'Precisely, and the Marshal only at that thought realised the impact of his selfishness,' the Young King said, 'even now he is brooding on his own somewhere. He refused to come here to bury a Martel and a man he sees as the blackest traitor.'

Bowman growled. 'Damn the peacock,' he said, 'and he abandoned us, maybe he's the traitor?'

The Young King looked at Richard. 'You know him as well as I do, he cannot help himself. We could have done with his help earlier than it arrived, but at least he is back in the company. I'm going to need him for what comes next.'

'What comes next?' Richard had a feeling it wasn't a rest.

The Young King's expression changed. 'Brother Geoffrey will come to speak to you soon.'

'I won't tell him anything,' Richard said, 'although there is nothing for me to tell.'

'He would sacrifice to pagan gods to hear my plans,' the young Angevin ran his hands through his reddish hair.

'But you won't tell me,' Richard said, 'in case I pass them on.'

'I told you before that I would trust you,' the Young King said, 'was I wrong to?'

Richard shook his head. 'I won't tell him anything, but I'd rather you revealed nothing to me in the first place.'

'I have a need of you,' the Young King said, 'I'm going to expand my household.'

'For another big tournament?' Richard asked.

'In a way.'

Richard groaned. 'Don't tell me,' he said, 'I just want to go home. I want no part of a civil war between two kings I am loyal to. Leave me out of it.'

'You are my man, are you not?'

'I can leave,' Richard said, 'and I owe your father directly for my land. You should release me from your company for your own good. You can't possibly trust me.'

'Do not presume to tell me what is for my own good,' the Young King said, 'you sound too much like my father.'

'You shouldn't quarrel with your father,' Richard said, 'I'd give anything for mine to be alive. And it is to my father's fate I should turn to now.'

'I know, you've told me about him.'

'The Holy Land calls me,' Richard said, 'may I leave your company?'

'To die in the dust in the east?'

'To find the truth and lay my father's spirit to rest,' Richard said.

Bowman sighed. 'My young lord made a promise. To your archbishop, no less.'

'Becket?'

Bowman nodded. 'And knowing my young lord, he'll go to the Holy Land whether or not you allow him to.'

'You are one of the most uncourteous knights I have ever met,' the Young King said, 'but I think you are probably right. However, Richard, you are right in the middle of what will soon be a war for the future of the empire.'

'I meant no disrespect,' Richard said, 'but which one of you and your father rules matters not at all to me.'

'You border on treason,' the Young King smiled, 'but there can be no peace until there is only one crowned king, and neither of us will surrender our crowns while we still draw breath.'

'I just want peace in my village.'

The Young King laughed. 'There will be no peace in Normandy, for that is where we shall strike. I have allies gathering, and they will lead their attacks into the duchy from all directions.'

'Into Normandy?'

The Young King nodded. 'It is the centre of our family's power. If I can force the duchy, then my father will have to at least recognise my supremacy and grant it to me.'

'Or kill you.'

'I doubt it,' the Young King said, 'but your village is in the heart of Normandy, is it not?'

Richard nodded. 'So that's why you think I'll follow you?'

'Help me take Normandy quickly and a devastating war might be avoided,' the Young King said.

'That almost sounds like a threat.'

'More like family politics,' the Young King shrugged. 'You can ride or sail east once I have resolved the differences with my father.'

'I can't help you with that,' Richard said. 'After Brittany I had one thing to do, and that was to go to the east to search for what happened to my father. For that I needed money, and my two plans for that have both failed.'

'Ireland and tournaments?' the Young King grinned. 'But the latter has not failed you. You will earn money from me for both Lagny and Corbie. And all those who serve in my Norman campaign will be paid yet more. I reward loyalty.'

Richard glanced towards the abbey doorway Sophie had left through. He shook his head firmly. 'I'm going home,' he said.

The Young King replied with a knowing smile. 'Are you sure?'

HISTORICAL NOTE

The twelfth century tournament was a world within a world. The playground of knights, counts, and kings, they excited the imagination of the masses, but taking part was the sole preserve of the upper class. Golden spurs were an entry requirement that would remain a barrier for squires for over a hundred years, so it was only knights who would arrange in teams to fight across vast tracts of land in the Young King's era. The tournament field at Lagny, not far from Paris, spread across fields from the river Marne to villages, across woods, pastures, and vineyards. In an ironic twist of history, the tournament site is now partly occupied by Disneyland Paris, and therefore must hold some claim to being one of the world's longest running entertainment venues. Tournament teams were based in two urban areas, the larger area being the base of the Within team, and the smaller site the base of the team Without. Teams were arranged along national lines, so English and Normans might line up against Hainulters and Frenchmen. In a nod to fair play, the sides were evened up to make things equal at the outset, but once the action began, it was quite another matter. In the twelfth century, these martial games took place with sharp weapons and at least to begin with, open faced nasal-helms. A sport it may have been, but there was no governing body or health and safety committee. Injuries to faces and hands would have been common, although deaths were rare enough that they were called out in chronicles and other written records. Occasionally the local clergy would even refuse to give dead knights a proper Christian burial, purely because they died doing something they viewed as unholy.

Capturing knights was the aim of the game, so preferred tactics included the snatching and cutting of reins, as well as singling out new and naïve knights to prey upon. Count Philip's somewhat dubious tactic of pretending not to fight until everyone else was tired, was one that he employed against the Young King's retinue for real. The Young King, rather than being offended, took up the tactic himself, and he and the Marshal both went on to profit handsomely from it. In the twelfth century, the end justified the means. Capturing a knight meant winning his horse and armour, which ensured that horses were off-limits as a target area. While this was a don't-do-to-me-what-you-don't-want-to-be-done-to-you rule, it meant that expensive warhorses weren't killed off for what was still essentially a game. In the later medieval period, a Spanish team journeyed to France to take on a French team, and in order to win, roundly killed all their horses. The defeated French were aghast, shocked at the appalling behaviour of the visitors, who were utterly disgraced in their ill-won victory. It is in the attempt to impose rules for horse safety and the taking of unharmed prisoners that we begin to see some of the more moral aspects of chivalry emerge.

William Marshal made his name on the tournament circuit to become as famous as any modern superstar, and a clerk in the Young King's household called Wigain genuinely recorded his victories for him. In a two year period he racked up over a hundred and fifty knights, which is a staggering amount of money to win. Wigain is included as a minor character in this book because I wanted to thank him for keeping his record - because without it we might think the Marshal's biography was exaggerating his abilities. That biography (and many other works) get mixed up with dates and places quite often, but this does not actually detract from its reliability in what matters: the deeds of men. Medieval writers and readers were relatively uninterested in dates and exact details of certain events. As modern people we live in a world where everything is categorised and recorded, and we're used to knowing all about an event. It is important to us to get the date of a battle correct, and the location for it. This didn't matter seven hundred years ago, and why should it? What mattered was the reasons for actions, the bravery and prowess of great men, and the consequences of what they did, right or wrong. This book therefore has followed the medieval spirit of history, and crammed twenty years of tournament stories into one. The stories are endless; Lagny was probably as big an event as portrayed here, carpenters could be paid in the lumber from their stands, there were arguments over ransoms and rule-following. The Young King's line about himself being the son of a king, yet his father only being the son of a count, is a quote, and during one party he did actually throw everyone out who was not called William. There are too many other tales to list, but William Marshal certainly got himself in hot water by riding away from his lord during tournaments, and later having to return to rescue him. Likewise, the plot to discredit the Marshal was real, although it involved many more men. Adam d'Yquebeuf was one of their ringleaders, and the village that bears his name is really right next to Cailly in Normandy. He was an important man in the Young King's court and hated the Marshal. His rehabilitation and death are invented - I cannot find a reference to what his ultimate fate was. William the Northerner was the Marshal's crude cheerleader, his fawning and sycophantic behaviour made some hate the Marshal who otherwise had no reason to, and the theft and twisting of the Young King's war cry was a real problem the Marshal seems to have created for himself. The alleged affair with the Young King's Queen is widely assumed to have been made up by his own biographer to cover the Marshal's problematic self importance, but if it was real, the Young King could have used it as an excuse to cut the Marshal back down to size. The young Angevin did recall his best knight and friend from his resulting exile after a reasonably short time, which suggests he didn't believe the accusation himself. His cousin Philip of Flanders did beat to death the man who slept with his wife, so I think if the Young King thought the Marshal had really done the deed, a recall would have been impossible. William's loyalty was probably never the question, and his substantial skill on the circuit made him worth keeping around. More proof of this is that Count Philip did try to poach the Marshal for a quarter of the rents of the city of St-Omer, a transfer-fee if you will, that in terms of value puts the Marshal up with Cristiano Ronaldo, David Beckham, or Lewis Hamilton in modern sport. And it is to Lewis Hamilton and Formula One racing that we find the most fitting modern parallel to the medieval tournament.

Spectators watched the grand charge in the same way modern crowds watch the start of a Formula One race. And probably for the same reason too, for the start of a race is where crashes are most likely to happen, and likewise the grand charge was where most of the action would occur in a concentrated and visible area. The fighting would break up and spread out across sometimes hundreds of acres of land, so some in the stands would simply leave after the charge. The parallels don't end there - racing is a team sport based around a driver and a car with a huge support team, and is not so different to a knight, a horse, and a collection of armourers, farriers, smiths, and trainers. If anything though, the money involved in the twelfth century was even greater than in modern sport today. Tournament teams such as those curated by the Young King, Count Philip of Flanders, or William Tancarville, were led onto the field by those men; stupendously rich men. Their wealth was stratospheric compared to the average medieval farmer, and the glamour and material riches on display made the bigger tournaments look like American NFL super bowls. But every two weeks. Two weeks seems to have been the standard period between events, and this is suspiciously the length of time the battered knights needed to recover their energies to do it all again. And that recovery was important, because tournaments were dangerous. The death-rate probably resembled that of Formula One racing of the 1990s, during which two drivers were killed. This isn't enough to put off the other drivers, but certainly enough to keep spectators on the edge of their seats. It also kept the participants serious. When we joust with balsa-ended lances in the modern age, we can be fairly certain of survival, but as soon as the solid pine lances with steel tips come out, the expression of modern jousters changes and the jokes in the morning before the event fade away. The higher stakes we face jousting with 100 percent real lances is heightened because of the genuine risk of injury, but in the twelfth century this was done with unarmoured faces and no metal plate armour on the body. It is said that William Marshal did introduce a face plate helmet for the tournament, although I am frankly surprised no one thought of it sooner. This danger kept knights coming back to the tournament in the same way that modern soldiers swear to leave the army after their current tour, then once they return home immediately sign up for another one. The tournament offered a unique chance to test skills against others on a scale that couldn't happen at home, and this applied to knight's horses too. It could also be quite fun. I know I find jousting without a tilt barrier and then drawing swords in mock tournaments to be the most enjoyable modern sport combat to take part in.

The medieval tournament circuit revolved around France, the Low Countries, and even the Empire (Germany). However, in the twelfth century it rarely made its way into England, for Henry II saw it as a malign influence. He suspected those who took part to be plotting against him, and wanted fighting knights to be riding with him, not messing around. Knights on their way to new sites were known to rob, party, and generally misbehave. In this book, William Marshal effectively robbed the merchant of his fifty pounds, but in real life the Marshal robbed a monk eloping with a woman in order to live by usury, or money-lending with interest, which Christians were not supposed to do. At the time, his actions were not seen as odd or wrong, indeed, another noble scolded him for letting the monk leave with his horse. This episode gives us a view into the medieval mindset and serves to remind us that their values and beliefs were quite far apart from our own. Tournament goers unsurprisingly got on the wrong side of the church for their behaviour. An abbot in Bury St Edmunds excommunicated a bunch of rowdy knights who took over his establishment and partied loudly all night just because he dared to ask them to be quiet. This didn't happen to the Young King's company, but it inspired the tale of Abbot Hugh in Knight Errant.

However, despite the downsides of the medieval tournament, they capture the spirit of twelfth century knighthood. Chivalry had not developed and Christianity was not yet fully intertwined with the knightly class, but change was on the horizon. Romance literature was in its infancy; Richard's tale of Eric and Enid was brand new in the 1170s but audiences loved this new kind of story, even if it was written down, and their subjects frequently included knights and tournaments. The character of Lancelot first appears (just as a name) in Eric and Enid, but stories about him and others created a self-fulfilling prophecy on how knights should behave. Another aspect of chivalric knighthood, heraldry, evolved on twelfth century tournament fields. It came from the need to differentiate knights from each other, to determine who was worth what, as well as who was on which side. It started with the geometric patterns we find in this series of books, and the repetition of the colours is used to show just how well this worked. I bet you can remember what the Martel colours are! Higher ranking men started to have more fun with these, as Count Philip did by adding the black lion onto his yellow banner, but even in the 1170s the royal English banner was probably just a plain red. The three leopards or lions first appeared only in the 1190s when the Young King's younger brother Richard was king.

Richard, the future Lionheart, is mentioned in passing in this book as the governor of the Lusignan lands in Poitou. He and his mother, the famous Eleanor of Aquitaine, butted up against the Lusignan family, and Guy is unlikely to have been on the best of terms with them. He wasn't known as a tournament goer, and his inclusion in the two tournaments in this book is fictional - but the rivalry was real. Similar rivalries simmered between families and dynasties across Europe, and these often spilled over onto the tournament field. Infantry guarded the lists, and some nobles would bring vast armies along on a larger scale than the Martel family did in Knight Errant. These infantry forces could be drawn into an escalating situation that ended in bloodshed, or brought along very deliberately to defeat an enemy, or win a battle under the cover of a game. The hijacking of the Corbie tournament by the Martels and Guy of Lusignan to take out an enemy didn't happen, but far larger and more menacing attacks did. Such tensions between and inside families were common, none more so than the relationship between Henry II and his eldest son, the Young King. The elder Henry loved his son, and really did get excited when he heard of his tournament victories. The £200 a day he allowed his son to spend on his knightly company cost the elder king a sizeable chunk of his royal revenues. Yet he continued to do it anyway, even as he faced down his first revolt, the rebellion that is spoken vaguely about in this book. The idea of having two crowned monarchs at once was not rare at the time, but would never again be repeated in England. What made the scheme go so badly wrong will be the setting for Richard's next adventure, King Breaker. But if you are interested in the world of the medieval knight, check out my non-fiction work: The Rise and Fall of the Mounted Knight.

Next up - Book Five in The Legend of Richard Keynes series:

King Breaker

Sign up to the mailing list on the author's website below to be the first to hear when new books are released.

But if you can't wait, investigate the author's non-fiction work:

The Rise and Fall of the Mounted Knight

www.clivehart.net

Printed in Dunstable, United Kingdom